A TRUCE
WITH TIME

A TRUCE WITH TIME

(A LOVE STORY WITH OCCASIONAL GHOSTS)

PARKE GODWIN

BANTAM BOOKS
TORONTO · NEW YORK · LONDON · SYDNEY · AUCKLAND

A TRUCE WITH TIME
A Bantam Spectra Book / February 1988

Library of Congress Cataloging-in-Publication Data
Godwin, Parke.
  A truce with time.

  (A Bantam spectra book)
  I. Title.
PS3557.0316T7 1987   813'.54   86-47891
ISBN 0-553-05201-2

Published simultaneously in the United States and Canada

Bantam Books are published by Bantam Books, a division of
Bantam Doubleday Dell Publishing Group, Inc. Its trademark,
consisting of the words "Bantam Books" and the portrayal
of a rooster, is Registered in U.S. Patent and Trademark
Office and in other countries. Marca Registrada. Bantam
Books, 666 Fifth Avenue, New York, New York 10103.

PRINTED IN THE UNITED STATES OF AMERICA
DH   0 9 8 7 6 5 4 3 2 1

This is for *Earl*, in his memory,
But most of all for *Doris Chase*
Whose caring insights helped deliver it alive.

Acknowledgments

I must thank a number of people for their generous professional help in the creation of this book: Donna Meyer and Kathryn Falk of *Romantic Times*; Carolyn Nichols of Bantam Books; Vivien Lee Jennings of Rainy Day Books, Fairway, Kansas; fellow writers like Morgan Llywelyn, Susan Shwartz, and Barbara Szold, and Pat LoBrutto of Doubleday, who took time to read the manuscript in draft and comment on it; Lou Aronica of Bantam Spectra, an editor who can roll up his sleeves and edit, a dying art; finally, Felicia Eth, my former agent and friend for ten years, who made me work just a little harder.

ACT 1
Winter, Spring

Manhattan—and certain
places in the heart and memory

1

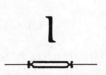

Caroline Cutler shivered in the wind knifing down Third Avenue and glared at the Doberman hovering indecisively over the gutter.

"Dammit, you silly bitch, we came out here to do your thing, so piddle or pack it up. I'm cold."

Dogger, the female Doberman, only trembled and looked apprehensive. Caroline sighed: if her heart had to go out to a stray dog, why did it have to be a Doberman? They always looked like they were in therapy or should be.

"Dogger—go!"

Dogger squatted miserably and went. When it was clear that was the extent of her inspiration, Caroline started back down East Thirtieth Street, Dogger alternately cowering against her leg and straining out at a forty-five-degree angle. The damned cold, Dogger's piddle, and Pat Landry's problems at least took Caroline's mind off her own for the afternoon.

"Caroline? You and Dogger look like seven o'clock!"

Caroline looked up past the row of renovated Federals to her own wrought iron gate and the tall man leaning against it. She tugged at Dogger's leash and lengthened her long stride. Pat had called that morning at the crack of nine before she was near awake, quieter than usual, to ask if he could come talk to a friend. Strange request for a loner like Pat Landry. He had a sound sense of courtesy about preempting people's time since he hoarded his own to write. Caroline said yes without hesitation, turned over to sleep again, and didn't think further about Pat Landry until her breakfast coffee.

Got a bad problem, Caroline. Need a friend.

"Hel*lo*, Pat!" Caroline squeezed her cheek to his. "Come on upstairs. My ass is blue from giving this silly woman her walk."

Pat Landry gave her a wan smile; definitely not his usual energy. "Hi, luv."

In her second-floor apartment, hats and coats dispensed with, Landry hunched on the edge of her couch and Dogger slunk to curl, shivering, by the remains of the log fire.

"Drink, Pat?"

"God, no. Just coffee."

"Left over from breakfast."

"Good enough. Hot and black."

"Coming up. Poke the fire for me."

From the kitchen serving port, Caroline watched Landry poker the embers and position another split log on top. A good description for him, she thought, would be an unconscious physical energy that was totally absent now, his movements minimal and deliberate. What would be normal movement for most fifty-year-old men would be restraint in Pat Landry. Caroline had known him well enough over the years. Sick or well, he never refused a drink unless he'd had too much the night before—altogether too often lately.

"Darling, are you hung over?"

Landry dropped back onto the couch. "Not that so much." His voice, stage-trained and clear as a trumpet, was now reedy with exhaustion. "My God, Caroline, what's happening to me?"

The urgency stopped Caroline's hand over the stove burner. She looked at her friend with as much puzzlement as compassion. She liked uncomplicated men for lovers; for friends she was tempted by the complex. Her sexual tastes ran to beefy English types, although, at fifty-five, she attracted wispy but successful men with an eleventh-hour urgency about sex. She and Landry had never been lovers, but from their first meeting as office temporaries eight years ago, they became more than friends, with a deep understanding. Both of them had been up and a long time down. They were on the way up again, but not forgetting how broke-lonely-and-scared could beat you if you let it.

Never lovers—Caroline idly wondered why sometimes and

concluded they just didn't ring each other's bells that way. Not that it mattered; you didn't have to sleep with everyone you loved. Pat Landry was handsome in his own way, the more so because he seemed totally unaware of it: almost six feet and with the remains of a good body just beginning to relax from youthful tautness into middle age. There he slumped on her couch, elbows on the knees of his worn jeans, the thick shock of dark brown hair graying faster than she'd remembered. He had the kind of face that intrigued but didn't ignite Caroline Cutler. With most men, what you saw was what you got, and she preferred it that way in a double bed. Pat Landry reflected different facets from moment to moment. He could sparkle or fade into the woodwork, delight or bore you to death.

From years of using his face as an actor to convey emotion and nuance, it had never set into the permanent lines of any attitude. He was not in the least photogenic, Caroline decided; the features were far too mobile to freeze in a still frame. He was attractive in motion, not repose, the most when he was rested, happy, and alert. Drunk, he could be a mean and unpredictable son of a bitch. Only fatigue robbed him of everything. Hung over and frayed like this, his features sagged, seemed to blur and lose definition. What you saw of Pat Landry was whatever claimed him at the instant.

Not one person but a whole slew. When I met him he was a skinny, out-of-work actor with one idea for a book. Now he's published seven of them. He's full of kindness and cruelties, he's hurt me without knowing it, and sometimes with malice aforethought. He's been my friend, and anytime I want to hear the straight score—and I do now, Pat, more than ever—I know I'll get it from you. You'd never ask without needing.

Caroline set his coffee on the end table. "What is it, baby? What's wrong?"

Landry took a deep breath, rubbing his forehead. "Caroline, I am one screwed-up guy."

"I was just thinking you're about five screwed-up guys."

Landry grinned. "Could be. You should have known my family. You going to the Bobby Burns bash at Crissy's?"

"Oh, sure. I promised to bring lasagna. How's the book coming?"

"It's coming." Landry rummaged inside his sweater for cigarettes, stuck one in his mouth, and snapped a Bic lighter to it.

"Smoking doesn't help a hangover," Caroline reminded him.

"Nothing will help this one. Denny used to call it the undying death. He showed very early talent for the family preoccupation."

Landry's rare references to his family whetted Caroline's curiosity. She had the lasting impression that they were, even in a negative way, very prominent in his memory. "Was he the brother that died?"

"No, that was my older brother, Arthur."

"It's confusing. You always speak of Denny in the past tense."

"That's where he belongs," Landry said tonelessly. "We haven't spoken for years."

The same stonewall reaction she always got when she asked about his family. Caroline's follies and wisdoms had a common clarity. Both were stated without hesitation. "Oh bullshit, Pat Landry. What the hell's wrong?"

He tasted the coffee and set it down. "I went out to a party in Morristown last night. I woke up at five this morning. In my own bed, dead sober. Cold conscious. And I saw something that scared me."

Caroline knew some of his Jersey friends. Artistic suburbanites to whom Landry escaped across the Hudson now and then for a weekend of therapeutic normalcy. Just an ordinary weekend party where Landry had been welcome for fifteen years, rising from always-reliable extra male guest to visiting royalty when his books became more prominent. He spent much of these weekends listening to the problems of writers manqué, most of whom would never start, let alone finish, a salable book.

"Among friends, Caroline. Old friends like you. Mature people, like I thought I was." Landry dragged deep on his cigarette. "A fun party, but somewhere in the middle of it, I stopped counting drinks. After that I didn't remember much except someone carrying me to a car."

"My God, Pat. How much did you have?"

"I don't *know*." He was honestly at a loss, bewildered. "The house was full of guests. They had to take me home. They drove all the way in town to the Seville and put me to bed."

"You can't say you don't have friends." Caroline took her favorite chair by the hearth and poured herself a sherry, looking into the fire. "Although I sometimes wonder how you can. You're fifty this week, Pat Landry. I'd say it's time you counted your drinks."

"One way or another, I count them."

Caroline heard the exhaustion in his voice, saw it in his physical passivity. Landry rarely sat in one place that long. On a normal day he'd be bouncing off the walls.

"I woke up at five this morning, and everything came back very clearly." He placed the words carefully before Caroline like evidence before a jury. "I called Mike's wife a stupid, uninspired sow."

Caroline winced.

"That's Rosalie. You've met her. Do you know how many times Rosalie's been my hostess? An old, valued friend, and I stepped on her like a bug. Another guy—he reviews books for a local paper—I called him a fucking hack with the IQ of lint." When he glanced up at Caroline, his brown eyes were muddy-dull with fatigue. "Those are the exact words I used. I can't even plead amnesia."

"You're a mean, unprincipled bastard when you're drunk." Caroline frowned. "I've seen it before. It's a wonder someone hasn't beaten you to a pulp."

"Like Connie . . ."

"What?"

"And why? What right have they—what right have I to do this to people?"

"None, baby, but you're my dear Pat and there's a reason, so let's have it."

"It's not the getting drunk, it's that I reach a point where I'm not drunk enough." He tried to grin. "Look at me, taking up your last free Sunday afternoon before Norman comes."

"Oh, he won't call until seven. Norman sets a schedule and sticks to it." Caroline smiled at Landry over her sherry glass. "Thank God, at least nowadays my problems are gilt-edged."

"Guilt-edged." Landry gulped the rest of his coffee and ground out the cigarette. "Honey, I don't want to do the Alcoholic Writer bit, the child-genius who has to be coddled by every woman he knows. Art as excuse for asshole. I despise people like that. It's not the booze, Caroline, not the drunks. This happened before when I was working on the magazine. The annual Christmas dinner. Twelve scotches after I started in—"

"Twelve! Good God."

"My date counted them. Don't you just love people who do your numbers for you? Anyway, the publisher got up to do his annual Bob Cratchit bit, and I told him to for Christ's sake sit down and shut up. Not the booze, honey, it's me. I'm not in control anymore."

"You're too damned much alone," was Caroline Cutler's blunt opinion. "Turning into a recluse."

"No, that's okay. I'm made to be alone. I was glad to get that last ditz-woman out of my life."

"The one that always smoked pot in my bathroom? What was her name?"

"Let's not remember. It's not loneliness, Caroline." Pat Landry looked straight at her, quietly serious. "There's something in me I'm scared of. I woke up this morning and knew I couldn't control it anymore—and I don't even know what it is. What the hell is happening to me, Caroline? I'm talking to the walls."

"A lot of things are catching up to you," Caroline said. "That's what's happening. You're fifty. I went through it. A lot of things are suddenly bigger and scarier, including success. Your books are making more money—"

"Oh yes, the books." The idea galvanized Landry into his normal restlessness. He heaved off the couch, prowling the living room with long strides. "The bloody books. A new career from nothing, phoenix out of the ashes. More money, better reviews. And I am talking to the walls."

Landry paused before the fireplace, grinning shyly at Caroline. Crissy James said once that he had a scruffy, Raggedy Andy sort of charm. The heavy fisherman's sweater was frayed at the elbow and under the arms, while his hotel closet bulged with good clothes rarely worn. He sat down on the hearth tiles, scratching Dogger behind her ear.

"Have you thought of breeding this neurotic virgin?"

"Easier to hump a nun, and don't change the subject. You're talking to the walls."

"And getting answers. I know some very articulate walls," he said in an odd tone; were she still a romantic, Caroline would have called it haunted. Both of them were past that, thank God.

"You got any aspirin?" he asked, mournful as Dogger looked.

Caroline fetched aspirin with a glass of water and fixed a plate of celery, cheese, and olives while Landry studied the rather good oil portrait of her over the mantel.

"You were about twenty when this was done?"

"Exactly. An Omaha debutante, far more sedate than I ever want to look or feel again." Caroline raised her sherry to the picture and made a face at it. "Corn-fed virtue; that's what dear Norman wants. I was born for New York and crazy people like you and Crissy and all the beautiful weirdos that hang out in my pub or come to my parties. But . . . Norman's getting impatient."

"You mean to get married?"

"What else? What'll I do in Tulsa? On a Sunday out there I'd be frying chicken or snoozing through Superbowl while the menfolk talk politics or money." Caroline smiled at her friend. "Where would I find an off-the-wall buddy like you to share his problems with me?"

"That's a blessing?"

"It could be worse," Caroline admitted. "At least you don't dramatize. Some of my gay friends are a bit of a trial that way."

Landry reached for an olive. "The greatest advantage in having been an actor is having been: past perfect, perfectly past. I've already played O'Neill; it's a big fat bore. I'd like to do the rest of my life for laughs." He unfolded from the floor and stood behind Caroline's chair, nuzzling the freckles on her cheek. "But it's good to have a hand to hold when a guy needs it."

"Only because I know damned well you'd do it for me," Caroline said. "But, *damn*, you're a complicated man. I wish you'd find a good woman. One you can keep awhile."

"Said the broad who don't wanna get married."

"Go to hell." Caroline bounced out of the chair and toward the kitchen. "Why am I drinking sherry, like I'm already training for Tulsa? I am going to have a scotch, and you're entitled to a hair of the dog."

Landry sat on the hearth, stroking Dogger and watching Caroline fix the drinks. If he was complicated, he admired her simplicity. With Caroline, everything resolved to a man: you had one or you didn't. She'd rather have Norman than no one. She did love her life here in New York but the men she attracted were hardly stellar.

Still, he felt he could learn a great deal from Caroline's earthy common sense. When he thought of their relationship, she fit perfectly as a staunch older sister, better casting in the part than poor Julia ever was. He could never talk to Julia like this.

What's happening to me, Caroline?

He hadn't told her everything about the party out at Mike and Rosalie's, barely able to understand it himself. He'd been enjoying himself, drifting from one conversation to another, escaping for a while from mid-book fatigue. The party had gravitated to the piano where an overripe soprano was approximating Sondheim songs. Landry drifted down into the den to freshen his drink at the bar and relax in silence. Leaning against the padded bar, trying not to hear the soprano's labored high notes, he became aware of voices in the kitchen just up the steps from the den.

Landry thought at first they were Rosalie and Mike—no, four of them. As he sipped his drink, pleasantly fuzzy, his ear detected a subtle, disturbing difference in the voices: clear and resonant, not New Jersey but deeply familiar.

"The hell you say!"

No one else in the world had quite Julia's husky tones or her nervous, explosive laugh. Landry's head turned toward the steps. He was either very drunk or not drunk enough. The other feminine voice came to him, stronger than Julia's, rising on its own rich swell of laughter.

"In your hat, Julia! Who needs another drink?"

Landry finished his in a strangled gulp and lunged up the steps to freeze in the kitchen entrance.

They were there, Caroline. Not figurative. Realities. All of them years dead, sitting around Rosalie's kitchen table as if none of them knew or cared that it was impossible.

Against the bright, coordinated colors of the kitchen, they looked anachronistic and wartime, Arthur in his dark olive green battle jacket and officer's pinks, Julia dramatic in tailored black, Jack Landry in shirtsleeves, Connie in her old blue housecoat, leaning on one elbow, pudgy palm to her cheek, and over it the marvelous, riveting eyes she used as skillfully as her voice, trained like Jack's in a day of large theaters, less light, and no microphones.

". . . his act was called Pardoe's Pooches, and Lord it was awful! The dogs used to beat the audience to sleep, and Pardoe was always wanting to get rid of them. The theater was Terman's old Rialto in K.C.—remember, Jack? The dressing rooms were under the stage with its boards all warped and loose. Awful . . . well, Terman brought in an elephant act, stolen from Kipling, no doubt. So, there's the music and this *used*-looking elephant lumbers out onto those old, warped stage boards—"

Arthur chuckled over his coffee; Julia guffawed: *"Jesus!"*

"All of a sudden I hear this *screaming* from Pardoe's dressing room next to mine. I opened the door, and there's Pardoe, wet as a washed shirt and this *deluge* pouring through the stage boards."

"The elephant, alas," Jack lifted one eyebrow, "was not housebroken."

"So about six months later I ran into Pardoe on Broadway and asked him how he was doing. 'Gr-r-reat,' says he. 'Remember the elephant that peed on me in K.C.? Well, I got a new act now!' "

Jack and Julia roared and rocked over their drinks, contained Arthur giving vent to his measured amusement in a silent grimace of a smile. Connie waited like a pro, cheek on her hand, then undercut her punchline with a shrug. "Then Pardoe hands me a flyer. Sure enough: PARDOE'S PACHYDERMS."

I remember that night, Caroline. Nineteen forty-three: Arthur was home from North Africa, Julia was down for the weekend, and for a change, the house felt happy. I wasn't that drunk, not near drunk enough. They were there.

The four of them, his parents, sister, and older brother, seemed to know he was there without caring, part of the scene but hardly its focus; that was always Connie. She poured more beer and raised her glass to Arthur and Julia.

"I'm happy tonight because—I just realized, Jack. I've got all my children under my roof again. I have the handsomest son in the world and a daughter more beautiful than I was."

Julia's smile lessened, tightened. She grew quiet. "Thank you, Mama."

Then Denny came into the kitchen, ten years old, grinning shyly, and Connie's glow of pride went warm with unbuttoned affection. "And here's our Ignatz!"

Hungry for attention, Denny let himself be hugged tight around his pudgy waist by Arthur, affectionate and vulnerable and always needing other people.

"All my children; not an ordinary one in the lot," Connie maintained. "Denny, is your shirt shrinking again?"

"Naw." Denny groped at the shirttail. "Just won't stay tucked in."

"I love you, Ignatz."

Then Denny turned to Landry in the doorway. "Monk?"

At the sound of that familiar, poignant voice, Landry's heart squeezed tight around an old hurt.

"I miss you, Monk."

Tell it like it was, Den. In your own way you turned out a bastard like the rest of them.

Jack raised gentle blue eyes to his son. "Be a little human, Monk."

Why did you come back? I don't need you people. I never had a life of my own until you were gone. I like it that way.

Arthur set down his coffee cup. "Why do we always get back to this?"

Julia slid cynical eyes to him. "Did we ever get away from it?"

Connie's voice commanded even at a murmur. "Maybe we need you now, Monk."

Why me, Mama? I'm fifty and I've forgotten you.

"You were the only one of my children I couldn't understand," Connie said. "I believe in destinies, but I could never see anything clear for you, Monk. But you're all that's left to remember us."

"Please, Monk," Denny pleaded. "They've gone, but I haven't. I only have the feelings of it all. You have the words."

Thanks no. I've spent years forgetting you, writhing out from under the weight of your egos. It's finished.

Connie only shook her head, sure of her truth. "Do you think we're here because you've forgotten?"

Finished!

Then, like a sound cue, Landry was again aware of the music from the party and how suddenly cold and angry he felt, and there was that stupid fat book reviewer at his elbow—

"Hey, Pat! What're you doing here talking to yourself? Listen, I had a great idea for a *Star Wars* kind of book, and I was wondering . . ."

Landry turned on him, wondering with boreal detachment whether to dismantle him on the spot. It seemed a wonderful notion. . . .

That was when he'd turned all his needless cruelty on the poor slob and his wife, and he'd awakened this morning to remember it all and the knot of them around the table.

Unfinished even now.

Caroline was talking to him and he'd missed most of it, staring past her shoulder and not hearing a word.

". . . always wondered how you can live like a monk with nothing but work."

He came back to her and the room. "My family used to call me that."

"What?"

"Monk."

"Did they? Well, it's typecasting if you ask me. Honestly, Pat, when it comes to women, you don't eat. You just pick, like Dogger. Woman-wise, it's time for you to sit down to a good meal." Caroline finished her drink and made the kitchen in three long-legged strides to get rid of the glass. "It's also time for you to get the hell out and leave me the rest of the afternoon."

She kissed him goodbye at the door, noticing another unusual thing: Pat Landry always looked directly at you, but now his eyes were—not evasive but focused on something she couldn't see.

"Hang in, darling Pat," she murmured against his cheek. "There's a lot of people would love to have your life."

"My life? Caroline, I don't have a life, I have numbers." He hugged her gratefully anyhow. "So many years since my wife left me, so many years in show business running away from being left. X number of women—hello, kiss-kiss-bang-bang, goodbye, out the door. So many books."

Landry plowed his fingers through the mop of his hair. "Honey, I'm a flagpole. Up top is a banner of a career getting bigger and brighter, but underneath that, very much at half-mast, is a dingy little dishrag of a life. That's the rest of me, Caroline. And I learned last night not even that's my own. Not . . . not yet. I can't control it anymore."

"You mean the drinking?"

"No." Landry stooped to bury his face in Dogger's neck. "Nowadays I think a lot about my family."

"I can't imagine you with a mother, Landry." Caroline pushed him gently through the open door. "You weren't born, you were published. Go home. Have a good dinner with milk, not booze."

Alone by the fire, Caroline opted for another drink herself, thinking on the kind of problems life handed one on a winter Sunday. She stretched out a hand to her least troublesome roommate. "Come here, Dogger. Let me beat you up a little."

She stroked the dog absently. *Well, it's here*, she thought. *The crossroads for Pat. Midlife crisis or whatever. Me too, come to that. I wish I could get along alone as well as he does, but I've never seen him so down.*

Caroline went to the kitchen for more ice and took from the refrigerator a plastic container, which she emptied into the dog dish by the sink.

"C'mon, woman. Dinner time."

Dogger approached the dish as if it were mined and sniffed without enthusiasm.

"Oh, dammit, eat. If you won't screw, at least eat." Caroline slammed fresh ice cubes into her drink. Norman would call at seven, neither early nor late, and there would be the question again.

"I don't want to live in Tulsa, Dogger."

But I've never learned to live alone, and who wants to? The way the world goes, you've got to have a man somewhere.

And you paid one thing to get another. Norman paid half the rent on this apartment and moved in most of the furniture. His taste was more correct than comfortable. He'd be in town in a few days, asking again. When would she move to Tulsa. Not if. When.

He'll come precisely on time and know just how he wants to spend each day here, dining me at just this or that restaurant and seeing just that uplifting, worthwhile show that he can talk about without embarrassment in Tulsa, and I'll have to spread my legs and pay my dues instead of hanging over the piano at my pub or getting blitzed with Crissy and talking about our friends behind their backs or telling garbagemouth jokes with Pat . . .

She was genuinely fond of Norman, she respected him. It wasn't marriage she avoided; she'd been there before. It was losing New York. And yet you needed a man.

Pat would never understand the problem. For him, being alone was easy. With some men, a good woman didn't help—but, Caroline reflected, there were none a good woman would hurt.

"And that's the truth." If she couldn't solve her own troubles, his might be easier. Caroline took a good pull at her drink, meditated a moment over the glass, then reached through the serving port for the phone, dialing from memory.

"Crissy? He*llo*, darling, how's Evan? Still playing with that new computer gizmo? Good thing it doesn't have tits. . . . Well, I wanted to ask you about the party . . . oh, yes, I'm bringing lasagna with everything in it, maybe even Dogger if she doesn't shape up. Something I wanted you to think about."

Caroline rattled her ice cubes, listening patiently to Crissy's breathy, bubbling party plans. It was going to be her usual blast—warm, crowded and thunderous, the last of the great buffalo herds.

"Crissy? Think a minute. Help me with something. Who do we know who's female, single, and interesting . . . all right, just single and looking. Well, frankly, for Pat . . . What? Not Nicole, she can't stand him and she's a flake anyway. Besides, she likes 'em young, horny, and controllable. Helen? God, Pat and Helen Storey've been friends for years, and they're both writers. They know each other too well . . . well, Gawd, there must be *some*one around who's not a bag lady or a basket case. I mean it, Crissy. It's time he got off his ass."

Please, Pat. Because I love you and right now your life's got more possibilities than my own.

"Lauren? Lauren who? Oh . . . her. Hell yes, I remember her. Who else would wear a lavender sweatsuit to a cocktail party and not give a damn? I know she's got balls, but does she have a dress?"

2

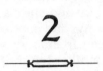

Lauren Hodge was small, sharp, and, where her art was concerned, a workaholic. She hurtled through her days looking competent, feeling brittle, and breaking only in private. Now and then since the breakup with Aaron, she allowed herself a one-night stand, always regretting the banality of it. Once in a while she drank too much, though not often. There were too many years of having to cope. Control was a deeply ingrained habit, even on days like this.

A beaut of a day, all hassle, phone calls, arranging for the delivery of this or that video tape, locating and heading off mistakes by some human sludge sitting at a desk in a university or museum office. Rush to the post office to get more stamps, five more time-consuming calls for miscellaneous reasons, and the day was eaten up. Creative work: zilch, five days out of seven, unless you counted the few blessed minutes at dusk watching the sunset from her window. One brief moment to renew herself in a wash of color.

When she found Crissy's phone message in her box, her reaction was: *Hell yes. I need to get out of the house and away from me.*

She dumped the mail on her dining table and sorted it swiftly. Most of it was art flyers, circulars, notices of film festivals she couldn't afford to attend, bills, something from a university in Kansas, and one letter from her brother in Portland. She set the letter aside with Crissy's note and the university thing and dumped the rest in the trash.

In the kitchen she wrestled ice cubes out of the jammed, overdue-for-defrosting freezer compartment, broke them out of the tray, and made herself a martini. Getting dark already, and she was still going at fever pitch, wound tight, trying to hassle the whole thing by herself when she desperately needed a good secretary. Key word: good. Young apprentices flocked to her, eager to learn video at the motherly knee of Lauren Hodge, full of their own dreams for brilliant works (all funded by the Tooth Fairy), and not a damned one of them could type faster than a turtle or file B after A without goofing up.

Lauren tasted her drink and tried to relax her tight shoulders. She could use a man now just to rub the tension out of her back. After the second potent swallow, she opened the envelope from the university.

> . . . regarding your second statement of rental due on
> the subject video tapes, our office has no record of
> first statement. If you would kindly resubmit . . .

"Oh, you dumb—fuck!" Lauren slammed the note on the counter with a yelp of impatience. More time wasted: another statement to make up and mail, more waiting to get paid.

"Well, I won't worry about you now." She swept the note off the counter and dropped it on her cluttered desk on the way to the window seat with her drink.

Watching the last of the light fade from the sky, she remembered the letter from her brother, Charles. It would be his usual matter-of-fact report on their mother. Good, dear Charles. Always the big brother, the grown-up, taking charge. *I'm grown up too, Charlie, I know the score. Mama isn't any better, isn't going to be any better.*

Alzheimer's disease was progressive. For several years before they committed Mary Halloran Weir, she would answer the phone when Lauren called, then forget it and wander away until Lauren simply hung up; or end a conversation with, "I have to go, dear. It's time for your father to come home," when Papa had been dead for years. Now, in the home, they put diapers on her, tied her in bed, sedated her outbursts of childish rage, and made sure she ate. There was no way for Lauren to escape the vague guilt, like a low-grade infection, for living her own life and not being there.

She missed Aaron, too.

Or is it, she wondered honestly, just the damned seven-year habit of him? Sure I'm edgy. I need sex now like aspirin for a headache. I need somebody.

Look, she snapped at herself: I know why I left. I drew a line. I loved him, but a time came when loving would mean erasing myself. If Aaron showed my films at parties, they were those with his music on the track. Then he'd plunk down at the piano and play his stuff again—what else?—while I passed drinks and *hors d'oeuvres*. How long was I supposed to be an appendage, with dance companies all over the country wanting to work on film with me? Aaron's a child, but I've already raised two of them. He needs a woman to flutter around him and lie down when he feels like it, and the hell with the rest. I walked out to save myself, and it wasn't disloyalty any more than refusing to go down with a sinking ship. So why do I feel guilty? Is it everyone or just women who get this guilt trip programmed into us?

The times and everything else have passed Aaron by. God, what a brutal business art is. They recognized him early, one of the bright young men along with Copland, but Copland knew how to deal with it. For Aaron it was all a big party that wouldn't end, except it did. Romantics were out. The critics would take swipes at him to build up some new *wunderkind*. The few times in the last ten years his work's been played, there was no press at all. He was like a kid no one invited to parties anymore. He never kept the rights to any of his work, or not enough of them. Cruel: someday when they've picked apart Glass and Rorem and Cage to a fare-thee-well, someone will rediscover the violin and clarinet concerti and the lovely pieces he let me use in my films, and the *Times* will do a nice something-in-depth on Aaron Feurstein, American composer. Columbia will do a modest reissue of his work, and if Aaron remembered to copyright the damned things, the royalties might buy him a headstone, because my love will be dead then. He's dying now.

The parade's gone by him and everything else has caught up. I see him sometimes around Gramercy Park, walking in that pained, stiff-legged way alcoholics develop over years of it, and I still care, still want to go to him, but there's more pity and sorrow than love now, mourning before the funeral. Artistically, his life or mine. He's already dead, but I've still got so much living and work to do, and there's steel in me that Aaron never had.

Why do women even have to apologize for strength? I'm me, paid in full. Free. I'm going to lay down the guilt and walk away from it. That's what you have to do if you want a life with your own name on it.

Get used to that, Mister Right, wherever you are. I need you and I'm looking, but that's the script and those are the lines. I'm not your mother or your bandaid. When the day's over and my work's done, when I sit down like this for a drink and a quiet communion with sky, stars, and sunset, then you're welcome. Come on in, I'm good at loving men. Been at it fifty-five years. Until then, you'd better have a life of your own going, because my line will be busy until closing time.

Lauren chewed the olive from her drink with a last, lingering look at the red western sky.

"The hell with it," she said aloud to Charles's letter. "I'll read you tomorrow, but now I'm going to put my bod in the tub, eat dinner, and go to Crissy's."

She looked around the studio apartment in which she'd lived and worked for ten years, her self-imposed solitary confinement. It was a glance of exasperation not without love or pride. "I am going to get *out* of here for tonight."

3

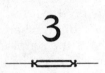

. . . the dreamer's knowledge that he dreamed, that it was happening exactly as he remembered it. He heard her slow, shuffling approach along the hall from her bedroom, and the animal sound of her pain. No, she didn't really want to live, but to die like this was a horror, with only himself alone in the house with her, sixteen years old and helpless in the face of her agony.

There was bright sunlight through the kitchen windows, splashing over the worn linoleum under his feet. You didn't need the dark for nightmare; you could writhe as well in sunlight. She was coming, groping her way through the dining room now, and what could she say when she couldn't make words anymore, just that sound, the dull monotone of suffering? Louder, nearer, almost at the kitchen door while he stood, powerless, unable to run or to bear the fact that she wouldn't even recognize him that last day of her life. Where would her sight be? The long, strange anger and the massive love between them was broken off, never to be completed.

The first thing he saw was the blue of her old housecoat, then the heavy-lidded, pain-protruded eyes and slack jaw, her mouth open as the sound of agony forced through—

Landry woke, twisting with a start onto his back. Still drowned in the dream's oppressive reality, he blinked at the alien fact of early morning light in the hotel room. He reached for a cigarette, feeling horrible. The dream had poisoned him from the inside out. He smoked the cigarette in absent drags while the fear and depression ebbed like a sluggish tide. Blue. Yellow sunlight on the dirtier yellow of the kitchen linoleum. More and more these days he dreamed in color, deep emotions coming closer to the surface.

The digital clock on the bookcase read 6:57. He couldn't sleep anymore and didn't want to go back into dreams like that.

Not just a dream, a memory. It happened that way. Haven't thought of that in years. We never forget anything. My mind is like an attic or a bank vault, all those memories drawing interest.

He butted the cigarette and pressed the BREW switch on his coffeemaker, always set and filled with water before he went to bed. While Mr. Coffee gurgled, Landry padded to the bathroom to brush his teeth and mouthwash away the sour-stomach aftertaste of the dream.

With his first mug of coffee, he sat on the edge of the rumpled bed, part of him still caught in the mood of the dream. He tried to identify the precise feeling behind the depression. Guilt? Something avoided, yet to be paid for, like the recurrent execution dream. He always escaped, but the dream kept coming back with its feeling of being trapped, ended, no way out. Gradually the concentrated depression faded as the day brightened and began to tug at the sleeve of Landry's awareness. A work day. They were all work days. When he took a day off, everything stopped.

In this impersonal room and others before it, his life had been pruned to essentials. Hotel desk with his typewriter, leather recliner, stereo and turntable on the dresser, small bookcase of brick and boards, coffeemaker, table with hot plate, bed, hotel color TV. Out of obsessive habit, yesterday's work on the book began to run through his head like a computer screen flashing menu. He had to make careful notes now. Good ideas slipped away, lost forever if he didn't snare them in the net of the moment. Time itself montaged, warped in his memory; a working idea might dissolve for no reason into a vivid picture of his brother Denny as a child, or something even more trivial, like a Mexican girl at an army dance in El Paso, years back, as if time had declared a truce with linear memory, allowing Landry to superimpose image upon image in complex chords of remembrance.

As it grew harder to remember present fact, the past became clearer and more emotionally detailed. Conversations, moments lived through rose again in startling clarity, wreckage from the bottom of the Sea of Landry breaking surface to float like derelict ships, rusted but real, before sliding beneath the waves again. What he had said to Caroline on Sunday was truer than she'd ever guess.

Nowadays I remember my family a lot.

Caroline was a good friend. He couldn't lay the whole mess of it on her.

His personal life was out of control, all the worse because the work suffered. All professionals knew this kind of sweat: Can I do it one more time? What if I wave the wand and nothing happens? He wasn't a newcomer anymore. The readers and editors knew his name. He got more money and his work was expected to pay off in return. From here on, relative failure and moderate success could look very much alike, both of them easy and comfortable. Play it safe, hit a certain level and hold on to it, minimize risk. If the talent's dead, cash in on the corpse. Sell a big, fat trilogy. The second and third books might be attenuated dreck, but the hell with that. Just count your fans and give them what they want. They made your living.

He'd never dried up before either on stage or on paper, but it was happening now, halfway through his almost overdue eighth book, not blocked but increasingly unsure about his daily output, unable to look at the pages without dissatisfaction. The only thing that got him through a thousand words a day was the discipline. His father gave him that early on, before he was twelve. Years of going to sleep with the sound of Jack's typewriter clacking away, comforting to hear through the wall when he and Denny were tucked in bed. Big Jack was at work, waving his wand, and morning would come, bright and safe and steamy with cornmeal mush.

From the time Landry was fourteen, he knew the difference between amateur and pro. Amateurs screwed around. Pros just slogged through it until perseverance became habit. A thousand words a day. Never mind if it's wrong or bad. Wrong can be fixed, bad improved. A thousand words a day, more if you could. Sometimes easy, but more and more now like constipation, the blank page a wall to stare at, for making reasonable excuses to yourself. Forget it for today. Do it tomorrow. And the older voice—

You know you can't finish anything, never had the guts.

"The hell I don't."

He had the stamina to last through tough seasons of stock

and repertory and still care at the end. Enough to pull his life out of the trashpile when his second marriage failed, to keep going when the painful affair with Janice washed out and left him in a grubby hotel room with hardly enough money to eat and only the seedling idea for a book to keep him going, when he'd never finished a book in his life and sold perhaps three stories twenty years before. Enough guts to sit on the hotel bed, the borrowed typewriter propped on a suitcase, and finish the book a page at a time. And the next one and one after that, a torrent of creation without stopping to breathe, but now . . .

It happened to others, why not him? He was tired, out of gas. The stuff looked stale. He detected old cribs, repetitions of bits that worked once but didn't now, just lay there disgusting him.

So work tomorrow. Is it such a big deal?

"I can do it," Landry challenged the walls. "I can deliver."

Can you? All you ever had was energy, now that's going. Less time at the gym each year to keep in shape, more goofing off, more scotch and less ice in the drinks. Old man. Fifty years old. You got lucky with the first books; that's not supposed to happen for a loser like you. You won't go the distance this time, and even if you do, what do you get but a little money to keep you running some more? And why? If you're good at historical fantasy, it's merely comparative. Most of the turkeys writing this stuff wouldn't know good, tight prose from lox. You only seem better because you know what works from playing the good stuff six nights a week and two matinees for years—

"Hey, enough already." Landry put down the coffee cup. "Let's go to work."

If he didn't start now, he'd piss away another whole day with nothing accomplished. That was part of what bugged him now, the way he wasted time. But, Jesus, it was painful to look at the pages when they read like pure shit.

He settled into the leather recliner and picked up yesterday's pages. The words looked foreign, opaque. He couldn't care about them. Landry tapped his knuckles on the writing board. "What's wrong with me?" *Do I need to lose?*

And if he did, when had it started? The only one of her children with no clear destiny, Connie said. Ironically, the only one who ever really had a life to call his own, freedom to be. Julia died complaining, unfulfilled, and miserable; Arthur slit his wrists in a motel bathroom in 1961 and left the answers

to coroners and silence. In their own way, each of them re-
treated into a shell and all the stupidities, brutalities, and
inexplicable waste of their lives stemmed from this. Denny,
twenty years lost down a trail of drugs and jail, never grew a
shell, only shrugged and stumbled from one inevitability to
the next.

And yet, Mama, you couldn't see a destiny for me. For all
the love we had, we were always adversaries. It's a pity you
didn't live long enough for me to really take you on.

"You'd lose, Monk," Connie stated over her beer with her
ingrained arrogance. "You never finish anything."

She was in the faded housecoat she never seemed to change
in her last years, the hem soiled and fringed with dust. Iron as
always, but rusting, gray wisps escaping to hang in strings
from the careless morning bun she made of her hair. Beer in
hand, Chesterfields within reach: Connie Hawkins Landry in
1944.

Here we go again. Even dead, you never bothered to knock,
Mama.

"Why should I? My family is my domain."

I can't even plead insanity; stark, staring sane and here you
are. You people going to make a habit of this?

"You were remembering us. Finally." Connie drank and set
down her glass. "The trouble with you, Monk, you're half-
assed. Why are you failing in school? Why won't you try?
Where's your character?"

Try for what? What was I supposed to be? Like you? Like
Jack?

"No." Connie gave it a stage pause. "Not like him. I wouldn't
have my son like him."

I'm his too, but I was the one who sat up with you while
you corroded and drank, listening to the same old injuries, the
tired injustices, trying to understand, trying to—I don't know,
find some kind of surety and maybe stop your bleeding for a
while. I can't take the load off you anymore, Mama, can't live
with it. A lot of things are catching up with me, and I've got a
feeling you're part of it, all of you.

Landry's mother snorted and drank. "You were never strong
as me. Arthur was skinny too but he built himself, made
himself into a man. He always had the thoroughbred look, if I
say so myself."

You never stopped saying it. You shoved my face in Arth's
perfection.

"You have to *finish*—what you start." She didn't say the line, she played it to the whole house, not forgetting the second balcony.

Did Arthur sit with you night after night while Dad and Denny just went to bed to get away from you? The two of us alone, sharing cigarettes, turning me into a night person for the rest of my life, listening to you because I loved you and you needed someone, and to me you were God.

"I wanted to understand you." Connie shook a cigarette from her pack and put a match to it with deliberate movements. "I wanted you to understand what's expected of our kind of people. A way of living."

It seemed we were aways broke.

"Broke is an inconvenience," Connie brushed away the notion. "Nothing to do with your values, your hopes. Poor is a different way of life. That's all there is." She swept her pudgy hand in a dramatic gesture of finality. "There isn't any more."

Thank you, Ethel Barrymore. What was I supposed to be? Half the time you were for Jack and half the time you hated him, degraded everything he was, but Arthur? The golden firstborn. Even when he committed suicide I'll bet his hair didn't muss. I wanted so much to please you, please somebody at something, but I never could. You had a soul like quicksand, Mama. Everything sank into it without a trace. Until I became like you, until love could never be simple but always cost a bleeding.

"You know what I want?" The maudlin tears were bright in Connie's large eyes. "I want you to be better than Jack, to make him look sick. Big man with all the sweet young things crazy about him . . . make him look sick, Monk."

Why? He was just a man and a long way from the worst. You could be generous, but Jack could be kind.

"Bastard."

If anyone poisoned you, Mama, it was yourself. Vindictive, possessive; down in the quicksand of you, I could probably find Julia and Arthur and part of myself.

"Listen to me!" The beer glass slammed on the table. Connie rose unsteadily. "You don't know what happened or what I could have been. What I gave up for you. You will respect me and what I stand for—"

. . . The cigarette ash powdered over Landry's robe. He brushed at it. Dreaming again. Why now, all of a sudden, was he remembering them so clearly? He'd loved better and kinder people in his time, but the ghosts of them still fought because fighting was the only way they could touch anything, and Landry still walked their rutted battlefield, turning up bones and rusted swords.

You have to understand what went into you. You can't live without understanding.

Who said? The unexamined life is what most people want. Julia scavenged the same field until she died, finding only what she wanted to find. She wrapped her life around it.

"But *I* knew them," his sister said with her old, irritating emphasis. "You never understood anything at all. My mother was a great woman."

Julia wandered Landry's room as she had the house in which she barricaded herself since 1942, wearily arch, a drink in her hand, lashing out at her captive children in an edged monotone of accusation and anger with no real energy behind it. *This house is filthy!* (It was surgically clean.) *None of you go out until this goddamned filthy house is clean, you hear me?*

Restless, self-condemned to solitary, rarely leaving her house in the last years, her voice worn to a whine and roughened by cigarettes and liquor. Julia was pale blond, the lightest of them all, her long body shapeless from eight live children and three miscarriages, protrusive blue eyes bewildered, reddened with liquor and frustration.

What time is it, Julia?

"What's the difference?" She couldn't care less. "Now or then. I'm dead anyway." Julia looked around Landry's room with her perpetual disgust. "How can you live like this?"

I live in me, Julia. The furniture's incidental. You never traveled enough to learn that.

"I didn't have to." Julia drank and wandered. "You're such an ass. My house was always a pain. It took everything just to keep it decent, and what the hell good did it do? Our whole street's guineas and spics now. Loud, trashy kids. And the kikes, they always get in."

Creeping democracy.

"The plot next to mine at Pinelawn is a Jewish accountant," Julia complained. "What can you do? Still, it's a lovely place. They always cut the grass and prune the trees. I was the only one of us properly interred."

That was the most anyone ever spent on you. I'll do it Jack's way, salvage the working parts for someone else and a note to the janitor, he should burn the garbage.

"How can you be so blasé about something so important?" Julia glared at her brother as she always had, condescending and yet bewildered, a trace of nervous insecurity. "I'm a Christian. I believe in certain things."

Julia, don't hang crepe, okay? You were always a career drunk. Drunk and fun I could live with, drunk and pious was dull.

"Very funny. And you? I didn't even read your books. If you must do historicals, *dah*-ling, look to Tennyson and Scott. The great writers. Artists with sweep."

You never read me, but you put the books out on your polished coffee table to impress visitors. "My brother, the author—but then all of us were artistic, you know." Your whole house was an identity card. *Your* mother, *your* family. Christ, I lost count of the heraldry hung on your frigging *House Beautiful* walls.

"She was your mother too," Julia accused.

And you were my sister once. I adored you, Julia: grown up and yet close enough to be friends with. Someone fun to be with, who'd give me the straight scoop, except you never really knew it.

Julia pronounced it to the walls like a judgment: "You grew up wrong."

No, just away from you, remember? Twenty-two years old, three thousand words a day pouring out of me. Learning to be *me*, Julia. Suddenly life was a feast and that summer I felt big enough to walk in without anyone's permission. Born to write like Jack never could. That was the year the New York agents called me a discovery.

"Going to be you," Julia smirked. "How could you turn your back on your own heritage? Your own history?"

Listening to you and Connie worry it to death. For the two of you, it was always then, never now. I went AWOL from your war.

"You never knew what was going on."

I was a kid; pardon me for that. I want to understand. Like Mama said, I'm all that's left to care about you.

"Is Denny gone?" Julia asked without much interest.

Might as well be. I haven't heard from him in twenty years. With luck, I can make twenty more.

Julia's smirk was oddly weak, never the strength to stab,

only scratch. "Arthur said you were both fifth wheels on a railroad track."

Because I didn't act, I reacted. I thought my family had all the answers. That's a laugh: half the time you didn't even have reasons. After all these years it's still a mess: pieces of you, all the missing pieces of me mixed up like two jigsaw puzzles dumped in one box. I didn't grow up wrong, just stopped believing your ludicrous fictions about Mama—

"Don't you dare talk about my mother."

Why wouldn't you even read my books? Were you jealous?

Drifting aimlessly about the room as her thoughts drifted, never anchored, Julia's aging whine complained, "Why should Arthur have all the medals? Why should you be published? I had talent myself. Why did I have so many goddamned kids? I was a model once. I painted for hours every day when I was young. And beautiful. The men were always after me." Julia flushed with the pathetic ghost of feminine confidence. "Even Jack."

No way. My father had an eclectic and wholly fallible taste in women, but that I don't believe.

"Oh yeah? There's a lot you ought to believe, brother dear." Even when she sneered, Julia sounded beaten. "You and Denny were too young to know how it was. Mama always let you do anything you wanted, smear the crap from your diapers all over the walls—

Expressionism.

"It's not funny," Julia snarled. "I had to clean it up, not her. Not her . . . wash Denny's diapers, the little shit factory, walk you around the block on your tricycle and you always went like a fiend, never got tired. I had such lovely books, and you ruined them with your crayons, into everything, never let me alone. I was glad to get away. Glad to marry Werner." Julia's bitterness softened to supplication. "Try to see me in 1937. You remember, don't you, Monk? The year I met Werner. I was nineteen and beautiful."

The age and thickness dissolved under the warmth of memory; as it did, Julia's body straightened out of its habitual slump to her youthful, striking height. The bright hair glossed again to a brushed-back sunburst: the Greer Garson look before Garson was ever heard of, the first rush of beauty out of the long, gangly adolescence. Landry could see the best of Connie in the high-bred cheekbones, all the grudge-holding

Hawkinses in the stubborn chin. Yet too pale, too delicate, not enough definition or determination to go any distance.

"I was beautiful, wasn't I, Monk?"

All of that. He'd forgotten under the dust of years; not iron like Connie but striking, the patrician look and husky voice could have given her as much of a chance as any television model forty years later. She painted and sculpted all her life, yet it was the voice, compelling as Connie's in its way, that Landry always remembered. Julia had the family gift for speaking, a dramatic immediacy that made you listen. When she was young, she could tell a ghost story to keep him and Denny shivering through many a dark evening.

But Julia was born too early for any of that. Long-boned beauties weren't the style in a day when a girl strove to be pretty, adequate, and married at eighteen. Like most thoroughbreds, Julia would have been stunning at thirty-five and handsome at fifty without too many children come too fast, or the booze and the corroding, life-long bitterness.

The loveliness faded, thickened, returned to the last truth of her: over sixty, slumped and dying, voice squeezed into a pitiful squeak from the cancer in her esophagus. Ravaged but still handsome: "The Parthenon by moonlight," Landry called her once. Truer than he knew. The fine lines were still there. And the glass still in her hand as always, drinking as much as she dared, on the way to another evening's binge, another useless fight with whatever daughter got in her way.

"What's the difference?" Julia wondered. "One day I just said the hell with it and died."

I remember the night I called and you told me it was coming.

Julia looked as vulnerable as she sounded that night, barely audible over the phone. Yet in the hard realization of death and ending, there was as awkward moment when they touched once more. Under all the time and distance, so much caring left.

Julia stood by the door, her pallid face congealed in defeat. "It wasn't that I hated you, Monk. You were very good about writing to me, coming all the way out to the hospital. I didn't hate your books, just . . . didn't have the energy to read any more. Pain does that to you, wears you down until all you can think is *let me out of here*. But I was so scared of dying, Monk."

Everything is said too late, isn't it?

"If it's said at all. One day you'll realize the truth of me."

I want to. What happened to all of us? We had such possibilities as a family. What drove us apart? Where did all the anger come from?

"Ask Mama," Julia husked. "Why her love always went to men and so little to me. With a little confidence, I could have been anything I wanted."

But you weren't.

"Any man I wanted. More than her, if I'd wanted them. There were plenty of chances, believe me."

Jesus, just once I'd like to meet a virtuous woman who didn't paste up her chances like green stamps. Connie enjoyed being a woman, you never did.

"Oh, you stupid—ass!" Julia yanked open the door, needing an exit line as usual, a triumph. "She never liked you, you know that?"

Why should she? We were too much alike.

"What did you have that I didn't?" Julia demanded of her brother and the years. "You, Arthur; what did any of you have?"

Nothing, honey. Whatever chances you missed, you didn't really want them. You had the talent, but that's only openers. You couldn't go the distance in anything.

"Go to hell!" Julia ended it as she always did, with a condemnation. "I'll never speak to you again even if I *am* dead."

She swirled her figurative cape in dismissal and vanished out the door.

"La de da, Julia." At the table, as before, Connie tapped the ash from her cigarette. "Where did a smart girl like me get such fools for children? It's depressing. Don't gape at me, Monk. You always look idiotic when you're surprised."

It's a bit of a jolt after all these years. I can't stop you from romping around my memory, and there's no one I'd rather be haunted by, but do you mind? I really have to work. And I assume you'll be back.

"Take all the time you want." Connie faded from the table with a Cheshire-arch smile. "Of course we'll be back. None of us have anywhere to go but here."

That was true, Landry thought. *Of all her children looking back into her eyes, she saw herself most clearly in me, reached to me, clutched at me when she was sinking. Where else would her memory fly home to roost?*

"I loved Connie very much," Jack reflected, "but in some ways she wasn't too bright."

At the desk, grizzled and huge, hornrim glasses sliding off the precipice of his broken nose, Jack peered at the marked-up green pages from the day before. "Monk?" he asked with his pervasive gentleness. "You gonna dream all day or get some work done?"

I'm scared, Dad. It's harder and harder to do, and what comes out looks rotten. I'm dried up, but it's my living; when I stop, the business stops. What the hell do I do? Help me.

"Like I told you," Jack said. "A line, a page, a day at a time. Don't worry about good now, just right and tight. Get it done and get paid, y'damn fool."

Landry finished the cold coffee in his mug and took up the pages. Embattled Connie dissolved out of him; cool Jack turned to the script. Yeah . . . the problems were clearer now. Landry slashed through whole sentences, scribbling over them, working faster and more confidently as time wore on. The basic lesson learned from his father: however you defined talent, it came down to this. A thousand words, that's what it meant to go the distance. Whatever unanswered questions or unpaid debts Connie or the rest of them brought back, Landry forgot them now and pushed on through another thousand words.

4

Too thin for most of her life, Crissy James, at forty-five, was suddenly and contentedly settling into agreeable plumpness. Busy at the kitchen table, she swayed her hips and shoulders to the soft rock from WRFM, sampling blue cheese dip on a sliver of carrot, darting her eyes to the clock. Almost party time.

Pat would come, he always did, but Crissy wondered if Lauren Hodge would really show up after so many polite refusals. She wouldn't have thought about it this time except Caroline asked. Made sense: Pat needed someone and Lauren certainly did. Crissy hadn't seen that much of her since Portland and still wouldn't if they hadn't collided at Alexander's before Christmas, when Crissy learned that Lauren had broken up with Aaron Feurstein. Finally. Her decision, not his.

You had to say that for Lauren, she was independent and as much of a loner as Pat Landry, but six months alone was enough for anyone, even those two oddballs. They should get along. You put good people together and good things happened. Mostly. Well, sometimes. Look at her and Evan.

"Ev*an*? Almost time and I'm working like hell. Don't bury yourself in there."

Just their usual late January party, but *every*one would be there to celebrate Robert Burns's birthday or Mozart's or even Pat's, which fell right in the middle. Pat had helped them move into this loft out of their claustrophobic studio after Evan got the contract for the computer software books. His first

view of the fungus-green walls of the erstwhile shirt factory
was absorbed in silence as he turned slowly around the drab
space, taking his time to believe it.

"Nazis used to gas people in places like this."

"Oh, we're going to paint." Chubby little Evan rubbed his
hands together. "You won't know the place."

"Isn't it *wonderful*, Pat?" Crissy bubbled. "Space! I can
breeeathe."

Bleached fore and aft, the loft breathed deep with Crissy.
White, open, quiet space, shelved along the walls for her
remaining sculptures and canvases, the last relics of a late and
unlamented time. She didn't even mind—much—Pat Landry's
nudging her about work. Not everyone was boiling to create
before breakfast or even after.

Crissy tilted her head to listen for Evan: still deep in dead-
line work at the word processor, and for the moment she had
the huge white loft to herself and Becket, their cat. The smooth
music caught her in its infectious beat. Carrot stick in her
teeth, Crissy spread her arms and let the rhythm take her. . . .

I really feel good in this place, she thought. Like maybe I
can stop running, and who cares if I never draw another line
on paper again? Pat's a compulsive worker. How can he live in
hotels all the time? What can you do in a hotel room but work
and screw and be lonely? I hope Lauren comes, she's always
vodka, we've got a barrel of that . . . so here I am, forty-five
years old, living in a whitewashed shirt factory in the Garment
District, married to a man who loves what he does and doesn't
have to kill himself to make a living, except he likes it. That's
okay. Evan's a yes. Who else would get a hoot out of me
throwing a party to celebrate our first one-night stand? You
couldn't do that back in Portland. My house in Portland was a
showplace, but then it was expected to be, and the fucking
bruises my husband left on me were showplaces, too. What is
it about men out there? I worked so hard at my art then, it was
the only thing that kept me sane, but here I don't need that. In
New York you can just be what you are and the folks downstairs couldn't care less unless your waterbed leaks. Downstairs is Josh Feder with his seventeen cats, I'm not going to sit
him down to lasagna next to anyone allergic.

Why does Caroline want to go back to all that? If she does. I
mean, across the Hudson and through the trees, it's like a
blight of normalcy. You get what you pay for, but Caroline
paid for New York, not Tulsa. Part of her needs what Nor-

man's offering, but none of her really wants it. It's not that I don't like Norman . . . all right, I don't. Tulsa's not that far across misery from Portland.

Was I beautiful then or just polished like the silver? Never more than a size 8. Who could eat? My stomach was always in knots living with that bastard. The price of liberty and a size 8 is eternal vigilance, but I do love sour cream with chive. I am going to pig out at my own party, and dance and maybe put a little catnip in Becket's 9 Lives, he's much too resigned even for an altered cat . . . now that's a gourmet dip. I don't mind getting a tummy. So what? Evan's got one, and he's warm on a cold night, and I'm entitled.

Buz-z—

Ohmigod, is that—? Hey, somebody's here already. Life can be that much of a gas.

"*Evan*? Push the button, I'm all sour cream. Let 'em *in*."

5

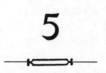

Landry nursed his scotch, trying not to get drunk and wondering why. The party was too loud. Half a hundred people, most of them dancing, made radiators redundant. Crissy and Evan scampered happily from popcorn making and lasagna cutting to the laden table, strafing in and out of conversations en route, greeting newcomers with effusions of joy, especially those bearing supplies.

The SoHo crowd had shown up in force, youngish and hirsute in tie-dyed T-shirts and jeans, jiggling about the dance space to chaotic rock. The older crowd drifted around the table and the rear of the loft. Landry wandered, content to observe from his writer's distance. A nice touch: Crissy had put a bowl of water at one unoccupied corner of the long table and drawn a high stool to it on which Becket, her black, altered tomcat crouched brooding over the party and perhaps his lost destiny.

There was Caroline, rawboned and redheaded in paisley and peach cashmere, talking to dark, patrician Helen Storey. *How would I describe Caroline?* Long legs and a cornfed Nebraska complexion. Glasses perched on an aquiline nose, merry blue eyes that might frost with anger or indignation but never malice. Handsome in a schoolmarmish way, and no appearance more misleading. Urban soul in a farm woman's body. She didn't want to go back to the corn, not for a minute, but Caroline wasn't made for alone the way he was. Pity; a talent for solitude, like a knack for cooking, could save you a lot in thin times.

And who am I kidding? Landry thought. Can't control my own solitude anymore. All the anger and memories boiling together, seeping out of me. Something in me is cooked and ready to come out of the oven, but I feel like one of the walking wounded.

Then Nicole Bramble chucked him in the ribs on her way to the dance floor. "Hi."

"Hey, Nicole."

"I can never get you quite sorted out, Patrick," Nicole tinkled in her cheery London accent. "You're absolutely unreliable. Either dead quiet or exploding."

"Said the kook."

"True, God's truth." Her laughter jingled again as Nicole moved off. "There's Nevil and I'm dancing. Cheers." She bobbed onto the dance space, giggling with her long-haired younger date.

People never understood that about writers. If you were quiet you weren't always brooding. You might be thinking of nothing at all. More often you were working, observing, noting conversations, tics, and attitudes like a voyeur-spy, shuffling words and ideas like a magician never without a deck of cards in his hands, until the feel of them became second nature. Much of the time around people, Landry was absorbing them like colors on a palette.

Like that woman there. What's the picture of her?

Lavender turtleneck sweater: not many women can wear lavender well, but she does. Thick hair cut in a page boy, not so much graying as fading. Used to be . . . auburn, I'd say, from the rest of her coloring. Wears that red scarf with a go-to-hell flare. Corduroy jeans, well fitted. About my age. Nice figure, petite, no more than size 6. Smallest feet I ever saw this side of a mouse.

Something more than the inventory of her, a subtle contradiction, made Landry look twice at the small woman. She was standing quite alone, absorbed in one of Crissy's sculptures on a shelf. Most women alone at a party would be self-conscious, would be moving toward someone, covering their singleness with laughter, judging the other women, aware of the men. This one was planted like a pint-sized Gibraltar, and everything about her stance said she was quite content to be there and alone, and she'd move when she damned well felt like it.

Then Caroline was at Landry's elbow, pressing her cheek

to his. "Listen, gotta go admire Evan's office, but count your drinks, okay?"

Landry put his arm around her. "You got it."

"Have you met Lauren Hodge yet?"

"Who?"

Caroline craned her head around, searching the party. "She's —well, she was just over there. Someone interesting, just got here a little while ago. Now don't get drunk."

"Aye, sweet mother."

"Fuck off." Caroline kissed him in parting. "And go talk to Helen. She really likes you and she's sick of all these noisy kids. Ciao."

There wasn't too much of a crowd around the nosh table now. Landry edged in behind a svelte, platinum-haired woman in kelly green and too much gold jewelry, earnestly cutting herself a square of lasagna. She jumped, startled, when he kissed her neck.

"Darcy Rambard, good evening."

"Pat! Hi-i." Darcy squinted at him through designer glasses and kissed him back.

"How's the tits-and-glitz market?"

"Getting better. Big things shaping up at Falcon Books." Darcy spread her arms. "Like my new dress? Bloomingdale's!"

"You look like a leprechaun pawnbroker."

"They didn't have leprechauns in Budapest. You should see the mink that comes with it."

Landry piled salad onto a paper plate. "Mink, no less."

"It's on the bed in back. I hope it's safe." The platinum of Darcy's neck-length hair glinted as she glanced apprehensively toward the rear of the loft where a knot of guests loitered. "Some of these people don't look solvent or scrupulous."

"Why not wear jeans?" Landry said. "Who'd get sneaky over a denim jacket?"

"Jewish princesses do not wear jeans," Darcy Rambard stated from her personal Talmud. "You never know when you're going to run into an eligible man in the six-figure bracket, and I will not have *him* see me in jeans. And you're dropping salad all over that expensive sweater." She swiped at it with her napkin. "Which you've been wearing since the destruction of the Temple; when will you buy a new one? Been keeping well?"

"Fine. How's by you?"

"You shouldn't ask." Darcy groaned under the weight of the world. "My two daughters are expensive heartbreak. The money I have to lend them to keep them out of debt . . ."

They found an unpopulated spot by the sink and, over the blare of the rock music, Darcy gave Pat Landry a five-minute monologue on the fortunes and follies of her ex-husband (the shmuck), her daughters (the idiots), and news of the only world that counted.

"Falcon Books!" Darcy's myopic blue eyes widened with revelation. "They're going into historical romances in a *big* way, a whole new line. High-class bodice-rippers, but the word is they'll pay megabucks for the right authors, and who, I ask you, *who* can rip a bodice better than me?"

"If the money's that good," Landry reflected through a mouthful of salad, "I might try it myself."

"Yah-h, stay out of it." Darcy shrugged. "You'd hate yourself in the morning. I don't always like what you write, but you don't write dreck, and dreck is what they want. Mind candy. And I am New York's leading literary confectioner."

Landry leaned closer to her. "You're cute."

"Don't give me the soft voice and big brown eyes, Landry. I might've bought it twenty years ago, but not now." Darcy patted his cheek. "I don't sleep with buddies, but I give'm good advice. Take care; I gotta check on my mink."

"Ask her if she's got a friend."

Landry watched Darcy slither around and through the press of people between her and the bedroom, ignoring the women, smiling at the men. He dropped his plate in the garbage pail and worked his way to Helen Storey, who was waving from the table.

"Patrick! Mah God, how've you been this long winter?"

"Putting on weight. Enough to have to choose between salad and lasagna. How's the cookbook business?"

"Gawd. They're startin' to look me up in the Domestics column." Helen Storey's Georgia-soft voice was a literate razor wrapped in honey. They'd been crossing at Crissy's or Caroline's for years. Landry sometimes wondered why it never came to more, except chemistry happened or it didn't, and it hadn't, and he'd loused up too many good friendships by sleeping with them. Anyway, Helen liked her men Latin and basic.

"Lordy, Patrick, for thirty bucks an hour, I'll edit subway graffiti, if that's what they want."

"So how's—"

"What?"

The rock music on the stereo had risen a few decibels; conversations around them rose to compensate. Landry leaned closer to Helen. "How's that Mexican chap you told me about?"

Helen jabbed a celery stalk into a plate of dip and crunched it. "In Mexico."

"From here you could throw your drink off the fire escape and hit ten Latins. Why go all the way to Mexico to find one?"

"Mainly so I can leave 'em all the way down there. Caroline says your books are doin' real well."

"Well, I don't dodge the desk clerk anymore."

"I've always admired people who could write fiction," Helen confessed.

She should try harder than she did, Landry thought. Helen was always waiting for someone else to steer her right, make her choices for her. She'd never find out how good or bad she was, never take that kind of chance. A ripe, dark plum of a woman with the lush beauty that Arthur always married. Hell yes, Arth would get next to Helen in a hurry.

"I've always admired people like my brother who could fly a plane." Landry finished his drink and rattled the ice. "It didn't help."

Did it, Arthur?

He got up to pour more scotch over the wilted ice cubes. When he got back to the table, Helen was gone. Landry tried not to drink too fast. *Count your drinks. Okay, this is the first one after the last one.*

Didn't help, did it, Arthur? A hundred and thirty-six combat missions, Liberators in Europe, B-29s from Tinian, Sabres in Korea, Air Medal, DFC. You bombed more real estate than I ever saw. Five beautiful wives: all gorgeous centerfolds, as if it wouldn't count toward your score if they weren't. You ended up bombing yourself in a motel bathtub in 1961, opening your wrists and doodling with your blood on the tiles. You, me, Connie, Julia—why were we born with the patent on anger? Somewhere in all the questions, there's a square root to it all.

. . . Party's getting too loud. Should I ask Helen to dance or just go home? I've just gone home too much lately. Getting used to being alone. Hell with it, one more drink won't hurt. Getting to drink too fast like all the rest of my blood. Arthur was the only one who never touched it. Easy; more water than scotch . . . you'll be hung over tomorrow, not a bit of work done, mooning out the window and wishing between aspirin you could meet someone. Warmth. Contact. You said you weren't looking. Bullshit, people alone are always looking, like gulls after fish. It's not that no one loves me. The awful thing is that I don't love anyone. The muscles are atrophied.

A sayable, livable word for love, that's what we needed. With all the wives and other women, Arthur never found one, yet he could always find somebody.

"Some body," his brother amended.

Maybe a body was all you wanted. But who ever knew you well enough to know what you wanted?

"Perhaps Julia," Arthur reflected. "I could talk to her sometimes. Now and then she might even listen."

Arthur Cole poised on the chair at the end of the table: blond as Julia, the blue Air Force tunic tailored around his trained body, silver wings and service ribbons beautifully set off between oak-leaved shoulders. Arthur had Connie's thoroughbred look, but cooler and more calculating. Only the vestige of a youthful stutter belied perfection. Arthur's voice was naturally clear and resonant, where Landry's had taken years of Shakespeare to develop.

Hello, big brother. What time is it?

"About '61. Close to the end." Arthur surveyed the party with more amusement than interest. "Where do you find people like these? They're out of Dickens."

They make more sense to me than you ever did. I could figure all of us but you.

"You were the one none of us could understand," Arthur countered. "Not good for anything. A fifth wheel on the railroad track."

I know. Things like that get back to you in a family. Julia enjoyed repeating it. She always loved putting me down, but you were a saint to her, like Connie. Did you ever love anyone?

Arthur's fine head moved slightly. "Of course."

I wanted so much to be like you. Someone took a picture of us in the backyard, remember? Me in my cowboy suit and popgun, you about eighteen. You were so big and safe to snuggle up to.

"No."

I never saw you much after that year. You went away. You were my hero for years. It was an education to learn how finite adoration can be.

"I loved you too, Monk," Arthur said with something like gentleness. "As much as I could. You were Mama's new family. There wasn't any room for Julia or me. There never was."

It seemed unnatural not to love my own blood, but I couldn't manage it when I knew you better. What happened to us, Arthur?

"Connie was always—" Arthur cut it off with a shrug of dismissal. Landry noticed the old nervous twitch of the mouth that made a false start before the words came, the only visible hint of tight-reined tension. "You're like Connie. Everyone had to have the same words for love as you."

1934: You went away that year, and somehow it was never the same when you came back to visit. Arthur's coming! Boy, when Mama used to tell me that, I'd wait in the window all afternoon. Is he coming yet, Mama? Is he coming soon? And then I'd see you get out of the car, so tall and magical, so sure of the far places you'd come from. But never the same after you left. Always a distance. Kids feel those things. What was it?

"Does it matter?"

Yes, it matters. Why are you, all of you, coming back now, old bits of memory like shrapnel reinfecting me? What made you into a piece of ice, Arthur? You lived tight and died silent. No one ever knew you, not even your wives. Not even in bed, I'll bet. That's a neat trick, but I'm sure you managed it.

Arthur only raised an eyebrow at Becket on his stool. "Terribly whimsical, setting a place for the cat. Damned thing will shed all over the food."

You took my father when he was washed up and thinking you were his last chance—

Arthur's mouth twisted. "Always counted on others, Jack did. Always had to be loved."

You set up that poultry business in Richmond and asked Jack to manage it. You made a laborer out of Denny and drove him like a field hand to earn his keep when he was sixteen. You ran your own house like your wing office at the air base. I had my own troubles then, but I didn't expect to see Jack get off the bus with Denny trailing behind, both of them flat broke. I never saw Dad so beaten. Sixty-three years old and lost, and Denny not understanding any of it except that his brother was a steel-plated son of a bitch. He told me about the "business," Colonel. You didn't know enough about chickens to point to a drumstick, but you knew how to shave a buck. Dive in, pull out at just the right time, and leave Jack holding the bag.

"He recovered," Arthur said coldly. "He always did. Never any substance you could bank on, but as long as there was a back to slap or a good-looking woman around, Jack would charm them all. Listen, Monk. Some lead and some follow, takers and the taken. You were all weak, all bullshit and beer. God, I got so sick of—you know why I never drank or smoked? Gagging on Connie's cigarettes, wearing a path up Corbett Road to the store to fetch her more beer—on credit. Even that I could have lived with. . . ."

But what? Connie adored you. I think if she could've figured a way to beat the incest rap, she might've balled you.

"That was Jack's department. He was always good at that."

Come on, Colonel. I've lived longer and deeper than you. Tell it like it is. 1934: the year you and Julia left. What happened?

"There was—"

For the blink of an eye, Arthur seemed to shrink. His body sloughed years, muscle, definition. The strong face went bony and callow, the mouth lost its firmness. *Were you ever that young?* Only the moment, a flicker in Landry's memory, then Colonel Cole was in command again.

"There was a word I never found," he said. "Never until I was phasing out in that warm, peaceful pink water. I reached up to write it on the tiles, leave something definite. A word."

What word? They couldn't read it.

"What the hell do you care?" Arthur snapped. "You were all alike, cigarette fog and the smell of beer and the lies. Leave my ghost alone," he finished unhappily. The tailored shoulders lifted and fell. "What's the use?"

Don't put me off, Arthur. You were never terribly bright, just shrewd.

"And you were always shapeless, soft. There was a word, but I've forgotten."

They tried to read it on the tiles when they found you, but it wasn't legible.

"Oh?" Arthur rose, carefully smoothing the blue tunic. "It made all the sense there was then. I saw friends go down over Germany, spinning in, one wing gone, the other on fire, no chance to bail out. Whatever they thought never got saved either. You ought to work out more, Monk. Getting a stomach. No woman wants to sleep with a soft gut."

Is that all you ever knew about women?

Arthur smirked. "Is there more?"

Jesus. You were human once, you must have been. What changed you?

Arthur stood up, settling the peaked cap on his head, ramrod posture concealing a slight curvature of the spine that the army doctors missed in 1941. "Everything is compensated for," he said. "A lot was taken; I took back. Lead or follow, get or lose." He looked down at Landry as he had all his life. "You were always a loser and Denny was a minus quantity. Why do you need to know?"

Because I loved you. Even now the deep-frozen freak you turned into won't leave me. All of you, you're a permanent stain. And you know what, Colonel? Someday I'm going to read that word you smeared on the tiles, and when I do, there won't be silence or arrogance or wild blue yonder enough for you to hide behind. I didn't want to remember, but I can't help it. I'm on your case because it's mine too; because I can't grow any more without knowing.

Arthur sagged a little from his parade ground stance. "I was never that cruel."

You were never that aware. You can't fly humans. You have to live with them.

"You—" Arthur faltered. "You and Connie were the haters. Jack was the taker. Why do you need to know?"

Not hate, Arthur. A sayable word for love. Your talent was planes. Mine is people. I'll write you so clearly, you'll never get away; so that if Denny or the world ever ask: was Arthur Cole human, the goddamned humanity of you will sing out yes! loud and clear.

"No."

I have to. You're part of me.

Arthur only turned and stalked away, shoulders swinging.

Don't go. Tell me what happened.

The cocoon of memory split, shredded, vanished. Landry shook his head to clear it, aware of the disco beat, banal but insistent. He stared at the ice in his glass.

Tell me what happened . . .

6

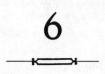

Lauren gave herself the marching orders: Finish this drink and go home.

The party had been pleasant enough, better than staring out the window and drinking alone. She chatted with Evan and admired the word processor that pleased him like a kid's new bike; caught up with Crissy, who really *was* putting on weight; said hello to Carrie . . . no, Caroline, who came to Aaron's once with Crissy and Evan. Very open and assertive, Lauren considered. Tells you in everything she says that she'll buy this Tulsa move because she's arguing so desperately against it.

And the writer, the one in green with all that gold rattling on her wrists: clever, funny, but it's one face for men and another for women. Breaks her neck to flatter men. Must be exhausting, even on reflex.

Odd going to a party without Aaron, she thought wistfully. I miss him, but I call the shots from here on. And the drinks. This is the last. I've talked, smiled, danced with that sweet boy who came with the English twit—not much conversation but a lot of energy—and whatsisface, the guy who smells of cat. Nice-looking, eager, and totally unavailable, a male old maid.

Are there singles' bars for the Geritol Set?

Crissy looks so happy running around. Thin little stick when I knew her in Portland. All her work on these shelves . . . old stuff, all of it. She hasn't done anything new in ages. Energy and ideas, she had them both, and a wry subtlety. You were good, Crissy. You had talent. What you didn't have was the discipline and the ruthless need for it, the drive that makes you grub at it, sacrifice, walk away from everything else for its sake, like I did. I'm that selfish, you're not. You want to be happy. Who doesn't? I'll never make a habit of celibacy, but I want to be the goddamned blue-ribbon *best*.

So we'll finish this drink and get home to it. Tough I am, young I'm not.

She'd noticed the tall man in the fisherman's sweater before. As Lauren edged to the liquor table for more ice, he was there, a few paces away, talking with Evan James.

A little young for me, she thought, but interesting.

About forty, Lauren judged, with a thick shock of dark hair falling over his forehead, graying as rapidly as her own. *Needs a haircut.* Her first impression was physical mass, bigness, but that could be the bulky sweater. His body moved as if he was used to balancing it all, not just dragging it around like an afterthought.

But he hasn't danced all evening, she thought, didn't even hover around the edge of the dance floor the way stag men do when they're making up their minds who to descend on. Married? Thought at first he came with the whatserface in green and glitz, but no, guess not. Swept out in her mink a few minutes ago . . . what the hell, he's too young anyway.

Lauren felt virtuous making this her last drink and meaning it. She found Crissy collecting abandoned paper plates in a plastic bag.

"Crissy, dear." Lauren hugged her. "Got to go, but thanks so much for asking me over. I enjoyed it."

"Oh, don't *go!*" Crissy implored. "There was someone I wanted you to meet, but the damned popcorn machine got polio or something, we hardly had a chance to *talk.*"

"Well, it's late. I've got a tennis date in the morning."

"The idle poor," Crissy admired. "Anyone interesting around since Aaron?"

"Not many," Lauren admitted with a giggle of confession. "My vibrator maybe."

"Be it ever so humble: science's boon to the separated girl. Hey, *listen!*" Crissy turned Lauren toward the rear of the loft. "There's someone you have to meet. Pat Landry. Down there by the table."

Without her glasses, that far was a blur to Lauren. "Where?"

"I don't want to point, but it's the tall guy in the sweater and jeans. Come on." Crissy tugged Lauren after her like cargo.

It was he: confidence and uncut hair, quite alone now, apparently meditating on the wall over the kitchen sink.

"He looks like an actor," Lauren muttered, hoping he wasn't. Most of the actors she knew were the dullest people in New York.

"Oh, he used to be," Crissy led her on. "Pat's my dear friend and Caroline's, you met her, 'n' he writes fabulous books that people actually *read*. . . . Pat! I want you to meet my old friend Lauren Hodge, who has much more ambition than me and actually *works* at art."

After Crissy introduced them and galloped away, Lauren was even more pleasantly surprised. He wasn't that young. The impression of youth derived from the line of the head and hair and the way he carried himself. Up close, the fine network of facial lines read nearer her own age than forty. The ease of his manner was genuine but overlaid with something else—not ego; she knew ego down to its socks—something perhaps troubled, but he looked at her and actually saw her.

She decided to have another drink after all. "Crissy tells me you used to be an actor."

"Until I repented and saw the light."

"Stage or film?"

"Stage mostly. You do film?"

"Video. There's a difference."

"Yes," he bounced back with unexpected energy. "Beautifully plastic medium. The things you can do with image, movement, and music."

The man was full of surprises. She noted his hands when he passed her the drink: large and square, incredibly warm to the touch. His whole body exuded energy and heat; Lauren could feel it standing next to him.

Before she realized it, he was drawing her out about her work instead of talking about his own, listening intently, head cocked slightly to one side.

Then, abruptly: "West of Nebraska."

"What?"

"Soft *o*. Clear vowels, no nasal. West Coast like Crissy?"

"Yes, I'm from Portland. You?"

"Born here," Landry told her. "Raised all over. D.C. and Virginia mostly."

"You don't sound southern at all."

"Virginia isn't real southern-fried, just lazy. Directors screamed at me until I learned to speak English. You can't say y'all in Shakespeare; it makes for a credibility gap."

"What do you write, Paul?"

"Pat. Historical fantasy, that sort of thing."

And that was all. Instead of launching into a monologue on his work, he brushed it aside with a trace of weariness. "You look Irish, Lauren." He had a disconcerting way of taking sudden right angles in a conversation, usually away from himself.

"Half, I guess. My father was a Weir. That's Scot. My mother's name was Halloran."

"Irish Catholic?"

"Oh . . . not really. My grandparents took me to Mass when I was little. I still go to Saint Pat's now and then to light a candle. You have the look yourself."

He grinned. "Partly. Sort of a mutt as far as I can tell. Pin the tail on the British Empire. Anywhere you hit, there was a Hawkins or a Landry dying for Good King Somebody or shooting at him. And a mick or two."

"Yeah-h." Lauren smiled at him. "You definitely have the look."

"I'd like to write for film." Landry leaned against the sink. "So damned plastic, so many possibilities. Like orchestration."

"Well," she said, "I've been looking for people who know their way around a typewriter. Come see some of my work."

"Love to."

Like herself, Lauren learned, his days were spent alone in the exile of work, and any voice was a relief from the nagging Narcissus of his own. She was intrigued; she felt at ease with him and invited Landry to a showing of her recent work in SoHo. The next day she found herself hoping he'd come because, as usual, she'd forgotten his name.

7

Landry remembered hers. He went to the showing in SoHo. With music by Aaron Feurstein, Lauren's piece was one of her last cross-form works, dancers interacting with open, elliptical sculptures. After the murky symbolism of some of the other pieces on the program, Landry found it utterly delightful.

After the showing he lingered for her as the in-crowd audience filed out of the theater, trailing criticism like cigarette smoke. Lauren firmly dropped her tape cassettes in his arms and announced she'd spring for a cab back to her place in Chelsea. A pretty woman, but in the gray February daylight of Wooster Street, the lines in her face were as evident as his own. Lauren rode the back of the cab like a tank commander, telling the driver where and when to turn. She had the fare ready when they pulled up at the Hotel Chelsea on Twenty-third Street, and tipped like Scrooge a week before Marley's return.

Landry's only experience with the Chelsea had been a two-week stay in 1969 between acting jobs. He recalled without warmth a dark cubbyhole and a hall bath, rock musicians wandering stoned through the lobby at all hours, followed by blond weekend groupies in from Long Island, fresh-faced and Apache-beaded, hustling change for their heroes on the sidewalk outside the hotel.

Lauren's apartment was something else again, a long studio that went from the hall door straight back to bay windows past

a couch, a fireplace, a small tidy bath and cramped kitchen-
ette, a TV monitor and cassette rig, and shelf after shelf of
hand-labeled tapes. Nothing stood in the middle of the floor,
nothing took away from the open, airy impression of the
place. In one corner near the bay windows a rubber tree grew
toward her small desk and antique stereo components on their
battered, paper-stuffed shelf. Large blowup photographs of
Lauren's sculptures and installations lined the walls above the
shelves. One of them showed Lauren much younger, hand in
hand with a heavy, balding man.

Lauren stowed her tapes and paused in the kitchen entrance. "Want some coffee, Paul?"

"Pat. And I'd love some."

Lauren winced. "Honestly, I'm so bad with names."

"Try listening to them." He blunted the reproof with a
smile, parking himself at the small dining table across from the
kitchen.

"Pat. Anyway, how do you like your coffee?"

"Black and strong."

"Good. I make it almost espresso." Lauren busied herself
with what seemed an inordinate amount of equipment. She
brewed coffee the continental way, directly into the cup. For
those with the patience of Job, it made a virile drink. "Don't
usually drink it after breakfast," she explained, setting the
mug down in front of him. "Winds me up too much, but I just
had time for a swallow this morning."

As threatened, the coffee was almost espresso. This would
be his last for the day or he'd be awake all night. "I liked your
film very much, Lauren."

"Thanks, but it's video, not film."

"What's the difference?"

"All the difference in the world when you're paying for
studio time."

"It was a nice surprise to hear Feurstein's music on the
track."

"Oh?" She looked up from her coffee, almost anxiously
pleased. "You know Aaron's work?"

"I have some of his old records from the fifties. Scratchy but
good. You knew him?"

"Very well." Lauren pointed to the blowup of herself and
the heavyset man. "That's him. Was him. He doesn't look that
good now."

Her tone answered more questions than Landry wanted to

ask. "There's a lot of Aaron's music on my tracks. He was very generous that way."

His hunch was right: they were or had been involved. "I'd like to see more of your work. Not that I understand all of it. Like listening to a new language that's almost but not quite like my own. I catch drifts of it. Interesting."

Lauren seemed pleased more by the definition than the compliment. "That's a good way to put it."

"I'm being honest. Good art excites me, bad makes me barf. Like that other piece, the one with all the carpetsweepers howling away." Landry set down his mug. "I'm pretty straight-life, Lauren. I like to know whatever I'm looking at or listening to has an idea behind it somewhere. And I've never been hot for vacuum cleaners, concrete, or symbol."

"Oh." Lauren plunked her elbows on the table. "I know the artist very well. Very young, still trying to find a form."

"Not on my time, please. I keep thinking of 'The Emperor's New Clothes.' Everyone saying how marvelous he looks and what a genius the tailor must have been, and only one little kid not afraid to say the king was naked."

"Speaking of which." Lauren finished her coffee and pulled an ancient projector on its stand out from the wall, plugged it in, and aimed the beam at the white kitchen wall. Quickly she threaded a film leader through it and snapped it on. When the title appeared, Landry applauded with raucous delight: THE EMPEROR'S NEW CLOTHES.

"Yay-y! Where's the popcorn?"

"I did this for a school library. Two talented dancers and a budget of nothing."

Landry sat back, grinning at the screen. He liked this girl; she knew who the hell she was. Before the film was over he decided to ask Lauren out to dinner.

A lovely idea, but not that evening, as it turned out. Lauren had an art opening to go to. Just as well, Landry thought. He wouldn't rush her. But he did leave a copy of his last book, *The Harper's Wife.*

"Sort of a historical," he explained at the door. "Never mind the cover, it's not all that romantic. More like Jean Anouilh on an off day. Call you, Lauren."

"See you, Paul."

"Pat!" He took her hand, laughing. "Ciao, Lorna."

*   *   *

Lauren suggested R.J. Scotty's on Ninth Avenue for dinner. Landry didn't know the place but took to it instantly: the long dark bar in front over which stretched a huge sign: TEMPER-ANCE, and the brick-walled, low-lit dining room, snowy linen and fresh flowers at every table. The waiters and waitresses were all aspiring actors, studying, making rounds, waiting for their break, full of that childlike hope that actors radiate even past the age of eighty. Landry's heart went out to them; most were personable, efficient waiters, annoyingly hard to find in a city known for its restaurants.

"Aaron and I came here sometimes," Lauren said.

"How long were you together?"

"Seven years."

Hardly the fickle sort. That was longer than his first mar-riage. In the soft light over the table, Landry began to flesh out the flat image of Lauren Hodge in his imagination. He learned of her long marriage to Walter Hodge, her background in Portland. There were two grown children, a son and daughter, both married and independent of her concern, unlike Darcy Rambard, who would do anything for her daughters except cut them loose. Lauren's main income derived from invest-ments made out of her divorce settlement with Walter, but even with her work known all over the world, a video artist had to hump like hell to get anywere. She was frankly curious and envious of the fact that Landry had an agent to do the selling for him.

"It's impossible for me to get anyone like that."

Landry squelched the swell of arrivée smugness. "Unless you're Harold Robbins, it's hard for a writer to sell himself right. Edith Fine does all that for me."

"What's she get?" Lauren asked.

"Straight ten percent."

Lauren shrugged. "Ten percent of me would add up to a fat hundred a year."

"Well, so did Edie's for a while, but she had faith in me." Landry savored the bouquet of his wine, then tasted it. "She comes on like an unshuffled deck, and her desk always looks like the aftermath of a tornado. On the phone she sounds like a Hadassah mother from Queens, but it's all camouflage. She's pure shark. I don't know what she does to editors to charm, cajole, or threaten my living out of them, but I'm very glad she's around."

When dinner arrived, the portions were delicious but seemed rather small to Landry.

"They're huge," Lauren contradicted. "Remember I told the waiter to split it? This is one dinner."

"Ye gods."

Lauren had a nervous stomach; while she cut, forked, and chewed each bite with meticulous relish, anything could kill her appetite, which was never ravenous, and splitting dinner saved money.

"And when it comes to saving money, *I* am a shark."

"I should learn that."

"You should, Pat."

"I don't know: money's there or it's not."

"That's foolish."

Landry felt a wave of irritation burn him; perhaps it was the drinks before dinner or the several glasses of wine with it, but he knew the quick, irrational anger that washed over him. Looking at Lauren over veal piccata, he wondered if part of his anger was the drudgery of the present book, whose late pages still refused to get up and breathe, stillborn words on a mortuary slab. The work never left him, not even during sex—not that he'd had that much recently—and for him to forget it completely, he had to be happy with the day's output. No writer in the dark night of his scab-picking soul was any better than his last few pages.

"I was up until two this morning, reading a fascinating book," Lauren told him.

"Oh?"

"The Harper's Wife."

The anger washed out of Landry; something relaxed and let him smile without effort. All through the evening, consciously or not, he'd been waiting for her to mention his book. When she didn't, he assumed she hadn't started it, or worse, couldn't get into it. He felt redeemed.

"I'm really glad you like it."

"You're a romantic," Lauren said. Then, cloudily: "Aaron was a romantic—my God, I'm talking about him as if he were already dead." She picked up her vodka and finished it. "I think I'd like another drink. You're not sticky romantic," she amended quickly. "Not gushy. There's a lot of humor even in the heavy scenes."

"If you cry," said Pat Landry, "you save the reader the trouble."

"Well, I'm impressed," she said gravely. Her fresh drink came and Lauren sampled it, keeping her eyes on him. "You write women very well for a man."

Landry warmed to the compliment although something niggled in his mind that he was being stroked. "I like women."

"Most men don't, not deep down."

"Most men are afraid of them."

"Are you?"

"I don't know, Lauren." He considered it seriously. "There's a lot of anger in me I'm just learning to recognize. You women are fascinating creatures who bear us, change our diapers, raise us, marry us. Love us and hate us, fight us, and what the hell do we know about you?"

Except somewhere down the long gauntlet of lovings, partings, and lacerations, we leave part of ourselves with you and come away with your fingerprints and scars all over us.

"I thought, when I had to make a choice between cliché and truth: here's a phenomenon. Let's take Woman and lay her out for examination. Most of the male writers I read wouldn't know a woman's mind from chopped liver."

"Playing it safe." Lauren nodded. "You could fail very easily."

"You don't fail, you don't grow. Did you learn to roller skate without falling on your tush? When I was in theater, I thought the consummate actor was the one who could play anything, people like Page and Brando. Hunter, Hoffman, Guinness. So I think the best writers are those who can write from both viewpoints."

"How?"

"Listening. Observing, as Flaubert said. Listen to the rhythm of a person's speech: what does it tell you? Watch their body language. Do they like their bodies, do they relate to them? How do they use their hands: to express themselves, or just awkward appendages to be parked or fiddled with. Or hidden. How do they come on, assertive, apologetic—"

Jack and Connie fighting each other through the years, instinctive masters of bitter or light hyperbole, eviscerating each other before the inevitable onslaught of flying plates. But never smothered, always expressive. Somewhere in both a confidence and an awareness of life—

"Jack."

It startled Lauren. "What?"

"No. Nothing. Jack was my father. He taught me to listen."

That was a lie. Jack never listened to women in his life.

"Women, Monk?" At the end of the table, sixty-year-old Jack hulked briefly over his old-fashioned. "Women are like going to the bathroom." He drank and vanished.

The hell they are, Jack. You should have listened. "It's just that . . ."

Lauren reached for his hand on the table. She had tiny hands herself, freckled and thin-skinned. Denny had small hands for the big man he grew into. "It's just that people don't listen to other people," Landry said. "Always playing their own theme song in their head. When you really listen, people tell you more about them than you really want to know. The trick is getting them to shut up."

Lauren left her hand in his. Her fingers were cold. He learned over time that they never quite warmed. "Have you been listening to me?"

"Not enough to tell me all I want to know," he said.

"We'll just have to have dinner again."

"Definitely."

When the check came, Lauren did a minute audit while Landry fumbled for his Visa card. It was a dollar too much in the total.

"Always add the bill for yourself," Lauren cautioned. "They're good kids, but you don't want them making mistakes on your money."

"Let's see." Landry checked the figures. Lauren was right. "Yep. A buck over."

Lauren gave him a too-bright smile. "Just as long as you're listening and watching, know what I mean?"

He felt a subtle touché. "Okay, lady."

"Am I right?"

"Right. Go play with the cobra."

"If you're into dessert," she suggested, "I've got some ice cream in the fridge."

8

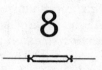

Landry continued to learn about Lauren Hodge. He'd been right about her original coloring: freckled redhead. From her early pictures, she had never been beautiful. At twenty, the face in the brownish photograph was not even interesting: 1943 hairstyle and nothing like life had yet happened to the eyes. Even at fifty-five, Lauren's features were very delicate, unable to take much makeup, and the little she used was subtly done. Everything attractive about her had been made, developed, become. There was nothing young about her except the resilient *sense* of youth that emerged, permanent and earned, when the first one wore away. She could be as bright and up as himself, but beneath it, especially when she drank, Landry sensed the same tight anger that smoldered in himself, though less acknowledged or understood.

He was interested. Learning about Lauren, he learned from her. Within a few weeks, she took him through a whirl of openings and showings, all a breath of fresh air to Landry. Unlike writers, who seemed to hang in closets like unused suits when they weren't working, the denizens of New York's film and video world were always on the move—seeing, being seen, in communication and/or warfare with the movers and shakers, the people who funded, ran galleries or film programs, criticized, or merely fringed the scene. Landry became familiar with the Guggenheim, the Museum of Modern Art ("MOMA" to the in-group), La Mama, mixed-media vagaries that grew like fungus in cellar theaters on the East Side and died as quickly, and the giddy, grimy, alleged charm of SoHo, where one could find, in an overpriced restaurant, a string quartet in a front window and rats by the garbage pails on the sidewalk. The Mudd Club on White Street with its air of a disreputable frat house, where the drinks were too expensive and most of the video incomprehensible. All wryly reassuring in a way. Of the battalions of artists introduced by Lauren, who might remember their names on a good night, none was as financially secure as himself. They were all on grants or clawing to get one, an art in itself. Party conversations centered not on who was doing what but who'd been funded or shot down in the middle of a project by running out of money.

"They've been talking money, money, all evening," Landry said aside to Lauren at one video showing. "What ever happened to *ars gratia artis?*"

"It got hungry, Pat. They get so little and the rent's always due."

"Remember that sculpture show last week? I admired a bronze and before y'know it, there's the sculptor tugging at my elbow to buy it. A steal at fifteen hundred. What a rat race!"

Quite true. Compared to this, publishing was fat and complacent. They were all anxious, concerned with money only to survive, but centrally concerned nevertheless, skating like Lauren on the edge with hope for a runner, some younger, more than a few middle-aged, many of them women, a few militant lesbians convinced that art was only a door to polemic, intense, committed, and aridly doctrinaire as born-gain preachers.

In her own milieu, Lauren had blessedly avoided becoming a grand dame like the gurus in the world of theater, where names like Stella, Judith, Julian, and Uta were uttered with awe and genuflection and whose presence at any function reminded one of an audience with the Pope. Lauren was solidly respected but no one kissed her ring or rump; no one could catch it in any case. With Landry often left to his own conversational devices—he was a curiosity to video artists; his work was paid up front—Lauren wheeled and dealt at parties, touching base with this person, dropping a word with that, knowing who was worth her time and who not, totally organized and in charge. Her neckerchief flashed like a sail following the prow of her martini as it navigated through the press of an arts party. Her medium fueled much more than Landry's on hype and contact. In the course of all this, he saw an incredible amount of new video in a few weeks. Compared to the best of it, like Lauren's, network television was the Stone Age with commercials, but much of what he saw downright infuriated Pat Landry.

"Goddammit, Laurie, what was he doing? What was his arc? Watching that tape was like a case of visual hiccups."

Lauren only shrugged, a veteran. "He got a hundred-thousand-dollar grant to do his thing. He doesn't go for ideas, just images. And he knows how to bullshit. He spends ninety percent of his time scrounging for grant money. And getting it."

Landry heard the mixture of disgust and envy. "Never changes, does it? The old bullshit factor. A lot of writers do their best work for peanuts. When they make it big, they get six figures for a laundry list. So who buys dinner tonight?"

"I'm broke," Lauren said. "I'll cook."

Lauren worked longer hours than Landry, waking early, revving up on coffee (one cup only but it would give ulcers to an Arab), then driving nonstop through phone calls, meetings, dubbing sessions, and storyboarding until well into the evening. Like Landry, she always heard a clock ticking behind her. Lauren rarely sat down for long; when she did, her slender legs wrapped about the chair base in a death grip as she drove herself on tension. The first vodka of the evening pulled her plug. Then and only then could she begin to think about dinner.

Landry honestly admired her work; once he shifted to a visual vocabulary, he respected it as much for the clarity of line and intent as anything else. Nevertheless, for all her brilliant visual sense, Lauren would freeze over writing a descriptive paragraph for a flyer or grant request. She usually farmed the chore out to eager young volunteers with indifferent results.

She was in his ballpark now. Landry would frown over the lame blurb: "Jesus, Laurie. I've read livelier descriptions on aspirin bottles."

"You don't think it'll work?"

"Work?" he hooted. "This dreck won't even walk. You've got beautiful, exciting images in that piece and this girl hasn't caught a bit of it."

"She does know what she's talking about," Lauren defended

without much conviction; the description didn't enthuse her either. "She has a master's in video."

"Hell yes. Grammar and terminology perfect. The whole thing is hopelessly correct. Gimme a pencil and run the tape, okay?"

He would watch the video for color and image, scribbling a word or phrase now and then. Over the years, Landry had learned to write book proposals like coming attractions, rejecting every static phrase, retaining only images of color and movement. When the tape was run through, Lauren would have a description of her piece that Selznick would have salivated over.

They hadn't gone to bed yet, although it seemed tacitly agreed they would. Lauren was available most nights when Landry called. It didn't bother him that she was probably seeing other men; in fact, it bothered him so little, he wondered what had happened to his old feverish possessiveness toward women. He and Lauren moved without haste toward intimacy, knowing they'd get there in time. As the weeks went by, they found not only the congenial but the irritating things in each other. Lauren was a former smoker, reformed after an intense bout with pneumonia. Cigarettes bothered her terribly. When Landry needed one, she banished him to the hallway. After a while, like a Pavlovian dog, he simply got up and wandered out on his own, causing a small panic. Lauren came bursting out of the apartment after him.

Lounging by the elevator, he looked up, startled. "Huh? Nothing; just wanted a cigarette."

"Oh Lord." Lauren wilted against the doorjamb, laughing. "I thought: he's mad at me for something and going home without a word."

For his part, Landry grated with silent unreason at her pathological concern over money; her too-tactful admonitions when he left a twenty percent tip instead of twice the tax—"Do you really want to leave that much?"; the inordinate time between dinner off the stove and onto the table, barely warm, or the sometimes several minutes between his knock on the door and her opening it. Minor irritations that came with the territory, like her obvious deference to him as a male that seemed more learned reaction than spontaneous. Among artists, Lauren had the chutzpah of a submachine gun; with Landry she was brightly attentive, laughed too quickly and often in the wrong places at his jokes. He wondered if she was

listening at all. At times when he was speaking, Lauren would
fix her eyes on him and murmur "um-hm . . . um-hm" rapidly
until Landry felt he was talking to an answering machine.

"Stop it," he said at last. "Stop deferring to me. It's an insult
to both of us. I'm not that stupid and you're not that shallow."

Lauren found his directness unsettling. There was no ambi-
guity in him at all. When his mind wandered, she was talking
to a vacant stare; when it didn't, she sometimes found his
concentration uncomfortable. He remembered almost verbatim
what she had said not only last but several lines before. To
Lauren it seemed rude and not a little eerie.

"Alcoholic actors," he explained, "or just people who didn't
listen or concentrate onstage. Never knew when they'd jump a
page of dialogue or just dry up. You had to listen or lose it."

As she became more aware of him, Lauren pieced together
his background. His family seemed all past tense, most dead,
none mentioned in the present. Theatrical parents, older brother
and sister dead, a younger brother somewhere south and
mentioned with no more warmth than the rest.

"That's Denny?"

"Dennis Hawkins Landry," he said with an audible sneer.
"Try not to meet him sometime."

That tone was so consistent in his rare mention of family
that Lauren felt sure there was more stunted love than indifference in Landry's feelings toward them. Patrick Stuart Landry:
colorful but shadowy family, sense of music from his mother,
sense of language from his father. Married twice, no children.
That was not a sadness in his life, she felt. Pat Landry seemed
oblivious to the very notion of children. He rarely referred to
his marriages and then only by their sequence. It irritated
Lauren's feminism.

"My first wife—"

"Did she have a name or just a number?"

"Norma."

"You ought to remember it."

"Believe me, I do."

"What was wrong with her?"

"Nothing. Norma was a nice girl who wanted a house and
babies. Unless you buy that whole package, you've got no
right marrying someone who does."

The second wife, Susan, was referred to only in moments of
whiskey-softened candor. "She was very much like you, Laurie. We were together three years. She left."

This much of him Lauren wanted to know clearly. "What happened?"

"New York. Everything was new to us. Trying to make it in theater. Maybe if we'd stayed in D.C. we'd still be married."

Lauren couldn't picture him as anything but what he was. His hotel room was functional as her apartment, everything centered about work. "Do you believe that?"

"Not really, no. Like a tin ear for dialogue, some people have no talent for marriage. I let her down."

Not the loss of the wife but that he had failed her. "Well, I was damned good at marriage," she asserted.

"So what happened?"

"Nothing. I resigned. Twenty-eight years. Even government workers only have to make thirty."

There were the things she didn't like. He had no sense of money; it escaped like air through the fabric of his pockets. He drank less than Aaron but at a certain point the easy smile might suddenly go cold, the soft voice turn hard and impatient, and Landry, who could charm a butch dyke when he felt like it, could offend with the same ease.

"I wish you'd speak faster and more clearly," he snapped to one of Lauren's less articulate but loquacious guests. "I'm listening very carefully to what you've said. Are you?"

Lauren, with murder in her heart, would leap to succor the offended. "I *really* want to talk to you about that last project of yours. Pat, we need some more ice from downstairs." Then in the kitchen, a virulent whisper: "What the hell are you *doing?* Go easy, will you?"

Lauren never sat down to consider if she'd take him to bed or not. They'd both seen that movie ten times over, to use a Landry phrase—God, she was talking like him now. More accurate to say she became more physically aware of him as a male, wished and suggested that he get better haircuts and a new pair of jeans, and one day found herself buying him socks in Lamston's.

"What am I doing?"

She knew exactly what she was doing. For all her new liberation, she had been raised to defer to and care for men. The truth of that always made her mad as hell after three drinks, but it was second nature. Lauren presented the socks to Landry after a candlelit supper in front of her fireplace.

He ran them through his fingers, even smelled them—he smelled everything with the olfactory curiosity of a dog—and put them back in the bag.

"Thanks for getting navy blue. Loud socks are like loud restaurants: I get out of both very quickly."

"Why'd you smell them?"

"I like the smell of clean cotton." He laid his hand lightly over hers. "You know, one of these nights I'm going to come over and bring my toothbrush."

Lauren felt gratified, more because he hadn't rushed it. "I'd be disappointed if you didn't."

They understood each other. Then Landry grinned with an uncharacteristic self-consciousness. "Well. Well, then."

"But can you wait a few days?"

"Oh. Sure. Bad timing?"

It had been so long, Lauren was slow to pick it up. "Oh no. I finished with that years ago, thank God. Just that, dammit, I'm coming down with a cold."

"You looked a little red and weepy." Landry leaned closer in the soft light. "I thought it was something I said."

"No. Just no one wants to do anything with a cold but poop out. And I don't want to be coughing and snuffling through a lovely experience. Oh—" Lauren grabbed at her paper napkin and sneezed explosively. "Oh . . . shit," she wheezed. "What timing."

Landry passed her a fresh napkin. "Have a good blow."

"How about one more drink and a sit by my fire, and then let me get some sleep, okay?"

"Fine by me," he agreed. "I'm a little shot down myself with all this good dinner."

By the fire, she nestled comfortably into his shoulder. "Isn't it wonderful to be our age?" She dabbed at her nose with a Kleenex. "Things that would be such a big ego deal for kids can be so simple." Another cataclysmic sneeze. " 'Scuse me."

9

Here we go, Landry thought: one more time.

The first time you go to bed with any woman, she's a whole new country to be discovered in all its variety, and that takes time. One-night stands are no more than setting your foot on the beach. You're not that close at all, no more than adjacent strangers exercising on the floor of a health club, each in his own bag. I've made a choice. *We've* made a choice. I want it to work right with Lauren; been so many years since love worked right. Susan, Janice, Myra, the demeaning, pointless one-nighters. The brief, bad, banal songs.

I want to know what Lauren wants out of this, but I'm old enough to know what I want: a little ease, a little rest, a little permanence, and whatever else we bring to our time together, whatever meaning we can make. Somewhere in any relationship you find some truth about yourself, and mine's not all nice.

For now, keep it simple, a little old-fashioned. I'll take her some flowers and chocolates. Never saw anyone take such delight in flowers.

"It's so nice to wake up next day and see them," she said.

I like that and the way she'll make a dessert out of half a chocolate, cutting it precisely down the middle and mouse-nibbling her half to make the enjoyment last. She can't understand why I eat so fast. Part of it's sloppy manners and the old army habit of having to eat and get somewhere else. Or just me, in my head already finished with dinner and moving to something else. Most of me is work, the rest isn't much. I hope we're not too much alike in that. Lauren *does* defer to men no matter how consciously she tries not to. Seven years of Aaron, decades with Walter Hodge. I'm glad she's not the worshipful, adoring sort of woman. That kind is emotionally expensive. They always expect you to be God Incarnate when you'd rather take a nap.

But she'll be thinking: *What's he used to, what does he expect?*

Just you, Laurie.

The truth of loving is hard to write, maybe because it's hard to face. You can cop out, diffuse the reality in a welter of euphemism (useful for romance paperbacks where every roll in the hay is the second act of *Tristan*), or go the pseudo-tough route for the macho postadolescents (spread her legs and watch her writhe under the ruthless male need of the hero). Or you take the hard way and be honest. The reality of sex is what you bring to it at the moment: hope, eagerness, need, tenderness, anger, fear, energy or fatigue, past failures or joys, all the former lovers remembered under your hands. In a culture obsessed with sex as an infant with its thumb, either too few people know this or know it too well and choose the fantasy for its anesthetic ease, like preferring Mantovani to Bartok—"ain't it pretty, all them strings?" The bullshit sells better. Darcy Rambard knows that and makes a good living from it.

All I expect from this is you, Laurie—whoever you are, whatever you bring to it, including your laughter. Bring that to bed with you. One thing about playing tragedy night after night: it builds up a hell of a hunger for laughs any way you can get them. I'm finished with bleeding.

I hope I'm finished.

He's not that perfect, Lauren told herself, but he could have been a lot less. In Portland you meet an attractive man, you wonder if he's married. In New York you wonder if he's straight. I guess I've found a good one.

There are things I *don't* like. He smokes too much. I wish he'd stop, but he's not a slob you have to follow around with a vacuum cleaner. Just now and then it ticks me off when he starts eating before I'm out of the kitchen, picky little things like that, and all it means is, he's been alone a lot. We always have to change them, and when we do we say they've gotten dull.

Pat said men and women are more alike than they're different. They'd argue with him in Portland, but maybe he's right. In a lot of ways I'm more like a man than Papa or Walter wanted me to be. If it's "masculine" to think work first and people second, I guess I am. Maybe I miss a lot that way.

So what do I know about Pat Landry? He's not as emotionally needy as Aaron, couldn't be and live the way he does, just a hotel room but everything's hung up or put away, nothing to clutter his work. He knows no one's going to pick up after him, and he's not calling and hogging my time every day the way Aaron did. All right, it was romantic and flattering, a nice pain in the ass that ate into my working time. I've got to be left some distance. All right, a lot of distance. Is that okay?

There I go again, asking of the walls and the world, is that okay? Asking permission to live, like Pat said. Will he be strong enough to be tender, to see how vulnerable I am? Will he know when to hold me without asking and go away when I need to be alone? Okay, I ask a lot but so does he. He doesn't want a clinger any more than I do.

And what does he want or need, two marriages and God knows what else behind him? The thing of it is, I'm not made for short-term romances; they're more exhausting than they're worth, and let's face it, I don't have the time to make an occupation out of man-shopping.

Still—I like you, Pat Landry. I hope we can make it.

The cold night Landry showed up with his toothbrush, Lauren brandished a party invitation from the Limelight.

"It's a new disco. There's an art show, seven to ten only, and I always get freebies. How long since you danced? I'll bet you didn't go to the gym today. It'll do you good." She pulled his head down for a kiss. "We can walk to Sixth Avenue."

Which was a mistake. The walk froze Lauren, who suffered intensely from any degree of cold. The Limelight turned out to be a retired Episcopal church of the dark-brick-and-stained-glass variety where Landry learned "Onward Christian Soldiers" in Sunday school and first heard about heaven—which glimmered as a prospect only when Jack told him ice cream and movies were free and continuous.

For the Limelight, the huge nave of the old church had been refloored for dancing under a multitude of Klieg and gooseneck spotlights. There were at least four bars on different levels, including vestry and rectory, where Lauren was shocked to discover that beer was three dollars, vodka and whiskey four, higher on weekends.

"Lord, it's Yuppie Land!" she protested. "Let's have *one* and dance. My toes are still frozen."

Since it was an Arts Council party, the crowd was older than usual, with a generous sprinkling of fringe people, ageless and hopeless, who went to any arts gathering for some kind of contact, and a colorful splash of punk rockers with green hair and leather costumes designed, Landry guessed, by an S & M type in terminal paresis. Lauren had disco-dressed herself: red silk shirt and black velvet slacks with something green sashed dramatically about her small waist. They stood at the bar at the rear of the dance floor, nursing their ungenerous drinks.

"I'm still shivering." Lauren jammed up against Landry's body heat. "Gonna light the fireplace tonight for sure." She whispered conspiratorially, "Bring your toothbrush?"

"I did."

"Hope I'll be thawed out enough. Oh, look at those two kids dance! Aren't they good?"

Under the deafening beat from oversized loudspeakers, Landry gave the couple a professional scrutiny. Compared to most disco dancers, who construed free-form dancing at its most tolerant interpretation, the slender boy and girl were marvelous, their movements precise and intricate. Connie would have enjoyed them.

"Professionals," he judged. "Chorus or ballet. You don't get bodies like that sitting behind a desk."

The boy whirled through an immaculate series of turns to sweep the girl in his arms, then froze to partner her through her own variations.

"Look at that," Lauren admired ruefully. "Honestly, the talent that goes begging in this town. It breaks your heart."

The roving pools of light swept over the dancers, spilled to the bar, and flowed away. Landry extended his arm to Lauren. "How about it, luv?"

"You wanta?" She grinned impishly. "Think you can keep up with me?"

"Listen to her." He set his empty on the bar and led Lauren out onto the floor. "I was wondering the same about you."

"Well, now." Lauren stepped into his embrace and they let the music take them.

In the shadows to one side of the bar, Jack and Connie stood together watching their son dance.

"He's better than she is," Connie decided, "but she enjoys it more. Doesn't it all take you back?"

"It does," Jack said wistfully. "Remember the old Palais Royal?"

"But that was music to dance to," Connie defined. "This is so loud every termite in the place must be shellshocked. What do you call this assault on the ears?"

"Disco."

"Dismal, I call it."

"It's an improvement over the sixties. You missed all that, Con."

"Missed what?" she jeered. "Civilization ended with Jerome Kern and myself. Now, wouldn't I love a drink." Connie yearned toward the busy bar. "But even dead I won't pay three dollars for a beer."

"Shall we dance?" Jack invited.

Connie considered it, looked down at her own lithe body, remembered at twenty for the occasion, then demurred. "Not to this outrage. There used to be a great speakeasy on West Fifty-second."

"It's the Twenty-One Club now, remember?"

"Oh, yes." Connie thought a moment. "All right, let's go in 1926. It was more fun then anyway." She bent a parting look on Lauren Hodge and smiled with anticipation. "God help Monk. I'll bet that little woman can be a handful when she wants to."

Landry and Lauren danced for an athletic half-hour, then caught a cab to Scotty's for a light supper. They walked back to the Chelsea through a zero windchill factor. Paralyzed again, Lauren spent a quarter of an hour lighting a log in the fireplace and shivering against Landry's chest while he worked to restore the circulation in her feet.

"I've had romantic first nights," he admitted, "but this is new."

"K-keep rubbing."

Lauren seemed tense and deliberate preparing for bed. She took half the throw pillows off the couch and fitted several others with fresh pillowcases. That done, she spent more time low-lighting the apartment like a movie set, turned on the FM to soft music, bustled here and there about too many errands, and finally retired to the bathroom.

In the haste of passion she's not, Landry thought. With nothing else to do, he undressed and got into bed. Time passed. And passed. He followed the patterns of firelight on the high ceiling. This was probably the way she got ready for bed every night: *so what else is new?* More time passed. He began to feel foolish waiting naked as a cadaver on a gurney table.

I wonder if she thinks waiting like this increases the pleasure. It might if I don't fall asleep first. Did she doze off in the tub?

"Hey, Lauren? You okay?"

From the bathroom, muffled but cheery: "Out in a min-ute."

What the hell, it's not the Olympics, but will she please get out of that tub before she goes down the drain?

In the fullness of time, Lauren emerged from the bathroom in a quilted robe. She spent more time cracking the windows just so, about half an inch each. The fire blazed cozily now.

"Want to dance, Pat?"

The way she asked pleased him. With first-time delicacy, he slid back into his briefs and went to hold her. Lauren's skin and hair were fragrant with her palm soap and cologne, and she was bare under the robe. Their legs brushed together as they moved with the slow, sensual music, and after a moment he drew her closer in a long kiss. Lauren responded with languorous warmth. He slid his hand under her robe to stroke her back—

The phone screamed. Landry jumped.

Oh God, who wrote this, Neil Simon?

"Prob'ly business," Lauren said briskly, as if they'd established no romantic mood at all. She snapped on the desk light and grabbed the phone. "Hello?"

From her end of the conversation, Landry gathered it was important, somebody she'd asked to get back to her. Lauren checked a note scribbled on her wall calendar and another in her doodle-scrawled appointment book. "Right, I've got it. See you there. Listen, I'm *so* glad you called . . . oh, before I forget—"

Sure, Landry shrugged to himself. *Anytime. I'm just standing here like the dangling loose end of a love affair that may never get off the ground unless New York has a power-out.*

When Lauren finally hung up and turned off the light, the radio had swung into a smooth arrangement of "How Insensitive." Lauren swayed into Landry's arms. They danced to the onda nueva beat, Lauren twirling on his arm, moving in closer to let him walk her. They danced the number through as if they'd been doing it for years. Then, before she could make another call, another note, pad to the kitchen, the bathroom, or any other diversion, Landry simply picked her up—"Enough already"—and placed her firmly in the bed.

"Are you nervous with me?" He slipped her robe off.

"A little."

"Don't be." Landry settled beside her, stroking her shoulders and small breasts. "The only thing it has to be is us."

"That," Lauren agreed, "is a lovely way to put it."

It was that: the two of them at that particular moment. Lauren was stiff and a little passive, like an accompanist working with a strange singer, and Landry felt somewhat inhibited himself. It wasn't *Tristan* or even Tchaikovsky. They simply weren't used to each other, and although Landry took all the time in the world, honestly feeling gentle and not pressured to prove anything, he knew it wasn't much for her either, and somehow that didn't matter.

After they rested, Lauren got up and made them each a nightcap. They drank them at the window, looking out at winter stars and the rooftops of Chelsea, and she was warm and relaxed in the curve of his arm.

"Like to stay, Pat?"

He would like very much to stay. "Just one thing. My problem isn't sleeping with women—it's *sleeping* with them. If I keep you awake thrashing around, just boot me out and I'll go home."

"Hey." Lauren's arm slid around his neck, her small body firm against him and warm at last. "No problem."

"Kind of new, aren't we?"

In bed, she murmured drowsily into his shoulder, "I'm so glad you didn't rush me through it. Takes a little time."

"Um-hm." Landry yawned, pleasantly surprised at the delicious languor systematically shutting down most of his body. "Thank you for a lovely evening."

"Mm . . ."

He thought: *I wonder if it'll take my usual hour to go to sleep. . . .*

The next thing he knew it was daylight, the early sun slanting on the windows. He'd slept the night through without even turning over. Only the top of Lauren's head was visible over the covers. Landry pulled them down to reveal the Lone Ranger, a black sock for a sleep mask draped over her eyes. Lauren yawned and purred:

". . . time's it?"

"Very early." Landry sighed, turned over, and woke again two astonishing hours later alone in the bed. Somewhere someone was panting with effort. He stretched and wheezed and sat up. Lauren was on the floor by the window, furiously pedaling her slender legs in the air.

"Good Christ. You do this every morning?"

"Yep," she puffed. "Make myself do it. Better get up. Got someone coming in an hour to look at some tape. It's a work day."

"Yeah." He eased out of bed with no enthusiasm for the prospect. "Me too."

Lauren bounded to her feet, arms pumping up and down like a demented oil rig. Landry lurched into the bathroom to brush his teeth. His mind felt full of cotton batting; he couldn't even remember which toothbrush was his.

I think it's the blue one. I hope it's the blue one.

He couldn't even brush his teeth with any energy. The realization hit him: he was relaxed. He'd forgotten how it felt to be this rested in the morning. Like a hangover without the sick. Landry rinsed his mouth and took a deep breath, relishing it like a novelty.

"Wow-w . . ."

When he stumbled out of the bathroom and groped for his clothes, Lauren was making the bed with no-nonsense purpose.

"Next time, breakfast on me," she promised. "Just that somebody's coming in a while."

"Will you be home tonight, Laurie?"

"Think so. Won't know till I look in my book. Hey."

"What?"

"Do I get kissed good-bye?"

"Lady, you sure do. C'mere." When he hugged her good-bye at the door, Landry asked, "Are we going to be something, Lauren?"

"I think we are definitely going to be something."

Landry ate breakfast in a coffee shop near the Seville, then went up to his room to shave. His eyes were bright and clear in the mirror; he felt twenty again, humming as he lathered his neck and chin, enjoying the unaccustomed relaxation of chest muscles that allowed him to breathe deeply over and over. In the mirror, Landry made a face at Landry.

"Okay, Monk." He winked with good-humored purpose. "Let's get with it."

He stuffed his gym gear into its tote bag and strode the fifteen blocks back to the McBurney YMCA on Twenty-third Street, ran two miles on the track, worked out into a satisfying sweat, showered, and walked home again, his whole body alive.

There was a familiar buff envelope in his mailbox. Landry read it over the first steaming mug from Mr. Coffee.

Dear Pat,

Well, I must say I'm very pleased. I did a little pre-liminary snooping at Trefoil Books. Looks like we've earned out on *Harper's Wife*. We ought to see a gratifying check next month at royalty time.

I think this is significant beyond the money. It shows the growth in your readership. Right about now you should be thinking of your next book so I can lay some groundwork for it. How's *Camlann* coming? Best—

Edie Fine/Artists Associates

Landry paced the worn hotel rug, spilling more coffee to add to the spot pattern of the last year.

How's *Camlann* coming? Slow and bad and full of potholes, Edie. You're asking about the next book when I don't know if I have the pizzazz to finish this one. I'm glad *Harper* earned out. All writers are optimists, we have to be. I don't have one small, foggy idea about what to do today, let alone tomorrow. But—a pat on the head from you, a night with a good woman, a workout . . . and somehow things don't look so bad—

"Wait a minute."

He stopped dead in the middle of the floor, eyes on the green plot notes by his typewriter, their too-familiar sense running through his rested, quickening mind.

"Wait a big-assed minute. *That's* what's wrong."

Landry lunged at the notes, spilling more coffee, stuck a cigarette into his mouth and fired it, puffing vigorously like a diesel rig getting under way as he scanned for the thousandth time the portion of outline that had seemed so logical when he sold it and so wrong since.

Try remembering a little of what Jack taught you, clown; what doesn't work doesn't stay.

The problem was clear glass now. Because a paragraph of exposition worked in the outline, he'd been trying to write it as narrative when the development of the actual text hardly needed six thousand words of a journey across Britain.

"Montage, you asshole idiot."

Slash. Scribble.

Which meant the last two thousand words of text had to go. It hurt to cut that much of work so painfully wrought and some of it not bad, but cutting meant the difference between plodding and real movement and sweep; ultimately, between the reader turning pages or simply dropping you in the trash. "Not bad" was what ended up on remainder tables.

"And now we can . . ."

His hands shook with energy and excitement. He picked up the recent pages and began to vivisect them with the pen, ashes spilling unnoticed over his shirt and jeans. The pen cut roadmaps across and down the pages, deleting whole paragraphs, trashing adverbs right and left.

"Where the hell did you learn English, in Minsk? Man, we can cut from here right to—"

The March afternoon darkened toward evening. Only when Landry was squinting did he remember to turn on the desk lamp. The pages spread over his writing board, the desk, and the floor. Hell, yes. It worked now, it was kinetic. He could do the whole transition in two thousand words or less and use the saved space where it was more effective.

Landry reshuffled the now incomprehensible mess of pages and scanned the day's work from the beginning, mumbling with busy contentment. The phone made him jump as it always did in deep concentration. He belly-flopped across the bed and caught it on the third ring. "Yeah? Hello?"

"Hi." A tentative pause. "Am I disturbing you?"

"Oh. Lauren?" He tried to wrench his mind back from the fifth century; it yielded with resistance. "No. No . . . not at all."

"Were you asleep?"

"No, I—no." He sounded like an idiot. "Just working."

"Don't I know?" Lauren laughed softly. "Just wanted to say it was a wonderful evening."

Landry turned on his back, phone cradled between shoulder and chin. "Would you believe? I went to the gym this morning and then worked all day."

"I went back to bed after my meeting," Lauren confessed. "Boy, am I relaxed. It's so hard most of the time."

"I know. Me too."

"Pat? I looked in my book and I can't make it till Friday night. Is that good for you?"

"Oh. Sure. You know . . . gotta work."

"Tell me about it." Lauren chuckled. "How's the book going?"

"Better today. I tore out some bad choices. It's like you have to learn to write all over again with every book, and I'm the class dunce, Laurie. I have to be wrong before I'm right."

"We have a lot in common," she said. "And the most important thing is, we're not anything without work to do. Without my work I'd be a genteel drunk in Portland. Or dead."

Lauren paused to yawn like a sleepy kitten. Landry's fingers drummed lightly on the phone. Already the corrected pages were running through his head. Another half-hour, all he needed to patch the ailing section into something organic.

"I just might go to bed early tonight," Lauren breathed.

"Me too. Meanwhile, gotta work." Over the line, Landry heard the raucous jangle of Lauren's house line.

"There goes the other phone. Put you down for Friday, Pat?"

"Friday," he agreed. "G'night, Lauren."

"Bye."

Landry raised his arms slowly over his head and stretched deliciously. *That's a good woman. So let's get it done, and I'll treat you to sushi tonight.*

Thursday afternoon, he received a note from Lauren on hotel stationery. She had a wide-looped, erratic but generous hand—

Dear Pat:

Wouldn't you know it? That other call was the Montreal Film Festival, and they want some of my recent stuff to show. Of course they don't want to pay much for it . . . well, it could be worse if no one called. See you Friday/L.

Beneath Lauren's broad-scrawled signature was a smile-button cartoon face with happy eyes and a very satisfied grin.

When you live on the edge, you're an optimist or dead.

10

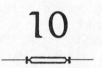

Dear Pat—I'm not writing this but resting at the end of the day with a martini and a sunset, watching orange go to copper to red to smoke and deep blue. We've danced and dined and finally made love. I've thought a good deal since about you and me and us. Thought, not spoken. The words don't come easily as they do for you, but the thoughts are there. So you can call these things I never say, letters I never send.

One night doesn't make a knowledge, but I know some of the important things about you. You were gentle, you gave me the time to relax. Although it probably wasn't all that much for you either, I appreciate you not trying to make it more than it should have been. Just . . . nice, a touching and a meeting, like eye contact between people who know they're going to enjoy being together, and there are those instant recognitions between artists that need no explanation. I've read your work. You know how to sing, Pat Landry. That's where you live.

I can feel the passion under your words and the anger so much like mine. We seethe, both of us. We have sharp edges that will cut the hell out of us someday. You're not as vulnerable as I am. Being a man, you never had to play anyone's game but your own. Nevertheless, you feel about your work those things I could never explain in Portland.

You take the pencil, the brush, the camera, or the musical note, and somewhere in your eye and hand, honed on a thousand mistakes, is the power to make meaning out of random experience, one stroke so clear and essential that it's inevitable to anyone who knows the same truth. Maturity and intelligence have nothing to do with it. You either know how to make that line or you don't. Aaron stayed a child and knew it. You're grown up—thank God—but you have the same knowledge. The critics can explain it. You and I can only make the line speak for us.

For all this understanding, we're still strangers, still only a possibility. I hope you can share my life without hogging it. I've lived with men, lived too much *for* them, because women are trained to that. Forty thousand breakfasts and dinners cooked, fifteen years of school lunches packed—and I somehow went on smiling through days when I didn't drive the car fast so much as aim it at a big red EXIT. Got out of that and into Aaron and the showing of my own work. I've seen you honestly studying my work, trying to understand it. That's the best kind of flattery. Did you know I've shown my stuff all over the world? Tokyo, Berlin, Paris, sculpture installations in several cities here. More accomplishment than most women dare in two lifetimes—and I still feel like someone's ex-wife, ex-girlfriend. Damned silly, I call it, but if I'm going to reach for the best of me, it's got to be now, Pat. So much to do and how long can I live? You've got to be secure enough in yourself that I don't need to define myself by my relationship to you. Got to have enough steel in you to stand on your own without me propping your ego.

That's what it's all about, that vague thing called talent. Steel. Being able to stick with it. Talent's the least of it, really. Crissy has talent, but she'd rather be loved. Not that you have to make an either/or, but you need to draw the line, so on one side I'll be—you'd better believe it—the best thing that ever happened to you, Pat. But on *this* side, that's where I work. There's a big, hungry shark in me with an appetite for being the best, and it's time I stopped trying to be Gertie Goodwife and *went* for it. I only hope the rest of me's tough enough to pay the dues.

Why do we have to live so long to see that the important choices are so clear? Sometimes I think we're not supposed to know, that the Great American Way of Life does everything it can in prizes and punishments to keep us from knowing who we are. They get you at puberty with the movies and soppy love songs, and say: "Get the message, kids? You need her and she needs you, and you'll have kids right away, and the kids need a house, and the GAWL just keeps rolling along."

Doesn't it just.

Maybe it was survival. Even when I was born, life wasn't that long. You had to get with it early: earn, breed, succeed, because the chances were you'd be embalmed at my age. So move it, kids. BETTY CROCKER IS WATCHING YOU.

Upwardly mobile: the chic new phrase for a bitter old truth. Grampa and Gramma Halloran were a couple of *shebeen* micks who knew what poor was like, and they weren't about to go back to it. You better believe they were upwardly mobile, like air bubbles in mud. The Depression was nothing new to them, but I grew up in it. Nineteen thirty-three, a lovely year. Made-over dresses and coats, Papa's clients paying him in vegetables. That leaves a mark. You make fun of me when I count out nickels and pennies for a cabbie's tip. Aaron used to laugh at my bargain-hunting, but I'd been in the game a long time then. For women, in some ways, it's always Depression. The Blacks weren't the only ones in the back of the bus.

Papa, I want to be a lawyer like you.

Girls aren't lawyers, honey. Girls are lawyers' secretaries.

I want to be a doctor.

Girls aren't doctors, they're nurses.

I want to be an architect.

Men are architects, sugar. Be an interior decorator.

Papa, I want to be.

Later, honey. There's a war on.

You remember the war, Pat. Women in slacks and snoods, ration stamps, crowded buses and trains. Let's Remember Pearl Harbor. . . .

Hell yes. Remember every damned thing but yourself, lady.

Moving from base to base with Walter, rooms with plywood walls still new-smelling from the mill. But look feminine, girls. Attract. A lot of them are going to die, so we gotta baby-boom the fifties. Turn up the music, turn down the lights. Hands across the low-lit table, Dietrich singing "Lili Marlene." He sails at dawn—hell, no one ever sails at noon—but get the breeding done first. Be a person later.

How much later?

Walter and I were married in 1943 before he went overseas. I had plenty of tagging after him from base to base before his division sailed for England. What does a wife say about a war except what it does to her husband? Looking back, that might have been the high and low and maybe the all of Walter's life. He never got over it.

Margaret Mary came in 1946, a quiet, serious child who looked more like Walter than me. She's always been the one with the problems of adjustment and identification which she covered by being painfully mature. The last time she came to New York, I took her to a SoHo gallery opening and a party afterward. It confused Margaret to see some people in black tie and some nondescript, even in jeans. "They're not *dressed*," she wondered to me. "Don't they feel embarrassed?" She sat there with one white wine all evening while that raucous crew surged around her like surf around a stone. She's never understood why I left or forgiven me for wanting a life of my own.

But you'd like my son Marsh. We had trouble with him in school. He was sort of like you, Pat. No one could figure out what Marsh was or what he wanted. He sort of ambled through school, bummed around through the sixties, opposing Vietnam because the other kids did, living with this girl or that. Lord, I was so worried one of them would get pregnant and Marsh would be stuck with some idiot. Not to worry, he married a fine girl. Marsh got his act together: his own ad agency. He didn't do it all on careless charm, either. When it mattered, Marsh could deliver.

Most of all Marsh was my buddy, *for* me all the way. I wish I could be as close to Margaret. That hurts more than I want to think about.

No one was ever that close to Walter, really. He came through D-Day and Omaha Beach without a scratch. Nothing that showed. Only years later the depressions became noticeable, more and more frequent. Became a condition. Until he had to go for therapy, hating it all the way as something unmanly. He couldn't keep a job. From a comfortable living we went to barely enough, and that's hard when your oldest child is ten. 1933 all over again.

To see us through, I taught art at a local college and tried to be everything at home. That's why I still have the "president" syndrome, the feeling that everything depends on me. I fed the four of us on ten dollars a week and watched Walter sink into the ruins of his pride, bitter with the children, miles from me. The love songs were done. They didn't write them like that anymore. In the great Togetherness decade, boy, did I have togetherness. I couldn't get away from it.

There was always my art. Trying to be me. Just in my spare time, nothing subversive to the GAWL. The first awards came, then the invitations to show my work abroad. People told me I was good. Somewhere along the line I began to believe them. Then, one day in New York, with a *live* city around me and Aaron holding out his arms, I knew I was just . . . not going back. Started to be me, Pat. The person you made love to the other night.

Walter never forgave it. Grown and married as she was even then, Margaret never understood. Marsh just grinned and said, "I'm with you, Mom." A lot of my love for Marsh is gratitude. Somehow without having to think about it, he knew I was a real person like anyone else.

So here I am, Pat Landry, and there you are. The two of us standing clear in Now, but with so many shadows behind us. I know who mine are. Who are yours?

Did you know I love your laughter? Like silver but there's an edge that turns sharp sometimes. I can't fault you for carrying your own anger when there's so much of my own, but sometimes I think it might have been better if one of us were a placid Swede. Duller but safer.

I can hear the rage when you talk of your family. You don't get that angry when you don't care. I hear it when you snap at me for nothing. Like you're responding to someone else I can't see. What happened that you feel so . . .

What's the word?

But that's not all of you, just echoes to the music. There are a lot of people out there in the GAWL who get to our age with no complexity at all. Sometimes I can envy them, but then Mr. Nice Guy will come down to breakfast and put an ax through his wife's skull and make the six o'clock news for an evening or two. So I think, Mr. Landry, that we have the best of it. We chose the way we live and damned well earned it.

Just, I *wish* you'd go down to the Gap and get some new jeans while they're still on sale. I told you and told you, and you just say: right, yeah, you'll do it.

So he will when he feels like it. Stop being president.

The sun's down now. Only a thin line over Jersey. I'm going to fix another drink and then my lamb chop or maybe go out to eat. My choice. Love (or a very good chance thereof), Lauren.

11

Dear Lauren—we haven't been together very long and carnal knowledge isn't much knowledge at all. You must be wondering, as I am: who is this I'm touching, who have I held through the night? I want very much for *us* to work, and yet I recognize in myself the perverse habit that needs to run from needing. That would be a lot to lay on you now, so these are things I don't say, letters I don't send.

I'm a guy who's past fifty and scared. I live on the edge like you, pumping away at a finite well of talent and energy that's just gone dry. I can't afford to wait for it to flow again, so what next? No one's going to hire someone my age for anything when so many sharp kids are coming up. *Peur de peur*, fear of fear. Fear of failure, of my own voice faltering into silence. Impotence.

I'm not sure by now I can have a lasting relationship with a woman. So many times since my second wife—sorry: Susan—left that I've started and ended, started and ended, something in me seeing clearer each time the end implied in the beginning.

When Susan walked out it seemed like the final proof that I wasn't worth a damn. I ran for two or three years, any show, any woman, usually younger. That's a bad mistake because the youth you're looking for is your own, long gone. They always love you, they always leave. You feel drained and had, but somehow you've got to shuffle the deck and deal again.

When Janice left—twenty-one and in some ways the best of

them—I wanted to crawl into a hole and die. You don't do that. Romance would have it otherwise and the truth isn't all that good for the music business: nobody dies of a broken heart. Nobody joins the foreign legion but Gary Cooper. I wrote my first book in a cruddy hotel room because it was the only thing that made sense or kept me sane. The book sold and got me a contract for another. When the dust settled, I had a chance at another career. One slim chance, Laurie, and I grabbed it. After so many years of failure, the mere whiff of it scares me now. I haven't stopped running.

By then I'd gotten out of the habit of permanence with a woman. One gloomy little therapist thought he had my number. I was living with Myra, who was not mad, just colorfully neurotic. Jewish, moody, and troubled, Myra joined so many self-help groups, she got hooked on them and never felt really secure outside of a therapy session, like the walking wounded who make *est* and Dianetics into Faith to Live By.

When our differences approached the terrorist stage, Myra enrolled us in couples' counseling where your own problems are hung on a very public line and you learn more about other people's sex lives than you ever wanted to know. The sessions were run by this careful little guy with a careful little beard who read my first book and told me that I had deep feelings of fear and anger toward women that would take *ages* to work through. He said there was no future in my relationship to Myra unless I did. He pronounced this very solemnly, scant inducement that it was, looking up at me as if I were about to burst into flame or reach for an ax.

By this time Myra had all the stability of a Shiite guerrilla. If she wasn't already around the bend, I would be soon. So I smiled back into the careful beard and said it wasn't good business.

"For a start," I told him, "I'd be paying you to listen to what people pay me for. Second, I'd end up so well adjusted I might never write a decent line again. And third, I'd end up with Myra, and I'm not that hooked on masochism."

He still didn't understand, but this was a guy whose idea of recreation was running the Boston Marathon.

"Look," I said. "You're telling me to take a neurotic silk purse and turn it into a normal sow's ear. The hell with it."

We gave up on each other. Mr. Careful went on to pluck needier psyches from the maelstrom of neurosis. I stayed maladjusted and prolific. Myra deserted me and married a bank clerk.

See, I wasn't a kid anymore. Ten years in theater makes pretty good therapy in itself. You have to find truth before you can play it. The truth is, I never really *felt* married to any woman. Happy for a while, I could say *yes, I've found it*, but it was a lie, even though the losses left me bleeding and I wondered why love had to have such anger and pain wrapped up in it.

When I drink enough to knock on the doors in myself where Connie still lives, there's something cold that won't give house-room to any woman. Needing them, drawn to them like a compass to true north, I've never trusted women, always had to get close and then get away. It could happen with you, Lauren. There's a hunk of me still fighting Connie because of old, unsettled scores. That war unended, I can't wholly accept any other woman. Walking away became a dangerous habit, being alone too easy. Why, Laurie? Why so hard for me to accept what's so natural for others?

Better than most, you can understand that a child is soft clay. Anything that touches him leaves a mark, and they mark you up thoroughly, tell you what you're supposed to be and leave you to grope for what you are. Like hunting a submarine without sonar; you have to guess from the torpedoes coming at you.

When I was a child, I searched for meanings and found only those the world left me. Nothing tailored, strictly off the rack. I bought the clichés and half-truths before realizing that off-the-rack is what the world accepts as truth, like Julia clinging to Tennyson's stained-glass cosmos because it was prettier than her own and anything else threatened her.

No one wrote a law against knowing who you are, but they made the game so easy to play without it. Jack said once that most people live lives without any real highs or lows, just gently rolling monotony. That may explain diamond wedding anniversaries and Emerson's Quiet Desperation, but you couldn't expect it in a high-octane outfit like my family. My perverse, hard-loved, hard-fought family who were—are—somehow the beginning of it all. They're still with me, unfinished. There's a last battle still to be fought.

So, if you want to know who you held the other night— someone standing between lost battles and last chances. There could be other women after you. There's always another woman somewhere, that's the ease and the horror of life. I'm not that selfish anymore. Scared as I am, life has got to add up to more than me.

That's why I'm going to bring you flowers next time we meet. Why I'm going to hope and try and love you as well as I can.

But bear with me, Laurie. Hang on when it gets hairy. I'm not the bravest kid in the neighborhood, and the old bullies are back on the block. Boy, are they back.

The difference is you. This time I can't afford to run.

12

Another slow, gritty day on the book, inching toward completion. Now there was light at the end of the tunnel. From here, Landry could see a clear line to the climax, the meeting of Arthur and Modred at Camlann. With the March sun long dropped below the buildings on Twenty-ninth Street, he turned off the typewriter, rested his head against it, and took a deep, tired breath.

So far to go yet when he'd run out of steam months ago, and as for enthusiasm, that demon energy that used to boil the pages out of him, that was a wistful memory. Getting there slowly, plot sturdy and inevitable, but there were subtle colorations that needed to be rubbed into the fabric. Arthur and Modred, father and son. Love and admiration and unspoken rivalry.

Jack and Monk.

There was all of it with Jack: love, shy distance, and the final betrayal of that strong but childlike man. Lord, but he could sparkle when he wanted to; throw back the years and stand suddenly in the follow-spot of his own imagination, the charming, handsome black sheep of the respectable Landrys. Burlesque performer at twenty, Palace headliner in his thirties, exulting in life and his body that would never tire, never age . . .

The typewriter frame cool against his forehead, Landry smiled with the memory. *How could Modred help but envy such a height?*

Or reach it, or even tell his father that he loved him. And yet the love was under it all.

"Oh, Jack wasn't all bad."

At Landry's table, Julia carefully painted her nails. "The plain men are more durable; that's why I married Werner. Hardly missed a day of work in his life. But Jack—"She blew gently on the bloodred nails. "Jack could make you laugh. Denny grew up like him: charming and insubstantial."

What time is it, Julia?

"1944. I'm down for the weekend, remember? You picked me up at the train station, all those GIs whistling at me."

Julia, slim and dramatic in tailored black with squared shoulders. She came through the train gate into the crowded station as though it were a stage proscenium, almost six feet tall in heels, coat draped like a cape, aware of the men's eyes on her. She walked straight and slowly toward Monk, taller than most of the men eyeing her, giving them a deliberate touch of class and enjoying it thoroughly.

Julia finished her nails and stood up. "Jack always had to be on, remember? But what fun he was. Come on Monk. After all, it's you remembering. . . ."

Landry closed his eyes to rest them, hearing the familiar melody on the piano: the languorous beat of Connie's inimitable touch.

> "When you're lonesome for someone,
> And just one will do . . ."

Connie swept the melody to conclusion with a graceful arpeggio and joined the family at the table, carrying her glass. She and Julia always drank more than they ate, but Denny and Jack were still eating—waste not, want not.

That was one of Jack's good nights. Lightly buzzed on beer, breaking up Denny every minute. As she listened, Julia molded a piece of green clay from one of Denny's abandoned Christmas kits. It had been a mistake to give Denny clay; they were natural aliens. Everything he tried came out looking like a tumor. He snuffled loudly over his plate with a bad spring cold, enjoying the effect on Julia.

"Den-ny!" She thrust the Kleenex at him. "For Christ's sake, blow!"

Denny blew with more noise than efficiency.

Jack was recalling Tyrone Power and the weeks they played the same bill on the Lower East Side.

"The moobie star?" Denny croaked. "I saw him in *Mark of Zorro.*"

"No, that's his son," Jack corrected. "I'm talking about Power Senior."

"Oh." Denny continued to ingest, less interested. "He do movies?"

"Nah, the old man was legit. Veddy, veddy legitimate and an old ham, genuine Smithfield. Now and then he condescended to a few weeks of vaude."

"Can you picture it? Shakespeare on Second Avenue." Connie chuckled, flicking ashes into the tray. "Jack, remember how all the Jews used to bring the whole family and stay all day?"

"Lord, yes." Jack rose from the table, glass in hand, gesturing. For the moment he seemed to slough aside his middle years. A wave of charisma flowed from him. "Stay all day, change the baby's diapers through the dog acts and the acrobats—"

"Pass the knish and salami around," Connie yipped. "Jesus, the garlic! Kill yourself to do a number, and the whole house smells like a vampire's nightmare."

"And the piano player who could never find your music—"

Connie rocked back and forth with the laughter. "And—oh God—the old drummer who went to sleep if the act bored him."

"Even if it didn't," Jack recalled. "Hell, he played his first engagement at Bunker Hill."

Julia's fingers kneaded expertly at the clay. "So what happened with Ty Power?"

"Well, now: Bernard and I were breaking in new material at the tryout houses, y'know. Proctor's, Keeney's in Brooklyn, but we needed more time to nail it down tight for the Keith time, so we book ourselves into this borscht house on Second Avenue. What the hell was the name of that theater, Con?"

"Damned if I know. I did a split week in February. Who wants to remember that?"

"Figured if we could make the *Yiddische* mamas laugh, we'd hit anywere. Lo and behold!" Jack paused, a stage wait, to gaze about the table. "Who has the same idea but Tyr-r-rone Power. Fresh from *Henry the Sixth.*"

Denny's head bobbed up from his macaroni. "What's that?"

"Early Shakespeare," Jack said dryly. "Early, long, and bad. Even the Bard had his tryout years. But a lot of blood, battles, and rodomontade. The gallery loved it and that's who Power played it to."

Warm laughter around the table, a smile in Landry's heart: a fading section of American tapestry, largely forgotten when radio and movies came. Julia refilled her glass and went on working the clay to suppleness in her knowing fingers. In a slight pause while Jack added a drop more of the devil to his glass, Connie hummed a phrase: "When you're lonesome for someone . . . great old number. That show should've opened. Baldy Slocum could really write 'em."

"Did you know each other then, Mama?" Julia asked.

"No, dear." Connie emptied her glass and gave it a fresh head. "We met at Keith's in Washington. On the big time. Second Avenue was five-a-day, most of it in Yiddish, and no vaude acts booked there unless they were trying out or dying out. Listen to Jack; this is a good one."

Standing before his audience, basking in his imagined spotlight, Jack limned with effortless imagery the mammoth, violent act with which Tyrone Power, Sr., descended on vaudeville, a clangorous succession of battle scenes strung together, like a war in an iron foundry, larded with Power's rendition of Shakespeare's longest and dullest soliloquies.

"And we had to follow this," Jack remembered mournfully. "The curtain came down on all that poetic death, then we'd go out there to work for laughs, for God's sake. In Power's act, everybody died—including Jules and me. Variety reviewed the first night. We got the best notices since the Black Death."

"What's Black Death?" Denny popped up.

"A lot of people died in it," said Julia with a meaningful glance at Denny's smudged nose. "Mostly because they never washed. Wipe your nose, you look like a spaniel."

"So anyway." Jack took stage again. "The manager comes around in the middle of the week: 'What's by you two? This is a comedy act? Power, the hamfaddo, is getting bigger laughs.' So I said maybe if we didn't have to follow the goddamned War of the Roses, it would help. 'What can I do?' he says, spreading his hands like a good little mocky. 'He's death. They don't know from Shakespeare, but he sounds like Jacob Adler, who is a great favorite here. And he's got a guarantee. You got another week, will I live through it? Take advice: don't play this act anywhere the lights are on.'

"Well, now," said Jack Landry. "What could we do?"

The manic and thoroughly irreverent heads of Bernard and Landry came together. Something had to give. The act was dying.

"It was so bad, Bernard was staying *sober*. The Thursday show was packed: mamas, papas, wet kids getting their diapers changed—and Power emoting from a mound of bodies. He outdid himself that day, bless him. He didn't chew the scenery, he swallowed it whole. War, death, destruction, chaos, and *gloom*. And not a dry eye in the house.

"But Jules and I were ready.

"The curtain comes down on this pentametric carnage, and there's a beat. The pit strikes up our music—but instead of coming out from the wings, Jules crawls out from under the curtain and me right after him with a big broadsword, and I chased him all over the stage and off left, yelling, 'Here's one you *missed*, Tyrone!' "

Jack tossed down his whiskey, wheezing with it. "And the *house* came down!"

Oh, he could laugh, Jack could. The cackle grew to a bellow, fanned into a roar to rattle the windows. Jack subsided only gradually, hacking from years of cigarettes. "Oh . . . oh, Lord. Pow . . . Power was fit to be tied. Livid! He clanked up to the manager, still in armor, and fumed—Ignatz, he sounded like an angry can of washers—"

It caught Denny with his mouth full. He sprayed food in the general vicinity of his plate. Jack stage-pointed at an imaginary door to oblivion. " 'I want those two gahd-damned mountebanks out of this theat-uh! Out upon the *in*stant. Do you hear me, sir.' And the manager—" Jack sat down again like a landslide coming to rest. "He just told Power to go to hell, it was the best laugh since the bill changed, and we should keep the bit in. And we did. We killed 'em the rest of the week. They laughed walking up to the box office."

Jack basked in Julia's helpless, braying laughter. "Ain't that one for the books?"

"That's beautiful." Julia's hands went on working the clay. "You should write it someday."

"I will," said Jack, mellow with whiskey and more with the feel of an audience again. "The memories . . . crowd back. God, we were funny in those days."

"Everything was, in those days," Connie murmured with a trace of sadness. "First acts should always be fast and funny. What are you doing, Julia?"

Julia presented it between thumb and forefinger, now a half-formed but recognizable human figurine. "It's going to be a dancer. The spirit of dance, the way you said you always felt onstage."

Landry remembered the finished, finely detailed form. The dancer, muscled, disciplined to complete freedom in that half-kick, arms flung back, all motion implied in the frozen figure. A freedom Julia's hands groped for through all her life, touched but never grasped. But the finest thing she ever did.

Her head lowered over the clay, Julia said quietly, "I always thought I'd be good on the stage. But in serious things. Tragedy."

"The hell with that, dear." Connie stretched out a hand to touch Julia's arm. "Make them laugh."

"Phooey."

"Make them laugh, Julia. They'll love you for it."

Denny dropped his fork with a clatter. "Oh . . . oh, guh—"

"What?"

Denny made the vague but spastic motions of a drowning swimmer. "Guh . . . guh sneeze."

Like a streak, Julia shot the Kleenex at him. Mouth already agape, eyes squeezed shut, Denny was committed to a nuclear sneeze. He grabbed for the tissues and missed, grabbed again almost too late, and most of the sneeze moistened the room at large. Denny never sneezed once; he was a double-play man with occasional triples, and tonight he exploded in triplicate.

"*Jesus!* The complete slob. They oughta send you out to be dry-cleaned." Julia winced.

Denny gazed, about the table, wet-eyed, his pug nose festooned with two swaying pendants that aspired to his shirt. "Eddybody wadda kiss be?"

"Sure," Julia groaned, "I'll mail you one."

"Here, Ignatz." Connie thrust a generous wad of tissues at him. "Blow your brains out."

"Speaking of no brains," Julia mused, "are you doing better in school, Monk?"

"Whatever he puts in that notebook, it's not homework." Connie lowered at Landry. "I don't know what's wrong with you."

"So what's he write all day?" Julia wondered.

"Who knows? It could be smut. He's just at that age, but I can't read his handwriting."

"I can," Jack confessed. "God, how you kill 'em off, Monk.

Violence and melodrama. Power would've loved you. But keep working." The humorous blue eyes twinkled at his son before flicking down to his own glass. "Yeah, I'll write that book someday. Maybe next year . . ."

You never did. A hundred sketches for vaudeville, the complete book for a show that never opened, dozens of radio scripts, a few late pieces for *Argosy*, but you never went that distance.

Landry rubbed his eyes, blinking at the pages by the typewriter.

So Modred rides to Camlann.

So sons learn from fathers. Whatever the lessons, our very lives betray you. I'm the writer you wanted to be, Jack. Perhaps not a loving or even a nice human being, which may be a pity, but I can make the line that means and make you care about it. If that doesn't pay the fare to Happiness Valley, guess I'll have to walk.

Can you hear me, Jack? Listen good. I remember the day, almost the moment when it all came together. That second historical, when I realized I wasn't writing one man's life in a pocket of time, but all life, the whole, soaring arc of the human marvel. Youth, age, greatness, failure, arrogance, and humility; the sweetness and the courage to love in the face of death and silence; the magnificent, belly-laughing defiance we throw in the teeth of mortality. And *I* had caught it on the page. Me, Monk.

I read over the pages, exalted and frightened by their power. Knowing it was there, now I had a responsibility to do it again. I thought of you and wanted you to read what I'd written, but that was another sad lesson: everything in life is an hour late or a dollar short. With yourself years dead, I finally understood Oedipus and the necessary, time-and-again murder of fathers by sons. Connie tried to make me hate you once. I never could. My murder was sharper and sadder than that.

I was better than you.

Somehow I felt that I'd betrayed you by that.

"Monk!"

The old man's slippered feet thudded down the hall with as much energy as eighty-two years could manage. "Monk . . . wait'll y'hear."

Yes, Dad. I'm here.

13

Jack shuffled into his son's room on thin, unsteady legs with the pinched, hard-spared movements of the emphysemic, shoulders hunched and wasted, his voice a rasping cough. He paused to catch what little breath was left to him, then dropped down on Landry's bed, the threadbare bathrobe slipping away from his varicosed legs. But excited: even in old age able to radiate that childlike wonder that never deserted him.

"Monko? Guess . . . guess what!"

What time is it? Nineteen sixty-three. I'm thirty-four and wondering if my life will ever mean anything; working all day at a job, all night in theater, supporting you, watching you die in front of me. Does anyone deal well with death? I can only draw my walls tighter around me, pay the bills, clean the apartment, and wonder how long it will be. As hard for me to show the love I feel as it is for you to breathe, Jack; if I crack, it will all come spilling out, ugly and incoherent, mixed up with my own problems. Denny is a petty thief, running with a crowd of losers, passing bad checks, heading for his first stretch in jail. Arthur dead, Julia aging in Queens, which amounts to the same thing. Only Monk to take care of you. I'm not a big-hearted guy in 1963. Love still frightens me.

"Guess what I saw, Monk." Jack's grizzled chin trembled in a quavering ghost of the old, dazzling smile. In his last moments, life remembered and touched him again.

"I was watching this thing on TV about Will Rogers. My

Lord, I'd forgotten all about it. They showed a shot of Rogers in front of this theater in Chicago. And there it was on the marquee: Bernard and Landry! Jules and I played on the bill with Rogers. Jesus!" Jack glowed. "There we were: Will Rogers, and I forgot all about it. I was just your age then."

Good years, Jack. Your best.

"The big time, two shows a day. Year after that, we played the Palace . . . the Palace." Jack dusted off the thought and let it shine again. "By then we were the funniest act on the boards next to Tate's Motoring. And me, Monk, I was the best straight man ever." Jack considered honestly. "Until Bud Abbot came along. It's all timing. Abbot set up those gags for Costello like a Swiss watch."

A stooped, shrunken old man, three inches shorter than he was in his prime, but the memory seeded a spurt of energy. Jack thrust himself up from the bed as if his shoulders still bunched with bull-muscle, found precarious balance, and was on again.

"You know the old routine: 'My Lord, the lady waits without.' "

Without what?

"Without food or clothing."

Well, give her a ham sandwich and send her in.

"Right . . . right. Doctor, when this finger heals, will I be able to play the piano?"

Of course you will.

"That's great. I never could before . . . yeah, you remember. Well, those punchlines would die without the setup. One beat late 'n' they die."

The moment passed, burned out. Jack wilted down onto the bed, pulling the bathrobe over his skinny legs. "I was never legit," he considered. "It takes years to do tragedy."

We all come to *Lear*, but comedy's harder.

"Oh . . . oh, Lord," Jack mourned. "They say you lose everything before you die."

Don't, Dad. I hear the reproof in it. I'm thirty-four and nothing much. No money, no Norma around anymore to please you and make you feel like a patriarch. Precious little warmth for my own life now, none left over.

But Jack never had that informed stoicism. A physical pain he could laugh at, but not this last, astonishing betrayal by flesh and life.

"I don't have anything left. I live in one room of my son's

apartment, and he's never home. My other son is a bum. I get
so lonely, Monk."

You could have friends over. I'd fix a party for you.

Jack looked away, even more reproof in the evasion. "I
don't want people to see me like this."

Like what? Old, broke? Not on top, not tailored and double-
breasted? You always had to make an entrance, be a big man.
I've been alone all my life. You never knew the meaning of the
word. For you, there was either somebody to say you were
wonderful or there wasn't.

"I don't understand you, Monk."

No, not in 1963. There are too many things we can't say:
that you're dying and I don't know how to deal with it, can't
stand to watch what's happening to you. So I go through the
motions. I go to work, I go to the theater to act because there
has to be something in my life to pass for meaning. I shop, do
the laundry, and clean house. With what's left over, I try to
make it as easy for you as I can. Sometimes I spend the night
with a woman because thirty-four isn't the age for a man to be
living with sickness and endings.

Denny wouldn't do it. He drops in for an hour, watches TV
with you, and that's it. If I were still with Norma, she'd
comfort you now as she always did. She adored you; didn't all
women? They lapped up your easy charm while you simply
accepted them at face value. Me, I had a lot of questions.

"You're thin and drawn, Monk." The old man looked at his
unfathomable son: not understanding, never to understand
beyond a basic commonality. "Why are you so hard?"

No patience, no humility, no success, Dad. You had all that
at my age and never heard the clock running behind you.
Whatever I'm supposed to be, it hasn't come yet.

"Be a little human, boy."

Jack made a feeble false start off the bed; he waited and
puffed and tried again, tottered a moment setting his balance,
then shuffled away to the memory of his own room without
looking back. Maybe they'd show the Rogers film again
sometime.

Not looking back, you never saw my tears. I had you in
that moment, Jack, knew you all the way down. You accepted
the world, men, women, and homilies as they came. There
was no real introspection in you, no anger, no complexity,
none of Connie's darkness. I had a love for you without
definition, realized far too late, as always, and now death was

washing you out from under me faster than I could frame the words—

"Human? Look who's talking! In your hat and over your ears!"

The dark young woman, heavier now than her dancer's frame was built for, leaned out the door to hurl her parting shot at vanished Jack: "Over your *ears*, Landry!"

Connie slammed the door and leaned against it—handsome as Jack but more vibrant, never able to conceal emotion, her heavy-lidded eyes red with tears, accusing something she couldn't reach but must strike out at. "No more . . . no more." The voice was still low and strong, compelling and musical. "Monk, will you grow up to be like me?"

I did. Damn you and love you for that, I did.

"Will you be faithful, Monk? Will you care? Will someone in this lousy family care? Little Johnny," she choked. "I couldn't even bring him home from the hospital. God, it hurt so much."

The brother I never saw, the last after Denny.

"I'm thirty-six." Connie barely controlled the pain. "Five children. No more. They said Johnny died of influenza. Who knows what happened in that rotten hospital?" She lunged about the room, still sinuous from years of dancing, but the beer-and-baby pot growing under the cotton paisley dress. "I was in the hospital having *his* baby—"

Connie clawed the Chesterfields out of a side pocket and lit one, weeping and puffing at the same time. Tears of rage, never defeat. Even maudlin drunk, Connie never whined, she raged.

That was 1934, Mama. The year everything changed. Why did you take Denny and me away after Johnny died?

"We should have stayed away. Why the hell did I ever have children? Why did I ever . . ."

Love anyone? Mama, the world isn't strength; it's frailty and fear. I had my share of it. You needed a Cyrano to love you. Most people can't handle that kind of need.

"Why did I ever stay after that?" Connie changed as she asked it, the body thickening by years, the lustrous hair dulling and wisping white about the temples, the strong face heavier and deeper-etched. Connie ground out the cigarette and massaged her temples. The headaches became worse in the last year of her life when the blood pressure could snuff her anytime.

"But I stayed," she said. "It was me who kept the family together."

That's true, Mama. After you died, I joined the army and Denny ran wild.

"Remember, Monk." The old woman reared back, fixing her son with an imperious glare, the Hawkins look. "Always remember what I did for you."

Tell it like it was, Mama. You loved Jack, but you could never love anyone without throwing plates at them. Most people want a little love to keep them warm, not a blast furnace. You needed an opera stage.

"There was a time. You should have known me then. Oh, you should have known me then." Connie lunged out the door of Landry's room, trailing her venomous prayer:

"I wish I could haunt that son of a bitch!"

We all haunt each other, Mama. Somehow I was the only one of us strong enough to contain it, like a combustion chamber, explode it to purpose in my heart. I've got to take you all and make one clear line that means, if only to myself. That's my trade. I can make the words sing. I need you for the music, but first I want truth laid out under a hard light. It had to come, always has to come. I've cleaned all the crap out of my life down to the hard bedrock of you all. I'm going to get you all off my back if I have to wring every one of you through my guts to do it. I won't dive back into a bottle like you or Julia, or try to find all salvation in Lauren, because she's got troubles of her own. For once, I've got a chance to win, and still everything in me wants to fail with all your old, plausible reasons.

So, it's war I guess; been coming all my life, because you were my first loves and my final enemies.

1934 . . . what happened that year? What *happened?*

14

"Pat! Hi—how're you keeping? Come on in."

The rangy, long-faced young woman slid two books onto a shelf and waved Landry to a chair by her cluttered desk. "I must say, you look good and rested for a change."

Edie Fine spoke with the nasal of a born New Yorker. The prominent teeth in her long jaw gave her a lateral lisp that swallowed half of her syllables when she smiled or laughed. She rooted under layers of paper, produced an ashtray for Landry, and buzzed the receptionist.

"Amy? I'm in conference, hold my calls. Pat, only got a few minutes but I wanted to show you the Trefoil figures. How's *Camlann* coming? Will you deliver on time?"

"No, but not that late." Landry said it with more confidence than he felt. "And it'll be good."

"Who doubted?" Edie found the object of her search, a letter bearing the Trefoil logo. "You really look good, Pat. Been getting out and around?"

"Thank God for small favors," he said. "Met a good woman."

"Another one?"

"I said good."

"I'm a little out of date," Edie admitted. "What happened to, you know, the one that always smelled of grass?"

"Dominique? Last I heard, she was raising it in Kansas with a guitar player. He works in the field and she spots for narc helicopters."

"I see: American Gothic." Edie passed him the paper. "Read something nice."

The letter was from Trefoil's accounting department. Edie had requested an early picture of the March royalties on *The Harper's Wife*. The book had earned out its advance and made an encouraging, if not robust, profit of three thousand in its first half-year. They'd probably see more in the fall. Landry felt gratified. He wouldn't have to sweat the rent or other basics for a while. Gratified but scared. Knowing from hungry had become a habit. Next year could be thin without another sale now. It didn't matter how tapped out he was: get a fat contract for cash flow *now*, and worry later how to do it.

He gave her back the letter. "I'm very glad, Edie."

"Well, now," she said crisply, "here's my thinking. Trefoil is going to ask how you'll follow *Camlann*, so I think we ought to lay the groundwork for the next book. Which should be another historical fantasy. How do you feel about it?"

Landry tapped a crumpled envelope against one palm. Sure, Trefoil would want more of the same as long as it sold. Some writers had spun out their lives doing more of the same; rich dinosaurs, tottering to convention rostrums to accept Life Achievement awards when they'd been artistically embalmed for decades. A comfortable way to die, but death was death. *Nothing stays, does it, Connie?* Some writers made their name (and said everything they had to say) in the first book, then went from fame to forgotten saying it over and over.

He was in the same boat; the difference was, he knew it. He gave the smudged envelope a final tap and jammed it into a hip pocket. "Can I level, Edie?"

She flashed the wide, scatterbrained grin that hid her shrewdness. "Sure. Lie to your mother before your agent."

"*Camlann* is the squeezed-out bottom of the barrel. I don't have a frigging thing left to say about Camelot or the tiresome but oh-so-musical Celts. And Trefoil has no option on the next book."

Edie nodded carefully, listening closely. "So? Any concrete ideas?"

"One. And it's a winner." *It means competing with a friend, but I'm empty and scared to stop. 'But at my back I always hear . . .'*

You better believe you could hear. That wingéd chariot was always loaded with kids coming up, some with talent and all with raw energy, like himself at twenty-two. It wasn't a matter of talent now, just how much time and energy he had left; go for the money now while he could, or get left. Try to keep Lauren out of it, she kept popping in. He couldn't be a loser again, not with her. That happened once before.

"Edie, I made all my bad mistakes in show business, and the worst was not shooting for the moon when it came up full and begged for it. There's no margin for error left, but I've got the track record and the reputation." Landry fired a cigarette, feeling reckless but determined. "I heard from Darcy Rambard there's a new project shaping up at Falcon Books. They're looking for the right authors." *And friend that you are, Darce, I'm gonna grab this from you if I can.*

Edie wrinkled her nose, contemptuous. "Bodice-rippers. Phony historicals with a lot of schlock sex. You don't do that."

"But I can, and I hear the money'll be fat. Look into it, Edie."

His tone surprised her. "You serious?"

"Very."

"I've heard talk around; they haven't even set the editor yet."

"Big bucks, luv. Find out." Landry crushed the cigarette hard into the ashtray. "I am very tired of a lot of things, but mostly of being very good for very little."

"Come on, Pat. *Camlann* went for twenty-five thousand: not rich but respectable. Most writers break their ass for less."

Edie, I'm dead, Landry screamed inside. *There's nothing left. Let me be a smart undertaker and make good money on the corpse.* He wanted to say that, but only rose to go, smiling at Edie Fine. "Remember how thin I used to be? Came from not eating all that often and wondering when I could. From going weeks on a can of tuna fish and a loaf of bread or a box of rice. From going to work in offices when I hadn't eaten more than three hundred calories in two days but still had to function. From having to decide too often between a cup of coffee *or* a pack of cigarettes. If suffering sanctifies, honey, I am Saint Patrick of the Paid Up Dues. So make me rich. I've developed the character to withstand affluence."

"All right, all right. I'll see what's up." Edie checked her watch. "Now get out of here and let me work—hey, you dropped your envelope."

The crumpled letter had slipped out of his pocket. Landry scooped it up from the floor. "Thanks. Something of a first, actually. From my kid brother."

"Didn't know you had one."

"Long lost but not long enough," Landry clipped. "We're not close. Let me know about Falcon."

15

Nothing on with Lauren until tomorrow night. For this evening there was only the eternal book to work on and the letter from Denny, who, after twenty years, remembered he had the remains of a family and wanted to be loved.

The last of them alive to deal with. Landry prowled back and forth across the room, coffee mug in his hand, muttering at the letter lying by his typewriter, crumpled but read three times.

"You're a loser, Denny. You always were."

And yet, ever since Connie brought the pug-nosed bundle home from the hospital, Landry felt more responsible to it than to any of them. Before he even knew why, that swaddled lump snoozing in Connie's lap was his to take care of.

A real loser.

"Yeah?" Denny laughed. "You ain't won any Oscars, Tyrone."

Denny lounged across the bed, thirty and handsome in a weak way, the good looks already collapsing into defeat with no character to support them. The ingenuous, charming smile remained; that would never leave him.

You always took the easy way out, Den.

Denny shrugged it off. "I got sick of the family crap, yours included. You were always gonna be such a big man."

I wanted to be more than just another slob. It was a matter of pride.

"Tell it like it is," Denny drawled. "You're nothin', man. Thirty-four years old and broke."

Because I take care of Dad. I don't see any bread out of you to help.

"That was your decision, not mine." Even defending himself, Denny had no strength in his face. He could deck some slob at a drunken party but nothing like a problem. "Sure, I feel bad about it—"

How bad? How about helping out?

Denny rubbed the end of his nose. "I ain't got the money."

Where does it go?

"Don't give me that shit about responsibility. You ain't doing all that much that I can see. Tell it like it is."

Okay, asshole, I will. What are you going to do with your life, Den? Live to be ninety, it's a third gone already. Face it, the only steady job you ever had was jail, and you're not exactly a master criminal. You're dumb enough to hijack an elevator.

Denny exploded in a staccato rush of laughter. "Take me to Cuba, gringo! Well, I admits I has not perfected a few points in my criminal technique."

In spite of himself, Landry was laughing too, the way they had growing up, lying in bed at night, telling each other gross-out stories to laugh themselves to sleep. Denny could always laugh; he wouldn't always see. He only wanted to remember the good times.

"Hey, Monk: remember when we were kids and there was this guy Billy across the street who always crapped his pants and carried it around all day . . . ?"

Denny was back remembering, trapped as Landry in his memories but unable to reach escape velocity. Always physically bigger than Pat but somehow the small one, the afterthought, too easygoing and soft in a family of hard egos. Denny never asserted, only reacted, avoided, ducked.

As Landry watched, the bulky man-figure shrank poignantly, rounded, softened to baby fat. Denny's vulnerable blue eyes filled with tears as he stared up at his sixteen-year-old brother and a world he never understood.

"My Mama's dead!"

It's okay. It's okay, Den. We're gonna get through it, you'll see.

The night she died I took the pain and locked it inside, because I'd already learned to be alone. You never had that defense. You grew up ducking and running, shrugged off Jack's dying as if that would make it go away, never able to do anything but laugh or sneer at me. I didn't understand then that some people can survive a lack of love and some will just break. You were a lamb in a lion's den, with no strength or center. You only tried to get along. I bullied and lectured and—Jesus!—somehow loved you more than any of them, and I remember that love now, but you killed it in sixty-three when you stole from me.

"I needed the money." For Denny, that explained it. "I had to get to Florida."

It wasn't the money, it was the trust broken. The last straw. You know what a big man Dad always had to be. For a few years after Arthur screwed him in Richmond, he made it back. An executive for the city, member of the Press Club, basking in the name his brothers made. It all came down to emphysema and empty pockets and one room in my apartment. And you didn't help at all. I'd look at you with the boy fading out of you and no man to replace it. A run-wild kid growing into a no-talent nothing. I kept hoping and hoping that you'd do something with your life, come back somehow so we could be brothers again, a family—

Denny was barely listening. "I never bought that old family bullshit."

No, you were the ashcan realist with street smarts. Anyone who tried to be something more was a phony, right? Don't ever respect anyone; you might feel like the shit you are. You let me know how you felt, stole from me and split.

"Hey, it wasn't that much money," Denny said. "I figured to get it back to you sometime."

You still don't dig it. That was the end. No more making excuses to myself for you. Nothing left. I opened my eyes and saw what a slimebag you'd become. Even Jack wrote you off. I remember when he said it; you could see the hurt in his eyes. He could never hide disappointment. He never knew the smell of the world.

Denny hunched on the edge of the bed with the vacant stare of the heroin addict. "I couldn't be like you all, I didn't know how. I'm sorry about Dad."

Try not to cry. *I* was the one who tore his vest like a Jewish father, you useless son of a bitch. Tore the love out of me and buried it. Go away, Denny.

"I can't."

What do you want of me? Love after all this time?

Denny studied his brother with something like expression.

"You were always so quick to judge, just like Mama. You think you're the only one got older?"

Landry was spilling coffee on the rug. He set the mug on the desk and picked up the letter again. Addressed in soft, smudged pencil, the envelope was postmarked from a town on the Texas Gulf Coast. Wide notebook paper clumsily folded and stuffed into an envelope too small, the handwriting an erratic mixture of printing and scrawl.

Denny's sparse history of the intervening years was salted with wry jokes usually turned against himself. He'd done eighteen months of a two-year stretch in '66 for bad checks and another in Florida on income tax evasion. Whatever happened on that count, Denny probably just pleaded guilty and went to jail with a fuck-it-all shrug.

> . . . I moved down here a couple of years ago to work the shrimp boats. It's a good living, keeps me in beer. I used to live with one of the cantina girls but she died. She was a real fuckup and a diabetic, and I don't think she really wanted to live. I really tried to get her to stop drinking, Monk. Hell, I remember Mom and what it did to her. Anyway I'm alone now and I've gotten interested in flying. Every day when I'm not fishing I go out to the local field. It's fun, but you have to be careful of traffic patterns. It's an unpleasant feeling to hear ground control tell you there's a Beechcraft gonna run right up your ass on the approach path . . .

And why he'd written in the first place.

> . . . a lot of time on my hands in slam, so I read. Most of the books get passed around so much they look like toilet paper. Used. One day I saw a copy of a book with your name on it. I almost shit. I read the book and loved it. You know, Monk, I did some writing myself in the joint. Not good, not anything like yours. Just bullshit short things. One born-again type said they were awful and blasphemous besides, and I guess they were. I wrote to Julia from jail way back, asking for your address. She sent it, but the letter had icicles hanging off it, and I got the impression she didn't want anyone to know she had a rela-

tive in jail. But I read your book and I was proud of
you, Monk. But if you feel like Julia, you don't have
to write back.

Hard to think of Denny as anything but a kid, but he'd be
forty-six now, and in the near-incomprehensible scrawl, Landry
gleaned the sense of someone older at last, tired, even humble. In spite of the old hurt, it mattered very much that Denny
was proud of him.

I guess we're all that's left except Julia, and she ain't
sending any invitations.

No, she's gone, Den. Even in death she went for appearances: wake, funeral, and a respectable cemetery where each
of us laid a flower on the casket and the girls broke down,
dealing with death for the first time. A few hours later they
were arguing over who got what out of her attic. I can't blame
them. There wasn't much love to go around in that house. The
kids had to settle for things they could hold. I put my flower
with the others and whispered *good-bye, darling*, and wished
there'd been more love, more warmth between us. A lot of
good things never got said in our family. Now they're buried,
and I'm out of the habit.

I won't blame you if you don't want to write to me,
but I hope you will.

No, I'm not going to love you, Denny. I'm not going to care
again—damn you, I'm not. There's no time for you. I've got a
life now, a chance to go all the way for the best of it. I'm not
going to drag you after me anymore.
Landry wadded the letter into a ball. He didn't answer it,
but somehow couldn't bring himself to throw it away.

16

━━━━━━━━

Their good times were marvelous, but there were evenings when they could be far out of touch with each other. Tonight, Landry admitted to himself, Lauren had every right to feel put out. She spent more time than usual fixing pork chops with stuffing, which he especially liked, a good wine and a cheery fire on the hearth to greet him, and he was miles away, attentive with an obvious effort. He felt guilty about it; this spring was a doldrum for Lauren's career. She was low on money, rentals on her videos were slow, and there was another letter from her daughter open on her desk. Margaret's letters were dutiful, warm as delayed toast, and seemed rather to upset than cheer Lauren.

The letter from Denny bothered Landry more than he wanted to admit; he couldn't put it out of his mind. Toward midnight, when he slid into bed with Lauren, she finally said it:

"Pat, are you mad at me?"

"What? No, honey, of course not."

"Well, something's wrong. I've been alone all evening."

Landry cradled her head on his arm, watching the play of firelight over the ceiling. "I got a letter from Denny."

"Your brother?"

"I haven't seen him in years. I don't think I want to."

"Maybe you do."

"Why?"

"They're always with us, aren't they, families? Maybe that's why you're so upset. Weren't you close once?"

"When we were kids. Real close." Enough to hurt saying it. Lauren whispered into his shoulder, "Be close to me, okay?"

Lovemaking was the last thing he wanted tonight, possible only when he simply devoted himself to Lauren's pleasure, but it released the tight knot inside him, allowed him to tell her about it afterward. Tracing his thoughts with one finger around the swell of her breast, he spoke from the far place in him where Denny still lived.

"It was good when we were little, before we were old enough to catch the fallout from Mama's war. I took Denny everywhere with me: Saturday movies, long walks in the park. Sledding in the winter when the hill across from our house looked like a big white cake with kids for raisins."

Lauren stirred in his arms, drowsy. "Grandma Moses winter."

"Winter mornings." Landry heard the tenderness in his own voice. "Dad always got up early and made a big pot of grits or cornmeal mush. And Denny would always come down late in one of my old bathrobes that he could never tie right, and try to navigate his way through breakfast. God, Laurie—"

He laughed suddenly, feeling free and warm with the memory. "I never knew how he did it, but Denny got grits in his hair and eyebrows and usually some on the dog. Oh . . . shoot. He was a good little kid. Sunny and very innocent. It was a big thing for him to go to the movies with me. I didn't learn for years that the Frankenstein flicks gave him nightmares, but he never wanted to be left home."

Denny always needed other people; never wanted to miss anything or be alone. The Sunday matinee movie was the high point of his anxious kid week. Two kids, ten cents apiece, a big item in the thirties. Jack and Connie couldn't always manage it.

Lauren understood. "If you didn't grow up in the thirties, depression is just something for a therapist."

"Boy, that's the truth. I remember doing my homework by kerosene lamps when the electric company turned off our lights. I had to lug the kerosene from the store in a big heavy jug. Ten cents for a movie could be a lot."

"Oh dear, yes," Lauren knew. "Major finance."

"So we scrounged. Every kid kept a sharp eye out for deposit bottles to take back to the store. The street bums and bag ladies do it now, but for us it was a cottage industry. A nickel? Man, you could *operate.*"

A nickel meant a Hershey or a Forever Yours or half a movie

if you could find another bottle. They scavenged in jungle competition with neighborhood kids and often closed in fierce combat over a disputed find.

"One day there were four kids from Sacred Heart, the parochial school a few blocks away. Well—you have to see this— *Robin Hood* had just opened at the movies, so everybody carried a stick, you know, for quarterstaves. And they jumped Denny and me."

Pretty soon the fight got down to Landry and the biggest kid. He never forgot that day or the exquisite pain when the stick hammered his fingers over and over. A mean fight, Pat sobbing with pain and rage, prevented from quitting only by pride. When he gave the big kid a good whack, the guy really lost his temper and swung the stick like a bat. It broke against Pat's staff but caught another finger as well. Screaming, Pat dropped his stick and waded into the bigger kid with bleeding, numbed fists, too full of murder to be scared anymore.

With the other kid's longer reach, he was getting creamed. Denny saved him. Standing on the sidelines for some time, he must have decided it was time to go. Thoughtfully he picked up his own stick, stepped up behind the big kid in the process of vivisecting his brother, wound up like DiMaggio at the plate, and half brained the bastard.

The blow sounded like an ax biting into wood. Landry's assailant grabbed at his bleeding head with a howl, trying to stay on his feet. He wove back and forth, blinking stupidly. All he could see was a small, silent assassin winding up to finish him and a screaming lunatic with red hands charging from the other side. Sensibly, he fled with the others in his wake, and the day was a Protestant victory.

"Denny had to carry the bottle because my hands hurt so much. That was a rough week, but we made twenty-five cents by swearing on my Cub Scout honor at the store that all the bottles came from there, and Den looked so incorruptible that the store owner must've believed us. And all week Den did clown imitations of the guy holding his head and running, until all he had to do was slap his hands on his head and make a face and I'd break up, too."

After Sunday dinner, dimes clamped tight in their fists (Denny never trusted anyone, even Pat, when it came to hard cash), they'd hurry to the movies, jiggling with excitement, jumping through the smoke from the raked and burning leaves in the gutters, daring the flames with Robin Hood's reckless courage, complete with music.

No wonder Den always wanted to remember then. That was a good time to be a kid, when a dime was a big deal and a bike of your own an adventure. I can remember the smell of autumn then, the way it wrapped around twilight with a smoky tang to the air, and the lights from friendly houses whose people you knew.

And always Denny trudging along, trying to keep up, grinning, encouraging his big brother to remember old times, remember when . . .

"He was always a nervous kid," Landry murmured to drowsy Lauren. "The way he rubbed the end of his nose with his dirty hand until it was black as the dog's. Or just walking along, all of a sudden his arms would swing wide and he'd kind of jig for a few steps. Sometimes I'd pick on him until he got mad and threw things at me."

But mostly, it was how they roared together over the absurd, gross-out adventures of characters they made up in bed to laugh themselves to sleep, a world of pompous clowns bent for lurking banana peels. Once, on the hottest night of a boiling summer, Landry couldn't sleep because something in their bedroom stank virulently. He tossed and turned and told Denny to take a bath because he had terminal dirt. By then, Denny was in spasms, choking into his pillow. Then Landry discovered that the corner of his sheet had been generously anointed with Limburger cheese. *I'll get you for this, Denny. Boy, just you wait. . . .*

"Good Lord."

Lauren opened one eye. "What, hon?"

"Nothing. Just it was all such years ago. He was never worth a damn after he got out of the army. Always found the worst people and the easiest way. Always went where the loud action was because he had nothing going in himself."

Landry shifted his weight slightly. "Years of it while I lived with Norma. Years of broke supporting Dad on very little. I saw less and less of Denny; when I did, I was always looking for the brother I knew. The landmark advice he gave me in those years was that I'd be great for passing bad checks because I had an honest face and spoke good English."

Lauren asked, "Was he married at all?"

"Yeah. A nice girl, but Den didn't take that any more seriously than he did anything else. Couple of children, a boy and girl. He split before they ever got to know him."

Landry was silent for a long moment, remembering.

"One night—1963 it was, with Jack wheezing in his room, trying to breathe a little longer and wondering why—Denny came up the stairs to my apartment, straight into the living room where I was learning a new part. He stopped right in the middle of the room and looked at me—I'll never forget it. 'Monk, I'm a junkie. I'm hooked.' "

Lauren rose over him, serious. "Dope?"

"Street-grade heroin. The weak man's suicide. I always wondered those last few years why all the personality had washed out of him; why he just collapsed in on himself. And that was it."

No, that wasn't all of it, Landry told himself. *I could never forget the kid I was supposed to take care of, but in those days I didn't have a vocabulary for mercy or the compassion to spare, not with an old man dying in the next room and problems of my own. Den made me sick, the waste of him, and I knew there was nothing in me to give. I'd gone as hard in my own way as Arthur ever was. No room for Denny's troubles. I was tapped out, and that was a kind of death.*

"A few days later he came up to see Dad. I wasn't there, so Den helped himself to seventy-five bucks off my dresser that should have gone toward the rent. He skipped town, didn't tell Dad anything. That was Den's goodbye. We never saw him again. I never needed to."

Lauren spoke in a curious, detached tone. "Maybe he needs you now."

"Sure, he always needed someone." He snorted and heaved over onto his other side. "Forget it."

"You never hated him."

"No, but—"

"He was so close to you," Lauren persisted in that odd tone. "You said there wasn't a mean bone in his body."

"Hell no." Landry twisted around to her. "Nor anything else. Zip. Nada. Empty. I don't want to talk about him anymore. Let's go to sleep."

Lauren slipped down under the covers, one arm flung over her forehead. "Independent, that's us."

"What?"

"You've never really been alone, Pat."

"The hell I haven't, lady."

"Neither have I, really. Solitude is choice, alone isn't. When someone like Denny says he's alone, it's because he feels it and can't do anything about it. He's not a kid anymore and you're all that's left of something he threw away. Who in this world would he need more than you? And I don't think it's all as one-sided as you make it sound."

17

Lauren Hodge was so structured by discipline and work that she wanted her off hours as loose as possible. The clock ran faster each year; she took the moment's spur, roweled it into the flank of the day, and galloped with it. For this reason, traits in Pat Landry that drove other women up the wall endeared him to Lauren. She gave Caroline Cutler low marks for general perceptiveness, but the woman was right on the money regarding Pat: he was the most inconsistent male on earth.

"Or not," Lauren quipped to female friends. "Depending."

In the clichéd thinking of the GAWL, inconsistency was a female failing; men of that bent were called "intuitive." Not so. Pat Landry was plain inconsistent, but the best of him cleaved to the best of Lauren, and the worst she could weather. From experience, Lauren was a long-haul weatherer, having that much in common with Caroline. They came from a generation for whom divorce was a last desperate measure, not the first, when women didn't give up easily on men. Lacking this perseverance, Lauren might have discarded Landry at his cantankerous worst and thought of it more than once. Sometimes, after a flareup as ridiculous as it was heated, when they made up over a drink by her window in the cool dark, Landry would take her hands and wonder quite honestly, "Why do you put up with me?"

Lauren knew the answer better than he ever would, not all of it complimentary. The young crave acceptance, to *be* loved.

When you'd had all that in spades, love was more important as a giving.

"Because I'm the best thing that ever happened to you."

Part of Landry knew this as a product of maturity; another part still roiled with old battles that sometimes stunted the giving in him. His passing remarks about his family had gone from caustic to downright eerie.

"Your mother *is* a difficult woman?"

"She was."

"You said *is*."

He spoke of them in the present tense sometimes, as if he'd seen them yesterday; which of course he had, although Lauren had no way of appreciating the fact.

For her, the marvelous thing about Landry was his utter lack of possessiveness or jealousy. He left her alone, allowed her space, and took his own. When they were apart for any length of time, he didn't sniff about the edges of her absence for the hint of other men, didn't hover over her at parties or tolerate it from her. If she spent more than sociable time talking to an attractive man at a party, she wasn't grilled later. Neither was there—thank God—anything perfunctory or dutiful about their sex life, nor anything ambivalent about Pat Landry in that respect. He was interested *now* or not. He might go a week or more, detached as a eunuch, and then descend on her in a tender avalanche of need. Lauren liked very much being told she was the first woman he could sleep with through a restful night, a confession of trust.

Only sometimes was there an unconscious violence in his need that frightened her.

When he asked about her work, Landry actually listened to the answers. If he was foggy or distant, Lauren never worried (after the first months, at least) that he was seeing other women. The object of his distraction was more likely a clutch of scrawled yellow pages by an unemptied ashtray.

Most of all, as spring warmed into summer, Lauren loved their Sundays together, one of the bylaws passed between them. However hard or rotten the week, they turned off the engines early Sunday afternoon and did something together, jaunting as far east as the Brooklyn Botanical Gardens, or north to the Bronx Zoo. Lauren always wanted to go, look, see and do, far more than the hermitic Landry, whose feelings for New York were stained with struggle and early failure.

On the weekends, lower Manhatten was a lusty carnival and frenetic flea market where the current of pedestrians eddied around sharp-eyed security guards perched on ladders in the middle of the sidewalk. Young Black men, eager to sell and be gone, hawked electronic wares at the corner of Fifth Avenue and Fourteenth Street—"Fo'teen dolla, fo'teen dolla, check it out, on'y two left, check it out!"—passing to the buyer high-risk goods from a questionable source. There was always a crowd of gullible Blacks and Hispanics around the three-card monte games set up on cardboard boxes, where money changed swiftly, most of it going one way to the rhythm of the fast-handed dealer's hypnotic chant:

"Here we go, here go. Red you win, black you lose. Twenny dollars, who gonna play? Who see da red? Who see da red?"

The female shill sees the red, wins twenty dollars for her dealer boyfriend, and looks around to encourage the males who think they see the red and finger the money in their pockets. On the corner nearby, lookouts chickee for cops and to shortstop anyone who might win too much, because monte is a house game with the gloves off.

The streets *smelled* like a carnival midway on warm Sundays: hot dog and sausage stands under their red and yellow umbrellas. The smell of summer heat, sweat, dust, mustard, engine exhaust, chili sauce, and sauerkraut. Charcoal smoke from shishkebob stands blowing over rubber-legged young Blacks break-dancing on a square of waxed cardboard, loud Puerto Rican men asserting their macho in the smallest matters, sibilant Koreans saving their energies for work and profit. Swarthy children hanging from the hands of tired but indestructible mothers in worn summer halters . . .

Sometimes Landry and Lauren walked south to SoHo to the aggressive swirl of Delancey Street, where the idle browser enticed into the store must not be allowed to leave unsold or at least unexhorted—

"This same article uptown would cost you twice. Sure, we got it in the smaller size. Manny, watch the *schwartzes* by the front bin, they'll take. . . ."

And on past the Brooklyn Bridge to Mott Street in Chinatown for the cheapest, best food in New York, ordered and eaten in tiny shops like loud hallways.

In a different mood, Sunday could be quieter. Lauren delighted in toys and gadgets like plastic fish and battery-driven carousels. It was inevitable when the kite spied in a

novelty show window whispered *fly me!* that they'd do just
that. The abandoned piers at the foot of the West Twenties
were a tranquil Kitty Hawk. People went there to read or
meditate, gay lovers sunned themselves on the bleached
timbers. Landry lofted the kite into the updraft, trading off
the line to unwrap barbecued chicken and potato salad from
his backpack. The Hudson flowed peacefully through the warm
afternoon, and their kite bobbed against the clouds while they
drank warm beer and shared bits of their lives, weaving
the tapestry of them tighter. Lauren had never been as
hungry as Pat Landry, but close enough (and longer) to develop her stringent sense of thrift. She remembered the grind
of budgeting a small income for two children and a bitter,
unemployable husband.

"Ten dollars a week. For a long time, that's all I had to feed
us."

She'd said it before, but it sank into him slowly. Their first
months were a continual process of discovery. "So that's where
you learned to make such great soup and stew."

"You better believe."

Landry believed with no athletic leap of imagination. There
wasn't an actor in New York who hadn't gone days without
eating more than once. "One day's a breeze. After two, if you
lean over too far, you tend to keep going."

"It's not good for you to go so long without food."

"No kidding, lady? Just like the army, you learn to eat when
it's there. Any more potato salad?"

A weave of understanding between them; gradually Landry
came to accept her attitude toward money, at least to tolerate it
in his better moments. Lauren wasn't tight. She would spend
to a purpose; she would never be careless with money. In
turn, Lauren saw how he could clean a plate even when he
wasn't ravenous. She'd seen the same caution in Europeans
long after the war. More like an abstraction, money never
represented security to Pat Landry. If he was out, he could get
more, but food was immediate, vital, not to be wasted.

Like as not, during a salad-flavored kiss, the kite would
escape them—

"Grab it, Laurie, grab it—oh, damn. Well, there it goes."

"G'bye, kite!"

"Write when you get settled!"

—floating higher and smaller, westering over the river to
descend on unsuspecting Hoboken while they finished the

warm beer and trailed home through the cobblestoned ware-
house streets of Sunday-quiet Chelsea.

When the weather grew warm enough to count on, they'd
backpack lunch and beer up to Eighty-first Street to wander
across Central Park, around the reservoir or past the Delacorte
Theater or across the Sheep Meadow, skirting softball games,
folk-dancing groups, the band shell and the busy tree-lined
Mall where street magicians set up and performed wonders by
the statues of Burns and Scott; where pickup jazz combos riffed
behind an open guitar case sprinkled with coins and the occasional bill (God bless the cheerful giver!), or a long-haired girl
with soulful eyes caressed magic from a Celtic harp for an
audience of bemused but enchanted Ukrainian tourists, and
riding parties in full to-the-hounds regalia jolted along the
bridle path, showing a dubious amount of daylight between
rump and saddle. To scamper across the Drive between dogged cyclists and joggers to Grand Army Plaza, where Landry
ferreted through the Strand stalls for bargain tapes, plunging
his glasses onto the bridge of his nose to read labels, brandish-
ing a rare treasure at Lauren.

"Look what I found. Clara Haskil." Astonished when Lauren
didn't respond to the name.

"Is she good?"

"*Good?*" Scattering deafened pigeons from the vicinity. "She
plays Mozart like Mozart wished he could."

"That's nice." By then Lauren would be hunting a bus to
ease her throbbing feet.

They admitted to quite different aesthetic senses. Lauren's
was visual, Landry's that of sound. Certain musical progres-
sions would raise the hair on his neck or rush his blood in
response to its beauty. The gorgeous legatos and restrained
power of a Haskil doing Mozart would not distract Lauren
from any other activity, whereas they produced in Pat Landry
the effect of a Hitler speech on Nazi Germans, while certain
passages of Bach and Prokofiev brought him to the edge of
insurrection. He carried this propensity into prose, reading or
writing it, always in terms of sound—rhythm, pace, fall and
resonance, movement and dynamic.

Landry listened, Lauren saw. She could never impart what
the masterful use of color and space did to her, much like his
response to music and prose. Sometimes at sunset they'd lean
over the brick parapet of the Chelsea roof, watching the sun
sinking over New Jersey, trailing subtle colors down the hori-

zon. The roof was part of Lauren's aesthetic, delightful as her end-of-the-day martini.

"I have to get up on top now and then to see how it all comes together."

When the Trefoil royalties came in, Landry splurged on a package tour of the Bahamas for Lauren's birthday. He learned to eat lobster, a food, he concluded, that did not live up to its rapturous reviews. They walked along the edge of the impossibly blue water under ravishing skies, had one major fight over nothing, as usual, and for the first time, to Landry's hooting delight, Lauren threatened him with bodily violence, storming at him with thoroughly Irish dudgeon—

"Goddammit, I wish I were a man. By God, I'd take you on and beat *hell* out of you!"

In peaceful moments Landry found the island picturesquely dull and scratched careful revision notes for *Camlann* while Lauren tripped out on dawns and sunsets.

He woke early the morning after their fight to find Lauren gone, and missed her poignantly. He hurried into jeans and a sweatshirt, knowing where to find her. There she was, a small, hooded figure at the water's edge, definite and sure as always of her own space in this or any setting.

He didn't call out to her. He always felt a keen pleasure in her joy, to watch Lauren at the still center of some secret communion, wordless and complete. At the core of them both was the inexpressible and the need to express it. All their difference resolved in this truth. There were moments when they were indifferent to or bored with each other, and others when each wanted to wrap the other in their own life, a center protected by love. Moments only; they were wise or selfish or simply old enough to know the wish was false for both of them. Their center was work. Quite possibly they were the compulsive freaks of Crissy's or Caroline's estimation. Knowing this clearly prevented either from ever feeling cheated, neglected, or taken for granted.

Landry reached her side just as the first ray lanced over the green water, turning it a steely hue not seen again until sunset. Lauren didn't turn when he touched her, just said:

"Look."

This was her music.

Idyllic, but neither could stand the bucolic in more than small doses. They were New Yorkers of the classic mold: imported, inured, and eventually addicted to the city. An absence of any length produced withdrawal symptoms and a desire to catch the first plane home.

They arrived at Kennedy in the evening with a typical argument over a cab or limousine to Manhattan, and compromised by each going their own way, both already thinking of tomorrow's work, clock-punchers on their own peculiar grind.

Lauren ran on wound-up nerves to an extent that sometimes irritated Landry. "Breakfast on me!" she would invite by phone, often as not with her other line ringing in the background. "See you in an hour."

And always-early Pat would sit in Wellington's on Seventh Avenue, fingers drumming by his twice-emptied coffee cup, wondering where the hell she was, *goddamn woman has no sense of time.* Another cup of coffee and a cigarette, and finally Lauren would dash in, out of breath—"I ran the whole way!"—arms loaded with mail, which she spread over the table, opened and shredded through breakfast. Lateness infuriated Landry, who imagined Grand Guignol punishments for her most maddening fault, though he grew to a teeth-gritted toleration of it after a time.

She was as swift with her mail as he was, garbage in one pile for the waitress to sweep up with her tip, important opened, scanned, muttered over, and scribbled on for reference in reply. Personal letters usually stuffed in her bulging shoulder bag but sometimes opened over her eggs. Landry came to recognize the creamy beige linen of her daughter's stationery and Margaret's clear but constricted handwriting and the dampening effect it always had on Lauren's brisk morning cheer.

"I guess I have to go home sometime this year."

"Trouble?"

"Oh . . ."

Lauren folded the letter and set it aside. "Time for me to go anyway," she reasoned. She never avoided or elided unless something troubled her seriously, the things too painful to express with his verbal ease. Lauren didn't have the safety valve of his quick anger, only contained silence. But then, growing sensitive to her, Landry would *hear* her silence and look up from his breakfast to see Lauren's eyes bright with brimming tears, one hand clamped over her mouth as if warning explosion back a little longer.

"What is it, Laurie?"

"Oh—" Dabbing at her eyes with a paper napkin, a discreet

snuffle. "I'm here and they're there. Everything. Yes, I'll go out, see Mama and . . . the rest of them."

Swatches in a lengthening weave of experience. In the long twilight of late spring, they sat by her window and talked easily in the disjointed fragments of people used to each other and needing fewer words. When the soft dark came on, Lauren would draw a bath in her small tub, which they shared dexterously after some practice, scrubbing each other with a loofah, absorbed as children with the progress of a plastic toy fish with a starboard list and no sense of direction.

Quite often they danced to radio music before bed, close and romantic or energetic free-style disco, Lauren clowning it up, coming to rest finally on the edge of the bed. Even in lovemaking they partnered each other like dancers, allowing distance and freedom. Early on they found the choreography that suited them best. Depending on need or hunger, the dance was brief or drawn out, never hurried, always satisfying. Lauren loved taking time over it, being gentled and wooed; or the fierce passion that could suddenly ignite Landry, but she couldn't deal with the inexplicable desperation that invaded that passion sometimes in this unique place made from the best of them both. It happened only rarely, a roughness in his lovemaking when he could hurt her without knowing it, driven by something she couldn't share. At such times, his fingers dug into her flesh for assurance that she was really there with him, and Lauren would be vised cruelly as he pulled her close, hoarse with need—

"Don't go away from me. Please don't go away from me."

—the pain of his grip blotting out her pleasure until the violence went out of his hands, the tearing need passed, and he realized he'd shaken her. Not deliberately cruel, he took no pleasure in the violence, sharply remorseful later when he saw the bruises darkening her flesh.

"Oh, hon, I *am* sorry."

"It's okay, just surprised me, that's all. What happened?"

"Nothing. Just . . . I don't know." Quite honestly he didn't. "Sometimes I need you that much."

But out of that shadowed well rose something older and hungrier with a stain that wouldn't wash or wear out, its intensity not all sexual, Lauren knew. She was used to men who bottled their feelings in the habitual supposition that it was the manly thing to do. Pat Landry never walked around his own insides but waded through the seething core and the

hell with the mess. When whiskey took the cap off his feelings, Lauren felt in him an ambivalent, warring love toward
his family and a blind spot that struck back at death as enemy
and thief. He mourned Julia in the midst of snarling at her
memory—

"Poor, silly bitch, she never understood anything."

But Lauren still heard in it the loss and the love. "You don't
mean it that way."

"No . . ."

"Then you shouldn't say it like that. Her name was Julia,
and she was a woman."

"I went to her funeral but not the wake. Why? What for,
to stand around looking solemn and stricken while someone
made hushed comments on how nicely they arranged the
wreckage of Julia? No, it's personal, like making love. I cried for
her alone, not onstage. Jesus, why do people get so theatrical
about death?"

Lauren thought: *because it's a relief and their due. For that little
time they're defined, they have a role to play and know what's
expected of them.* But she saw Landry's tears and knew as well
the things she couldn't put into words as he could. Death was
an enormity no one could answer, and the frustration made
families turn on one another as if death were a plot. At least
Julia was cleanly dead, not babied and herded like her own
mother, womanhood and dignity shredding in petulance and
dirty diapers.

"The same bit when my father died."

Lauren heard the tightening edge in Landry's voice.

"Some guy on the phone said I'd better get down to the
hospital. Hell, I knew Dad was dead; dying for years, it wasn't
a flash. I had to ask the son of a bitch three *times*: Is my father
dead? He wouldn't say it. All this schlepp knew was that
death makes families go to pieces on cue like actors in a trite
play, so the standard way to break the news was that . . .
obscene delicacy. Couldn't even read the line right. Christ,
dead is dead. Give me the fucking *fact*. I'll handle the feelings."

Which Landry did with his own left-handed but deep affection. Going through St. Patrick's Cathedral one Sunday, Lauren
saw him lighting a votive candle among dozens bending in the
draft.

"It's for Julia. She always liked the trimmings."

While he was lighting his candle, Lauren had knelt when

she prayed for her mother and crossed herself from childhood habit. They could both be inconsistent.

Yet, for all her balm to his visible wounds, he was the same to her own unreachable hurts. When tapes were lost by a dense university clerk; when the tenth refusal of a grant arrived from foundations known for a decade to have funded the trendy garbage of opportunistic hacks; when she planned a studio session for weeks only to find a ridiculous, wholly avoidable glitch on the finished tape; when she was keyed up and impossible to be with, unable to sit or even be civil because she was fifty-six and still running on the same treadmill as the kids from Wooster Street; when there was yet one more letter from Margaret with its dutiful affection and unspoken reproofs for the life her mother dared to live—when all these sucked Lauren down in a mire of futility and she *felt* the middle age of the middle class she'd fled, there were blessed times when Pat Landry knew when to hold her and what to say.

"The hell with them out there. You mean something, Lauren. They love your work in Paris. First prize: you don't get those with boxtops."

"Oh, no," Lauren sputtered against his chest. "But—"

"And they're going to love you in Berlin. You're a *fine* artist, but something's got to give sometime. You have to be mother of the year as well?"

"B-but hell, I look at my work sometimes and don't even know where I'm going."

"None of us do, sweetheart. Like tail gunners, all we see is where we've come from. Here, have a Kleenex."

"I just get so—"

"I know. All twisted up in a ball and no way to undo it. Hold on to me."

"And Margaret . . . honestly, sometimes I just want to kick her."

"Tell her to fuck off. Politely."

"She's not that mature, Pat. She can't just shrug things off."

"You're all tense. Lie down, I'll rub your back."

"My shoulders ache."

"I know." He kneaded them gently. "That's where you carry the world. Give it a rest, hon."

But I left them, Lauren brooded under his hands. *When will I be paid up for that?*

"Feeling better?" he asked, working over her.

"Hmmm . . ."

"Let's take a bath and go to bed."

They would make love then and sleep like exhausted children. For all Pat's private war, Lauren wished she could find more in their lovemaking than relief and satisfaction; that primal spending of joy, anger, grief, fear, that he sometimes could. She would clamp her mouth to his like a lamprey eel, ride him like a stallion, crying not to God but the primitive mother-goddess plunging with her, drive him on long past pleasure to the expulsive need in herself. And when she came, screaming like a banshee, her nails would stripe his flesh, draw blood from it to soak into the stupid sheets. But for all her tolerant wisdom that could put its surgeon-sure hand just where family ached in Pat Landry, he had the key to that simple, blessed cleansing and she envied him.

"It's not all on you," he whispered, covering her up before sleep. "You don't always have to be God."

"It's hard not to play God when I had to do it for so long." Relaxed and restored, Lauren laughed softly in the darkness. "Especially when I'm so right for the role."

ACT II
Late Summer, Early Fall

18

Caroline Cutler was back in town from Cape Cod and points west, and bluntly suggested it was Landry's turn to buy lunch. He chose Joanna's on Eighteenth Street. Cuisine aside, the decor didn't poke one in the eye: pre–art deco chic, unisex waiters in crisp white blouses, black bow tie and slacks. Joanna's was mostly an expense-account lunch place, but worth an occasional visit. The wine list was impressive and the steak tartare actually edible. While lower Manhattan sweltered through August, Joanna's remained a bright oasis in the midst of decaying bookstores, delicatessens, and abandoned business lofts.

Landry waited for Caroline at a red-leather-lined corner spot between two huge mirrors and a blown-up photograph of a begonia, rubbing the gritty feeling of too little sleep out of his eyes. *Camlann* was in the home stretch and preoccupied him like a growing tumor. He didn't feel quite sane.

Caroline gusted in punctually, square-shouldered and breezily confident, as if she'd just bought the franchise. She spotted Landry and slid in beside him, beaming.

"He*llo*, my dear Pat! *Lumme!* If you have to hate New York, August is the month for it. Don't kiss me yet, I'm all glowy."

"Glowy?"

"Ladies don't sweat, we glow. I'd better start remembering the difference. Don't you ever wear a tie?"

"Sure. Funerals." Landry leaned over and kissed her anyway. "You're not glowy, just sticky. Where've you been, Caroline?"

"Oh, going the expensive route." Caroline settled back. "Flitting back and forth to Tulsa, a month on the Cape. Giving Dogger away to a Methodist minister. Are you still with Lauren?"

"Sure," said Landry.

"My God, eight months? With you, that's serious."

"Oh." Landry squeezed the bridge of his nose between thumb and forefinger. "We have our problems, but—"

"You look harried," Caroline observed, hoping for gossip.

"Not by her. The damned book."

Caroline's eyes widened. "It's not done *yet?*"

"No, it's not done *yet*, dammit. It's late," he added in a hopeless tone. He could never imagine writing the last page of any book. The task stretched into fog and infinity. "Won't even let me sleep. Want a drink?"

Caroline extended a tanned arm to commandeer his wine and sip at it judiciously. "Well, it's not the Connaught, but at least they know the difference between chilled and frostbitten. I'll have one of these."

"You do look good, Caroline." She always did in public. Her makeup was discreet and the summer shift was a flower print in mostly pale blue and violet to compliment the hair that stayed red without help. Nevertheless, Landry sensed an edge in her today, a testiness that brought out the stern German in her face.

"I don't feel great, Patrick. Decisions, decisions." She scanned the menu. "Christ, this joint is pricey enough. Can you afford it?"

"There's no tomorrow. Want to split a lox appetizer?"

"Sounds perfect. My darling Pat, you're gorgeous as ever, but get out in the sun more. You're pale."

"Tell me about it."

Their waitress came—tall, blond, and crisp as her linen, with pointedly perfect diction: an actress or singer, Landry figured. She took their orders, brought Caroline's wine and ice water, and swept away. The restaurant was ebbing out of the lunch rush into the predinner lull, but half the tables were still occupied. There was more talking than eating.

Caroline looked around. "When did you discover this place?"

"Edie and I come here sometimes. The food's good and you can hear yourself think. Most of this crowd's expense account."

"How can you tell?"

"All the friggin' Perrier. Half of them are trying to sell and the other half's trying not to get hustled. One friend of mine found out after a three-martini lunch that she'd agreed to a three-book contract."

"So." Caroline sat back, revolving the stem of her wine-glass. "Tell me the news. Have you moved out of the Seville yet?"

"Hell no."

"Oh, why not?" Caroline shot at him. "I hated that place. I had to wash my dishes in the bathroom."

"I still do," Landry admitted.

"Why don't you get an apartment? A guy like you needs a salon to entertain in."

"So what's today, a wake? Here comes the lox."

Caroline was decidedly moody, picking at the salmon. Her business with the duck salad entrée was mostly a rearrangement on the plate. She finished her wine and ordered a double scotch/rocks.

Landry said gingerly, "I'm getting the impression Tulsa wasn't all that great."

Caroline kept her eyes on the duck salad. "Not great; just the future, baby. What should I do, Pat?"

"You're asking me? About what?"

"Well, it's here. The ultimatum. I move to Tulsa, we get married."

"Oh . . . yeah." He filled in the blanks. "That's why Dogger got a transfer to another outfit?"

"No love lost. If Dogger were a woman, we'd be talking behind each other's backs." Caroline took a healthy nip of her scotch. "I told Norman I wanted to keep the apartment. I *like* him, Pat. I don't love him. I don't want to leave New York, but . . ."

Not that surprising. Lauren said months ago that it would happen. Amazing, the bottom-line instinct women sometimes had for each other. He ought to learn it. "Sounds like you've already made up your mind."

Caroline made an I-don't-know gesture. "If I could be like you and Lauren. You don't live together; you get along."

"We get along because we don't live together."

Because each of them had a center in work, not in each other, their loving, sometimes pugnacious relationship maintained its balance, like a drunken high-wire act, through this saving distance. Caroline was of Lauren's generation; she could long for the same freedom, even relish it, but in the end she defined herself in terms of men.

"Well," she temporized, "Norman is very old-fashioned."

At seventy-odd, Norman would be. Landry had met him once or twice at Caroline's, as a forthright and determinedly social man who hosted parties in a red blazer and played the piano as if there were a blood feud between the two of them. A creature of die-stamped habit, Norman retired at a certain time, party or no, to reappear in pajamas, landlordly hammering on the door to the bathroom, which might temporarily house someone sensitive and unforgiving like Crissy James, who implacably loathed him. Landry gleaned two equally strong impressions over lunch: (a) Caroline didn't want to marry Norman, but (b) she was damned well going to.

"But only if I can keep the apartment," she insisted defensively. "Oh—I don't know." Caroline finished her scotch. "What d'you think, Pat?"

"What do *you* think?" he deflected. "You were always a sucker for men."

"Some men. That's been years. I'm just tired, Pat. I'm really very tired."

"So. Tulsa."

"That's right." Caroline pushed away her half-finished plate and dabbed the napkin at her lips. "I've had the adventure and the grand passion. I just don't want to feel I'm—hell, I respect Norman a lot. There's a lot of affection."

"You don't want to feel mercenary."

Her eyes flicked to him and away; Landry knew he'd hit the sore spot. "The trouble with saying there's no tomorrow—there is. I've been hungry and I've been full, just like you, and you fucking well know which feels better. What do I have? Social security and not much of that. One step up off the street from a bag lady. Done a lot of running, seen a lot of broke. I don't have to run anymore if I don't want to."

"Still, it doesn't sound like something you want. More like settling."

"You're a man, it's different."

How different, Landry thought. *Why do you invalidate yourself by making a difference? You have the strength to be, like Lauren, but you never wanted it that much.*

"It isn't good-bye, baby." Caroline took Landry's hand. "I keep my place, I'll be back in town once or twice a year to throw a wingding. But, Lord, I will miss you, you uncombed bastard. I really will."

Landry held on to Caroline's hand. "I can feel you're ambivalent about this."

"I am," Caroline said. "But it's reality. Norman wants me and he wants to give me what I need. Right now it's the only deal in town. It's hard for a man to understand."

"I wish you'd stop saying that. I feel like a scab in a union shop."

"Oh hell, Pat Landry, you know what I mean."

"I'm trying," he said honestly. "Least I won't miss Dogger too much."

"I always had a soft spot for stray dogs." Caroline ran her fingers lightly through the thick hair over his ears. "And odd, interesting men, and the view of Central Park at dusk from the windows at Nirvana. London pubs at a certain hour in the afternoon, full of black bowlers, umbrellas, and noise. But you gotta have a man. That's what it's all about." *Isn't it?* "You I'll miss, but Dogger deserves a Methodist."

19

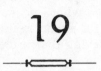

For Landry the three most miserable states of existence were hangover, toothache, and not enough sleep. In the Korean government crisis of July 1948, he'd gone seventy-two hours straight duty in the battalion radio shack. Afterward there was some talk of a commendation ribbon. He would have settled for ten hours' sleep. The way things worked out, he didn't get either, and went home after two years with his nerves screeching like wire in a high wind. His body very quickly offered its own sensible compromise.

"Look, turkey," it said, "early or late, give me at least seven out of twenty-four hours to sleep and we'll get along fine. Seven straight. Under that, I get flakey."

Doing *The Harper's Wife* had been easy compared to *Camlann*. His sleep pattern inched forward around the clock until he was rising at sundown with the rest of the vampires, working all night, and falling asleep after breakfast. But he was alone then, no Lauren to accommodate. She was a day person and he struggled to keep his schedule somewhere near sync with hers and naturally resented her for it. Lauren signed off promptly at midnight and was usually asleep in minutes. Landry was lucky if his mind would leave him alone before three.

The book was very late. Like a long-distance runner, he knew he needed a reserve for the finish, a third-act punch, but who could have predicted a slow spot in July? *Bad. You're getting old.* He kept telling himself that the outline was sound, the end of the book well plotted. If his wind held out, that's what it came down to. He was deathly sick of the book, and yet the thick pile of pages obsessed him unhealthily, reaching a cruel green arm even into his sleep to jerk him awake at odd hours like this, his mind already running dialogue and plot.

Please let me have one good night's sleep, Landry prayed to whom it might concern. *Just once let me come at this thing fresh. I've forgotten what it feels like.*

Just like Korea: he probably wouldn't get the sleep, and for sure no one would be handing out medals when he finished.

The ancient hotel air-conditioner worked just well enough to earn its title, an asthmatic whisper in the corner as, once more, Landry gave up on sleep, heaved out of bed and turned on the lights. He stared at the forever pile of green pages spiderwebbed with cuts, scribbles between the lines, and notes in the curling margins.

Four A.M. Nothing looked good at four in the morning, especially this ratty clutch of pages on the writing board. Landry jiggled the last cigarette from his pack and snapped the lighter to it, wondering why he worried over tightness like a mother over a sick child. Sloppy writers who wouldn't cut a line on a court order were cleaning up now, and most of the readers wouldn't know the difference anyway. Why bother? The book was clean enough.

Because Jack would bother. Jack taught him that. There was tight, tighter, tightest. All of them could read well, but tightest *played.* Kinetic. You could feel it work, feel when it didn't.

Four-seventeen A.M. Landry read the same page for the third time, wide awake now with a grisly clarity to his judgment. This beast was not only late but too fat by a hundred pages. Fat was inherent in dramatic prose; you couldn't think lean when you were digging for truth, that came later.

But it's later now.

Even lean didn't give movement; that you got by cutting every static phrase, making every word count, letting punctuation work for you. Semicolon half-stops rather than full periods whenever possible, weeding out past-perfect tenses like crabgrass from a lawn. No brakes, no drag, all the thrust forward in a kind of piquant imbalance where each moving image fell forward to engage the next.

When the pages looked more like a graffiti wall than narrative, Landry clipped them together and laid them by the typewriter for another draft. Five pages out of hundreds, beginning and ending nowhere like that road the prisoners were always building in Devil's Island movies, but ultimately a smoother road, the difference between five hundred bloated pages and four hundred with more meat.

If anyone cared.

Landry stretched, scratching his sweaty stomach under the pajama shirt. Outside the window, the summer sky was lightening from ink to something paler. He leaned on the sill and watched New York come up to morning, hoping he could sleep just a little before the damned book woke him up again.

"I hope you fuckers care," he whispered to no one.

"Don't worry about them."

Hulked over his own radio script at the table, Jack Landry picked up the stopwatch, read the last line on the page, and . . . *click*. He jotted the playing time at the bottom and peered over his glasses at Landry. "You care first, then they will."

That was back when people really read, Dad. You never think of reading as a habit like brushing teeth, but it is. And it can get lost. Julia's kids don't even read the *National Enquirer*.

"The hell with that," Jack rumbled around his cigarette. "Don't go arty, Monk. I taught you to be a pro."

Jack snapped the stopwatch at his son and faded out.

Sure, all the old excuses. He could make a living working for the magazine, check every Tuesday, the way it was for four years. Drink his lunch and throttle the impulse to shoot his boss.

Stop feeling sorry for yourself.

Landry turned out the lights and went back to bed. The air-conditioner gave the room the smell of canned air. He used it only when the heat was too much for comfortable sleeping, not that he could anyway. He stared, red-eyed, at the ceiling. Still a long time until the coffee shops opened for breakfast. If he drank coffee now, he wouldn't sleep at all.

Lauren would be back from Portland in two days. She called regularly to keep him posted, to touch him. She was dear that way. He'd never heard of her mother's problem, Alzheimer's disease, until he met Lauren. Used to be called senility, but you didn't have to be that old. Charlie Beaumont went that way, fading out in the middle of script conferences, unable to remember from one day to the next what he'd done or said. And Rita Hayworth—hard to think of her in diapers, forgetting to eat, hitting out at the nurses like a child, no Astaire to waltz her away with lilting music and sparkling dialogue.

Boy, you do get morbid before sunup.

If his sleep pattern had to go so ragged again, better now than when Lauren was home. There wasn't much left over for her.

I know she notices. Most of the time now I feel as sexy as a sponge.

And yet he needed her as much as ever. No walking out this time. There was some stability to his life now . . . and the letters from Denny, regular as his brother never was about anything before. Denny had his pilot's license and was working toward a multiengine rating, as natural a pilot as Arthur ever was. Perhaps a natural lot of things if Denny'd ever given himself the chance. He should have found it young when it counted; now he did it offhandedly, flying the wrong kind of cargo for the easiest buck, with vague ideas about cargoing shrimp inland. The big money was in flying contraband electronics into Mexico—

> . . . where the field is so small and grungy, I think they got scorpions in charge of the tower. First time I landed and saw this old truck tooling out to meet me, I wondered if we'd get nailed by the morales. Shit, it turned out the police were driving the truck because they got the racket sewed up. I mean, these were BAD motherfuckers, they looked like extras from *Treasure of the Sierra Madre.* You don't carry a gun because they'll take it away and use it on you. They come on and unload you quick and tell you to go, and you do. What scares me, Monk, I always wonder what will happen when those guys decide they need an airplane. . . .

And always the same refrain toward the end—

> You don't have to write back but I hope you will. Everybody's gone but us, and this ain't much of a town to be lonely in.

He only answered Denny's first letter, a brief note to tell him Julia was gone. Only that, but he still couldn't bring himself to throw away Denny's letters. Sometimes he read a little here and there to Lauren. They kept coming, the most determined thing Denny had ever done. Now and then from the painfully awkward handwriting, a phrase would leap out—fresh, sensitive, like a run of notes played idly by someone with a feeling for music, and Landry wondered if not only life but an equally stubborn instinct for language were finally catching up with his brother.

> . . . going to quit flying soon. It's an easy buck, but I don't know, I don't somehow feel like an easy guy anymore. Does that make sense? Phrases of your stories keep echoing in my ear and sometimes some of my own. Don't laugh but—I really want to write.

Five forty-three A.M. Exhausted, but still he couldn't sleep. The compulsive Puritan in Landry rasped its discontent: *Don't just lie there. Do something.* Just a little more, until he was able to sleep. He'd retype the revised pages. He got up, turned on the lights and the typewriter, fished the largest butt out of his ashtray, lit it, and fed a fresh green sheet over the roller.

He did three pages, what the cuts boiled down to out of five, and read them like a surgeon doing postop on an incision. Good he couldn't say; no one knew from good at 6:00 A.M. But the pages were tighter.

Around 6:30, with the sun well up and traffic beginning to boom beyond the windows, Landry drifted off. The floor maid came in later and cleaned around him like the rest of the furniture.

20

Lauren let herself into the apartment at 1:30 A.M., wrinkling her nose at the stale air. She set the heavy suitcase by the closet and went to open the windows. There was a mountain of mail on her table, dutifully accumulated by the bellman. Too tired to look at it or even unpack, she ran a hot bath to wash the plane trip off her.

The apartment smelled flat. After her bath, Lauren cracked the door with the chain on to circulate fresh air, then poured two shots of Absolut over ice. On reflection, she added a third shot, hell with olives or vermouth, and carried it to bed. Propped against the pillows in the restful dark, she let the vodka work, trying to unravel the knot of tension in her, trying to define it.

Her whole life—career, family—felt suspended, here a maybe, there a perhaps. *Thank God for Pat.*

Her mother was dying; peacefully perhaps, but all the pain was felt by the people who loved her. Even with cancer you could suffer a long time before God and the American Medical Association let you check out. With Alzheimer's, your family felt the death every day for years while you floated, swaddled, spoon-fed, and oblivious through twilight toward the dark.

In the old days, Mama would be sheltered at home, a genteel widow, "Miz Mary," not quite right, you know. Senile, second childhood, dotage: all the polite euphemisms to label and sweep it under the social rug. Now the disease had a name, even a charitable foundation, but no cure. How did you

cure a mind with a billion circuits shorting out and disconnect-
ing? The patient became infantile and incontinent, forgot to
eat. . . .

*Mama was always tiny. She only weighs eighty pounds now. One
bad cold could finish her. It's a blessing that Papa's estate pays
the bills, but that won't last forever.*

When her mother was finally taken to the home, Lauren
used to call her every Sunday as it became harder and harder
to speak to Mary Hodge, a grueling five minutes just to say
hello, laboring the simplest phrases over and over again—

"Hello, Mama. Hello, Mama. This is Lauren. *Lau-ren.* How
are you, Mama? How *are* you? I *love you.*"

—and hanging up to weep a little in Pat's arms: *Please, God,
take her now, let her go. There's no justice, I don't expect that, but
could we have a moment's mercy?*

Letters, to her mother became as painfully elementary, re-
duced to large-printed postcards: HELLO, MAMA. I WENT
TO CHURCH TODAY. I LOVE YOU. LAUREN.

*Take her now. She's not suffering but we are. It hurts to sit with
Mama on the dreary sunporch with the other old women beaming
from their own limbo, and know she doesn't recognize me; only that
someone nice is holding her hand. I watched Walter sour and die
inside and Aaron drink away his talent, and you know something,
God? I'm not suited to handle death. Who is?*

Lots of women, Lauren supposed, finishing her drink too fast.
*Hordes of them, the family types who think Togetherness is a religion.
The cow-goddesses of the suburbs who haul their best black out of the
closet and head for the funeral like a holiday parade, and sit there with
the fat of them straining against girdles and black wool, overfed life
bulging out of symbolic death, looking solemn and important. Why
not? Something is finally happening, a corner turned or an old score
settled in the casket, and their stagey solemnity is measured to the
black-bordered occasion. Later on they'll eat too much at brunch and
get on with life. You need more milestones than the weekly copy of*
TV Guide.

Margaret was with her this last time and seemed to handled it
as she did everything, with arm's-length competence. One
wondered where joy or anger hid in Margaret; against her
will, Lauren was reminded of the taste of thin broth on a
stainless steel spoon. She spent as few nights as possible at
Margaret's house and escaped to Marsh, whose "Hi, Mom!"
still had as much love and acceptance as the day he first
learned to say it.

But first there was that long drive back from the nursing home with Margaret when Lauren realized that some kind of spiritual boundary had been drawn between them.

The vodka hit Lauren's fatigue with a soft rabbit punch. She felt light-headed and a little maudlin, but the anger beneath was undulled. *They won't do me like Mama. When I go, I'll choose the way, no one hanging on me or me on them. No nursing home, no funeral bills, just down the chute quick and clean.*

One more drink before sleep. Easier on the vodka this time, a little vermouth. Lauren fixed the nightcap and wove back to bed, feeling a hundred pounds heavier.

Let Mama go in her sleep tonight. Somebody, please let her.

"Fat chance," Lauren muttered.

No, the GAWL was very uptight about both ends of life. Legally, you could abort an unwanted or unaffordable child or the result of a rape, but not without a lot of moral bullying and maybe your clinic being blown up. You couldn't let your mother out gently at the end; couldn't fast-forward God's will or a fucking bunch of doctors already terrified of malpractice suits.

Lauren lay back and let the helpless tears spill down her face. Men were such pompous cowards, not moral at all, just covering their sweet little asses. So Mary Halloran Hodge could go on shriveling the Christian way as long as the bills were paid.

Margaret had called her selfish this last visit. That surprised Lauren as much as it hurt, that Meg could be that open. In the car coming back from the nursing home, some of the tension boiled over in Lauren. Thinking of Mary and the waste of Aaron, she muttered to the windshield, "Why do they tell us suffering ennobles? Nothing comes out of suffering but misery all around. It does nothing. It's random and meaningless."

Margaret steered carefully onto a city-bound ramp. She drove efficiently as she did everything else. She had Walter's height and coloring and more of his temperament than Lauren's. Lauren wondered how much of herself there actually was in this child out of her body.

"She's not suffering, Mother," Margaret pointed out.

"We are," Lauren grated. "And we endure it because there's nothing else to do short of a gun to the head."

"We're used to it," Margaret said with her eternal common

sense. "We're closer to it here than you are. I see it every week."

They rode in silence for a while. Lauren was grateful to be moving to Marsh's today. She always felt a distance in Margaret, an accumulation of impressions and signals over the years that added to disapproval and resentment. Now that she thought about it, Margaret had always gone silent at any mention of Aaron. She'd met him in New York, and Lauren always felt there was a polite repugnance toward him. But this morning she'd mentioned Pat and got the same reaction—a perceptible stiffening as Margaret veered away from the reference with the look of a martyr suffering one more wound.

My daughter doesn't like me. Or can't.

Once accepted, facts rushed in to corroborate. Unlike Marsh, Margaret was only politely interested in Lauren's art as more of an overgrown hobby than lifework, and had been physically repelled by New York people. "Don't any of them speak *English?*" Lauren's cozy apartment with its rooftop view of Chelsea passed her by for charm—

Margaret, come look at my sunset!

Margaret emerged from Lauren's bathroom: "Your bathroom tiles don't match."

Guilty not only of unmatched tiles but dirt around the edge of the kitchen sink, smudges on the wall behind her garbage pail, grit on the window sills, grime on the panes. Roaches, discovered and announced with the implications of a nuclear meltdown.

"This city is filthy, Mother."

Meaning disapproval not only of where Lauren lived but the way she did it.

"You really ought to stay longer," Margaret said now, her eyes on the road.

"No, I can't." Lauren was glad for the truth of it. "Work to do. There's Berlin coming up. My last video's in line for a prize." She waited hopefully for some reaction and received none. She might have noted that the weather was a bit cloudy. "And I do miss Pat."

By God, she did it again. I saw her. That perceptible stiffening as at a dirty word. *The man I sleep with who isn't her father or even my husband. Grow up, Meg.* Lauren felt a rush of anger, even— after all the months with volatile Pat, mind to mind and sometimes sword to sword—a savage urge to lay it on the line with Margaret. Useless. Her daughter would turn it aside as always, as if her feelings were none of her mother's business since she was no longer a real member of the family.

Turning off the freeway toward her house, Margaret said, "I don't see how you can stand New York."

What's the use? She couldn't hurt her child any more than the past made necessary. There was a rift between them, a boundary line. Maybe in ten years Margaret would forgive; perhaps in ten more, she'd understand. A thin perhaps. Suffering didn't instruct life, wisdom didn't always come at the end. Meg could live hermetically sealed like Pat's sister, Julia, until she was eighty if she chose. But on her own side of the border, Lauren would fly her own, hard-won flag.

"Sometimes I can't stand it," she said more casually than she felt, cushioning her head against the back rest, pretending it was Pat's arm. "But there's my work and Pat, and he's part of me. That's one thing I've learned being there. You pay one thing to get another."

Margaret braked a little too hard at a stoplight. She vented a small, sibilant rush of disgust. "That's so selfish. I don't believe that."

Lauren closed her eyes and tried to relax her shoulders. *No, I don't suppose you do.* "Are you ready for lunch before the children come home, dear? My treat." She thought of her mother on the sunporch. *I wonder if Mama knew it was me holding her hand. I hope so. . . .*

She was too exhausted to be startled when the phone rang close to her head. "Hello?"

"Hi-i, sweetheart. Knew you were getting in late. Didn't think you'd be asleep yet."

"Hi, dearest." Lauren wiped at the tears, hoping Pat wouldn't hear them in her voice. "Just having a nightcap before fading out."

"Glad you're home." He sounded like it. "Dinner tomorrow?"

"Well, I certainly hope so. Been two weeks." And they both needed sex, Lauren knew. Neither of them ever knew when to turn off, resisting relaxation like cranky-tired children. "Working on the book?"

"Just not ready to sleep yet. And I missed you."

"Tha-at's what I wanted to hear." She smiled. "I missed you, sweetheart." At times like this, when they called to say good night, she loved his voice, like a pillow under her head. "How's the book going?"

"Oh—" A deep breath of resignation. "Not as good as it could be. Probably better than I think. How about Scotty's tomorrow night?"

"Yeah-h."

"How's your mother?"

"As good as she'll ever be. They don't know much about Alzheimer's." Her own, sudden intensity surprised her. "I hate that place, Pat. I fucking *hate* it. So damned hard to sit there, holding Mama's hand and smiling when . . . oh, wait a minute."

Lauren wiped her eyes and blew her nose. When they were back on, Landry asked gently, "Okay now?"

"Yes."

"About your mom?"

"That . . . and Margaret. It came through loud and clear this time. She still blames me for everything. With Mother and the rest of it, I was miserable. Honestly, sometimes I feel just plain mad enough to cut Meg out of my will."

"Why not?" Landry laughed. "She'd just spend it on something sensible anyway."

Lauren yawned, suddenly very ready to sleep, needing desperately to close her eyes now that she was home with Pat and the world on track again.

"We'll be together tomorrow and work it out," he promised.

"I was thinking on the plane," she drowsed over the wire that connected them. "You know how I'd like to die?"

"Two o'clock in the morning and you're getting philosophical about death."

"No, just sanitary." Lauren yawned again. "I thought . . . if I ever know I'm finished, on the way out and nothing ahead but some nursing home, I'll just take a plane to Miami. Everybody goes to Miami to die," she expanded dreamily. " 'Specially if you're Jewish, you can get great food. So . . . I'll check into some nice, overdecorated place on the beach, have a good dinner, leave a neat letter absolving God, the flesh, and the AMA, and maybe on the second night I'll go for a long swim." Another yawn. "Yeah, I really think . . ."

"I think you're falling asleep," Pat murmured. "A very sleepy little girl."

"Love you, dearest." Lauren kissed the mouthpiece.

"Love you, baby. For once I know what I mean saying it."

"Y'better. G'night."

Lauren put the phone down on the headboard and got up to

turn off the kitchen light. Unpack in the morning, do the mail, start the whole grind over again. Just before falling asleep, she thought of her mother again and the scenario about her sketched on the plane home. Maybe, with the right actress, she could do something with it in video. . . .

21

Outside the Seville, the Labor Day weekend was sunny and dry, the humidity washed away by yesterday's cloudburst. Inside, Landry hunched in his leather recliner, back and rump numb, scowling at the scribbled yellow page, most of it slashed through and written over. Four thousand words yesterday, two thousand so far today, running on the last of his wind. He hadn't bathed in a good twenty-four hours. The room reeked of him, stale cigarettes, coffee, and the flat air pumped from the ancient air-conditioner. He had a dull headache from going through a pack of cigarettes since breakfast. But the book was almost done.

He got up stiffly and went to the bathroom cabinet, chewed two aspirin to pulp, and swallowed them with water. Boiled-egg eyes in an aspic of wrinkles looked out of the mirror at him.

"You look embalmed," said the image.

I should feel that good.

He felt schizophrenically distant from the world beyond his windows, the sunlight a pallid intrusion on the fringes of consciousness. He should have called Lauren this morning after missing last night. His hands shook lighting a cigarette, and his throat was lined with sandpaper. Odd pains flashed across his chest and neck. If he were hypochondriac or even sensible, he'd swear off cigarettes and see a doctor, but he'd been here before. No one felt human on the last stretch of a book. The aspirin would kill his headache, so screw it, sit down, and deal.

Last page. No need to drag it out. The Battle of Camlann was as well known to fantasy readers as Waterloo. Arthur and Modred died there, locked in the final combat. No need here for the mythical tags of Excalibur or the Lady of the Lake. Other, older myths were at work all through the book. Modred's emotions were clear and strong enough to play without comment as he drove down on Arthur, his father. Analogies— Zeus and Cronus, Oedipus and Laius. Monk and Jack.

Despite all else, a love never spoken before the ax comes down. Modred couldn't help feeling the weight of this, cutting down, obliterating what could somehow never be attained. What his wronged, vindictive mother sharpened and pointed him to.

> I feel a weight like history itself pushing me forward to this moment. Cronus-Laius-Arthur-father. So we come once more to the demanded sacrifice, the necessary murder. Was it all for her, my mother, or is this time and again chaos a part of the illusion of order?

Landry paused and closed his eyes against a throbbing pain behind them. Forget sharpness; he was struggling to join simple words now.

Wait, rest. Keep your eyes closed. Don't force it, let it.

Analogies. Connie and Jack. Was it all for her, the distance you put between yourself and Jack? Connie was a kind of Morgana, a black sheep. So was Jack, come to that. Never thought of it before but both their names come from near Morgana's birthplace, Devon and Somerset, the Landrys out of Cornwall. Like Morgana, Connie held on to grudges, shaped her life around them. Like Modred, I believed her causes and reasons for years without question.

Before I ever read history, Connie and Julia gave me the Hawkins saga, truth sweetened with romance and bad memory. Prideful, quarrelsome, arrogant men and women, prudently commended (or escaped) to the New World, one foot on a slaver's deck, the other behind a pulpit. You could never beat the English for combining piety with self-interest.

Emotional, volatile men: I remember Mama's stories of her father, Elijah, who fought the South and still loved it despite the loss of two fingers at Chancellorsville and starvation in a Confederate prison camp. A peremptory, passionate man in the habit of stumping over to Congress and berating in person those representatives he disagreed with. He knew of Francis Landry and disapproved of the whole Landry clan without having met any of them. Landry's editorials influenced Washington opinion on everything from Spain and the *Maine* to immigration.

"God damn it to hell!" he bellowed over the breakfast table, throwing the newspaper to the floor. "That young pup Landry has gone too far this time. Damn if he doesn't think he's related to God!"

Not entirely true, though it would be typical of the Landrys to consider it God's misfortune and not theirs.

Elijah's wife, Sarah, never disagreed with the Major. She was a Kentucky McLeod—fluttery, thoroughly southern, implacable only on the worthiness of her husband and the scalawag nature of Yankees in general.

"*Now* what!" Elijah thundered long before his daughter Constance saw the light of day. "Sarah? Francis Landry has condescended to marry." The paper rattled disdainfully. " 'Annie Eithne Steele of Boston. The daughter of Andrew and Fiona Steele.' " A *humph* of Hawkins contempt. "Sound like a brace of smart micks on the make to me."

"Bog trotters," said Gramma Sarah, whose Highland ancestors had righteously inoculated Ireland with Protestantism.

"Goddamned immigrants," rumbled the Major, whose ancestors had inoculated the colonies with slavery, never particular as to what color they were.

Annie Steele was "black Irish" like her mother—blue-black hair, fair skin, and a fine color to her cheeks. She brought more steel than her name to the complacent Landry blood; she made her house *the* place for Washington society to meet and was more than a match for them, to her husband's pride. She introduced a Gaelic turn in the naming of her first sons, Patrick and Dennis, allowed another Francis—all to be successful journalists—and compromised on one last, spoiled, too-handsome boy christened Stuart but never called anything but Jack. At which point, Grampa Elijah roaring in his grave, the clans collided. Connie was the last of the Hawkins swashbucklers, but I'd love to have turned Fiona McGowran loose on her. Fiona had all of Mama's talent for hatred but more survival sense.

She came off the boat lousy from steerage like all of her fellow passengers, to do seven years' indentured service, the condition of her passage from Ireland. The silences and omissions, the laconic references, are more revealing than reams of romance. The year Fiona escaped starvation was called the Black 47. As Annie told it to Jack, Fiona would rarely eat a potato and then only if it was scrubbed and quartered, because she'd survived the famine on blighted potatoes and nothing else. She developed a fetish for silk underwear and never mentioned the English in their own tongue. Fiona was beautiful (when she finally got enough to eat) and took steps to make it pay. She married a manufacturer, Ulster Protestant though he was, briskly tucked away most of the sacraments, became dutifully Episcopal, raised her daughter Annie as a Boston debutante—but always left the drawing room when her husband's guests sang Irish songs written this side of the water. She'd seen girls like herself eat weeds before they starved to death in ditches or lean-to *shebangs*. Fiona had no more nostalgia for Green Ireland than a Jew for Auschwitz. When Annie married Francis Landry, Fiona blessed the union even though her son-in-law had the English in him, because there was real linen and full-weight silver on his table, his house was not common brick but gleaming white frame, and her daughter would never have to wear a potato-sack shift.

That's what Connie and Jack came out of. I could see it all in their eyes and mouths. Always there in the old pictures, but I understand it now. Mama's mouth was more sensitive but with a downturned brooding, the ghost of a feud old long before she was born. Jack had Annie's mouth, so surely caught in Monty Flagg's pen-and-ink portrait of her: thin, humorous, sardonic, always hovering on the edge of mischief. Perhaps like Arthur the King, too easily forgiving, trusting the world to have his own warmth and share his motives. Only occasionally that delicate mouth went hard, not shaped for anger but apt to flashes of it when Connie went too far—

"Damn you, Con, why don't you stop! You've confused one of my sons and turned the other against me. Lay off!"

"You lie, Jack! Oh how you lie!" Played to the gallery but bitter truth for all of that. "Ask my reasons. Tell your sons why I hate you. . . ."

Analogies. All those years, Morgana nurturing Modred on her pain and hatred for something so old, so far back, and the boy, loving and defenseless, pointed and loosed like a missile.

. . . and it was years before we ever embraced, before I could tell my father I loved him. There was a humanity in Jack for all his failings. He simply waited and opened his arms when I came. Or maybe love wasn't that white a heat in him as it was in Connie. There was a child in him as well, who wondered and never fully knew.

How did she come to make me such a battleground?

Questions.

Landry opened his eyes, brushed cigarette ashes off the page, and read the last lines written:

> Was it all for her, my mother, or is this time and again chaos a part of the illusion of order?

Modred didn't know, only wondered.

> Now my father sees me; wondering's past, for all it answered, and now we close and strike. In time, the bards will beat our fury into what passes for meaning, but now the indifferent fog swathes Camlann and the ruin of us. The son of the carpenter weeps, the older gods yawn and look for other sport. My father dies with his certainties, I with my questions.

The page blurred before Landry. He squinted at it through a cloud of cigarette smoke: not too bad. Good enough for now at least. His head was full of tapioca, unfit to judge good from pure dreck. He dragged deep on the butt, put it out, and slashed a bar beneath the last line.

Done.

He felt nothing, neither fatigue nor elation, only sat for long minutes, a bleary-eyed lump staring at the phone, wanting to call Lauren and tell her. Tell someone. *I did it. Went the distance one more time.*

"Oh?" said the uninterested world beyond his window. "You want the medal or the sacktime?"

Landry shuffled the yellow pages into order. He wasn't really finished anyway and didn't have the energy to call anyone.

22

Crissy James invited Landry to dinner at the loft on an October night when Lauren was busy, and found him friendly but a little absent, and said so to Evan before they dropped off to sleep.

"You have to admit that Pat Landry can be very strange. I mean, he finished that book—what's the damned title?—but it's like he's still in outer space."

Evan yawned. "Maybe he had a fight with whatsername."

"Lauren? Nah, they fight three times a week, weird as he is." Crissy giggled softly into her husband's shoulder. "And *she* is. Art is such a hassle. I'm glad you write software books."

"Pays better. Less angst."

"True." Crissy settled herself for sleep. "And tormented artists are pains in the ass."

And she said as much to Landry, not knowing the only thing worse than having to finish a book was not having another to begin; when pressing the CREATE button elicited only a polite negative like an empty soft-drink machine. SORRY, WE'RE OUT. PLEASE CALL THE MANAGER AND PANIC.

Landry didn't panic at first, at least not visibly. He told himself he'd just finished a book (six *weeks* ago!), that he needed time to fill up again. For all the logic, panic seeped through the walls of rationality like water into a basement, to stagnate at the bottom of his mind.

Around the middle of the month, Edie Fine sent the fall royalty check on *The Harper's Wife* along with a newsy note: she'd sized up the Falcon Books project, how about lunch at Joanna's?

Here we go again, Landry thought stoically. *One more time*. But this time the gravy would be richer and so would he. It never got easier; that's why he didn't grudge the six-figure contracts to dinosaurs like Peters and Halverstrom. They'd both survived the old cent-a-word days to become Grand Masters in the genre boom of the seventies, and rich ones when the young movie audience discovered science fiction and fantasy for serious. Of course, Peters was a compulsive, afraid to leave his typewriter lest it turn into a pumpkin, and Halverstrom, hippie-hailed as another guru in the sixties, had declined from his early and best work to a kind of philosophic paresis with delusions of intellect. Both of them and their grateful agents were very well off now. Blessings on their heads, mazel tov, they were entitled.

Get the money. They forget you so fast.

What was the name of that great book by whatsisname?

Who?

Oh, you know who I mean.

I'm lousy at names and titles.

So is the world, man.

Landry found himself being evasive with Edie when she asked about ideas of his own, which made as much sense as lying to Lauren; disgusted at his inactivity and sloth, skipping the gym day after day, not even able to read. After ten minutes, his fingers started to drum. He'd close the book, put on a record, listen a few minutes, then switch it off. Bored with himself, a mechanism made to function continuously, without work or the supportive props most men could take for granted— home, children, or a varied social life—he corroded rapidly. For the first time in years, he kept whiskey in his room and counted the days he could leave it corked.

He was restless and querulous with Lauren, who began to look a little peaked. Knowing the best and worst of him now, she began to count his drinks like a worried wife and felt the strain of smiling when she didn't feel like it. The fidgety absentness in Landry sent her off on her own tangent toward irritation: was he bored with her? Was he seeing someone else? He was younger and certainly knew enough eligible women. She wished her dinner conversation could sparkle effortlessly at the end of a gritty day, but her spontaneous wit had gone down the drain with twenty-eight years of dishwater. Was she getting frumpy? She didn't even feel right in a dress anymore, whereas Caroline Cutler would look soigné on welfare, Helen Storey was always cool and gorgeous, and Darcy Rambard's wit was sharp as her lacquered nails.

Lauren knew Pat's redeeming sense of the absurd. He could usually save himself with laughter, but even that seemed to have gone limp in the wet fog of his depression. They even spatted in public, something neither would do on principle, in the small dining room at Danieli's. The argument was ridiculous; neither could remember how it began, but their voices went suddenly sharp and Lauren saw the maître d' look over, startled. She leaned across to her gloomy lover and muttered:

"We'd better keep our voices down. We'll get sixty-nined out of here."

The bitchiness in Landry tripped and fell on its butt. He blinked at her: "What?"

"We'll get sixty-nined. Thrown out."

He began to gasp with it, then the cleansing laughter boomed out over the small dining room as Landry shook his head helplessly.

"Honey," he sputtered, "you . . . you mean eighty-six."

The mistake was quite innocent. "Oh? What's sixty-nine?"

"Oh. Well . . . well, I'll tell you later," he managed through a fresh convulsion, "but we never do it in Danieli's."

Like oil in a hardwater bath, laughter could take the curse off him. Nevertheless, his lovemaking afterward and his goodnight kiss had a rather remote quality to it. Landry wandered to the door as if he'd forgotten something and couldn't bring it to mind, mumbling about a meeting the next day.

"Lunch with Edie," it sounded like.

"I know you feel written out." Edie took a bite of seafood salad, washed it down with Perrier. "And I know you're unhappy about it."

Landry let his gaze wander over the lunch crowd at Joanna's, marveling at the perception of good agents. "What about Falcon Books?"

"Let me finish. There are writers who turn in two books a year—schlock, mostly—and who will be turning in two books a year from now until I get tired of Mexican food. Why not quit awhile, wait it out?"

"Because I can't afford to wait it out," Landry said. "What about Falcon?"

"Yeah. Well." Edie pushed away her plate and rested on folded arms. "You know Bethany Harris?"

"Seen her. Looks like an NFL fullback?"

"That's her," Edie confirmed.

"Thought she was at Random House."

"She was. Got the ax last year. Bought the wrong books at the wrong time. I should complain," Edie confided. "I sold her one of them. Well, she's at Falcon now and the word is she's bought into a new co-op apartment, guessing very right and ve-ry carefully about acquisitions, commercial as toothpaste now. Got clout and a budget to match." Edie swigged at her Perrier. "I had lunch with her last week. She thinks the time and the market are ready for another family-saga-type series, set Elizabethan or later, but the accent on romance."

"Gee," said deadpan Landry, "why didn't I think of that?"

"Don't be a smartass, just listen. Harris is talking a multibook contract, far as the market will take it, and she's looking for a Mallory Maine or a Darcy Rambard to do it."

"Maine!" Landry's knife clattered on his plate.

"Now, now, that's window dressing. She knows she can't get Mallory Maine for less than—" Edie shrugged. "What? A hundred and fifty? But Rambard is definitely a contender. So last week I sent her a copy of *The Harper's Wife* and a stat of *Camlann*. She liked them and wants a lunch date with you whenever."

Landry relied on Edie's bottom-line frankness and her nose for the business. "How's it smell to you?"

"Straightforward," was Edie's informed assessment. "They're pretty good on contracts. They don't have Trefoil's sales force but they're building toward it and know they have to put their budget where their mouth is. But—I get overtones," she reflected. "You know: a word here and there eventually adds up to a sentence."

A very clear sentence that Landry understood well enough as Edie outlined it. Falcon Books was owned by an overseas conglomerate that didn't read anything but year-end statements. A lot of people had been laid off in the last six months, and the new series had the faint ring of a very scared editorial board out to grab a large enough hunk of a growing market to look good in the front office where the carpets were thick and the charity thin.

"But I can ask good money for you," Edie said.

Landry nodded. "Set it up, Edie."

She wadded her napkin and dropped it by her plate. "Sure."

"What's the matter?"

"Nothing." Edie Fine uttered a heartfelt non sequitur. "When I retire, I never want to hear another telephone as long as I live." She looked at her watch and flagged the waiter. "Come on. I gotta get back to work. I'll call Harris this week. She's a good contact, but just one tip from experience. Don't try to outdrink her at lunch. She's got four hollow legs."

About the time he drifted into the Caroline-Crissy circle, Landry met another writer named Joan Vogelman, a Ph.D. from Columbia. They enjoyed talking history and trading source books and both considered themselves blessed, in those early, anxious years, to get four thousand a book with six percent royalties. Vogelman's first, fine historical novel garnered respectful reviews and anemic sales, but with the robust success of her second, more erotic than historical, Joan Vogelman became Darcy Rambard, waxed her legs, platinumed her mouse-brown hair—"When you got it, flaunt it"—and moved into an East Side high-rise.

"I'm too old to be a yuppie," she defined herself then to Pat Landry. "I'm nouveau riche. That's French for the longtime poor."

If the money was new, Darcy's ideas about men went back to her girlhood in Jersey. "Don't make a pass at me, Pat," she fended off his first and only exploratory advance. "I stick with Jewish men."

"Bigot."

"I understand them. Well-off Jewish men I understand even better. You, Patrick, are a buddy. Let's have another drink."

And so they flourished as friends where they would have made abysmal lovers. They drank, laughed, and bitched together at parties, conventions, lunch, or wherever they crossed trail. The day Edie set up his lunch with Bethany Harris, Darcy called him, breathy and excited.

"Pat! I love you. Listen, I have to *tell* you. D'you know Beth Harris at Falcon?"

"Uh—yeah. Yeah, what about her?"

"I just had lunch with her at Rendez Vous. You gotta try it, their desserts are illegal. Almost didn't make it . . ."

And Landry listened politely while Darcy described her tortuous progress to the restaurant, very late because her daughter called with problems, what else, she needed root canal work and of course she couldn't afford it, and Darcy *finally* got her off the phone and then there were always cabs on Third Avenue except when you needed one . . .

"So you had lunch with Harris," Landry edited.

"God, is that woman big! Wears a hat to lunch, always looks like she's about to make an arrest. But what a *deal* she's talking, right down my alley."

Landry waited for the punchline, wondering if Darcy had the series sewed up.

"Only thing is, I think they're considering someone else, too. No reason why not, I guess. She was all compliments and what-all but not very specif—*cat!*"

The phone clunked on something hard. Landry heard a muffled splintering of Rambard invective, then she was back. "Merlin was up on the counter fressing on my salmon steaks. Listen, my boyfriend's coming for dinner, gotta run. But isn't it *fabulous,* Pat? I mean, if I *got* it? Ciao, baby."

Landry lay back in his leather recliner, listening to Puccini and finishing his scotch. He'd have another, maybe two, and wallow in the silver sorrows of Cio-Cio-San as an antidote to his own.

If he got the series, he'd make money, if nothing else, and since he didn't have any ideas of his own going for him, money was the name of this month's game.

I remember the familiar, stale taste of failure in my mouth, and Susan believing in me. Later she tried to believe out of loyalty and habit while I withered away with shame and the man of me faded with it. Until she couldn't believe anymore and left me for a guy who at least looked at her as a woman to be loved. I'll never blame her for that, but Christ it hurt.

But it hurt then for the last time.

So why aren't you smiling? You get it, you'll be set.

"What the hell's wrong with you?" Jack roared at his son, glowering over his hornrim glasses from the table. "Grab it, Monk. How many times did I tell you?"

Yeah, you told me.

"Don't be an author, for God's sake. Authors starve, writers eat. Grab it. Two minutes, ten . . ." Jack made a notation at the bottom of his own script page and vanished under the aura of Madame Butterfly, *Un Bel Di,* and scotch. Landry scowled boozily at the turntable, then snapped it off.

"Shut up, Jap. You think *you* got problems?"

23

Bethany Harris's fedora was as familiar in midtown restaurants as Bella Abzug's sun hat, though she favored Rendez-Vous on East Fifty-second Street, which ran to hushed waiters, dark leather, large drinks, and small portions for lunch. Bethany was a big woman, more burly than fat. She smoked continually and had a direct manner that might intimidate any author new to lunching with editors. Her tolerance for Jack Daniels was awesome. Landry began the long lunch virtuously enough on Perrier, but relapsed to scotch as Bethany's drift became clearer. Predictably, the history series Falcon wanted amounted to no more than a glitzy backdrop for the erotic romance that would sell the books.

"I see the setting," Bethany explained, "oh, somewhere after 1550. Rapiers and lace rather than broadswords and mail." Her smile failed to warm Landry. "And of course the accent on romance and sex rather than the history. That's what I admire in your books," she expanded. "The background is *in* the background and the characters are down front."

"Well," he parried, "you never play a show in back of the scenery."

"Right, right. And the readers want romance. That's what the cover art will emphasize."

Hell, yes. The title would be embossed in scarlet or electric blue over a flame-haired beauty with 38C boobs losing herself deliciously, wantonly, in the embrace of a broad-shouldered,

151

black-haired stud in a white Hamlet shirt whose strong mouth was usually described as "plundering" or "implacable." Landry pictured a metaphoric hybrid of Dracula and an anteater. Feeling dismal, he ordered his second scotch.

"We plan to launch this with a large press run," Bethany told him.

"How large? Quarter of a million copies?"

"Oh, well, that's a decision for when we have the first book in house," she dodged nimbly, the fedora bobbing in punctuation. "But we plan to do the full promo: dump bins in the stores, posters, which means—"

Absolutely nothing, Landry knew. *Unless the advance is big enough, you're just dazzling me with footwork.*

He finished the scotch too fast.

"Of course, this is a package," said the Great Burly Harris through a cloud of smoke while a woman at the next table coughed reproachfully. "I hope you can work closely with an editor."

There it was. The Kiss of the Spider Woman. No one had ever messed with his stuff; no one had to. He gave Bethany a smile of reassurance even Jack would admire. "Hand in glove."

Nice going, wimp.

"You write women well," Bethany was saying. "Good love scenes. Not enough of them," she amended, iron in velvet, "and generally not the kind I want. I don't want truth, I want romance." She stubbed out her cigarette and reached for another. "We know our target reader. She has enough money to buy ten or more of these books a month, and she does."

"Ten?"

"Or more."

"Like chewing gum."

"Just like chewing gum. It's her fix. She's loyal to the genre. Romance is her trip."

Landry listened without joy as Bethany Harris expounded on the reading tastes of her target customer, hoping he could pull it off without too much compromise. He tried a feeler. "I can't even think of—well, what I call Wagnerian love scenes without tending to comedy."

"Neither can I," Bethany admitted, looking like a weary owl under her fedora brim. "I imagine your taste in comedy is rather astringent."

"Yeah."

"Mine too, but forget it. To the lady we're trying to reach, comedy is TV sitcoms, and no one laughs in bed. Now, you did a beautifully steamy love scene in *The Harper's Wife.*"

"Thanks. I worked very carefully on that scene."

More desperate than careful. His editor had wanted much more Wagner in the love scene, where Landry tended to Prokofiev. The disagreement bothered him to the point where he finally said the hell with it, wrote the scene half-drunk, scored it for a hundred violins to make the editor happy, and always skipped over the scene when paging through the book.

"I know you could deliver what I need, working with an experienced romance editor. Tell you what they told Victorian wives about the unpleasantries of sex." Bethany swept up her drink in a catcher's mitt of a hand. "Put the flag over your face and do it for Old Glory." She nodded at his glass. "Could you use another?"

"Yes," said Pat Landry. "I believe I could."

Before he went to Lauren's that rainy evening, Landry heard from Bethany through Edie Fine that Falcon would go with him on the series, contract negotiations to follow. He had it, then. He didn't know the contributing truths to the fact and was, perhaps, the happier for it. Bethany Harris might be a hard-bitten near-alcoholic, but she was clear-sighted about writers and agents and stoic about both.

A half-dozen writers had been considered for the project, starting at the top. Mallory Maine—the two of her—was sewed up tight in another house and far beyond the Falcon budget in any case. Number two, for the money they could offer, was quite viable but experiencing a difficult pregnancy and making skittery noises about going mainstream.

"Lots of luck, dear. Let me know when the baby comes." Bethany Harris put down the phone and forgot it.

Number three had become a Fundamentalist since her last book, aspiring rather to speak in tongues than marketable prose. She wrote a long, soul-searching letter to Bethany in which she praised Jesus fulsomely and doubted the spiritual value of erotic romances. Peace be with her.

Number four was Raven Sharpe (Melvin Smith to his wife and children). Melvin was putting away more whiskey than pages lately, so consistently late on manuscript deliveries that his books always had to be rescheduled. Melvin was a *kvetch* who whined or raged in person or by mail, pestered editors on the phone, and made passes over lunch. His previous editors, when they met on the cocktail circuit, told "Melvin stories" and felt like a convocation of therapists.

Two reasonable choices left and the front office bugging Bethany to firm it up and start rolling. Darcy Rambard or Patrick Landry. In the very small world of New York publishing, both had good track records for product and dependability. Both knew the historical period. Rambard would give it lush sweep and steam, Landry a compelling intensity and grain. They'd make a beautiful team, but then the advance wouldn't be enough for either of them. Rambard seemed the right choice.

When she sat down to lunch with Landry, Bethany Harris had forty-eight hours to nail in her author and had just been informed that the advance for the first book would be in a range about twenty thousand dollars lower than first estimated, and less negotiable. No way over sixty thousand top. It wasn't the first time she'd had the rug pulled out from under her and told to do miracles anyway. This made Rambard all the harder to get, since her agent had floored the last book at eighty in another house.

Bethany Harris hated dealing with Rambard's agent. He had a tendency to dictate and make waves without consulting his clients. On the other hand, she did a lot of business with Edie Fine, who could fight for her points without sending an editor up the wall.

Bottom line: Pat Landry was an equally good writer she could get for less. She called Edie Fine and, after a brief, cordial exchange (much more cordial than the one they would conduct over the advance), Edie called Pat Landry and told him he had the series.

When they were finished, Edie said, "Pat?"

"What, Edie?"

She paused longer than usual. "If it's what you want, I'll get every dollar it's worth." Edie clicked off the line.

"Y'know, Monk?" Jack Landry retrieved his butt from the ashtray and gave it second life. "Dorothy Parker made five grand a week working for Metro, but she died broke trying to do it her way. I always said you'd click, but watch it. Even when you were a kid, you had to be a goddamned *ar*tist, y'know?"

Not anymore, Jack. They're giving me a chance to check out rich.

"That's the ticket, Monkey." Jack winked over his glasses. "Rich and slowly."

I made money today, Laurie. Remember all the crap we talked about the unlimited vistas of our artistic estate? Well, someone's bought mine to subdivide, and the why of it all—oh, that would take so long to explain.

Lauren had her own problems that day. The Berlin Festival was getting close and the committee hadn't sent her airline tickets yet, which meant another expensive phone call to light a fire under some minion. She'd gone uptown to meet a producer at two-thirty. He didn't make it until well after three. While waiting for the producer to get back from lunch, Lauren had flipped through a video journal and found a belated and negative review of a piece she'd done two years back, praising the young performer and scathing Lauren Hodge for "intrusive" camera work. She knew the reviewer, an instructor in film and video at New York University, whose own work in the medium was radical and utterly without heart.

The review hit a vulnerable spot. Her work in that piece *was* intrusive. She was changing directions from dance and image to working with ideas and words, learning a new language and still thinking in the grammar of the old one. *Of course there were wrong choices; being right* starts *with being wrong, you sterile—*

Lauren tried not to let the piece depress her, telling herself the work was transitional and far behind her now; while *you*, she addressed the reviewer with righteous venom, are still sitting in your little ivory tower with your head in the sand and the sixties, still crying "Revolution!" when I've moved beyond it.

Coming home, she emerged from the Twenty-third Street station into a chilling rain without her umbrella, wet through as she trudged to the supermarket, dispirited when she reached her place. She hoped Pat would be in a good mood and not compulsively early as usual. Lying in a hot bath, Lauren asked herself: *why do I feel so rotten?* The sum of little things, all having to be borne without the ego or the resilience of youth, and deep under the corroding pile of it was a word.

"Selfish," she said to the bathroom tiles.

She'd admitted the fault a hundred times in her own context and definition, but when Margaret had said it in the car, it was a condemnation that pierced with a lasting pain.

What happened, Meg? Through all the trouble with your

father, I tried so damned hard to shield you and Marsh. He rolled it off his back, but you grew up so controlled and careful.

Lauren felt close to tears.

A few tears might help. I can fight the world but not you, she thought. I can tell myself it doesn't matter, but it does. Poor Meg, you saw so much of Walter's rage. You couldn't wait to grow up into your own place where you could lock it out, deny it. You always went for the cautious, sensible way, married right out of school and even at twenty-five you wore matronly hats to church. Children need security, and they'll find it one place or another. Your father put one rent in your reality and then I tore it in half by leaving.

But I never wanted to hurt you, Meg. Hurting's easier when you're young, and you hurt me with that one word hissed out, one tiny jet escaped from a pressure tank. I've tried to explain so many times that it must be boring to you now. Time gets precious at this end of life. Every tick of the clock is one less to live and *mean*. Every sunset one less wash of color to brighten my soul, one day less to create, and when I can't do that, it won't matter when you bury or scatter me, because I'm already dead. And—oh, my dear, it's going to be so long before you forgive me and even longer until you understand. I hope I can last it out.

Lauren ran more hot water, lay back in the tub, and surrendered to a brief but thoroughly satisfying cry. Tonight she and Pat needed love and touching. They hadn't gotten to bed nearly enough lately. Shouldn't make each other whipping boy for what couldn't be helped, but they always did.

And then, of course, *just* as she was getting out of the tub, there was the phone. Business, what else, more possibilities, more maybes, but something that had to be handled immediately, and before Lauren knew it she was revved up and tearing around the apartment to get something at least started so she could pick it up tomorrow, forgetting the time. . . .

24

. . . **A**nd Pat walked in *early*, at least fifteen minutes before she'd begun to get ready, glumly shedding his wet raincoat and dropping a sodden manila envelope on the floor.

"From Denny," he mumbled, kissing her absently. "It was in my mailbox, didn't feel like taking it back upstairs. Don't let me forget it." He surveyed the chaotic condition of the paper-strewn table and floor. "You don't look ready."

"No kidding." Lauren quelled the urge to mayhem. "I wish you'd come a little later."

He wasn't in the relaxed mood she'd hoped for. Lauren went to the kitchen to make him a spritzer, smoldering. *I only needed a few more minutes. If he says one more time that I'm disorganized, I'll scream.* He had an agency and the whole publishing industry to pick up after him; she had to cut it alone. He couldn't even give her time for that?

"Did you work today?" she called from the sink.

"No, I didn't work today," came the dogged response. "I had lunch with an amazon editor. Outside of that, I had the pleasure of doing absolutely nothing."

It hardly sounded like pleasure. If he was quirky under the pressure of work, Pat Landry was impossible without it. Where he could be by turns sweet and irritating, now he was sometimes a downright bore. A month or more since turning in the book. He wasn't working on anything new; he'd have told her about it. The check was in the bank, so of course he'd spend it

157

like a sailor on leave and not think of economizing until he was almost broke again. Helluva father Pat Landry would've made.

She started to cut up some cheese and celery for a snack while Landry hovered like a troubled spirit in the kitchen entrance, watching her. He was putting on weight again, not exercising, probably drinking alone and too much, distant and tense as herself. He hadn't even called to say good night for three days. That was okay, busy as she was now, barely nibbling at breakfast before charging at work, but there was a screening at Millenium tonight she'd planned to catch with some women friends until Pat called and suggested dinner. She should have said no, but dutifully canceled the other date, then wondered why, angry at herself. Putting herself at a man's disposal again: all the things she said she wouldn't do. *He's taking me for granted—and now he's reaching for the plate before I'm even finished—*

She boiled over. "*Damm*it, Pat—"

"What?"

"What a clod! Just come in and take over. I'm fixing the plate for you, and my own work's not done, and—oh look, just take your drink and go by the window. I'll be out in a minute."

While he sat brooding over Chelsea, Lauren swept up the scattered work and shuffled it into some kind of order for tomorrow. Nothing ever worked out right.

With a strong martini she felt more human except for the tight knot between her shoulders. Lauren took her drink to the window and bent over Landry.

"Hey, give us a kiss?" They could start with that much at least.

He smiled at her for the first time since coming in. "Hi. Have a rough day?"

"Oh, honey." Lauren sank into the chair with a deep sigh. "Don't ask."

Because he asked, she recited the litany of woes, knowing how dull they sounded. Worst was the flawed video tape she couldn't afford to redub before the Berlin Festival.

"I remember that tape," Landry said. "The glitch is barely audible."

"It shouldn't *be* there."

"I can loan you the money for a dub."

"No. Thanks." Lauren said it into her drink. "I pull my own weight, same as you."

"I said a loan."

"It isn't that, it's—the whole damned Catch-22 situation. I've got a new piece written. About Mama. I want you to read it—you can tell me what it needs—and it's perfect for PBS, but even then there's no money in it. Figure out how to get me an agent I can't pay and the name talent to make someone look at it, someone I can persuade to work for a delayed percentage of peanuts, and I'll be in business."

"It takes time, Lauren."

"I'm fifty-*six*," she lashed back too hard. "How much time is there?" Lauren lunged out of the chair and went to the kitchen for fresh ice, angrily bashing it out of the tray. Landry followed her, filling the narrow entrance. "Laurie?"

"What?"

"You think it'll be easy just because they give you a lot of money?"

"I'd like to have that kind of problem for a change."

And what would he know about it? Lauren glowered to herself. Sitting on his ass, not even working out to keep in shape, dust on the typewriter, none on the whiskey bottle, and the machinery still worked automatically for him. Finished his homework like a good little boy, so he can go out and play. *Nothing's automatic for me. I'm cranking by hand every day.*

He was just as distant at Scotty's, fingers drumming on the tablecloth, ordering scotch instead of wine with dinner, conversing without any spark. Most of the effort fell on Lauren; she resented that too, and ordered her second martini, her fourth for the evening. Somewhere behind the thickening anger, unfocused as Landry's, was the fading hope that after dinner they could relax and make love, touch somehow. Make it right. One of the foggier areas in Mr. Landry's awareness: he enjoyed sex but never seemed to know when he needed it.

The turning point came with the check. The waitress put it between them; automatically, Lauren reached for it to review the addition. Landry's hand covered it too quickly.

"Leave it."

"Just wanted to see if they added right."

"I'll do it." He fumbled on his glasses and looked it over. "Right." He dropped it in front of her. "Here. If it'll make you happy—live."

Lauren studied the bill. Correct, but they'd added the split.

"Of course they charged for the split," he told her with condescending patience. "It's on the blackboard: split entrée, three dollars extra. Nothing furtive about it, and I'm paying tonight, so what's the sweat?"

"Why don't you call the girl over?"

"And what? Tell her we don't usually pay the split because we're old customers? Look, when it's on you, you can chisel all you want. Me, I'll pay the three bucks."

Lauren bridled. "I only—"

"Every time we go through this. You split a dinner, you pay the split charge because the portions are larger." Landry dropped his Visa card on the tray with the bill. "You want to start a war over three bucks, do it on your own time. Let's go home."

He's always saying how he feels married to me, Lauren smirked to the mirror in the ladies' room. *Tonight he sounds like it.*

She made him wait longer than usual while she did and redid her lipstick, using the time to cool off. She ought to send him home. If they went back to her place, she wouldn't offer him another drink. Pat Landry was getting to be a big fat bore.

They walked silently under the dripping trees, past the lamplights and renovated Federals on Twenty-second Street to the Chelsea. In the lobby, Lauren slapped the elevator button too hard. "Coming up?"

"Yeah, I guess."

"Don't do me any favors, sweetheart."

The elevator slid open. Landry slouched into it.

In the apartment, she spent a good deal of time brushing her teeth without offering him a drink first, much too tired to be understanding now. Emerging from the bathroom, she found him sprawled in a chair at the table, still in his coat. He'd helped himself to wine and soda.

"Are you staying?"

"I guess."

"You don't have to," she hoped.

"I'm sorry." He sounded more preoccupied than sorry. "Didn't mean it the way it sounded."

"Look, honey, I'd love to have you stay." She really wouldn't just now. "What's wrong?"

"What do you mean, what's wrong?"

"All evening. I can't reach you."

"I can't reach you." Landry swallowed half the drink in one gulp. "You and your neurotic fear over three bucks."

Lauren felt herself go white all the way down. God, they went through this stupid argument constantly. This time it exploded, the razor tip of a very large iceberg.

"Look!" she snapped. "I don't have your kind of money. Even if I did, I wouldn't throw it around like you do."

"Here we go: Up From Depression," he returned with sharp sarcasm. "When the going gets tough, the tough get tedious."

"You're not used to money. You're an easy mark. You always pay too much and tip too much."

"I do *not* overtip. I've worked in restaurants, lady. It's exhausting, sometimes demeaning, and you take a lot of crap for every dime you earn." He emptied the glass. "You are so pathologically *tight*."

"I have to be. Oh—shit," Lauren gave it up. This wasn't their night. "For an interesting man, you can be an awful strain."

"That's mutual." Landry looked at her like a stranger. "Maybe we need a vacation from each other."

Lauren slammed the ice tray on the counter. "Not a bad idea."

"Go sleep with someone else for a change."

That was unfair and hurt. One of the less attractive things about him was his way of going for the jugular when he didn't need to. It would have hurt more if he meant it, but they'd played this bitchy scene before. "That's large of you. I have your permission?"

"I mean—" Landry heaved out of the chair, knuckles white around the glass. "I am very sick of being asked: did you work today? Did you go to the gym today, take your vitamins today? Did I do this or that, like I have to report for your approval."

Not the words but the taut, cocked-pistol fury. She didn't know him, absolutely didn't know him. He quivered with something far beyond their argument.

"It never gets easier, lady. Never stops, does it? You all want the work to go on churning away, on and on. Did I work today? Work at what? Snap my fingers and turn it out, right? Think at eighty words a minute, seven hours a day, seven days a week, and who *cares* if it's pure shit? Least of all, the hydrocephalics who ingest shit with the discrimination of a public toilet. What the hell—turn it out, get paid. Click, click, snap, right? I would dearly love you and Edie Fine and Bethany Harris and Trefoil and Falcon Books and the whole world to get off my—fucking *back!*"

The hand with the glass snapped back and loosed. The glass shattered against the wall. Lauren froze, dully aware of the splintered shards scattered over the floor. No more distance now. He was there, hurting with something.

"Laurie, I'm empty."

She said the only thing she could just then, drained as she was. "Go home, Pat."

"Empty," he slurred, foggy and drunken.

"I don't know what you're talking about." She edged around him for the broom in the closet. "All I know, you've been impossible for weeks."

"Guess I just had to . . . say it out."

"Say what? I'm not your enemy, Pat. I'm not against you. Say what?"

His hands lifted to her, then dropped helplessly. "Right. We need a vacation."

"I'm going to sweep up this mess and then I really want to go to bed. You're drunk and feeling sorry for yourself. At least you get money thrown at you."

" 'Bsolutely." Landry hulked to the door. "They can make me lousy rich. Very rich and very lousy."

"What *is* it, Pat?"

He opened the door with his self-mocking grin. "That, luv. I got sold out today, and I did the selling. And tha's not the worst of it. The worst of it . . . part of me can't be sorry. I know if I turn in pure shit in the right kind of neat little piles—'s a fact. Numbers—they'll pay me twice as much money's when every page had my heart in it. And I hope Susan will be very proud of me."

The door closed behind him; he didn't even slam it.

Silently and with considerable invention, Lauren cursed the world of art, men in general, and Pat Landry in particular. Maybe if he'd really tried to get close, told it to her instead of throwing it at her—well, there'd been other nights like this, but never so violent. A stupid argument, a door closing. After a day or two, one or the other would call, contrite. There was a rock-bottom love between them, but they were both pretty ridiculous. They deserved each other.

He'd forgotten the manila envelope. Something from his brother, he'd said. Lauren kicked it under the film projector. If he wanted it, let him call.

She was getting into bed when an odd shard of memory nagged at her. Susan. Something he said about his second wife.

Lauren couldn't remember and was far too exhausted to try.

25

Long past midnight, Landry sat swirling the melting ice in his scotch. He'd had too much today; shouldn't have drunk at all with Lauren. It soured the whole evening, spoiled him for some kind of fight. Just like Connie.

Vestigial common sense told him he couldn't treat Lauren that way. She'd walk. He'd done it himself more than once, as when Dominique and Myra tried to do their numbers on him. *Tomorrow I'll apologize.*

No, said his demon. *If I feel like it, maybe I'll apologize.*

It always came down to this with all the women he'd ever known. Anger for equals, contempt for the airheads. Sometimes he envied men who could live for years with one woman and keep her happy. The trick of that simplicity eluded him all his life, turning it into a stylized dance of pulling close and pushing away, and always the undertone of another failure a dissonance through the music.

"Failure," he stated to the walls. "Fear of. That's the magic word."

A bathroom wall kind of word scribbled on his soul, like Arthur dabbling his blood on the tiles. Everything he did since finishing *Camlann* was in response to this. He was going to take the Falcon contract because he was tired of stretching his money thin from one royalty check to the next, heartily tired of watching turkeys with less talent making much more money.

Passionately and profoundly tired of hotel rooms. Of being temporary. Of failing.

Susan was the failure that scarred deepest. A hundred times over, he told himself that theater was the roughest business in the world, that thousands more failed than made it, but, like Lauren's personal responsibility for the world, he felt it like a blot. Susan saw the end coming—

"Either make something of yourself in this business or get out of it. It's *killing* you, Pat. It's killing us! You'll lose me."

Miserable, unable then to separate one failure from another, he did lose her. It all began with Connie, who never forgave any kind of failure.

"Never," she intoned from the table, setting out the last of the dishes for dinner. Denny was already reaching for the platter of hamburgers.

"Dinner, Monk," Jack summoned. "C'mon, Monko. Get it while it's hot."

They always took the same places at the old round dinner table, forming a cross: Monk to Denny, Connie to Jack.

"Denny," Jack suggested delicately, "if you pull your chair nearer the table, you might get more in your mouth."

Denny barely paused over his churning fork. "You call me slob, Masked Man?"

"I think you've got definite talent for it, yeah."

Dinner as usual: Connie barely bothering to eat, another full glass of beer in front of her as she pondered her husband, chin on one fleshy hand, the glance darkening gradually with the same unfathomable anger that rubbed off on Monk.

Eat some dinner, Mama.

She tapped the ash from her cigarette. "I had something in the kitchen. And I don't need advice from my son who doesn't even pass in school."

Denny gobbled hamburger, carrots, and potatoes, listening to expansive, enthusiastic Jack telling stories from his finally begun showbiz memoir, *Ham & Yeggs.* "Writing's hard work, Slobbotz." Jack gestured dramatically. "I'm cudgeling my brains to get it out." He liked the image, clutching his shaggy head, twisting handsome features into a parody of superhuman effort. "Cudgeling my brains!"

"God, how he suffers." Connie's tone was an essay in acid. "You haven't read it to your secretary yet?"

The implication hovered over Jack like a guillotine. She

wanted a fight but he wasn't buying. "Now, don't start, Con. I don't have time for that at the office."

"That's a first."

With Connie as emotional pivot, so many evenings went that way. She could ignite with laughter or turn sour in an instant with that treacherous anger. Connie never knuckled under to a fact. If she no longer expected any return from the world on her invested life, neither would she forget or forgive the debt. From long experience reading her weather signs, Jack and Denny fled the table as soon as they finished eating, Jack to the typewriter in the bedroom, his two-fingered staccato echoing down the hall through closed doors. Denny retired to the room he shared with Monk to play his Spike Jones records.

Landry remained at the table with his mother as he had for years. All his life, this was his picture of her: aging, the face gone fleshy but still striking. She would have made a better serious actor than Jack, having all the turmoil of deep, feelings without the power to stand apart from them. Jack knew all the words without ever really daring the depths beneath them. He accepted the world as it came. Connie fought it and him to the end.

I like what he started on the book, Mama.

"He's always starting."

It's funny.

"Always." She drank, sighing over the sudsy residue in her glass. "Jack is a funny guy."

Think he'll finish it this time?

Connie poured more beer into her glass. "I hope so, Monk."

You wanted to believe. Couldn't bring yourself not to, even after years.

"Yes, I hope he finishes it." Connie turned her head toward the rattle of the typewriter through the door. "There's some fish have to swim near the top. Can't take the pressures of the deep."

You were so different. How did you ever come together, ever last this long?

"Once upon a time, when there were such impossible things as Coolidge dollars and bathtub gin, your daddy lived rich and your ma was good-looking." Connie drank. "Lord, we should've stayed that way." Her expression altered slightly, lost its habitual bitterness as once more she tilted her head to the sound from beyond the walls. Connie put her fleshy palms to the table top and pushed up from it with a visible effort to crack the hall door a few inches. "Jack?"

The typewriter barely paused. "Yeah?"

"Don't strain your eyes, you damned fool. I'm coming to bed soon and you've been at that since you got home. You hear me?" Pause. No answer but the rattle of keys, thud of the heavy carriage. "Stubborn bastard. Always thinks he can do anything."

Connie hesitated in the doorway, then moved down the hall toward the sound of the machine. "Jack?"

Landry finished his scotch and pondered the wisdom of another before bed.

"Why not?" Julia shrugged, leggy in summer shorts and blue halter, the ubiquitous glass in her hand. "Have another with me. I'll be up all night anyway." She grimaced after Connie. "Gone to sleep with him again, I suppose. Can't see why. Mama always said she didn't like sleeping with him. She only stayed because of you and Denny."

Twenty years is a long run for self-sacrifice. There must have been a payoff somewhere.

"Oh, what the hell do you know about it." Julia dismissed the notion as not worth consideration. "You should've known Mama young."

Yes. I would have understood more.

"So bright and warm, so full of verve." Julia looked through the wall into the past, painting the sentiment there. "My father was the only man she ever loved. Jack broke her."

You should have known Mama old, day after day. It was in her to break herself. If there was a brightness, there was the dark as well. Destructive, bullying, sadistic. She never faced that in herself.

"Was it Mama?" Julia charged. "*Was* it?"

(A song for Julia. Primetime rating forecast: EXCELLENT)

When I was old enough, Mama used to talk to me a lot when I came back to visit for the day. A woman to talk to, drink with. She told me about her first husband, Arthur's father, and how he used to slap her around out of jealousy. A real louse. And I'd say, "Mama? Wasn't he my father, too?" And she said yes, of course—but in such a way that I never believed it. What could I believe? Mama was always on the road when I was little. The nearest thing to an official father I ever had was Jack, and he wasn't my own. God, I wanted that so badly, living with Mama's sister Alys. And after she married Jack, there wasn't room for Arthur and me, and we went back to Alys, and I still didn't know who I was.

Then one day after I was married, Mama showed me a picture of a handsome young boy in a navy uniform, World War I. He came from an old family with a lot of money, and everything, but he was Catholic and his family wouldn't agree even to an Episcopalian like Mama. It would have disinherited him. Mama never said much, but the way she handled the picture, I knew she was talking about the love of her life; how she touched it and then very carefully put it back in tissue before laying it on top of the other pictures. She didn't have to say any more. I knew then who *my* father was. I'll always believe it. It's something to hold on to, being a child of love. Arthur came out of misery, and Monk and Denny from that bastard Jack who'd grab any skirt going by, but my father was her real love. I just know it.

You need something like that when you grow up not really wanted, pushed off for months at a time on relatives. You need some picture of a man in front of you. An ideal, like Lancelot and Elaine. I'm owed that for all the things that didn't work out. A dead end in modeling, the dust on my paints, no encouragement from anyone. Monk said my pastel of Jesus looked like a fag decorator. Always cracking wise like his father. I wanted a gentle, soft Jesus. A Gentile Jesus. I can't think of him as Jewish, because he really wasn't, being the Son of God.

It's just that you need some kind of a dream to get you over marrying a hardworking man like Werner who never satisfied you in bed but gave you kid after kid all the same. And the old house that always needs work and too much money to keep it respectable. I remember always that I was a child of real love, not like Monk or Denny. It helps a little, remembering how Mama got so tired and frumpy and beer-fat, such a slob she wouldn't even take care of her appearance.

When Mama died, I took my father's picture from her collection, and as much other stuff as I could find. I'll have him always now, and my own real name. All of my names hung on the wall—Hawkins and McLeod, Pickett and Lacy, back to the Kentucky days when one brother went Union and the other Confederate; all of them pouring their blood and names into me. And Monk, who used to love my telling about them, turned his back on all of it to find himself? Where? He wouldn't *be* without them.

I began to think of Mama as Elaine, her black funeral barge floating down the river to lodge where Lancelot could see it. Men always hurt you; you're always stuck and they're always free. Mama should never have married Jack. We could have been a family without him. Elaine, lying in a barge where Jack could see what he did to her life. It's the truth of *romance* I wanted, since I never found the beauty anywhere else. Mama would laugh at that. She got terribly vulgar living with Jack. Don't you laugh at me, Mama. My anger's not for him alone. I had a beauty too. If it broke like a Christmas tree ornament, was it any less than yours? I could say a lot of things about you, but I'll think of you as Elaine and tell my daughters what a great woman you were, a saint, because that's less painful.

"Ask your dear father why we had to leave. Why Arthur always despised him. Big Jack," Julia snarled. "He never finished that book, never finished anything good." The nervous laugh brayed out of her, ebbing away in the habitual snicker of disgust. "Jack the hack."

He was a man, Julia. Not the best in the world, a long way from the worst. I'd like to have known him young, before the platitudes became his whole truth.

"They always were," Julia said. "Everything he wrote sounded like Haggard or Hilton or whatever he was reading at the time."

No. Before he knew what losing was—

"For he's a jolly good fail-ure . . ."

—while he was still singing and couldn't know he'd never have the talent or the luck to be Horatio Alger's white-haired boy. Don'tcha just love the American Dream? It convinced him he was a failure because he died broke. I hate it for both of us, Jack and me, because I'm going the same route and can't stop myself. Why the hell do you think I'm drunk? I can understand and mourn and forgive a lot of things now. Swear to God, Julia, sometimes I think we're all a bunch of shawlheads fresh off the boat needing to get and keep before we starve to death.

"What are you talking about?" Julia asked with small curiosity. "You're so half-assed. What's wrong with a beautiful home and nice things. You never knew what life is all about." She drank, hiccupped, and disappeared, still snickering. "Jack the hack . . ."

That's right: steady, reliable, eager to do whatever they wanted and do it their way. The rest, the aspirations, the failures, all bundles of yellow pages turned dark and brittle before they were thrown out years ago.

And what the hell am I doing?

"What are you doing?" Connie challenged from the table. "Look at me when I speak to you—"

26

She was drunk enough to be abrasive, the school report card on the table already marked with a wet ring from her glass. "What do you do in school all day? You used to be so good in school. Now . . ."

Connie picked up the report card and performed rather than read it. "Math, F. Physical Education, D. You could always trip over a match. Now you can't even catch a whatd'ya call it basketball? Science, F. From what I know of Mrs. Bergson, that's an understandable lapse—but D minus in English? A boy who writes as well as you? History, C. There's a switch. You must have worked for a day or two. Social Studies, the familiar F. My son fails again and doesn't graduate into senior high school."

I'll transfer to high school next year like the rest, Mama.

"Oh yes. Transferred. Not graduated. No diploma, no accomplishment, no pride. No one in this family knows what to *do* with you," she declared. "I mean *my* family, Arthur and Julia. Mr. Landry, of course, making indifference into an art, had nothing to say except that I should leave you alone."

The usual late-night scene: Connie drinking by herself, Jack and Denny fled to avoid war. Monk on the griddle because he chose to be there; because Connie was the only person he trusted.

But even that was changing in her last year of life.

He couldn't tell his mother how useless or shamed he felt, how hopeless, since so much of it was bound up in her. Some truths Connie wouldn't take. The turmoil and the balm of his life, such as it was, began with her. Confused and demoralized, he gave up trying in school, a neurotic child who showed only the worst of himself to all comers, an incoherent dreamer with a desperate need to be recognized. A habitual truant given to music and movies, disrupting classes with clowning and stupid wisecracks. An adolescent years before the age group became exploitable in film and television, when teens were only half-people wrung through schools staffed by aging civil time-servers who no longer hoped to educate, only to keep the traffic flowing.

Monk lacked the maturity to direct himself. By this year he knew direction would never come from anyone in the school, nor any longer from Connie, who was on her downhill slide toward the end.

He believed, for lack of evidence to the contrary, that he was as worthless as Mrs. Bergson said. She was his homeroom and science teacher and always reminded Monk of the portraits of Frederick the Great or Grant's *American Gothic*. Mrs. Bergson imparted no enthusiasm for her subject or anything else under the sun: tall and severe, utterly devoid of humor, patience, or the palest spark of imagination in her job. Her face had frozen and thawed through countless winters of school and summer vacations until it was potholed with bitterness and indifference. She hated teaching and was as lazy as Monk in her way, but those protrusive, colorless eyes would never see any flaw in herself. Even Connie had to admit Mrs. Bergson looked thoroughly German in the worst sense of the word.

That morning he'd received his dismal report card and notice of transfer. His father wouldn't demand an accounting. Jack had a hands-off understanding of what it was to be a boy. But Connie would. The rest of his class was graduating that day, enjoying the dress-up, party-promised rite of passage somehow always to be denied him. Monk felt failed enough as he started away from the school office toward the main exit.

"Landry!"

There was Bergson with her Gothic look, advancing on him, pale eyes gleaming with vindictiveness. As if she'd been waiting. "Where do you think you're going?"

Home, Mrs. Bergson. *Never at least to see you again.*

"No," she denied him. "Not the front doors, not you. You go out the back way."

She marched him through the halls and empty cafeteria and opened the rear door with the finality of an executioner: *Behold the head of a traitor!* He left meekly, miserable with defeat, not to realize for years how much of a defeat the act implied for her, that she had to do it and take pleasure in it.

How could he tell that to Connie only hours after it hap-pened? How could he tell her anything now? There were so many changes he couldn't share with her this last year. Life itself was breaking up, thin ice under his unsure feet, shooting him taller and stalk-thin, tearing his voice between perilous baritone and squeaky soprano. Forcing him to see with the first cruel clarity of a growing mind that the world and its truths were larger than Connie.

"Well?" she demanded. "What's the reason for this report card and all the others for the last two years? No Hawkins has ever laid down and quit, but *you* have. Just *quit!*"

Mama, I—

"Why!"

So far beyond words. The emotional need once focused in her had become a seething hunger for other women—not that there was any hope there, either. The class "slam book" told him that. The page assigned to PATRICK LANDRY in that thumbed, eagerly annotated notebook told the story. He was an un-kempt mess. What did it mean to be a Hawkins or anything else when he'd been tried by a jury of his peers and their verdict rendered with no recommendation of clemency. He wasn't strong enough to disbelieve them.

"Oh, Monk," Connie beseeched wearily, "why didn't you try a little?"

Try for what?

Because—

"Because *what?* Stand up straight. Look at me. I'm waiting."

He felt rock-bottom defeat, and his mother couldn't hear the cry for help in it, lost as he was. Years later, reading the statistics on adolescent suicide, he was struck by the fact that death never occurred to him as an alternative. Which was quite reasonable even to Monk's embryonic intellect. Dead, you were out of the game. Didn't matter who cried for you or how much or long—you were canceled. He knew that much without words, the way he had to grope for every clear mean-ing available to him. He never had the words with Connie until that night. Something tore between them. There were later nights, the few remaining to Connie, when harsher things were said and done, but that night began it.

I—I'm not good enough, Mama.

"What do you *mean* you're not good enough? I can't under-stand you, Monk."

But I was beginning to understand you; in a world with more imperatives than reasons, to understand you beyond blind loyalty and love. Beginning to see and question.

Mama, why do you have to drink so much?

That last year he'd looked at her from a widening distance, loving her still but seeing a shrewish bully, old before her time and as much of it her own fault as through any fault or indifference of Jack's. He grew increasingly disgusted with the condition of their house—dust thick on the floor, dirt worn into the kitchen linoleum, the housecoat Connie never seemed to change. Something in him turned for the first time and gave it back to her.

I mean, look at you.

She wasn't ready for that. Connie would battle fiercely for her own but demanded a blind devotion Monk couldn't give anymore. "What are you saying to me?"

Look at you, look at this house. I don't even want to come home to this. That's why I stay out late and don't even call. That's why I never bring anyone here. I can't.

Cold now, deliberate, playing the moment, Connie rose and moved toward him. "So it's all me, is it? As usual, it's all me."

I didn't say that.

"Didn't you? Look at me! Didn't you?"

I have been, Mother.

"Are you ashamed of me? No doubt you'd like me to be a conventional mother. A stage mother—sweet, lacy, and graying in velvet. Is that what you'd like?"

Sputtering and tearful, he could only stammer because it was what he wanted then. Some clear, acceptable image of a mother. He was learning realities but not master of them yet.

Connie moved closer to Monk. She winced. One hand went to her temple and her voice turned harsh with effort. "I'd love to be out working. In a store, even a sandwich shop. To see other people besides you three sometimes. But there are plenty of younger women for that. *You* don't like to look at this place? Well, neither do I, and I won't be judged by you. *I won't be*—"

Connie's heavy arm shot out and caught him by the throat. He couldn't move. Breaking her hold would be easy, yet he was paralyzed with ambivalence. If anger was new, the love and obedience were years deep. He could only hover there, and she knew it, enjoyed it, needed the victory as Bergson needed hers.

"You think you're stronger than me?"

Don't, Mama. Stop it.

"You think so? You think so?"

Stop. I swear, Mama, I'll hit you—

"You will?" The fleshy arm released him, drew back, and slapped Monk stingingly across the mouth—

Landry's eyes snapped wide open, like a sudden rush of blood to the head on the brink of sleep.

If there's cruelty or desperation in me, he thought, I learned it from you. The senseless anger, the need to destroy, all from you. All but the why. Years it took to know even a piece of the truth. You loved me by your edged, clawed definition of love that became mine. Caring as anger, love as laceration. If you tried to shape me, like Julia's clay dancer, you tried as hard to break me, Mama. Somehow I wouldn't be broken. Crippled, yes, but not devoured. I was healthier than that. Sure, you wanted me to try, wanted me to be everything except my own person. You saw me growing away from you, and that threatened you as it did Julia later. Your last anchor, fifteen years old. I looked at you with that slap stinging my face and said the truth because you knocked it out of me.

How could I ever love you?

Connie took a step back as if she'd been hit herself. "What. . .?"

How could I?

"Because you're me, Monk."

Half my lifetime, never able to accept love, but tearing at it like you—

She was shifting, changing—

"Because I'm you."

Blood pounding in his ears, he blinked at the blurring image of Connie. The lights in his room rose to sudden brilliance as he stared at his mother. She seemed to grow taller as the weight and years melted from her. Connie's back straightened, shoulders squared under the maroon silk dressing gown that caught the light, rippling with the fluid movements of the tight-muscled body beneath.

She was no more than twenty-five, the lustrous dark-mahogany hair bobbed short but catching light like the material of her gown. She hummed as she moved, brushing small imperfections from the costume hung near the mirror, tilting her head to hear the faint music from a pit orchestra.

"Grace?" she called through the wall. "Hustle it, we're on soon."

Connie bent to the mirror, inspecting her makeup, then shed the robe and tossed it on Landry's bed, totally unselfconscious in her underwear as she rummaged the dresser top for something.

"Grac-eee? If you took my new mascara, don't use it all. This one's almost out."

She was not beautiful but animated, the face never in repose. She had the long, ropy leg muscles of a dancer. Over the waistband of her silk underpants there was no slight bulge of softness, only the clean articulation of firm midriff rising from navel to ample breasts that jiggled slightly as she swayed, humming, before the mirror, with the sheer, irrepressible need to move. When she turned to Landry, it was impossible to think she'd ever been ill or even fleetingly sad in her life. The smile was direct, warm, and often misread as invitation by men.

"Nice of you to drop back. Connie Cole," she introduced herself. The large, expressive eyes swept over Landry, not displeased with what they saw. "Your face is familiar. Have we met?"

Not yet, Miss Hawkins.

"Mrs. Cole." The smile didn't alter but the point was made. Connie swung back to the mirror, unconscious energy and grace in the movement. Under the stage makeup, Landry recognized the familiar profile and strong mouth remarkable even in youth. "Mrs. Connie Hawkins Cole. Nice of you to come back, but I never go out with older men. Even gentlemen," she amended in the mirror with an ameliorating smile, "and they are the ones to watch. Dah-dah-*dee*-dum . . ."

Your pictures don't do you justice, Mrs. Cole.

"No, they don't." She stated it as a fact. "Attractive but not beautiful. Onstage, energy makes them forget that. There are showgirls walking a runway for Ziegfeld who fade into the scenery because they don't have a speck of it." Connie lifted her costume from the rack and stepped into it. "Long as you're here, hook me up in back—*what*, Grace?"

She listened through the wall; the face became an imp's. "Oh, yes, I saw him at rehearsal today, and I'll tell the world: is he a sheikh, Gracie. A shee-eek! Jack Landry is against the law for looks. You can forget Jed Harris, know what I mean?" She listened again. Her laugh was robust and very young. "Valen*tino*? No-o. Very direct, a little pleased with himself. But charming. I think he's interested. I heard him talking about me when we were marking the number without the piano. There sits Mr. Landry with a mile of legs stuck out, and he says to the stage manager: 'Who's the young Dempsey?'— dah-dah-*dee*-dum—*got* to get that entrance right."

A short knock on the door. "Two minutes, Connie."

"Thank you." Connie pirouetted away from Landry and

presented herself to him in frank feminine pride. The emerald gown was designed for movement, tight at the waist and slit high. Connie took up a prop fan, batting her lashes at Landry from behind it.

" 'Tell me, pretty mai-den, are there any more at home like you?' " A twist of the fan; she was a wry Fanny Brice. "No, we were lucky. Only one black sheep to a fold."

Connie's verve was infectious, impossible not to enjoy. As Landry watched, she wilted into a parody of feminine help-lessness. "Kind sir, do not condemn my Constance. Vanished though she be into the hard world, yet my child sends money every week to maintain pride and proprieties. The Major's dead, suh, and our fortunes dragging in the dust, yet are we true ladies of the South, my daughters and I. Only must I weep for where she's gone. To make one among thieves, rogues, and CAH-mon players." The fan sailed at Landry. "And does she LOVE it!"

Again, two sharp raps at the door. "Places, Connie."

"Thank you. I'm on." She winked at Landry. "Didn't catch your name."

I'm a relative of Jack Landry.

"Yes." Connie observed him with judicious pleasure. "I see the resemblance. Jack's relative is a very distinguished gentle-man. I'll tell him at dinner." She touched his lips with a polished fingernail. "Which he doesn't know about yet. It's quite all right. I'm separated from Mr. Cole. The ring and the Mrs. keep the dogs away—but I'll always make an exception for thoroughbreds. Are you out front tonight?"

Wouldn't miss it. Don't you know me, Mama?

"Not yet," Connie denied with a vast tenderness, "but I will. It's only 1924. You'll look more like me when you're young, and no matter how much of Jack Landry a camera finds, you'll always have my heart."

Connie gave her hair a final pat and flowed to the door. "All my children are in the house tonight. Don't let Denny get lost. I hope you like the show; you wanted to see us young. To-night is for all of you."

Keith's Theater, all right. He and Denny used to see movies here during the war. They still had the old loges from the vaudeville days. Under the music from the pit, Landry heard muffled footsteps clumping down the aisle. Denny pushed across him and dumped into the next seat, stepping on his toes as usual—

THE KEITH-ORPHEUM MANAGEMENT

presents

AN ENTERTAINMENT ENTR'ACTE

starring
That saucy specialty girl of the Passing Show of 1922

CONNIE COLE

and

BERNARD & LANDRY

Their last appearance before opening at
New York's Palace Theater

(Ladies are requested to please remove their
hats. Small children should be left at the
lobby office where one of our uniformed attendants
will cow them into silence)

"Watch it, stupid!"

"Hi, Monk."

—his shirttail hiked up over his baby-round middle, rubbing his nose to darken the perennial smudge, clutching a butter-stained box of popcorn.

"They gonna show a serial, too?"

"Den, with this show, you don't need movies. Hey, look who we've got with us. Visiting royalty."

Arthur swung down the far aisle to take a seat at the end of the same row. Arthur at thirty-five, in air force blue, silver wings bright on his tunic, blond hair still a proud crest.

"Christ." For an instant, with the houselights at half, Denny looked old as Arthur and more ravaged. "Our official big brother. And here's Julia, fashionably late."

Late but fashionable: Julia at twenty-six, before she stopped leaving her house at all, wearing navy with a flare, the wide-brimmed cavalier hat setting off her fair complexion and careful makeup, sweeping down the aisle, always conscious of an audience. She kissed Arthur in greeting and settled into the seat next to him.

Denny offered them his grease-stained treasure. "Want some popcorn?"

"I don't even want to be here," said Arthur.

"I wouldn't pay two cents to see Jack Landry," Julia sniffed, "but Mama will be stunning."

The overture ended in a roll of trapdrums and cymbal crash. "Ladies and gentlemen—Miss Connie Cole!"

She strode out from the stage-left wing, overheads catching sequins in the emerald gown. Connie Cole took the stage and filled it, extending her arms to the audience.

Do I have a *house?*

From Monk and Denny: "Yay-y, Mom!"

"I love the gown," Julia allowed. "She could always wear green."

"Mother," Arthur protested in plaintive boredom, "do we really need this?"

Do we need it? Do we need this show? I'll tell the world we do. Hit it, maestro!

In the pit, the piano rippled an arpeggio.

'Just like a gypsy . . .' No, wait. That's Nora Bayes. Just like a black sheep, I've wandered away from the flock. My sister Alys—tall, elegant Alys—was the lady daughter, I was always the ham. I'd rather do a cross for the comic's take than twirl a parasol on East Capitol Street.

That's respectable
But not delectable.
I'm not a tease,
But if you please,
A tremulo for a start.
I wanted to be
A Duse, you see,
But vaude was made for laughs.
You have to bleed for comedy,
You have to break your heart—

Or someone's. We were the Major's lady daughters, and when the Major died—I won't do Lillian Gish, but you get the picture. Alys was a hothouse orchid, but I was a dandelion made for the sun. She went to work in an office. I got a job in *The Red Mill*. That was 1915.

Alys married a banker, a man so calm he could fall asleep in a dentist's chair. But me? Somehow there was never time for that. When the music played, who could keep still? And my show was booked for the road.

Cali-forn-ia, Here I Come—

A great traveling number, you can vamp forever. Those were the days before Equity, and your mother got stuck more than once when the stage manager ran off with the payroll. Any of my children ever been in Ogden, Utah in the winter? Don't. When they shot the buffalo, they killed all the comic relief. The stage manager was gone with the money, all of us stranded, and our boardinghouse was not a charitable institution. I got a job waiting tables there in Ogden, then Denver, K.C., Columbus, and points east back to New York. Home on my birthday with a dime in my pocket and no one casting. A little Jerry Kern, please.

Poor Pierrot—

I used half my dime to call Alys, who came through with alms and a missionary lecture: where was I going and what was I doing with my life? I listened for once. Not from common sense, but slinging hash halfway across the country in winter, fending off propositions, my shoes worn out and my feet never warm. I succumbed to respectability, which has even tempted my son Patrick in his weaker moments. You know how it goes, sing along.

Tea for Two—

Bert Cole was handsome. Bert was solid and twenty-seven.

Bert was possessive. Bert had a steady job and I had my moment of weakness or simply fatigue, so play the wedding march and let's get on with it.

Bert gave me—oh, a lovely son. I want to say it. Arthur was a champion from the first, all legs and arms and feet too big, but it was marvelous to see him fill out from awkward colt to thoroughbred.

Bert gave me other things too. It wasn't easy to raise a little boy, be a wife and mother with the music still in my ears and that great, big, lovely *stage* out there waiting for me to fill it. Bert gave me ultimatums and several black eyes. He was jealous of the men I worked with, and the johnnys that came to the stage door. That was 1919; it never occurred to men that a woman might have a sense of taste and choice. And of course, the usual refrain from Alys—

> When will you ever grow up, Connie dear?
> When will you properly care
> For that bee-yoo-tiful boy of yours?
> While you forsake him,
> Let me take him,
> Just till you're straightened away?
> Arthur, oh Arthur, come home to me now—

Sang guileful, childless Alys.

"Mama!"

Connie paused *en attitude*: A request from the house?

"This isn't the right song," Julia protested. "Sing about my father. The only man you ever loved."

Who was that, dear?

"Hugh. The boy in the old picture."

A little Gershwin, please.

The Man I Love—

This is my song, Julia, not yours. Nineteen seventeen: there I was, a battered wife. We weren't called that then. A battered wife with a little chee-ild, learning to be one tough, self-reliant woman because I had to—and there was Hugh in his navy uniform, tender and shy and eager, all kindness. Definitely a new act, and there are times when violins, wine and roses can make a moment of indecision very easy.

"You loved him!" Julia wailed. "The love of your life."

At nineteen, no one knows who to love for a lifetime. Hugh was a nice boy, and if I were Alys, I might have thought him a catch.

"He was *my* father!"

Was he?

"Wasn't he?"

Well, I was there, dear. Frankly, you always looked more like Bert.

"Do you know how I felt growing up without a father?"

Don't heckle my act, just enjoy it. Unless you're a Baptist, nothing is black and white. Hugh wasn't always there, Bert wasn't always mean. This my song, Julia. Maestro, a little through-the-years music.

Your children never forgive you for being a woman as well as a mother. There's something sad in that, but we won't lean on the strings. You all wanted me to be your picture of propriety, which was always dull but not always possible. My dear children, did it ever once occur to any of you that your mother was ambitious? That I wanted to star, to be next-to-closing on the big time? Not to have the needing bunch of you hanging on me? I could have made it. Bayes, Miller, Greenwood, Tanguay, they had nothing on me but salary, and who cares about money? You bear a child because there's one inside. You create beauty because it has to be born.

You hear that, Monk? Because it *has* to be born. Even Jack felt that once, that excitement over something that could be beautiful, and the hell with money.

But I did have you. Diapers and circumstance. I was named for the men I married, measured by them, so I could never quite put men second to career. If I was angry, Julia, a lot of it was for myself, for gladly leaving you with Alys when I went on the road, guilty because I wouldn't do anything else. If I'd been born fifty years later, there'd be no problem, but if wishes were horses, we'd all have saddle sores.

And then Jack came along.

I could never put men second to work, and nobody put Jack Landry there. I'm talking about a man, children. He could take a bullet without a whimper, and there were a lot of them flying through the crowd he ran with, as many bootleggers as show people; but he could be sick for a day over drowning unwanted kittens or taking a stray dog to the pound because we already had too many. There's the charm of inconsistency.

The lights came down to a spot on Connie. The piano turned torchy with a flippant twist.

Brice does this with a shawl and a lot of rubato, but let's underplay—

Bert was mean, Jack was unreliable.
Hugh was a nice boy, Jack undeniable.
Some scared of women, some needed mothers,
But Jack loved me—why bother with the others?
When he opened his arms, there was no doubt
I could be warm in there.
But then you get on and then you're old,
And who remembers you young?
It makes you think: why blues are sung
By women more than men.
I never missed a man I left,
I never left the one I loved.
But I missed the place beneath the lights:
A spark of me that wouldn't fade.
But you get on and you get old;
Depression comes, and Pat and Den,
(Brother, can you spare a dime?)
Vaudeville dies, you're broke and then,
With no surprise, you're out of time.
Lost somewhere when the spotlight dimmed,
Washed out with the dishes
And the diapers changed,
Shook out from the oil mop,
Down the drain—
And death looks just like Monday.
I never left the man I loved,
But the heart went out of Jack
And out of me to see it go:
A great big bird with wings too small,
Who'd never make it back.
Lost like me when the spotlight faded.
I always wondered why I traded
This for what life gave me back:
The four of you, Bert, Hugh—and Jack.
There's those for whom to live's to fly,
Or life's a bitter word;
And none, my dears, who mourn the sky
So much as a crippled bird.

Connie stood at the footlights, head bowed as the last notes
of the piano died away. Denny and Monk leaped up, applauding:
"Yay, Mama! That's selling it!"

"Gol-lee," Denny marveled, "ain't she good?"

But Julia was weeping. "She's disgusting. Cruel."

"Wasn't it all?" said Arthur.

"Oh shut up. I hated it."

Thanks, folks, you're a wonderful audience, but no encores tonight. I want to introduce my children. Follow-spot, please. Ladies and gentlemen, my eldest, Arthur Cole. Take a bow, gorgeous.

The spot lanced across the darkness to pick up not Colonel Cole but a sullen boy of eighteen with the callow beginnings of fine carriage and features. Connie held out her arms to him—

Forgive me for stubbornly loving you the most. I couldn't help it. Forgive me for goading you to be a winner in a world where you can't always win. You were never a fool, and that's a pity. It denied something I always missed in you.

The boy's head came up, glaring at Connie. "I was taken once, Mama. Never again."

The house stands by its statement. Julia, my neglected daughter, take a bow.

The spotlight caught Julia at nineteen with the first flowering of her brief beauty. Her long, slender hand fluttered to her hair. "Why didn't you love me, Mama? What was wrong with me?"

I did love you, Julia. You were dutiful and good, but I was never much for women. My love always went to men, you know that.

"You bet I know it."

Forgive me that—and yourself for what you couldn't give your own children.

"It's hard to love someone when you don't know who you are," Julia reminded her.

But you stuck. You were the steadfast one. As far as that goes.

"Don't say it like that."

What do you want, dear? Acrobats?

"I didn't know what love was, Mama. There wasn't much practice at home."

No, there wasn't. And the amenities weren't among my talents. Don't milk it, dear. Take your bow and sit down. And now, folks—the one thorn in my bouquet. Stand up, Patrick.

The spot flowed along the row. Landry rose into it.

My most disappointing project—lazy, spineless, undisciplined, undirected. The most like me and the least cut out for it.

"Spineless? I was the only one who ever fought you."

I know . . . why, Monk?

"Why what?"

Why did you turn on me?

"Our way of showing love, remember? We brought out the best and worst in each other."

The family failure, folks, our expert in atrophy who took forty years to discover he was alive!

"No." Landry could only shake his head with the sad truth. "I was so like you, you had to fight me for being the same miserable bastard."

Ladies and—

Connie hovered, sequins flashing in the light, but her vibrance flickered and dimmed. For a moment, she didn't fill the stage but looked small and lost.

Of all of them, Monk. Of all of them . . .

"I know, Mama. I loved you too. Take the light off me."

Well, then!

Connie's smile dazzled once more, if a little forced.

I usually try to get off with a laugh or at least gracefully, so I saved a crowd-pleaser for the last. My dearest hooligan—Dennis Hawkins Landry.

The light caught Denny hunched down in the seat, munching contentedly, one hand deep in the popcorn box.

Forgive me, Denny.

"What for?"

For dying before I really had a chance to see you grow.

"You didn't miss a thing," was Denny's dry solace.

You had the eyes and the smile of an angel, Den. I saw Jack every time you looked at me. That wasn't a bad sight on a cold, broke morning. You'll always have his charming innocence about the world. I couldn't always keep you clean, but you always got an extra hug when I tucked you in. Good night, lambkin.

Landry heard the rising pulse of Connie's exit music. "Den, say something."

In the hard light of the spot, Denny's face twisted with emotion. "Mama?"

What, baby? I'm almost off.

"I never knew what to say. All I could do when you died was scream."

Sweetheart, once you've played Roanoke, death's an improvement. But I should apologize for my funeral and the pansy who did my hair in a blue marcel wave. I looked like a dead poodle. And all of you behaved typically: Arthur in dignified silence, Julia dramatically stricken, Pat weeping alone—and Denny could only scream. That was as good as a kiss, Den. I knew what you meant.

And so, kids, it's time to get off. I hope you liked the act—oh, I do think of you all sometimes, but more often of the night I opened at the Winter Garden. I should never have left that, but you know how it goes. "That's all there is. There isn't any more."

Connie bowed and blew them a kiss. As the music came up, she swept lightly out through the wings right.

"Damn!"

The door burst open and Jack lunged into Landry's room.

"If he ain't the tail end of pee time!"

Jack slung his jacket on the bed, prowling the room with the furious grace of an agitated cat. At thirty-five he was just that: a handsome, uncomplicated animal, the raw power mellowed by an obvious good humor. The cool blue eyes and satirical mouth couldn't express anger without a comic turn.

"Jules Bernard is the funniest man east of Stan Laurel," he informed Landry and the world, molting shirt and tie. "But he's gonna pee it away like he's always done."

Jack crouched on the side of the bed, pulling off his shoes. "We open at the Palace in two weeks, best big time in the country. We're on *here* in five minutes, and that son of a bitch is BOILED! Ah, Jesus!" Jack Landry beseeched heaven for help. "What am I gonna do with him?" He barked a glass-shivering laugh at the hopelessness of it all. "What can I do? Lock him in a closet until showtime?"

He jumped up and banged thunderously on the wall. "Jules! You hear me, you little rummy bastard? I ought to throw you under the sink for the rats to get. You couldn't work a dog act. They gotta be able to sit up." *Bang!*

Jack snaked out of his pants. The legs were as muscular as Connie's but slenderer in proportion to the broad chest and boxer's shoulders. He expelled a vast sigh of suffering and took his tux from the clothes tree. "I hate doing a single. Never work with drunks," he advised with tragic authority. "I'm always hauling him back and forth to the alky ward, drying him out. Paying his bills half the time. Oh . . . shit and carry eight."

He looked closely at Landry for the first time. "What are you, a gag man? I write my own material."

So do I. I'm a relative of Connie Cole.

"Cole? Yeah-h." Jack studied him judiciously. "You have her look, like you disagree with the world on principle. You on the Keith time?"

No, I was legit.

"God help us, hams never die." Jack finished dressing and bent to the mirror to smooth the glossy black waves tight against his scalp. With a camel's hair brush he bordered his eyes in a thin line of clown white and underlined it in brown pencil. "Me? I want to write more, do my own book and lyrics for a musical. Made seven-fifty a week last year just on the side, writing for other acts."

A sharp rap on the door: "Two minutes, Jack."

"Thank you! Broadway's the place to be. What you can *do* now with lights and words and music if you think of them as a whole, an orchestration. I'll get Baldy Slocum to do the score. He's the best—"

And you'll die forgotten and broke.

The notion amused Jack Landry. "I can't even imagine dying, let alone broke. Never been flat more than a week in my life. Never tipped less than five bucks. Forgotten? Hell, they all forget you. Get the money and the hell with the rest."

Don't you know me, Jack?

"I will." The admission was absentminded, not the center of Jack's concern. "But you wanted to know me young." Jack gave the tux a last approving pat and mirror-glance. "You won't be as easy to love as Den."

But that powder puff in your makeup kit, I carried it in my own kit for years. Always touched it for luck before I went on.

"Didja now?"

A sort of continuing. The touching we always denied each other until too late.

"A mother can hug and touch," Jack said. "But men, fathers and first sons, there's always a distance. Love's a hard word to say. What did you do best?"

Comedy. I had your timing.

"And all of Connie's ham. Gotta go. I'm on."

He was at the door in two long strides—arrogant, amused by an absurd world. He would feast on life as a gift but never understand or take it seriously.

"Hell," he summed it up, "what do I know now? Thirty-five and on top. Women are just nights along the way. Top billing, center stage under the lights, bringing a house down and five bows at the end. Being told I'm wonderful, getting laid—that's what matters now. You were the same at my age, long on charm and short on heart. Nobody gets smart until too late in the last act. You never had the temperament for an actor, but you could write."

Once more the wall-shaking guffaw erupted from the prime animal who was Jack at thirty-five. "God, you were awful! You did everything wrong except quit. Just now and then, there'd be a phrase or two that made me think: I only reached so high, but maybe this kid can stand on my shoulders. And I knew *I* had a son."

Another knock: "Places, Jack."

"Thank you! But you wouldn't have been worth a damn if I hadn't made you work at it. *Care* about it. Think about that when Connie knocks me. You out front tonight?"

Wouldn't miss it, Dad.

"Well, then, I'll do this one for you." Jack hurled the door open, grinning at his son. "But don't come back later. Cole doesn't know it yet, but she and I are going to wine and dine. That woman wasn't just built, she was *designed*. Olive oil!"

Break a leg, Jack.

"God *damn* Bernard. JULES!" Jack roared down the hall. "Not that it matters, but your act is on."

"Oh?" the boozy voice rasped through the wall. "How we doing?"

The house lights were at half. Julia rose to go, setting the cavalier hat at a studiedly rakish angle.

"I wouldn't stay," she announced to her brothers, "to see Jack Landry walk on water."

"A number of women thought he could," Arthur muttered.

Julia swept up the aisle without a backward glance.

"Why all this, Monk?" Arthur demanded. "At least we were peacefully dead."

"I'm not the stage manager," Landry confessed. "Just remembering you."

"And now you can do what you like with us."

"No. I've got to know what happened."

"Why?"

"I want to understand."

"The final irony." Arthur's mouth twisted in a cold grimace. "Out of this brood, a moralist."

Julia charged back down the aisle. "Oh, that's annoying. I can't find an exit anywhere."

"There isn't any," Monk said.

Arthur got up and settled the peaked officer's cap on his head. "I don't need to see Jack."

"Hey, Arth!" Denny hooted across the row. "I don't think you got much of a choice."

Julia put a protective arm through Arthur's. "He was hurt worst of all."

"Lady, don't bleed on me," Denny snorted. Monk saw his brother's features fast-forward through years, the lean jaw thickening to jowl, the voice so like his own but wearier. "Somewhere in Texas, I'm a lot older. Sit down and enjoy the show."

"It's cruel," Julia protested. "Just because we're dead . . ."

"Yeah, yeah. Sure," Denny growled as Monk settled beside him. "If it was us dead instead of them, we'd be lucky to get a walk-on. This show is a great idea, Monk. Shoulda done it before."

The follow-spot lanced through the dark to illumine the call card at stage left.

BERNARD & LANDRY

A dark sleeve with gold links winking at the white cuff reached into the light and stripped away the card to reveal another.

TONIGHT
LANDRY ALONE IN
"$750 A WEEK"
AN AMERICAN TRAGEDY

The orchestra swung into a fast 2/4 as the spot caught Jack Landry dancing out toward center, cane twirling, straw hat at a jaunty angle. He moved effortlessly with the tempo, movements tight and clean. Jack danced with infectious enjoyment, conscious of his sleek body and its effect on an audience.

I like 'em young, I like 'em sweet;
Long, long legs and dancin' feet.

When I'm low, nothin' can fix me so fine
As a dozen gorgeous lookers in a cho-rus line—

"Jack!"

The music cut mid-phrase. Jack stepped nimbly to the footlights.

Do I hear a request?

Arthur was rigid, gripping the seat arms. "You're a dirty bastard, Jack."

And me a nice boy from a good family. You're right, Arthur, but this is a family show. No blue material allowed. Are my kids out there? Hey, Slobbotz?

"You know it, Dad!"

Monko?

"Give 'em hell, Jack!"

Okay, then, we got a SHOW! Little song of my own, folks. Little song entitled, "She Was Only a Fisherman's Daughter, But She Never Went for My Line."

Sunburnt Sal-om-ee,
Sunburnt Sal-om-ee,
Pack your grip and take a trip
With me across the foam.
Don't take along your overcoat,
Just leave your clothes at home—
And you'll top the bill in vaudeville,
My *sun*-burnt *Sal*-ome.

Jack took off his hat as the music turned lugubrious. He laid a hand on his breast—

"Oh my God," Julia groaned, "he's going to be sincere. And not an exit in sight."

Here we go, folks. The trouble with growing up spoiled is, it doesn't prepare you for much. Every family does its own casting: the bright one, the sensitive one. And the black sheep, guess who? But a chorus for my father, an honorable man.

Son, said my father, whatever you do,
Though a man is a man, a suggestion for you.
Remember, wherever you lay your head down:
Next morning don't bring her to THIS side of town.

Denny held his nose. "This material sucks."

"Jack respected appearances," Monk said. "Didn't matter what you did, just don't bring it home. He was afflicted with propriety."

"Now, that ain't nice."

"None of us are *nice*, Den; we never were. What we are is true."

And the gleaming Apollo in tux and black waves was as true as the snuffling, shuffling old man whose ragged breathing filled Landry's apartment until the final trip to the hospital. Now Apollo commanded his audience, laughing at them, with them—

Well now, there I was in 1905: twenty years old and every door open to the scion of Francis and Annie. Only a matter of time until I opened one I couldn't shut behind me. The wife of the secretary to the British ambassador.

My father was grave but unshaken. My mother was sick for a day. The scandal was all over Washington, and Annie's rival hostesses were chortling. Well—if Dad was king, Annie was Richelieu. She was the state, and *l'etat* was tottering. Relations with England had not been so strained since the *Trent* affair. Annie reached for her bank book. In G Major, maestro. Something for a mother's love.

> Though you leave a place empty at table,
> Your mother will ne'er let you down.
> Take this thousand, dear Jack, while you're able,
> And *do* please get out of this town.

So off I went and got my first look at a tough town. New York was fast even then, with a powerful beat that a kid could feel deep in his belly. I had some thought of a job, but none of the going concerns needed a president. I couldn't do anything well but play the banjo, and there was an opening for that, a burlesque company going to Alaska, and I'd never been in either.

I played the king of a cannibal island in a blackface sketch and the banjo in the oleo like everyone else. Burly was more minstrel than Minsky in those days, and Alaska was still gold-rush. End of the week they paid us in dust. The saloon had so many bullet holes in the floor, all the mice had sprained ankles.

Then there was Birdie Belmont. She made me into a dancer, helped me cross over from burly to vaude, one of the few that made it. Birdie worked the livin' jeejee out of me, but when we opened on the Keith time, I was crackerjack. They were great years with Birdie. Yeah . . . when you get old, you remember. So many years like a dusty collection under glass. And . . . you see so clearly what might have been . . . can you hear me, Monk?

Louder, Jack.

From Julia: "And funnier."

Truth is, none of it's funny. I never made the right moves at the right time. Birdie got an offer from Hollywood, wanted me to go with her, but I thought movies weren't all that much. She went and I stayed—and then there was Slim Barr!

The music blared up-tempo. Jack strutted, the cane whirled—

> You got'ta give 'em the jazz,
> Give 'em lotsa pizzazz;
> Gotta set up the gag,
> Give it a tag,
> Get off to the rhythm of a RAZZamatazz!

Slim Barr, king of the small time: half comic, half crook. He needed a straight man. I fed him his laughs, paid off his bookie, sobered him up, tried to keep him out of jail. We played, guzzled, and conned our way from one end of the circuit to the other. Slim couldn't even breathe honestly. He'd come into town on a variety bill and skip out on a wanted poster, with me running right behind him—

> Bricks in the suitcase nailed to the floor;
> Scram out the window with the law at the door.
> Running through the grinder of the five-a-day,
> (With lawful jokes and awful jokes)
> Lookin' for a bookin' on the Gay White Way
> (Throwin' waiter jokes and later jokes)
> Waiter! There's a fly in my soup!
> (Not so loud, everybody'll want one)
> Waiter, don't seat me near the hoi polloi.
> (No, sir. We don't serve no Chinamen in here)
> Stealin' new gags when your time is tight,
> Catch it at a matinée, use it that night.
> Slim lost his timing but he never could see
> The funniest thing in his act was me.

He ended up working for his own bootlegger in Chicago, and died full of holes in a disagreement between Al Capone and Hymie Weiss. Still, he taught me comedy, Slim did. But the master was Jules Bernard.

Jules was the funniest man on two legs—when he could stand up. Had a little piece of string he used to wind around his finger when we were on. It bothered me at first. I thought: the son of a bitch, I'm feeding him and he's still trying to upstage me. So one night I hid his string. Drove him wild, muffed most of his gags, funny as a plague notice. He told me: "Jack, I gotta have something in my hand when there's no glass." So I gave him back his goddamned string and he wowed 'em all the way to the Palace.

The booze got him, same as Slim. After a while the funniest guy in the business couldn't think funny anymore. Our last two seasons, he didn't get a single laugh I didn't write. I found I was better than him. That was strange. Embarrassing. Almost like . . . I don't know.

"A betrayal?" Monk suggested from out front.

Just like a betrayal. But time was passing and so was Jules. Gimme the beat, maestro—

Charles-*ton!* Charles-*ton!* Charles-*ton!*

Fall, 1927. A hundred shows running on Broadway, stock market crazy, money falling out of the sky. I was in demand all over the Street, seven-fifty a week and no taxes to speak of. People said vaude was dead even in New York. "Hell with that," sez I—and married Connie Cole. There we were, sitting pretty and me writing my own show with Baldy Slocum. God, that was a beautiful show! Baldy's music was genius, the best he ever wrote. My book was solid; it was *about* something, production concepts and numbers *years* ahead of their time. I backed it myself for fifty percent. The scenery alone cost an arm and leg, but Jesus, it was stunning. And Connie . . .

I'd never loved anyone quite like her. She didn't just sit back and wait to be loved. She was a bright, intense light, always the one men gathered around at a party or told their troubles to. She had style, panache, and no more sense about money than I did. We lived high and the sun would never go down. No reason at all to think about tomorrow.

And then suddenly there was.

Every dime I had was in the show, but we needed a lot more to open. Backers came around, but they were the kind

that Runyon used to write about: two-hundred-dollar suits
and hardware under the left arm. Maggots in silk shirts who
never carried less than a grand and kept showgirls in mink.

We came down to it one day in Lindy's Restaurant. Me and
the backers: all palsy-Italian, fat cigars, and too much jewelry,
hugging each other. Couple of the younger goons at a different table, watching the door.

The money man gets down to cases. These girls he's thinking of for my show—it ain't just a favor, I should know that.
They're daughters of good *Siciliano* families, and they deserve
a break like anyone else. But they won't put out for the lousy
directors because Italian girls are raised right, and he feels a
duty toward their parents, so they will work in my show. It
ain't the money, it's loyalty.

No, I said. It's the money. I want to protect my investment
the same as you. We need solid talent, specialty types. You
got an Eva Tanguay or Charlotte Greenwood, we'll talk.

Oh, the dismay: *Landry, be reasonable. I like doing business with
reasonable men.*

No again. I do my own casting.

The meeting got real Sicilian then: *Look, you son of a bitchin'
mick. You want the money, you do it our way. A few small favors,
everybody's happy, okay?*

I looked at him and knew all I had to do was nod my head
and there'd be the cash by my glass. But *I* wrote that show, me
and Baldy Slocum. The finest thing I ever did.

I said no for the last time and walked out of Lindy's.

Jack stood before his audience, the straw hat raised. He
dropped it on the stage and squashed it with one foot.

I sold out, Monk, and I was sorry every day while you and
Den were growing up. I sent your future down the chute for a
spasm of integrity. Cleaned me out. Paid off the bills, never
opened. Then Connie was pregnant with you. That was fine.
Wonderful. We still laughed as much as we loved. When you
came along ten months before the Crash, I knew Connie'd
given me something I'd missed all my life. Meanwhile, Hoover
said the country was fundamentally sound. Famous last words
at the soup kitchen.

That attack of so-called integrity ruined me. When I walked
out of Lindy's that day, I walked out of the big time forever.
The road was dead, vaude dying; who remembered a song-
and-dance man named Jack Landry? I never got used to that or
the eight-to-five grind afterward, for all the years I did it. The

same with Connie: we were race horses sold to haul a milk wagon. Yesterday's winners down to squeezing out change for the rent and a seven-cent loaf of bread.

But integrity, principles? I used to think about them when you and Denny were out playing in the backyard. What I might have given you little guys. The maggots were right. What was one lousy show? More than the money, there was nothing to show for my life. My brothers all made it big as newsmen, but me? Forty-seven and finished, youth fading out of the mirror every morning when I shaved, all gone and not coming back. Connie and I tried not to let it change us. It wasn't that she nagged—not then, anyway. Just that I needed something in the middle of all that failure to feel like a winner one more time.

Going on fifty, selling soft drink mixers from door to door, bar to bar, carrying my samples like a delivery boy in places where I used to stand drinks for a dozen guys at a time. Guys that still came in sometimes.

A song for Jack, maestro. Keep it simple, it's already sad.

> Hello, Charlie! Put 'er there!
> Great to see you. Tell the truth,
> I'm here to see the manager.
> *(Manager's new, doesn't know me*
> *Or the gang who used to drink here)*
> Oh, big things, Charlie, really big.
> Writing for radio now.
> Buy you one for old times' sake,
> But I forgot to go to the bank.
> *(Carfare home, that's all I've got)*
> Thanks, Charlie. Don't mind if I do.
> Next time's on me, y'hear?
> Cigarette? Thanks, I seem to be out.
> Oh, big things, like I said.
> Got a nice little house in Queens,
> A wife, two kids, one on the way.
> You remember Connie? Sure, you do.
> Weren't those the days, old kid?
> This bar saw some great old times,
> Remember? Breakin' 'em up with routines.
> Baldy Slocum died last year,
> Rummed himself out like Jules.
> Hey, let's not talk about that . . .

(Keep your eye on the manager;
Don't let him go without a sale.
Make a buck somewhere today)
That there? Someone's samples, I don't know.
(Drink up and go; don't see me like this)
Yeah, radio's the coming thing.
Just breaking in, but the networks
Are reading my stuff and they love it.
(Manager's leaving, gotta catch him now)
Well, Charlie, thanks for the drink.
Glad you're working. What the hell,
Split week in Trenton's still a job.
You need material, give me a call.
For you I'll work cheap. Ha-ha, sure . . .
(Now or never. Pick up the samples. Jesus . . .)
Ha-ha, pulling your leg, Charlie.
My sideline and a good one.
Best mixers in the business.
Here, try one for taste.
See you, kid. Kill 'em in Trenton . . .
(But Charlie stands there watching
While the manager listens ten seconds
And says no sale today, maybe next week.
Your arm is numb from carrying
The sample case, that last sad hope.
Talk about bad split weeks.
And you hope Connie stays sober tonight.
It's not good to drink with a baby coming,
And the last thing you need is a fight)
Yeah, sure. So long, Charlie . . .

Jack's voice trailed off into a gritty whisper on the last words. Piano and sax retraced a chilly fragment of the melody, faltered, and fell silent.

The lights had come down to a dim indigo that carved deep shadows into the unmoving figure onstage—no longer young but thickened and sagging with defeat—

You older kids, Arthur and Julia, you were there. You know how bad things got by 1934. They took the heart out of me. You wonder that I wanted a little of it back, even for a moment?

Denny nudged Monk. "What's with the lights? I can't see anything."

The lights were fading even lower. A muffled sound from

down the row made Monk turn. Julia and Arthur were leaving. "You can't get out," he called. "There's no exit till it's over."

"I'll make one!" Arthur snarled. "I've seen enough. I don't have to look at any more of this." He lunged up the aisle with Julia after him. She turned at the last row to spit it at Jack: "Sure, *Daddy*. We know how it was—"

She disappeared in the gloom as the orchestra swung into a languorous foxtrot. Monk could barely see the stage. The indigo deepened to murk, highlighted by touches of bluish silver. Barely visible, Jack moved alone to the music.

"I gotta get closer," Monk said. "I can't see him." He groped his way down the aisle, bumping against seats as the orchestra swung into the refrain—

Dancing in the Dark . . .

He could barely see Jack now in the gloom, but it seemed the white tux shirt turned, phantom arms lifted in invitation to a hint of movement at stage right. Another dark form slipped toward Jack's waiting arms as the lights went to total blackout.

Monk stood alone in the dark as the music cut like the needle lifted from a record. He felt the sudden panic of disorientation. The dim outline of the nearest seat grew impossibly larger.

"Denny?" His own voice cracked—piping, child-thin.

Silence. Somehow he knew Den wasn't there. His next breath inhaled the mustiness of a small, closed space. He wobbled with a dizziness like vertigo as his center of balance plummeted and his body shrank, mind blurring as years of memories bled away and maturity crumbled out of his voice.

"DEN-NEE . . ."

Without yet knowing the word for memory, he remembered. He was very small, playing in the attic twilight, the world huge, daunting, and dim about the edges of awareness as the light in the dusty attic on Corbett Road. He loved the attic, a place of imagination with Arthur's old Lionel train set up the length of the floor. Sometimes Arthur came up with him to show him how the trains worked, let him operate the transformer to make them go. Today Monk ventured up alone, trying to fit the wheels of a freight car to the tracks—

Sudden sound, frightening, getting louder and nearer. His child-awareness heard *wrong* in the stumbling steps thumping up the stairs. *Wrong wrong bad scared—*

The attic door burst open, slammed hard against the wall.

Arthur there, swaying in the entrance, not seeing Monk or anything else, but making a sound Monk never heard out of him before. He looked terribly hurt, like someone hit him hard for no reason. Monk was frightened, glad Arthur couldn't see him huddled scared at the other end of the railroad tracks, the freight car clutched in front of him—

Julia's voice. Julia running up the stairs, and Arthur wavering there in the doorway, holding on to it like he'd fall if he let go. Big, safe Arthur that nothing could knock down—but if something hurt him so bad he cried like this, it must be the worst, terriblest thing in the world. Monk shrank from it back into the shadows. His back wilted against the door, Arthur slid down it to sob into his hands. Julia knelt beside him, her thin face hard with fury.

"Leave me alone," Arthur sobbed. "Please go away. Oh God, it's so—uh—un*fair*. How could they do it?"

"Because they're shits, both of them," Julia savaged through her own tears. "We can't stay here, Arth. You're the only real brother I have, and they want us to go."

She saw Monk then in the shadows under the far window. "*Pat*rick! What are you doing up here? These are Arthur's things. You are *never* to come up here alone. Come here. Now!"

Timidly, Monk edged out of the shadows, sure of a spanking, holding the toy freight car against his chest like a shield. Julia advanced, threatening. "What are you doing up here?"

"Nuffin."

"You get downstairs." Julia pointed, imperative. "You little—I have to look after you every *minu*te? Can't I have a moment's peace?"

"Arth fall down?"

"No, Arthur didn't fall down. Just sick, that's all. Sick of you as I am."

So it was his fault after all.

"Mama lets you do anything you want. We don't have anything you don't break or spoil. Get *out*."

"No. No, wait." Arthur uncovered his face, wiping at the tears. When Arthur looked up at him, Monk thought he was going to be mad about the old train. He held out the freight car, hoping it would be all right. After a terrible moment, Arthur took it—gently, not mad at all. He put it down and curled that big hand around Monk's arm, so big it could grab around anything.

"It's all right, Monk. Hunky-dory. I'm not mad at you."

"*Pat*-rick," Julia nasaled her tired drone of warning. "Out."

"Go on, Monk." Arthur gave Monk's arm one last squeeze and turned his face away.

You were a human being, then at least. You cared about something enough to cry. Why did you have to go? It was that year, 1934, the year Johnny was born.

Closer than that; the *month* he was born.

Wait a minute. I remember. Jack's diary . . .

Landry became conscious of the light in his hotel room.

Something in Dad's diary.

"Den." His own voice jarred him in the silent room. He said it aloud to the only other person left alive to question or care. "Den, I—"

The empty glass slipped from Landry's fingers, thumping on the rug.

"—remember."

He stared at the glass, then got up to retrieve it, the memory a single bright spot in his tired mind already closing down for the night.

The diary. I remember.

The scene came back clearly as he pawed his clothes off for bed: ten or eleven years old, short pants and dirty knees tucked under the side table in Jack's pipe-acrid workroom. Shoving his own scribbled pages aside to raid into his father's diaries—

Just that, nothing else. He was too tired. Already the thoughts were dissolving, washing down to the bottom of his mind. He turned off the lights and fell into bed, just able to pull up the covers before the memory fragments, already illegible, sank under heavy sleep and dreams like white noise.

. . . Not so much a puzzle piece missing as an error in closure. All the pieces were there, needing only to be pressed together, and the diaries were the key. Something on a page he'd read and reread as a child, vandalizing his father's life.

Landry walked across Murray Hill to the supermarket on Third Avenue and back with groceries, trying to join the pieces as he had for the last three days, the wind whipping at his scarf ends. At Park Avenue, he waited for a WALK signal in a fog of concentration.

Jack's diary entries were never more than bare facts. He'd worked too hard selling his words to spare many for private reflection. Monk was reading years ahead of his school grade then, insatiable, everything from Dick Tracy to De Maupassant, Jack's slush pile, scanning the diaries with innocent voracity. He read them like the Sunday comics, starting at the back: 1938, 1937, 1936, the flat, declarative lines of a weary man, stretched beyond his talent and already forgotten, who couldn't afford to quit. Even after years, Landry could almost see the pages.

> Saw Raskin at Mutual about the summer sustaining show. No dice. Barnes, CBS. Sweet guy but nothing for me.

No, it was further back, along with Jack's scornful notes on the WPA and its ridiculous Writers Project—

> . . . no talent, half of them Commies. Use ten writers to do a one-act play.

Further back than that, when it was really bad: 1934.

> Connie went to the hospital today, baby anytime. Ten bucks in the bank. Another tight month. This script has got to sell. Arthur's friend Shirley came to help with the typing.

> Connie had the baby. We have another son, John. Shirley still typing. Says she wants to write. Who doesn't?

> Can't bring little Johnny home. They say there's influenza in the infant ward. I prayed for him. Connie at the hospital most of the time. Rent bill came today.

That's right, I remember. Connie couldn't bring the baby home, always away at the hospital. Even at five I could feel things weren't right.

> Shirley worked extra to finish typing the script. Don't know how I'm going to pay her for this.

Not the exact words or order, but the gist of it, and there was another entry on one of those pages, sharply recalled because the handwriting was different. What *was* it?

Just before the light changed, a flashy young Black woman spoke to Landry once and then again. Something about time.

"Mm?" He came a little way out of his fog. "No, sorry, I don't have a watch. It's about four."

He was halfway down the block toward Madison Avenue when his memory replayed what she'd actually said, a hooker making a quiet pitch. *Time to go out?*

She must have thought him a squirrel case, definitely not with it.

There was a phone slip in his box: call Edie Fine. He wished it had been from Lauren, but then he should call her and apologize for being a damned fool. Three days of silence; it wasn't right to let her fly off to Berlin for three weeks without an evening together and getting straight.

Up in his room, Landry stowed his groceries and called Artists Associates. Edie clicked onto the line immediately.

"Pat? Hi. Just wanted you to know: Falcon gave us a firm sixty."

Landry sat down slowly on the bed. "Sixty?"

"I had a feeling that was tops, so I pushed for the last buck."

There it was. Sixty thousand dollars. "How . . . how'd you know?"

"That's what I do for ten percent. Listen, the contract will be delayed, but Bethany wants an idea of your heroine."

Right, Landry thought. *It begins. For sixty grand, does she want a hint of plot or ideas? Just bring on the broad, the maguffin.* Landry jiggled a cigarette from his pack and lit it. "Right now, my heroine looks like four hundred pages and feels like sixty thousand dollars."

"Come on, Pat. She wants a description, a couple of pages. Is that a problem?"

"All right. My heroine is Radcliffe Storme—a proud, tempestuous, head-tossing beauty with hair like a forest fire in a Prell commercial and a subtle, smoldering sensuality never fanned into flame until she meets the moody, dangerous hero, Studley Hormone. He of the shadowed past."

Edie squawked. "Stop, will you? I'm serious."

"And until he presses his merciless maleness into her, Radcliffe knows that no matter how often she's been screwed, blued, or bodice-ripped, she's *never* felt this way about a man before, dot-dot-dot. How does that grab you?"

"Awful." Edie chuckled. "What's worse, Beth will love it."

Why not? One of us should.

"Got another call coming in," Edie said. "Send her the description, and play it straight. Talk to you later."

Landry hung up and squashed out his cigarette, feeling like Cagney in *White Heat*.

Made it, Ma! Top of the world!

(LONG SHOT: THE WORLD BLOWS UP UNDER LANDRY)

"Damned right they'll love it," Connie snapped over her beer. "If you *have* to work a dog act, it'll be the best they ever saw. You're my son, aren't you?"

"Attaboy, Monk!" Jack swung around from the typewriter. "I knew you'd hit the big time, like when I made it to the Palace. How's it feel to be a headliner?"

The Sicilians were right, Jack. What's one show? I've got an even better question. What happened in 1934?

Jack only turned back to the typewriter. Connie contemplated her drink.

Mama? You two gave me songs, snappy patter, and even the old tug-at-the-heart, but where's the point to it all?

"You're the one who's remembering," she said and vanished with Jack.

"You at a loss for words?" Landry asked the empty chairs.

Something always talked around in the long anger afterward. The root of it all, left to him like a Gothic family curse handed down in a sealed letter, one generation to the next. Somehow it began when Johnny was born, in his own childhood where the deep lessons were learned. He was still playing their script, even with Lauren where he couldn't afford it anymore.

He took a shower, brushed his teeth, and mouthwashed away the day's cigarette and coffee taste. Then, after a few moments' hesitation, he called Lauren.

"Hi." Like a guest unsure of his welcome. "It's me."

"Well. Hi." Tentative, a little cool. "Feeling better?"

"I'm sorry, Laurie. I am the prize ass of the world."

"It's funny you should say that."

"I've missed you." Saying it, Landry realized how very much.

"Well, I was pretty uptight myself. We shouldn't do that to each other, Pat. We mean something."

Don't we? Couldn't we? "How are you?"

"Oh, still working. Cleaning up odds and ends. Flying out early in the morning."

"I know, that's why I called. We ought to be together."

"Yes." After a slight pause, Lauren volunteered, "I can cook if you like."

Good for her, he thought. She could take a stupid blowup and not run for the emergency ward. "No, how about I treat for Mexican?"

He loved the sudden, honest delight in Lauren's voice. "*Wouldja?*"

When Lauren opened the door, he stood there in his wet raincoat holding out a sheaf of roses. The scarlet buds, peeping gay and hopeful over the paper's edge, underlined his contrition. "Hi."

"Hi."

He put the roses on the table and hugged her small body to him, loving the smell of her skin and the feel of her in his arms. "Laurie . . ."

"I know." She laughed softly. "We're both jerks. But flowers, even. They'll be all gone when I get back."

"No. Give them to someone nice."

"After I wake up and see them at least once."

Still he held her close, tight. "Laurie, am I crazy good or crazy sick?"

"I get a choice? Well," she kissed him again, "I'd say within tolerable limits, you're quite insane. Hey, my plane leaves at nine. Let's not stay up too late."

They had a marvelous evening, the kind that could happen when they let themselves sparkle: Mexican food at La Cascada, where Lauren's margarita came in a salt-rimmed goblet and the burritos were tastier than hot. They drank draft beer in the back room of the Eagle Tavern on Fourteenth Street, clapped hands and sang along with raucous reels and Irish jigs, listened in pin-drop silence to penny whistles and a breathy flute that sang of an Ireland no one really remembered; a girl who played "Six Green Fields" on a limpid Celtic harp.

"Margaret called today," Lauren mentioned as they walked home through the cool damp.

"The usual?"

"About Mama, yes; she'll go anytime now. But . . ."

She let it hang too long, didn't pick up the dangling thought. "What, Laurie?"

"I felt Meg was *trying* to be close to me. Something she wanted to talk about and couldn't quite manage. Meg's so on top of things usually."

"About your mother?"

Lauren tried to reconstruct the disjointed conversation on the phone: the rapid litany of little things, then long, pregnant gaps between false starts before Meg gave up and said goodbye. "I don't know."

Her instinct said trouble. Without a name, it nagged at her.

They enjoyed a bath before bed and their lovemaking was prolonged, sweet, and very needed.

"When we get around to it," Lauren purred against his shoulder, "we do it right."

"I need you, Laurie."

"Damn right." She yawned. "Who else could live with us?"

"No one; not even us."

"You want to stay?"

"I can't sleep this early."

"Well, I'm gonna fade out in about two minutes." Lauren yawned again, slipped out of bed, and pattered to the bathroom. When she came out in her nightgown, she picked up a large envelope from a pile on the floor. "You forgot this last time."

"What?"

"The letter from your brother. It was open."

Landry remembered opening the envelope briefly in the Seville lobby, not then in the mood to decipher Denny's spastic handwriting or whatever else it contained.

"I picked it up when I was cleaning," Lauren said. "The pages fell out. It's a story."

Landry slid the pages out of the envelope. "Denny wrote a story?"

"I read some of it. Hope you don't mind."

"No, no . . ."

"It's crude and kind of raunchy," Lauren smiled, "but there's a pull to it. You keep reading. He's very real."

The messy pages had been typed on a manual with a weary ribbon. "Denny wrote a story?"

"Hey, you got the family franchise? Read it at home. I have to be up at seven. Go, Landry."

He finished dressing. Lauren draped the raincoat over his

shoulders and dropped the tweed hat on his mussed hair. He was still bemused by the envelope. "He really did it."

"I'll call you from Berlin," Lauren promised with a final hug.

"Please. If you miss me, leave a number and a time. I'll call back."

"Not to Berlin!"

"Why not? I'll plunge, romantic-transatlantic. Good luck with the krauts. Win a first prize for me."

"For who else?" Lauren pushed him toward the door. "And read the story. Your brother doesn't know a thing about writing except how to do it."

"He's that good?"

"No, not yet." Lauren considered it. "But he's *funny*, Pat."

ACT III
Fall, Winter

27

Landry exploded—roared long, loud, and deep. He bellowed, hooted, subsided into sustained giggles as he wiped at the helpless tears running down his cheeks, wondering if they were all from laughter. Gasping, he picked up the pages to read on, only to bounce out of the chair, guffawing at the outrageous but undeniable truth on the page.

Denny was funny. More than funny; under the clumsy syntax and overdone hyperbole, Den had the truth of comedy, human pain turned inside out. He bombarded the reader with simile and metaphor on a nuclear scale, a sidewalk Vonnegut clutching haplessly at the thrashing tail of a language always about to shake him off.

Landry chuckled, admiring. "You're a gas, kid. Who'd've thought?"

The story was as universal as a head cold: a lonely loser, in Den's words "inept as a pickpocket in boxing gloves," looking to make contact with girls. As he read, Landry began to recognize the roots of the style and the forlorn protagonist: the stories they used to make up before sleep; all the years of listening to Jack, absorbing the one-liners and exaggerated figures of speech. Much cruder here, all from the underside Denny knew too well. All-night saloons, jail cells, street people with beer hangovers, wincing against the flat, hard light of

morning, scrounging change for a Burger King breakfast, trying
to make it through one more day without knowing why.

Denny's protagonist didn't ask why, sharp enough only to
be forlornly aware of his neglected teeth, unchanged socks,
and the stains on his underwear. A Russian writer would
weep over him. Denny made you laugh.

For the first time in years, he could touch the Denny he
loved, scolded, and worried over. The pages cried for an
editor, but they were funny and true; you kept reading. The
story faltered toward the end, as if Den didn't know how to
wrap it up, but it was good enough to be fixed by an editorial
janitor who could sweep out the debris, pare the images to
lean meat, teach Den how to use one word for the five he
wasted.

Why didn't he find this years ago?

He tried, Landry remembered, seeing the pudgy little figure
bent over a pad of paper, mumbling to himself, creating a
story in clumsy panels, a few lines to a sheet before tearing it
off to attack the next. Trying to make pictures that moved
because he didn't have the words. Now he'd found some of
them. Somehow Denny had shuffled his fly-specked life and
dealt once more.

> . . . don't know why I wrote this, but it gets dull on
> the boat or when I don't want to go drinking, and
> that shit is getting very old. Is this story any good,
> Monk? I don't want to bother you. I know you don't
> have any reason to write me, not the way I treated
> you. But just tell me if I should work on this or make
> paper airplanes out of it.

*Do that, Den. Why should I get involved with you? You weren't
worth a damn when Dad and I needed you, stole from me when I was
broke. You'll fuck around with writing and drop it when it gets too
hard, looking for the easy way out like you always did.*

Landry tossed the pages into the wastebasket and lunged
about the room, muttering to the walls. "Go away. I don't
have time for you. I'd be the one breaking my ass trying to get
you to work. I got tired of hoping for you twenty years ago."

And, Christ, that still hurt.

"The woods are full of talent that can't go the distance.
Fuck off," Landry snarled.

It would be easier if Denny had no talent at all. Landry

couldn't deny the excitement and pride he felt in reading the pages . . . but no. Denny didn't have the strength. He was trying too late, years too late.

"You are a big fat pain in the ass."

He washed his face in the bathroom, massaging savagely with a towel, then flopped across the bed and glared at the ceiling, wanting and not wanting to call his brother. Denny's number was in his address book, sent with the first letter. Landry fingered the book open and looked at the name before flinging it away. No way: he was too old to go looking for extra grief. Den was just that.

But still . . .

"Aw, hell."

Landry snaked off the bed with a sigh of disgust, plucked the pages out of the trash, and dropped them on the desk, not clearly knowing why except that he couldn't ignore talent any more than he could spit on the flag—and Lauren would want him to give it a chance.

Damn!

He said it again: "A royal pain in the ass."

28

Landry hiked himself onto the stool and high-signed the bartender. "Dewar's on the rocks."

Beyond the bar entrance, the younger fans of fantasy and science fiction racketed through the lobby of the Sheraton La Guardia. MOON BASE, the yearly convention of the Manhattan Science Fiction Society, always produced a lively crowd of fans with a raucous substratum of film buffs and costume freaks. Since these rarely drank, the bar was bastion and refuge for the pro writers, editors, agents, and the older fans privileged to buy them drinks. They hung over the horseshoe bar in pairs or moody solo, refugees from the day's frenetic programming—readings, panels, formal and informal autograph sessions. Here in the shadowy bar, one didn't have to smile.

"Bartender," said Landry in prudent revision, "make that a double."

He'd already greeted the writers he admired and tactfully avoided or parried those he didn't read, including the Very Serious Writer of Celtic fantasy who trashed Landry's work for polluting the hallowed myths with comedy and anachronism. They'd crossed swords in a panel discussion that afternoon, Landry maintaining that it was fine to be historically accurate but better to be interesting, and the Very Serious Writer wrote him off as trivial.

After hours of this, Landry gravitated to the bar to find his peers like displaced persons in silent, desperate communion, wondering, like him, why *they* were here.

He had taxied from Manhattan on a moment's impulse. Lauren was still in Berlin promoting her films, bitching cheerfully when she called—

"I'm eating like a pig and coughing all the time. These Germans chainsmoke in their sleep. Love you!"

—and Landry had come to MOON BASE to fill an empty Saturday, done his panel, signed copies of his books, and shown that he was a just-folks prince of a guy, but now he wanted to go home to his cave.

He heard the jewelry before the voice, audible yards away. "Pat!"

Darcy Rambard pounced to the bar beside him, beaming through her glasses. "Gimme a great big kiss, Landry." She planted one on him, swiveling to command the bartender. "Jack Daniels on the rocks, lots of water. Pat, honey, how've you been keeping? Caught a flash of you in the hall this afternoon but you dashed off the other way."

In the cool, dim light of the bar, Darcy Rambard was very feminine and sexier than fifty-odd had any right to expect this side of Jane Fonda. Wide, frank, perennially astonished blue eyes took Landry in behind tinted designer prescription glasses. Darcy's trimmish figure was flattered by wheat cashmere under a tweed jacket thrown with careless but fine effect over her shoulders. Her manner was earnest and rueful, direct as a fire alarm. Listening to Darcy, one could get a very clear picture of the raw female psyche working at full blast.

She dumped the Daniels into the tall glass of water. "Didn't think you'd be here."

"Or you," Landry said. "Didn't know you were a fan."

"I'm a Trekkie from way back. And there's some agents here I want to touch base with. You look good." Darcy peered closer through her glasses and modified the estimate. "Sad but good. Kiss me again, I need it."

"My pleasure." Landry brushed her lips with his own, realizing how much he missed the known intimacy of Lauren. Strange how you got used to one woman's mouth over a long time. Lauren's was thin-lipped and delicate. Darcy's lips were full and soft, like cushions.

"You even kiss like a WASP," she said.

That came out of left field: "How's that?"

"No tension. Like you never had to look over your shoulder or excuse yourself for living. It's all how you're raised. I'll bet your family's idea of liberal was lunch with a Catholic." Darcy tilted the glass and drank, little finger carefully unextended. "What kind of name is Landry anyway?"

"Cornish, I think."

"Yah-h . . . what the hell ever happened in Cornwall but Tristan and Isolde?" Another gulp of watered whiskey. "My first drink since the last at lunch. See what I mean? Why am I explaining that to you? Landry: who would doubt such a union-card name? But Vogelman? Don't ask: a dash for guard dogs. Jewish men have tension. Tension is sexy. Oh, maybe you are a little in a *goyishe* way. But you are a sneaky bastard."

"Ouch."

"A-and I feel like hell." Darcy draped her heavy, cashmered breasts over the bar, gazing after the young bartender. "I feel—she sighed with mournful lyricism—like sad songs on a blue piano, black coffee and three o'clock in the morning. My daughter's got the hots for a nogoodnik with a great track record for wife-beating and not much else. And I just broke up with a man dull as a stock report but as reliable."

Landry squeezed her hand. "Why do you do romance? You'd be great at comedy."

"And," she plunged on, unassuaged, "my good friend Pat Landry just got a series I would *kill* for. Bread out of my children's mouths."

As always, Darcy overstated the *tsouris*. Her daughters were down to their last Gucci handbags. "So with everything else that's gone wrong, a lovely week. First I hear from my soon-to-be-dumped agent that someone else got the series. Then I find it's *you*. 'False, fleeting, perjured Clarence!' you know damn well I should get it. I mean, I know history as well as you. I've got a Ph.D. in it. Su-re, she has." Darcy's shoulders scrunched in resignation. "A brilliant thesis on Shakespeare's sources in the Columbia U. library where, like John Brown and my serious historical novel, it lies a-moldering."

Her heavy bracelets clanked against the mahogany bar.

"I've never heard jewelry quite like yours," Landry admitted. "Sort of Zulu."

Darcy rattled the hardware at him. "I can do Susie Shiksa with the best of them, but a week like this my JAP comes out and I go all jangly at the wrists. Jewish princesses you wouldn't know from. Buy me another drink; it's the least you can do."

Landry signaled the bartender. "Treat you to a cab home?"

"Got a room here. I put extra tuna in Merlin's bowl. Hell with it," Darcy brooded into her ice cubes. "If I get blitzed I only have to go upstairs to pass out. Where's Lauren, anyway?"

"In Berlin, hustling the krauts to show her films."

"I admire Lauren's discipline. She's so . . . austere."

Their refills came and another after that while the bar babble sank to dull white noise beyond them. They watched a buxom lady novelist, too well dined, teeter past them with a school of fans and a small husband like a pilot fish in tow. Landry waved in response to her polite nod. She made the conventions regularly with a pro's faultless demeanor, fatigue upholstered in graciousness.

"That's whatsername?" Darcy grunted. "Won the whatsis award last year?"

"The Hugo."

Darcy gave the woman the swift, steely assessment her sex reserve for one another. "Not the best dye job on her hair."

"It's real," Landry differed. "Seen it up close in daylight."

"Only her mortician knows for sure."

"That's rotten," Landry sputtered into his drink. "Funny but rotten."

"Who feels funny?"

"Who needs? My funniest stuff was written when I wanted to walk off a subway platform."

"Then I'd be a riot." Darcy dug in her bag for a filtered low-tar cigarette and let him light it. "Because that's the color of the week. I mean—"

She took off her glasses and polished them on a bar napkin. At fifty-two, she still had a luscious if overblown ripeness enhanced by subtle makeup. Landry wondered why the boyfriend hadn't worked out. The guy could do a lot worse.

"I got a bundle for my last book, which helped because my daughters were both in financial trouble—*vey*, what else is new? And that agent of mine, you'd think I worked for him."

Darcy's youngest was twenty-seven but she still felt she had to lavish on them. By her own admission it was an *esse, mein kindt* kind of love, but what could a mother do?

"I'll bet you got the series because my *shtummie* agent wouldn't lower the price. We usually floor at eighty. Why not? Hell, I'm good as Mallory Maine, and I can spell a lot better, and I don't need editing. Honey, I'm not putting you down as a writer," Darcy mollified quickly. "You're good, Pat. Just you're not ro-*mance*."

Landry absorbed the remark, which rankled the more being true. He'd never been able to take sex out of context in life or work. His characters enjoyed lovemaking as they did good food or any pleasure, never blasé but not always the Twilight of the Gods. Darcy wrote and sold her books on the American myth/romance apotheosis of sex, somewhere between paradise and nervous breakdown. Landry wondered if it was just business with her or if she really regarded sex that way. Janice liked to screw to Wagner; very nice if he was in the right mood, though his mind tended to follow the music in the better passages. Frantic Myra read every new sex-therapy book dripping like sweat from the self-conscious seventies and assumed they ought to be in on it. Even in bed, Landry never knew what game matrix he'd landed in.

Once Myra asked solemnly, "Will you tie me up and pretend to rape me?"

When he laughed, she got furious. "What's so funny?"

"That."

"You are the most insensitive—it's a *fantasy*. Fantasy is necessary." Accusing as always: "Couldn't you do *that* much?"

He told her honestly, "Not with a straight face."

"Oh, you—fantasy is very important to the female psyche."

"How do you pretend a rape?" Landry wondered. "You pretend you don't like it?"

Myra turned over toward the wall with a hopeless sigh. "I just thought it would add a little—*stop laughing.*"

"Okay, okay." For the sake of peace, he tried to go along, sliding out of bed. "Where's my bathrobe?"

Myra bounced around toward him. "Why do you need your bathrobe?"

"For the belt."

"Je-*sus!*"

"Be fair, Myra. How often do I need a rape rope?"

"This is one of the reasons we should go to therapy. You're not taking my needs seriously."

"I *am*—but help me with the knots. All I know is a granny."

"Oh, never *mind*."

They went from abortive sex fantasy to the therapy group like Hitler to the last bunker.

"So I don't write good fantasy sex," Landry conceded to

Darcy Rambard as soberly as the scotch would allow. He planted a conciliatory kiss on her gold-armored earlobe. "Still love me?"

"Yah, course." Darcy was feeling her own drinks now. She focused on him muzzily. "In sex scenes, the earth's gotta move. With you it just turns."

"Like in real life."

"They don't want real life," Darcy exploded in a breathy rush. "They want three ninety-five worth of *orgasm!*"

The emphatic sweep of her arm tipped her drink over the bar. Instantly she was all sincere regret and charm to the muscular young bartender who mopped up efficiently and smilingly brought her another. Darcy put out a dollar tip for him, following the surge of his shoulders under the white shirt and black vest.

"Now, there's a stud," she decided. She placed the fresh drink precisely in the center of the new napkin and nibbled cheese crackers from a nearby bowl. "You're cute too in your way."

"Aw . . . I wunnered when ya'd notice."

Darcy played with his hair. "A great big, snarly, growly sheepdog. Oh hell, I could write great comedy now, Patrick. I feel like making it to that subway platform: a ninety-cent suicide. My daughter's in love with a prick—and the rest of him isn't very nice either. And I'm wondering where'm I gonna find another man who isn't half dead or all boring."

Landry stroked her cheek. "Hang in, Darce. Will you entertain a radical thought?"

"If it's male, I'll entertain."

"People have been known to stay alone for a while without lethal effects."

"No." There was suddenly something like panic in Darcy's eyes. "I don't want to be alone, Pat. I get weird alone. I look at my cat sometimes and think: are you the rest of my life?" She shifted closer to him, her voice unconsciously intimate as bed, lacquered fingertips resting lightly on the back of his hand. "Baby," she breathed, "I never had any luck. Ever try to kill yourself?"

"Me, the thinking man's coward? Forget it."

"I did," Darcy confessed. "Twice. When I found my ex-husband, he should die with herpes, was fooling around on the side. We were skiing in Vermont. I went out in the woods and tried to freeze to death. No luck, you wouldn't believe: the woods were full of helicopters with bullhorns. Zotz!—down come the goddamn rangers."

When Landry observed that freezing would take unpleasant hours, Darcy, with airy inconsistency, said she'd brought along a brandy flask, her feet always got cold first.

"So after that my sister descends on me from Albany. A vigil. I go to the bathroom, she sits outside: Joan? Are you all right? Are you getting depressed in there? When she finally gave up and went home, I popped all my sleeping pills with a whopper drink and went to bed."

Darcy revolved her drink slowly with red-nailed fingers. Her hands were no more relaxed than the rest of her. For Darcy, angst was a hometown. Whenever she called to say hello, the first five minutes were always a litany of complicated griefs.

"My husband, the rat, was still at the office. I lay on the bed thinking bye-bye thoughts and after a while I called and told him what I did: shalom, you bastard, I'm checking out. 'Stay right there!' he yells—like I might go shopping—'I'm coming with the paramedics.' So at least he cared that much. So time goes by and I'm wondering when I'll start to feel sleepy, and I call my sister in Albany, very dying-fall even if I didn't feel it, and I tell her what I've done. She starts *laughing* at me. I said, 'What are you laughing, Esther, I'm saying good-*bye.*' She says, 'Like hell you are. Your sleeping pills looked just like my vitamin C, so I switched them.' " Darcy's shrug was eloquent. "What can I tell you? Suicide? I couldn't even catch a cold. Lady Luck, that's me."

She looked so forlorn that Landry felt a warm rush to comfort her. "You're quite a woman, Darce. That guy should've appreciated what he had."

She opened like a flower in the sun at the compliment. Darcy planted a kiss in his palm. "And you are a very sweet man, Pat Landry. Did Lauren ever tell you that?"

"Oh, now and then."

"Well, you are. She's lucky. Sometimes I wish you were Jewish."

"There you go again. Darcy, you're a snob."

"No, just . . . habitual. Jewish men know what the world's about." She shook her head as if to clear it. " 'Stime to go t'bed. Mus'be close to eleven."

She finished her drink and levered her hips off the bar stool, weaving a little trying to focus on Landry. "Oh, that last one did it. Gimme an arm, Pat."

Landry guided her out into the lobby, Darcy clinging to his arm, navigating with a slight starboard list through the garishly costumed fans spilling out of the adjacent ballroom like a coffee break in a Mardi Gras parade.

Darcy marveled at them. "God, Halloween is over. What kind of cockamamy call you this?"

"The costume contest." Landry steered her around the leather bat wings of an overweight demon in black tights— "Watch them elbows, Beelzebub!"—and toward the elevators. Somewhere in their wake, someone far too shrill was paging Ursula Le Guin.

"Oh, Miz Le Guin? Miz Le *Guin?*"

A pudgy, paste-jeweled hand arrested Darcy and a very short woman whose immense hips began just below the shoulders surged around to confront her. The woman's hair was unbound under a copper crown and billowed over a flowing tent of a gown waisted, if the term applied, with a witch's knotted cord. She smiled expectantly at Darcy, showing a gapped expanse of horsey upper teeth.

Darcy tried to focus on her. "Yes?"

The sorceress stepped back, less certain. "Aren't you Ursula Le Guin?"

"Honey," Darcy confessed tremulously, "this week I'm not even Erica Jong."

"Oh." Interest dropped like a plate on the floor. "I thought you were—are you anybody?"

Darcy swayed into Landry for support. "I was gonna ask you that."

The woman managed a flourish that jiggled all her bulk. "It's my Con personna. I'm Lady Eirian, sorceress of Castle Dore."

Darcy looked gently pained. "I knew we'd met somewhere. Excuse me, I'm not well. Get me to bed, Thorndyke."

"Take care," the sorceress warned after them. "I might cast a harming spell on you!"

"How?" Darcy mumbled into Landry's shoulder. "She could fall on me? Oh, that last drink was a *mamzer.* Punch the elevator, eighth floor."

Landry shoehorned them both into the crowded elevator car that smelled of unbathed sweat and marijuana. Still clutching his arm, Darcy was sardined between a Gandalf with a troublesome six-foot staff and a black-hooded ninja, her nose at chest level to a tall blond boy clad only in leather loincloth and Bowie knife. Darcy beamed at him.

"You look like a Nazi Tarzan. Who's your tailor?"

At her door, Darcy fumbled interminably for her key before getting the door open. She hadn't mussed the place much. Except for her tweed overcoat draped on a chair, the room was virginal.

"Indifferent," Landry decided. "This room doesn't care whether you stay here or not. How much did Sheraton pay to make these rooms impersonal as a subway?"

"Ah, stop writing," Darcy snarled. "You're lousy at descriptions."

"I am *not.*"

"You're better at epitaphs."

"You mean epigrams?"

"For me it's an epitaph." Darcy sat down heavily on the bed, removing her glasses. She massaged her temples. "I can kid about it, but I really feel lousy about that series. Or maybe just about getting old. Old*er.*" She couldn't resist the correction.

"Aw, come on. You're a doll, Darce. Didn't I just say you were the most attractive woman here?"

"Yah-h . . ."

"And I can too write descriptions." Landry paused a moment. When he spoke again, his voice was modulated and mellow. "Standing over the forlorn droop of her shoulders, he knew she had never been this beautiful as a young woman, that her quiet radiance was a sum of days."

When Darcy looked up, he knew she'd appreciated it. "That's what I mean, Pat. Very good, very literary, but—"

"A bit lush."

"Not lush enough," she said. "Better this way: the sleek curves of her lush body sent a sudden, urgent message to his manhood. *Tags*, baby. Descriptive tags are everything in romance. Like—She looked up at him and felt a tingle of electricity course through the deep, secret places in her body and soul. His massive shoulders filled the coat he wore. He moved toward her with an animal grace."

Landry sat down beside her. "Grace was his sister?"

"Shmuck." Darcy leaned into his shoulder. "But she was glad for the comforting male warmth of him beside her."

"His granite features softened with pleasure when she smiled."

"Tha-at's the idea." Darcy nodded. "Gets 'em every time. Hell, it gets me." She smoothed a stray wisp of hair behind his ear. "His dark tangle of hair was threaded with irresistible gray."

"Lightly," Landry did it, "he fingered a loose tendril of hair on her cheek."

Darcy stiffened. "She felt a sudden, fear-ridden urge to jump away."

"But then he swept her up in his arms as if she weighed nothing."

"Don't try it. I'm heavier than I look and you're older than you feel." Darcy frowned. "Aw-w, his eyes were dark and wounded."

"Like an unfed spaniel. Her eyes seemed pure azure and trusting innocence."

"His voice was deep and gentle, unconsciously seductive." Darcy's sardonic smile softened, the difference between electric light and candles. "That's true, Pat. You have a lovely, soft voice. It's the sexiest thing about you." She yawned and wilted down on the bed with a sigh. "That's not a tease. You're a sweet man with a turn-on voice and I have absolutely no intention of doing anything about it. I'm just making a point about descriptive tags. Like: she wasn't listening to his words. His voice came to her like the sound of distant, lulling surf."

Landry stretched out beside her, tired as herself, propped on one elbow. Darcy opened her eyes and looked at him.

"Pat," she said in a little mouse voice. "I really didn't mean to give you a come-on."

"I know, luv."

She curled naturally into him, aggrieved. "Just I feel so rotten this week, you know?"

"Sure." He rubbed her shoulders the way he did for Lauren when she needed to relax.

"His eyes raked over her boldly," Darcy overplayed in a throaty whisper. "You mustn't, dot-dot-dot, she gasped."

"Boldly over her, Darce. It's tighter."

She nipped his nose. "Stuff it, I'm being lyrical. Her stomach tingled at his nearness. The air around them seemed charged with terrible energy."

"The destined mating of electric eels." Landry kissed her hair. After a moment, Darcy slid her arm around his neck.

"She hungered for his plundering mouth," she said.

"Plundering, sundering—"

"Ravaging, savaging."

"Tragical-historical."

Darcy punched him in the ribs. "She breathed in the pungent male suh-*mell* of him."

"Sweat!"

"Hair!"

"LIEB-ES-NACHT!" Darcy sang like a harp glissando.

"Alex North!"

"Whozee?"

"Wrote the score for *Streetcar Named Desire*."

"Yah-h—decadence and rotting roses. Give me life! Give me love! she prayed."

Landry bear-hugged her. "Not her innocent love he wanted—"

"Get off my *el*bow, klutz!"

"Oh. Sorry. Not her love he wanted, only her charged flesh now—"

"And she gave it gladly, offered up all of her to his r-r-ruthless need."

"No goddamn ruth at all."

Darcy's heavy soft mouth crushed to his. She came up for air, giggling. "Dig this: Her breasts, like milky globes—"

"Yuk."

"—strained upward to his touch, his hot kiss, to be devoured, the nipples erect, rosy messengers of fire."

"Darcy—that's obscene."

She blinked up at him: "What's obscene?"

"You wrote that indigestible line in your last book."

"Damned right I did!" She bounced off the bed, offended. "It got me a Bergdorf wardrobe, a month in Bermuda, and my daughters out of debt. Publishers don't want my serious work? Too bad. I happen to be very good at this. Indi*gest*ible?"

Darcy stalked into the bathroom, slamming the door. From behind it, her final comment: "I write ten *times* better love scenes than you."

"Darcy Rambard and her All-Schmaltz Orchestra."

"AAAAGH!" A long silence. Then: "Why am I always defending myself through a bathroom door?"

The toilet seat banged down, the plumbing gargled. In a few

moments, Darcy emerged carrying her shoes and stockings. "And you?" she attacked. "No excitement, no tingle. All in the day's routine."

"Well, ain't it? It can't always be first-time fireworks."

"Okay." Darcy hung up her coat with quick, angry movements. "Okay, you're honest. Honest I'll give you. It's honest when the phone rings or stupid side thoughts creep in. Landry, do you have any idea who you're writing *for?*"

"Ah, go wax your legs."

"Go write a cavalry charge!" Darcy scooped up a shoe and hurled it at him. "You big dumb fuck, you're better with horses than women!"

"My horses are more believable than your women. I haven't heard that much heavy breathing outside an asthma ward."

"Pat, Pat." Darcy shook her head helplessly. "Tell that to the girls on the subway or the yenta who buys you to read under the hairdryer. The nervous little girls who haven't had a first time yet, or the Weight Watchers over forty or maybe fifty who never had one to speak of. They buy ten of these books a month, they're looking for real? Real is her kids. Real is what comes home from the office. They want to relive the feeling about sex when it was something to look forward to. Or the way it should have been but maybe never was and never will be."

Darcy sank down on the bed, very tired now, her words slurred but the bitterness unblunted. "The richest writer in this genre—Mallory Maine, First Lady of Romance—is a husband and wife team. Herbert and Gertrude Fleeson. They take turns at the word processor, but when they get to the love and sex stuff, Herbert takes a walk and lets Gertrude do her thing. Because women know what's sensual. Once a man comes, he can get just as interested in the eleven o'clock news. But a woman knows . . . I know. To me a man is the ultimate, first, last, and always turn-on, and I know a woman keeps hoping for the kind of magic she wants to really happen. She believes it will. Maybe I keep believing it, too."

The admission wrung something painful from Darcy Rambard. Glasses shed, massaging tired eyes with a nervous claw of a hand, she looked more myopic than ingenuous. And a little more *zoftig*: she'd left her girdle in the bathroom.

"I wish sometimes it wasn't so. These last couple of years when half of me wants to spend more time writing or just to hear myself think, the other half screams, what are you saying? There's a lot of jokes about Jewish princesses, but we're born into a religion where men used to say—and dammit, they still think—'Thank God I was born a man.' My first summer job I got on my own and I loved it, until my father marched into the store and dragged me right out of there because *his* daughter would not work. Didn't matter *I* loved it. That's a princess, Pat. We don't get our own lives, all we get are things. No wonder we're nudgy pains in the ass. My whole life has been men: listening to them, doing what they told me, marrying them, needing them. Praying they'll need me, don't laugh, so I can feel like *some*body. Maybe that's all I know. But, baby, I know it good."

Darcy heaved herself up with a deep sigh. "I want a spritz of plain soda before I crash. How 'bout you?"

"No." Exhausted himself, Landry folded down on the carpet, resting his head against the bed quilt. "Gotta go home."

He studied Darcy while she dredged the last of the ice from the plastic bucket on her dresser. Part of her wanted out from under a male thumb. Unlike Lauren, she could wriggle free just so far and no further. The keen-minded scholar who won a doctorate on her own and wrote a fine novel that went begging on its way to obscurity. Unbeaten, she turned herself into a commercial winner, yet always kept holding out her credentials as if she didn't expect to be taken seriously. The other part, the JAP she played compulsively rather than felt, was an older Janice—inordinately thrilled by men and sex as a sensual candy store, always waiting to be approved and validated by a man, ultimately wanting it that way, not unable but unwilling to understand anything else.

Darcy sat above him on the bed, offering her drink. "Sip?"

"Little one."

"Then go home and let me sleep. I'm having breakfast with a possible new agent tomorrow. I want to look good."

"Who?"

"Henry Steinberg. I like a man for an agent. I deal better with them."

She would, Landry thought. *I'm only a woman. Authority figure, tell me what to do.*

Darcy draped an arm over his shoulder, stroking his mussed hair. "I should've got those books, you know that."

"Hey, Darce—"

Landry nestled his cheek into the warmth of her hand. Hell, he was no better off than Darcy, just a different kind of scared. Looking for approval, waiting for someone to validate him, ready to sell anything now that the good stuff was gone. Like a comic falling back on shtick and dropping his pants to get a laugh. *Why can't you once believe in yourself? Hell no, don't trust your talent, never that. Just run scared.*

Like death, failure was a thief that stole from him, and everything he'd done since Susan left was to avoid the horror of failure, as a man once starved will hoard in the middle of plenty, even starve again to keep from spending that vital security. Like Darcy, part of him could see the absurdity. The other part only ran faster.

He said it precisely. "You're right, you should have. Because you really believe in it. I'm going to do it because I'm scared not to."

"You'll be lousy, Pat. You'll be writing down to a market, and that never works."

"You're not hearing me. There's some things you don't know about men. Take away a man's effectiveness, his ability to perform, and you leave him impotent. That's not just sex but the whole range of what he can *do*, Darce."

"My wife Susan left me because I failed. No—not true; because *I* thought I failed. Man, I was so green and scared of New York. After she left, I went on running. Then I got lucky with the books or maybe just desperate, but the talent poured out of me like it'd never stop. Now it's stopped, and I'm back to square one, tapped out, shit scared, still a living to make and no idea how to do it."

Landry shifted around to look at Darcy. "But I am not going to wait, like it was with Susan, until I see that baffled contempt in Lauren's eyes. I got on a roll and I'll do anything to keep it rolling. Anything. I swear to God, Darce, I'll never be a loser again."

Darcy leaned down to kiss his hair. "Better you should hate every minute?"

"You got it."

"That's what I said. Baby, I could cry for us both." She gave him a push. "G'wan home, I'm dead. Tomorrow morning I have to make Hank Steinberg think I'm Virginia Woolf with bigger boobs."

She trailed Landry to the door, yawning. "Gimme a hug."

They embraced as tired as they felt. "Call me next week, lunch maybe?"

"Sounds good."

"You know any interesting Jewish widowers, bring'm along."

He managed a weary grin. "Talk about prejudice."

"Nah." Darcy patted his rear. "It's like these damned old jeans of yours: look like hell but they've learned to fit your *tuchuss*. Give my best to Lauren, I only hate her because she never gets cellulite." Darcy surrendered to a last, terminal yawn. "Ciao, baby."

29

Lauren was jet-lagged, her stomach distressed with airline food, nerves jangled by the long cab ride from Kennedy to Manhattan. For the evening she'd much rather have had a quiet dinner with Pat—but Aaron Feurstein called and pleaded with her to come to his birthday party later. That was Aaron, she thought: married to someone else, yet still needing to know Lauren cared. Child-oblivious to everything but his own needs, innocent, maddening. But he looked awful the last time she saw him. She should go, put in an appearance at least. Gramercy Park was five minutes by cab.

By late afternoon she'd completed the Chinese-checkers process of coming home, unpacking, winnowing important mail from three weeks of junk. There was a letter from her brother Charles, a thick sheaf of phone messages (several from Charles and Margaret), business cards from the Berlin Festival sorted into three piles: follow up, maybe, and forget it.

When sense began to glimmer amid chaos, Lauren called Pat to let him know she was home. After a three-week separation, his enthusiasm was ear-splitting and lovely.

"HI! Hey, love, it's so good to hear your voice. I'll be over."

"Lots to tell you, sweetheart. Listen, there's a party at Aaron's later. His birthday."

"Why not?" Pat boomed.

"If you want to go, but I really should for a little while at least."

"Should I dress?"

"Aaron's always come-as-you-are and everyone does. Six-thirty?"

Around six, Lauren fixed a weak martini—*go easy, you're tired*—and opened the letter from Charles. It was postmarked ten days ago. Under the no-nonsense black block letters of the heading CHARLES AND LEONA WEIR, straightforward as a dentist's bill, the letter was brief and very Charles, a constipated family affection spread too thinly over business brusqueness.

> . . . today from the nursing home that Mother has lapsed into bronchial pneumonia. We called you as soon as we knew, but your hotel said you were in Europe. Please call as soon as you return. I think you should be here. And of course, we miss you . . .

Ten days ago! Lauren calculated time: near six here, about three in Portland. She picked up the phone and her address book from the desk and punched Charles's home number. Maybe Leona would be in. She let it ring ten times before breaking the connection and trying Margaret's number. There were only two rings, an automatic click, and the familiar recorded message—

". . . not at home just now, but if you'll leave your name and number, I'll get back to you."

Shit!—well, she'd be getting the children from school. "It's Mama, Meg. I just got in from Berlin and wanted to know about Mama. I'll call back later this evening, or please call me."

Lauren hung up, the gray feeling in her stomach more to do with fear than the airline lunch. She'd probably have to fly out immediately, which was no fun to contemplate. Her mother weighed eighty pounds—less now—and any infection would be critical.

I saw it coming and prayed for it to be quick. At least she doesn't know what's happening, and yet—

And yet, an odd, primordial sense of maternal responsibility wrung its hands in Lauren: *It wouldn't have happened if I'd been there.* Something deeper than thinking: to love was to protect. *It wouldn't have—*

Stop it, she snapped at herself. *You'll call, you'll find out. You'll catch a plane. You'll be there.*

It wouldn't—maybe it already has.

I said stop it! You're not president. Neither are you, Charles, so you stop too. Stop being older brother for once. Don't make my decisions for me.

Absently, Lauren cut some cheese and celery for Pat and put the plate in the fridge.

As if she couldn't decide for herself. Families handed out guilt like religious medals, and they all wanted their piece of you. Even Aaron. She gave him years, not all bad but not all easy, and he married Anna only weeks after their breakup. Aaron couldn't be alone. He wouldn't reflect as Pat might, just reach for someone else like a dish of salted nuts. Anna was perfect for him, a little younger, well off on her own, and happy to provide what Aaron needed. There were women like that, needing someone else's life to lose their own in.

Aaron and Pat: so different. Aaron the eternally excited child, compulsively performing his own music at parties—*listen to this! Isn't it wonderful? My God, I've done it again!* The child's unselfconscious demand for attention, the driving need for the reassurance of sex in the ruined, dying body. The innocent, unclouded mind that had no word for shadows or alone.

Pat the diametric opposite, more acute and difficult, needing solitude as much as herself. If Aaron had been easier to love, Pat was easier to live with.

Lauren found herself glancing repeatedly at the clock. Hours before she could get anyone in Portland now. *Mama looked so frail the last day I spent with her, holding her hand, hoping she'd recognize me. She smiled now and then, like brief sunlight through clouds. Yes, Meg, you were right, right, RIGHT. I should have stayed. It wouldn't have hap—*

Yes—it—would.

"It's me, hon."

Pat Landry looked huge and marvelous in her doorway. Healthy and alive.

"Hi-i, sweetheart." Lauren wrapped herself tight in his rain-sodden arms, loving the feel of him, the tobacco smell that clung to his skin and clothes.

"Missed you a lot this time," he murmured.

"Tell me about it." After a long kiss, like cool water on a hot day, she said, "Want a drink?"

"No, later." He held on to her. "Just let me hold you."

Over his shoulder, Lauren's eye was drawn again to the

small traveling clock on her dresser. Just past six-thirty. Three-thirty in Portland. Meg would have called back right away; Leona might have met Charles somewhere for dinner. Hours to go.

"There's lots to tell you." Lauren skittered to the fridge and set out the plate she'd fixed. "Have a nibble. Honestly, I haven't washed since Berlin. Need a bath before I'm condemned."

A few minutes later Landry perched on the closed toilet, nibbling cheese while Lauren revived a little under hot water, oil, and soap.

"Mama's very sick, Pat. They said pneumonia."

His eyes met hers with a tacit understanding.

"I'll have to go out."

"Lord, you just got off a long flight." After a moment he asked, "Do you want me to go with you?"

Lauren pulled him to her with a soapy hand and kissed him. "I love you for that. But no, I'd rather you came at a happy time."

"Well, will you be okay for money?"

"Fine. Did you go to that convention wherever?"

"MOON BASE? Yeah," Landry said. "Darcy Rambard was there."

"Oh?" Lauren purred. "Should I be jealous?"

"I'd like you to be," he ruminated around a bite of cheese, "but I can't think of a good reason."

Probably not, Lauren reflected with tidy comfort. If something had happened, he wouldn't mention the glitzy bitch at all. She smiled up at him. "It's good to be home."

"How was Berlin?"

"No prizes, just an honorable mention—which got more attention in the right places than the others. Good contacts, and did I work for every one. A madhouse. God, those Germans! Eat, eat, eat, smoke, smoke, smoke. My throat's still raw. The whole town's under a cigarette fog."

She told him about the contacts and sales she'd made. She was good for more showings in Berlin the coming year and most likely in Paris again, an important one. But she'd eaten too much and felt like she'd gained five pounds, parties all over the place, the last at a big marble barn of a place she couldn't pronounce and wasn't going to try. The Germans were acquisitive as ever.

"Talk about *Morgen die welt*. They used to want to conquer the world. Now they'll buy it if it goes with the rest of their furniture. Grab the loofah, you get to scrub my back."

Landry knelt at the edge of the tub, working the loofah over Lauren's slender back in long strokes. "You might have put on a pound or two."

"Does it show?"

"No . . . and it'll help you fight colds. It's good to have a couple of extra pounds in winter."

Mama could have used them, Lauren thought bleakly. "You look thinner."

He kissed her freckled shoulders as he worked over her back. "Maybe."

"Is something wrong?"

"No . . . nothing."

But it was something. He never lost his appetite unless something worried him. He was smoking too much; Lauren heard it in his breathing. He ended the scrub with a kiss on the ear. "Hey, lady? Wanta wrestle?"

Lovely idea. Lauren melted her mouth into his. "Two falls out of three?"

"Optimist."

It turned out a single, gentle fall. Fatigue and the hot bath made Lauren's body sleepily sensual. Their lovemaking was a long floating upward toward a lovely height and a slow, drifting return. Before she fell asleep in Pat's arms, she thought of her mother again. When they woke up an hour or so later, it was time to go to Aaron's party.

Before they left, Lauren tried Charles's number; still no one home. For one reason or another, perhaps to forestall the inevitable, she didn't call Margaret.

The phone rang a little while after they left.

30

For Lauren's sake and a respect for the man's genuine talent, Landry always tried to be polite to Aaron Feurstein on the few occasions they met. Not without difficulty, since Aaron seemed to place him firmly below the artistic salt as a "popular" novelist. Lauren was always "pleasant" toward Anna and wanted Pat to be "civilized" toward Aaron, the quotation marks quite audible in the wish.

The party was wall-to-wall when they arrived at Aaron's penthouse. The crowd eddied around the grand piano, spilling into the kitchen and bedroom with occasional forays onto the terrace overlooking Gramercy Park. In twenty-five years, Aaron had never thought to angle the piano into a corner for more living space. It resonated better in the middle of the room and remained there, like Aaron himself, crowding everything else toward windows and walls.

At Aaron's, come-as-you-are was literal. Between the occasional tux and Landry's casual denim, costume ran riot through every degree from business suits to punk rock. Anna greeted Lauren in one of the few uninhabited spaces between the foyer and living room, a tiny woman who held out both hands to her guest.

"Lauren! *So* good of you to come. Drinks and whatever in the kitchen, if you can bull your way through. Hello . . ." She smiled with vague graciousness at Landry. "Sorry, I don't recall your name."

"Pat."

"Oh yes. I don't think anyone can get to Aaron just now."
Anna glanced at the crowd around the pounding piano. "Coats
in the bedroom."

Aaron was playing a number from a show produced in the
fifties. Landry had bought the album new and replaced it
twice. After they stowed coats, Lauren made for Aaron immediately for a quick hug. He glowed at the sight of her, barely
acknowledging Landry.

"Lord, that's so old, what he's playing," Lauren mourned.
Her expression just then was hard to interpret. "Go circulate,
sweetheart."

Landry squeezed through to the kitchen and made a moderate scotch. An out-of-town aesthete, he reflected, might compare Aaron's party to a Bosch canvas, a cross section of dark
fantasy or merely New York's working art world, from the
successful down through the hopefuls to the fringe hopeless
with a filigree of unclassified. Landry relaxed into his natural
party mode, content to listen and watch. A number of people
from the Chelsea had come. He recognized the Israeli artist
Juki Baraz, and Miloff, the Italian miniaturist with the overgrown Dali mustache, gulping red wine like lemonade. The
co-owner of a disco whom Landry knew vaguely from the
Chelsea buttonholed him to expound on a religious fantasy
idea he wanted to sell to films if he could just find a good
writer to work with.

"It's tremendous. We could cast Anthony Quinn as the
Pope."

"Quinn already played the Pope," Landry said, looking
furtively to escape.

"It'll gross a hundred million!"

"Lotsa luck!" Landry called as three shrieking women separated them forever.

Not to be jealous, but Lauren was certainly spending a lot of
time with Aaron. Hell with it. He managed his way back to the
kitchen for another drink, elbowing past a tall brunette in too
much makeup but still striking. The statuesque woman looked
Landry up and down as he moved past her. She seemed to
like what she saw. Nice someone did.

Knock it off. Just I wish Aaron would keep his hands on the piano.

Armed with a fresh drink, Landry made a slow circuit of
the party, tuning in to conversations whizzing past like
asteroids—

"Sid Vicious shot his girlfriend at the Chelsea. They're going to shoot the film on location there."

"No, you've got it backwards. Harry was my therapist *before* I married him. Now we both go to a group."

". . . belonged to the Party all through the thirties. Then he made a pile, and went Republican."

". . . not like *we* have a religious problem. Myron agrees with me that neo-paganism is the only place for an individualist. Just his mother wouldn't like it."

The music was on tape now, mostly drowned in party din. Landry recognized Aaron's violin concerto, recorded once in the fifties. No one listened to it then, either, fine as it was. Aaron had Lauren in a corner in a boozy-serious exchange.

She's never looked at me like she looks at him. Well, they had years together. Just I feel like a tourist.

Landry continued to prowl.

". . . I said to her: I don't see what letting a guy pay for my dinner has to do with selling out feminist principles."

"Feurstein was eclectic, but in such a narrow way."

"But I *love* Aaron's music; especially the commercials. I mean, they have a lot of substance."

"I wouldn't say Rona was a nasty person."

"No? When I had the flu, she sent me a get-worse card."

One of us ought to stay sober, Landry thought. Lauren was already listing slightly in Aaron's arms.

"Bullshit!" The masculine sentiment exploded close to Landry's ear. He winced.

"I'll have to *see* that, sweetie." An office type in a three-piece suit looming over a thin, bangled woman whose electric pink stole managed to clash with everything she wore. "When it comes to Women's Lib, I am from Missouri."

"Harry, Missouri is an Indian word for *thick*."

"Grace," said the three-piece suit, "I am not an insensitive man, but you've been crabby since dinner. You know egg roll doesn't agree with you."

"It's not the egg roll, Harry. It's the whole last year."

Sometime later, over a dozen heads, the tall brunette caught Landry's eye and winked. He couldn't help feeling appreciative and was edging toward her from the kitchen entrance when Lauren materialized and pulled him down to her for an off-center kiss.

"Hi-i." She wove precariously.

"How's it going? Getting tired?"

"Oh," she shrugged, "just one more and we'll go. Been getting around?"

"Sort of eavesdropping."

"And all the women making passes, I suppose."

"Only one confirmed," Landry told her with a tinge of pride, recalling the long time she'd spent in the corner with Aaron. "Warmed the cockles of my pacemaker."

"Oh?" Lauren plopped fresh ice in her plastic glass. "And who's that?"

"Big one over there with the operatic sense of makeup."

Lauren glanced at the brunette and drowned her ice in vodka. "Sweetheart, his name is George."

"George?"

"And he's in drag," Lauren informed him redundantly. "He usually goes for the punk rock set. See the kid with green hair? That's his date. And he knows you're with me."

"Glad you told me." Landry felt ridiculous. "I was beginning to think he was cute."

"He is." Lauren smiled blearily. "Dear and pathetic. He's a composer, wanted to score one of my films, but he's too off the wall. Go talk to Aaron. Be civilized."

"Hey, lady—" The implied reproof irritated Landry. "You already said that."

Lauren drank. "Lord, I'm tired."

"I know. It shows. You've made your appearance. Why don't we say good night."

"Soon," she promised. "Just have to touch a couple more bases. Gimme a kiss. I like it that I can leave you alone at a party without you sulking in a corner."

Landry tried to say it without the edge he felt. "It's called poise."

He watched her slight figure writhe into the crowd and be swallowed up. Landry made himself another scotch, wanting to leave. . . .

He was standing in a corner sometime later, contemplating a languid turtle in a lighted tank, when a contra–tenorish voice at his ear said—

"*Excuse* me, but do you *hap*pen to have a light?"

Landry turned to find the statuesque brunette posed beside him, elbow crooked on one palm, cigarette poised. George/Georgianna's dramatically mascaraed eyes were on a level with his own, intense and just a little too near. He snapped his

Bic to the pink Sherman, edging backward. The turtle tank blocked him.

"Lauren tells me," the voice was pitched and paced for effect, "that you're a writer."

"Uh—yes. I'm a novelist."

The cigarette flourished à la Bette Davis. "Serious?"

"I wouldn't say I was kidding around. Science fiction, fantasy: that sort of thing."

"We all have our secret sins." Georgianna's eyes swept him up and down like a vacuum cleaner. "I read Jackie Collins and Judith Krantz in the bath."

"Lauren says you're a composer."

"Quite." The cigarette had become semaphoric. "Are you into music?"

"Secret sins," Landry said. "I listen to Saint-Saëns while shaving."

"Oh dear," Georgianna vented a stagy sigh. "Do you know *modern* music?"

An eternity later, wedged against the turtle tank, Landry regretted that he knew modern music at all. An incipient headache was not helped by drinking too fast, but Georgianna would not relent. Besides an intense, discomforting stare, Georgianna had severe opinions, dismissing Prokofiev with contempt and most composers after Berg as minor and irrelevant.

"There was Blitzstein and there is Cage," Georgianna allowed. "They knew how music must relate to the space in which it is performed. After Cage, the only valid music is mine"—a virtuoso sweep of the cigarette—"or utter silence."

Landry suffered.

"I don't see *how* you can argue for Prokofiev, Mr. Lundy. He was such a fence-sitter, a musical mugwump, an exhibitionist at the beginning, sentimental at the end. If you knew *anything* of Moscow in the thirties—"

Landry felt a sudden sensation like a rush of blood to his head. As if a cold, naked bulb had clicked on in his brain, the sight of Georgianna became sharper but neutral as a stone and as disposable. *Careful,* the last ghost of caution warned him—as Aaron Feurstein wedged between them, a rotund punctuation mark, very drunk, the ash from his cigarette brushing off against Landry's jacket.

"Sorry 'bout that. Georgie, do I hear the sound of musical debate?"

"Dispute, darling. One needs two equal sides for debate."

Grinning at Aaron, Landry felt numb, free. "Happy birth-day, Aaron. Blessings on your head. This masculine Mae West was badmouthing Prokofiev."

"Don't be gauche," said Georgianna.

"No, don't," Aaron reproved woozily. "Sarcasm is the low-est form of humor. Georgie is a qualified critic. Prokofiev was an opportunist with no heart. Ditched his wife because she was a Jew. And furthermore . . ."

Time to leave, Lauren knew. Shouldn't have had that last drink. It hit her hard, draping a wet sheet over her mood, which wasn't good when she arrived. She should call Portland and didn't want to. Given a choice, she'd like a good cry or to throw her drink at someone.

Leave me alone, Meg, she raged silently. *Don't tell me about selfishness.*

Aaron's apartment was even more crowded with latecomers and disagreeably smoky now. Lauren left her drink on the floor and edged around the crowd toward the blue blur of Pat's jacket between Georgie and Aaron. She felt a sudden, poignant rush of sympathy for Aaron: his eyes closed, looking tired and unhappy.

Poor Aaron. Poor, ruined Aaron. Another operation coming up and he knows it won't help any more than the last. He knows he's dying. Lord, how I tried to keep us together . . . and there's Pat towering over him, never sick a day in his life. Mama, Aaron: the world's taking pieces out of me, everyone I love is dying . . . 's not fair.

Nearer, she heard Pat's cutting voice rise over the party babble. "Aaron, where do you come off saying that? Prokofiev and Shostakovich were both victims of the cultural purges."

"Shost'kovich," Aaron slurred contemptuously. "Music with no heart, no feeling. Bloodless."

"You knew the OGPU scene, you've read Seroff." Pat Landry faced Georgianna and Aaron like a sergeant chewing out re-cruits. "Or you should have. Khrennikov and his slimebag wife screwed them both—"

Lauren's muzzy anger focused suddenly and irrationally on Pat. *There he is, old Total Recall, laying into the wrong people as usual—*

"Damn, Aaron," Landry said. "You're a talented man, enough to have a little charity."

"Genius has no need to be charitable," Georgianna snapped.
"Oh?"

Lauren cringed as Pat turned to the transvestite. *God, I know that look. Don't be cruel to Georgie, the world's already done it.*

"Georgie," Landry said too precisely, "if I lived in a glass house, I wouldn't throw anything but parties. The world will be listening to Prokofiev when no one remembers you as anything but an inverted George Sand."

Georgianna was stung enough to step out of character. "Back off, mister. I'm not as helpless as I look."

"Maybe not, but in three-inch heels I'd forget it."

Lauren plunged in like a lifeguard, hooking her arm through Aaron's. "Darling, we have to go. I'm exhausted. Take care now—and don't mind Pat. He gets very serious."

Aaron draped an arm around her. "Oh, he's just showing off."

"Again?" Lauren tried to lighten the whole thing. "He's very good at that."

Wrong; she saw Pat stiffen and knew somehow she'd put her own foot in it. The coldness in him was naked for an instant before he masked it.

"Aaron, I was paying you the courtesy of speaking in your discipline. Which is more than you could do in mine."

Lauren tugged at him in earnest. "Pat, we have to go."

"Of course." To Aaron, taut: "I'll say good night to your lady."

"Don't bother." Aaron turned away in dismissal. To Lauren's irritation, without a word to her, Landry moved to Anna, took her hand politely, then started for the bedroom to get his coat. Then Aaron kissed her once more. He was very drunk now, barely able to stand up. "Thanks for coming, darling. But where in the world did you get *him?*"

"At Gimbel's." Lauren pecked at his cheek. "G'night, dear."

Good-bye, Aaron. God, I'm always saying good-bye, always leaving.

31

He was waiting for her at the elevator like an ambassador about to break off relations. His eyes were queerly bright and black. He was ominously quiet in the elevator. Lauren felt his stare boring into her. They came out onto the park square in a light rain. Lauren went to the curb to look for a cab, not wanting to cope with her own knot of emotion and fatigue. Pat was cold drunk now; she'd seen it before, saw it when he turned on George. Pure cruelty.

"Thanks a lot," he said finally.

"You didn't have to insult Aaron. Or George, he's been hurt enough, and Aaron—"

"Was with you for seven years, yes, I know. Seniority."

"Yes he was. He was also brilliant."

"I was listening to Feurstein when you were making school lunches in Portland." Landry wrestled into his raincoat with angry thrusts of his arms. "The drag queen was—"

"His name is George."

"And George was—well, if he had one, he'd be one. Talking arrogant, ignorant rot. Then Aaron got into it and all of a sudden I'm the Devil under attack from two musical fucking Jesuits."

"And all of a sudden you're putting Aaron down about courtesy." A taxi sailed by, ignoring Lauren's imperious wave. "And that bit about saying good night to his 'lady.' "

"You said be civilized. That's how it's done."

239

"Beauregard Landry. Anna didn't even remember your name."

"That little snob said I was showing off. And you agreed with him. That's your courtesy."

God, she was tired. "Pat, Aaron is a child—"

"Is that how you lasted seven years, catering to a spoiled child?"

"There was more," Lauren flung back in a ragged voice. "There was a fine person there once."

"And it was easier to let me feel like a dog on a leash than hurt his feelings."

"I've always had to do that for him," she admitted, tasting the bitterness.

"I suppose you did. "Since I'm not a child, I don't need the consideration."

"He's living thirty years ago. He could never take reality. And he's dying."

You don't know that much about women, she thought. *That's inherent, part of loving. Leave me alone.*

"No, come on," Landry persisted. "I'd really like to know."

"Pat, I'm tired." Lauren looked away into Gramercy Park. "I want to go home to bed, and I have to call Portland and find out something I really don't want to hear anyway."

"I despise jealousy," he said. "Tonight I really tried not to feel that way."

"You know you can't drink."

"And you're an expert? I know about selling out, too, and that's what you did to keep baby from crying. I don't own you, Lauren—"

"Damn right you don't!"

"But that hurt. That's an achievement. I have to love someone a lot to be that vulnerable, but you hurt me."

The dismal feeling in Lauren's head and stomach turned savage. She wanted to drop the world from a high window. *Why do I have to be mother, lover, and saint to all of you?* "Go home, Pat."

"I'll get you a cab."

"I can do that. Just go home."

"Fine, if that's the way you want it." He turned up the collar of his coat. "Call you."

Lauren turned away toward the street, smoldering. "I may not be here."

"Then thanks for the loyalty."

The word tore something in Lauren. "Leave me alone!" she lashed at him. "All of you, leave me *alone!*" The rage whipped her around, flailing out to slap his face. Almost part of the same movement, he caught her wrist and twisted it hard, wringing a cry of shock and pain from Lauren. He let go instantly; they stood apart, Lauren holding her wrist.

"Get away from me, Pat."

He might not have heard her, looking at his hand as if it belonged to someone else.

Lauren felt cold and dead. "I had to take that from Walter. I had to watch him take his anger out on Marsh until Marsh was too big for him. But not from you."

He seemed to stare through her at something else. He took an uncertain step backward. His lips moved silently.

"You men think you have so much *right*. You're pathetic." If anything surprised Lauren, it was the virulent rage in herself. *"Who gave you the right?"*

Pat Landry came a little way out of the strange fog. "I'll— "

When he raised his arm, she thought he might be going to hit her, but he stepped off the curb to flag an approaching cab. When it pulled over, he opened the door for Lauren and closed it carefully after her, then simply stalked away toward the corner. Lauren leaned forward to the dim figure of the driver beyond the partition.

"Chelsea Hotel . . . Twenty-third Street."

I wish I could talk to you, Mama. Wish you could tell me what to do. How much do I have to leave to live?

There were two phone messages in her box. One was from a woman friend in the hotel; the other was from Charles.

Mother passed on this afternoon. Please call.

Lauren leaned against the elevator wall, trying to realize what the slip of paper told her; trying somehow to keep it at a distance.

She let herself into her apartment and snapped on the lights. At the desk, she just let the damp coat fall from her. Her hand went out to the lamp, but faltered. Feeling as if she weighed four hundred pounds, Lauren slumped into the desk chair and put her head down on her arms.

She didn't suffer. Just went to sleep. She didn't suffer. . . .

Lauren began to cry softly, then harder. Warm as the room was, she felt cold. A violent shuddering took her. When she tried at last to punch Charles's number, she hit all the wrong buttons.

Landry walked home through a chill rain and the colder turmoil inside him. Lost again. Told to leave again because of the same senseless, vicious rage he hated in others because he despised it in himself. He hurt Lauren physically, something he'd never do sober, no matter what she did.

He felt sick when he lurched into his room.

He started to hang the wet raincoat over the tub, but just let it drop and ran hot water to wash the heavy, tight feeling out of his eyes, avoiding his reflection in the mirror, but it caught him. He looked Landry up and down.

"I don't like you," he confessed with fervent loathing, "and I am very tired of you."

It happened once with Susan just before the end. He was very drunk then, too, and he hit her hard. All her pent rage boiled out then as it did from Lauren.

I hate you. You've killed everything I ever felt for you.

Lost again. He told himself he could live through her leaving, but how much could you lose and still call it a life? Connie's kid, right enough. Drunkenness was the trigger, like the night in Jersey when he turned on old friends with a cold pleasure in his ability to inflict pain. His moral right to hurt them—

Click.

Wait a minute. I said that before. Where?

To Caroline, almost a year ago.

Absently, Landry dropped ice into a glass and opened the scotch.

Moral right?

Look at me when I speak to you.

Connie slapping him back and forth, Monk trying to duck away, his bewildered love for her paralyzing the will to strike back, but the rage growing in him like a demon fetus.

Connie's own, right enough. Beautiful. She wrote the script and I'm playing it—

Something clicked again like a subliminal frame in Landry's head. Script—

Writing . . .

What lit that rage in you, Mama, and how did you pass it to me?

Click.

"Because I let you," he said.

Landry put down the glass. The truth struck him like a slap in the face.

Because we let you, all of us. Me, Julia, Arthur—even Lauren. Because, even when we grow strong enough to write our own scripts, we still let you star.

The elusive image flashed again, clearer—

Script. Something about the word.

—began to play on the screen of his memory.

Ten years old, raiding into Jack's diary for 1934. And the single line in Connie's hand at the end of one entry, heavy as the pencil bore down with her vindication. He'd read that line a dozen times before he was thirteen, let it fade to illegibility under almost half a century of living, and only understood it now.

Click. The puzzle closed together and fit.

Landry picked up the scotch bottle, went to the bathroom and emptied it down the sink. He dropped the bottle in the trash and settled into his work chair. Ready for them.

Act three, Mama. Julia, Arthur, Jack. Places, please.

And they were there, had been there always: Jack at the desk, peering at his son over horn-rims and the eternal cigarette. Connie and Julia at the table, the beer between them. Arthur erect and apart at the door.

"I do like to visit," Connie bit off the words. "I don't like to be summoned."

The production number, Mama. Everybody on. All the hole cards face up.

"Some writer," Julia commented. "I told you when you were fifteen, don't mix metaphors." Her hands were busy with the clay dancer, using the point of a hairpin to work the last tiny lines of definition—waves in the hair, the subtle definition of flexed muscle; the piece was almost finished.

Arthur undid his battle jacket, relaxing a little. "Why can't you leave me out of this?"

Can't, Arth. All of a sudden it makes a sad kind of sense.

"I was buried at sea," Arthur said. "I've gotten used to the quiet out there." He sat down lightly on the bed. "Well, we're all here. What's this about?"

This is the last scene, where everyone has their best lines.

Jack blew out a cloud of smoke. "What lines?"

The zingers, Dad. The maguffin. Straight truth.

Connie gave her son the Hawkins Glare. "Are you challenging me?"

Don't worry, Mama. You'll be brilliant.

"Anytime," she accepted with audible relish. "Pour me one, Julia."

Have a drink, Arthur.

"No." Arthur shot a disgusted glance at the bottle between his mother and sister. "I always hated the taste and smell."

Break a rule. You're going to need one. All of you.

32

Pat Landry composed himself in his work chair/conning tower and faced his memories.

Last act, family. We're going for truth, so anyone with a delicate ego better brace yourself.

"You're speaking to a family known for its courage," Connie retorted. "Some of us, anyway."

Don't sell me short, Mama. Been a lot of years.

"Perhaps, but if you're taking me on, you'd better pour one for yourself. Scotch, isn't it?"

That was part of the problem. Tonight I began to lick it.

"Down the sink," Jack noted with a tinge of regret. "Twelve years old, not a day less."

It was a choice. I'm an alcoholic. Speaking of courage, just saying that took a little, but getting it said I know I don't have to drink. And while I'm giving out medals, maybe the bravest thing Den ever did was coming to me and admitting he was an addict. Looking for help I couldn't give and he couldn't take. But he said it, something Mama and Julia never managed.

"Phooey." Julia shrugged, working with her clay. "We drank a little."

No, dear. You drank a lot, both of you. You never fell down or passed out, but most of what you were and did came out of it.

"You think I had no good reason to want a drink now and then?" Connie said.

That was your life, Mama. When it spills over into mine, *I* can do something about it. Tonight it did, and I may have lost the best woman I ever found, because, in one way or another, all of you planted germs in me. Tonight we isolate them and find a cure. So it's 1934, everybody.

"Tragedy as virus." Jack considered the figure of speech. "Nice idea."

And a nice way to put it, Dad.

"Thanks. I liked it too." Jack swiveled his bulk in the chair. "Pour me a short one, Con. Let's see what the Monk can do."

Connie passed a beer to her husband. "What would he remember about 1934?"

Everything. Finally. I can misplace a memory in an attic full of junk, but once it's there, it'll turn up. I remember so much: toys, Christmases, candy eggs and jelly beans at Easter. Mama using a breast pump to feed Denny, Jack bringing me lollipops, Arthur playing with his trains in the attic, or bitching at Julia to get out of the bathroom, he needed to go. The way Julia's clothes hung loose on her before she began to fill out. My first nightmare, filled with the color red and the sound of crying and someone pulling at me. It took me forty years to realize I remembered being born. I used to sit on the floor, playing with my blocks, *straining* to understand what you were saying to each other. And nothing was really forgotten, just went dim around the edges. That's what a baby's memory is in a world of giants and gods, a little light in a lot of darkness. But it's all there.

Arthur shifted with a trace of unease. "Do I have to stay for this?"

"It's old trouble, long past." Even Jack looked oddly vulnerable then. "It was years ago."

"Monk. Please don't." Julia kept her eyes on the clay dancer she was gluing to its pedestal. "I never got over it. You don't grow out of these things."

You can grow up. We're doing it now, all of us.

Julia looked helplessly to Arthur. "It's cruel."

When did I learn kindness from any of you? All the crosscurrents, the unspoken anger that never faded: like why Arthur never had any love for Jack; why it was so easy to screw him in that business deal in forty-nine—

"It wasn't meant to be that," Arthur slashed back. "But whatever I did to you, Jack, it wasn't enough. I lived through this once. I won't do it again." Arthur was trembling. "Whatever happened, I made a life. I functioned."

"With distinction," Connie reminded him.

"Don't do this to me, Monk."

I played the family game for years, Arth. Tonight you play mine.

"Very well, then." Connie straightened in the chair, resolute. "Do your worst."

"That's my Con." Jack gave her a rueful grin. "The original Spartan Boy."

"You don't expect me to whine, do you? This will be as interesting for you as any of us." But the cigarette shook in her fingers.

Jack only looked tired. "I don't need this."

"*You* don't!" Julia flared suddenly. "You incredible shit, you caused it all."

"Is that all you remember of me? I was a good stepfather. That wasn't easy in 1934."

"You?" Julia hooted in derision. "You even made passes at me."

"Oh, Jesus." Jack could only shake his head. "I feel sorry for you, Julia."

"You sanctimonious, hypocritical—"

"Julia, sit down." Without raising her voice, Connie commanded the scene. "I believe him. We may have been bad tragedy but never farce."

"Thanks, Con. I love the way you play disdain." A subtle thing passed between Jack and his wife. "Julia always reminded me of a rhinestone duchess."

"Yeah?" Julia fired back. "And what was Shirley?"

"Costume jewelry." Connie's eyes slid to Pat, cool and ironic. "We are talking about Shirley, aren't we?"

That's right, Mama. Not a star but a helluva cameo. *Shirley White? Five minutes, please.*

"No." Arthur lunged for the door. "I'm not going to—"

Yes, you will.

Arthur wrenched at the immovable door. "No!"

Places.

"*No* . . . Monk." The anger softened to a pleading note. "If you ever loved me."

I did. Love's what this is all about. Everything you were became a part of what I am, and I can't afford it anymore.

Mama wrote it at the end of one of Jack's diary notes for that year. There's no mistaking your hand, Mama. Cue, Jack.

Jack took his line bent over the typewriter. "Shirley still typing on the script. I don't know how I'm going to pay her."

Cue, Mama.

Connie's voice gripped tight around a note of pain. "You found a way, but she typed herself right out of your life."

Yes, those were the lines. Didn't mean much to me at ten, less at five, but life was somehow all downhill after that. So we're going to run the scene one last time. 1934! Astaire and Rogers shoot *Top Hat* at RKO. Police shoot Bonnie and Clyde in Oklahoma. A little traveling music . . .

Except for Arthur, the change in them came swiftly. Connie's hair darkened and took on luster as she swelled with pregnancy under the cotton maternity dress. The flesh on her arms and legs tightened and toned. She toasted her children. "Mud in your eye! I'm in the hospital having Johnny. Thirty-six now; not as easy as it was with you kids."

And Jack hammered away at the ancient typewriter. The paunch melted from him, flesh from his jowls, the mild good humor from his eyes. Behind his glasses they gleamed with concentration and desperation. He grabbed a pencil and slashed at the page.

"Too long. Out."

Good script, Dad?

"It's a hundred and fifty bucks." Cigarette smoke curled around Jack's glasses. "They want it quick. The rent's due and the hospital and gas bills. I'm working fast, and that's how good it's going to get."

The machine spattered words onto the paper.

Like a flower closing in time-lapse frames of film, Julia's curves went angular, the whole image raw and unfinished. The blond hair flattened down in a limp Dutch girl cut. She poked hopelessly at it and frowned at the mirror as if she could force growth from it by an act of will. "I'm skinny now, but I'm going to be a knockout. Arth's good-looking already. All the girls are after him. Silly twerps." She gave the hair a last prod to no effect. "Get the phone, Arth. It's for you anyway."

At first there was no change in the sleek figure staring morosely at his shoes. But the tailored uniform seemed not to fit quite so well, wrinkled where it had been smooth over trained muscle. Arthur hung between boy and man, struggling not to go where he must.

"I won't."

Don't be afraid, Arthur. You were never afraid of anything.

The blond head came up in defiance. "Damn right I wasn't. One hundred and thirty-seven missions, never a scratch or a crewman lost. Berlin, Frankfurt, Messina, Ploesti. B-29s off Tinian. Give me a paper kite and I'll fire-bomb Tokyo. I'm the best."

"You were a young god," Connie said lovingly. "You weren't afraid of anything, not even death."

"Why should he be?" Jack drawled. "You filled him so full of that young god stuff, he knew he'd be up for Easter."

Last mission, Colonel.

"Why, Monk?"

Because you were a part of me, and I loved you. Love was natural for me then.

"Yeah." Arthur glanced at his younger brother. "It was easy for me then, too."

Remember it.

Arthur let go and let it happen. The body regressed from athletic to rangy until it balanced between well-built youth and the last of gawky boyhood. He sprang off the bed, movements still jerky. Arthur at just eighteen in white ducks and polo shirt, even more a male copy of Connie than he was to be later on. In the stance of that frame, Landry saw his own at the same age: lanky, durable, late coming to prime, even later in leaving it, age an impossibility. Arthur didn't move, he loped. As the room's illumination came down to pools of light, he hummed and duh-dummed "Love Is Just Around the Corner" in an unstable baritone, snapping his fingers as he lifted one long thigh over a chair and sat down to an unfinished model of the new P-35 pursuit plane. The smell of boy, sweat, and glue pervaded the air.

Julia stepped into her own light: sixteen, in a fuzzy sweater and pleated slacks, unsure of what to do with her large hands. She planted them on her hips as Connie so often did, then picked up the jangling, old-fashioned phone and lifted the receiver off the hook.

"H'lo? Oh. Millie. Arthur? Yeah, just a minute. Arth? Hey, lover boy, it's for you."

Arthur tipped a slim length of balsa with dope and set it into the fuselage. "Who is it?"

"Millie Cavanaugh. To no one's surprise, she wants to talk to you."

"Tell her I'm sick."

"She says when did you get sick?"

"When she called. I'm all gluey and I just had a fart attack. She could smell me over the phone. I'm just getting in the tub."

"Millie, he's taking a bath. By popular request. See you in study hall . . . bye. Listen, Arth: I'm tired of being secretary for your dumb girlfriends."

"Why?" Arthur blew on a dab of glue. "I'd do it for you."

"Sure, all the calls I get." Julia sat down, inspecting her nails with bitter attention. "There's no one around I'd look twice at, but it would be nice to get a call for a movie *once* in a while. What do I get? I get to change Denny's diapers, the little crap factory. Or take Pat out to the park or around the block on his tricycle, and the little fiend goes like a squirrel on a treadmill, never gets tired. I get to answer the phone for my stupid brother when the stupid girls call, because he doesn't give a big rat's ass for any of them."

Julia shot a resentful glance at her preoccupied brother. "Boy, what's he got, anyway? Even Mama and Aunt Alys are like cats over Arth. I wish someone would be a little jealous about me. They will be, someday. I know a looker when I see one, and one of these days, boy, I am going to be a lulu."

She yearned wistfully toward the silent telephone. "In-for-may-shun? Could you please tell me where the goddamned future is?"

Arthur rose from the table and slipped into a clean white shirt, knotting the tie carefully, attacking his stubborn hair with comb and brush. The operation took some time and enormous care, redone three times before his cowlick surrendered to order. He squared his shoulders and chest, checking the view in the mirror.

"That year," Julia remembered, "it was all of a sudden different with Arthur. I mean everything. Quieter, mooning around, borrowing my Russ Columbo records, for God's sake, that he used to hate before. Mama had little John but there was influenza in the infant ward. She couldn't bring him home, and she was frantic, barely home to eat or change clothes. Jack was upstairs most of the time, working on that damned radio script. Cudgeling his brains, as he liked to say. That's when Shirley came around."

Shirley White stood just inside the door in a paisley dress with short, cuffed sleeves, tentative and unsure of herself. Her features coalesced from the deepest parts of Landry's memory: darkish hair worn in the bobbed wave made popular by Ginger Rogers and Myrna Loy. The face was soft, small-mouthed, and not quite pretty. At twenty she had nothing more going for her than youth, but nothing less. Her body sensed its maturity more surely than any awareness in the girl's mind. She hovered, hushed, as if she were in a chapel, not daring to touch anything, her need and vulnerability like a lighted sign.

Jack turned from his work to give her a casual assessment, but Arthur had been riveted to her from the first moment. As she passed him with a bright smile, his eyes followed her, never left her. Arthur swallowed and suddenly seemed awkward in his careful clothes. There was an eloquent difference between his adoration and Jack's concise appraisal. Jack took Shirley in at a glance, saw her whole, knew everything she was or would be. In one form, face, name or another, he'd had Shirley White ten times over. In Arthur's magnetized stare, it was poignantly clear he'd never been so affected by any other person in his short life. His boyhood ended in that look, vanished forever, gusted down the past with Boy Scout merit badges, model planes, and most of what he'd heard, thought, or dreamed.

"There's her sweet self." Julia dropped the words like something unpleasant. "Arthur met her at a picnic and mentioned Jack's writing. Now Daddy has a wide-eyed, willing typist. Go ahead, Monk: take a good look at a rotten shame."

"It wasn't meant to be like that." Shirley worried at her nails in the circle of light. Arthur hovered close, enthralled. "It wasn't meant like that."

In a barely lit corner, worn coat over her shoulders, Connie turned in, drawn tight with strain and a doomed waiting. "The genteel tramp with scruples."

"No . . ." Shirley looked around the room to find some person to batten on for security. Arthur moved closer, touched her. "Hello, Arthur. I wanted to be an actress, and I got to see some talent scouts, but my teeth would cost too much to straighten, and you have to smile a lot in close-ups. Then I tried to write, but I got all the stories back with just printed rejection slips. People who create things are different from plain people. And to think one of them lives right here two blocks from me. Somebody who writes stories that I actually heard on the radio. I'd do anything to learn from him."

"Arthur?" A jet of smoke from the vicinity of the pounding typewriter. "Can she type?"

"It's her job in New York," Arthur volunteered, painfully eager. "She lives just down the street."

A wheezy cough. "Send her up."

Suddenly clumsy, Arthur tried in the same movement to shake Shirley's hand, get closer, and back away. "My stepfather is—uh—yeah. He's upstairs. In his workroom." He adored her openly. "Upstairs."

Shirley moved to the desk as Jack got up and handed her his pages. She took them like an acolyte receiving the Cross.

"I want to be a writer, Mr. Landry. I have so many things to say that I really *feel*, but the words won't come."

Around the cigarette, Jack's smile was patient and not unkind. "Talent's a pump, Shirley. You have to work the handle as hard as you can."

Arthur appealed to Connie hunched in her coat, lighting a fresh cigarette off the last. "Mama, I've met a swell girl."

"That's nice. I can't come home now. The baby's not doing well."

"Her name's Shirley. Shirley White. I'd like you to meet her."

Connie was barely listening. "Yes. Bring her to dinner when we can afford it."

"And he did." Julia grimaced. "Shirley became part of the furniture. Upstairs typing for Jack or out in the yard with Arthur, waiting for Jack to need her. Arthur always had the girls after him, but now he was—I don't know. I wish we'd had time to sit down and talk, but I had my own problems. Anyone who wasn't blind could see it was all one-sided. Not that Shirley was worth it. I mean, at least we had some style. Shirley was like bread without butter."

In a soft center light, Arthur and Shirley danced a slow foxtrot. The girl followed better than Arthur led, but he held her like delicate crystal.

Shirley faded out of the light.

Arthur was alone and radiant. He looked off to Connie absently turning the pages of *Collier's* in a waiting room chair; to Julia trying, with grim determination, to tease her discouraged hair into some kind of body.

The irony transmitted itself to Landry watching. Connie's golden boy, never ignored by anyone for the rest of his life, totally alone now when he cried to share what he felt. He stood alert, vibrant in the soft light. After his death, people remembered a glossed, contained magnificence about Arthur Cole. In this brief moment, there was a beauty as well, perhaps his first and last before the polished doors closed. Arthur looked around expectantly.

"Won't someone *listen* to me?"

No sound but a ticking clock, his own breathing, his bones lengthening. The rapid pattering of the typewriter in Shirley's rhythm, and her sudden, marveling laughter at something.

"Listen . . . someone. Monk?"

Right here, kid. You look great.

"Remember me like this," Arthur pleaded. "You and Connie were the singers, but there's a time when anyone can hear the song. All of a sudden a life just . . ."

Gets bigger.

"Bigger, brighter. Comes together. You can feel it moving in you like Mama did when the baby was big enough, and you know who you are and what you want. And all the songs are possible, and any one of them can be yours. With Shirley, I feel like—I can see the whole future stretching out like a bridge from here in my chest. Boy, have I been a dope! You know what Jack always says about sex being just like going to the bathroom? Okay, it was that way in rumble seats or in the woods, sure, but that's not all. I mean, when I saw her I saw the whole future."

You had to lose her.

"I won't lose her," Arthur denied, joyfully sure of himself. "I never lost anything. Nothing has changed, but it's like all of a sudden everything sparkles. You saw her, Monk. Isn't she wonderful? You would have loved her yourself."

At eighteen I could die over her. Now I might just buy her a drink and invite her to bed.

"Don't talk like that." Arthur glared at his brother with outraged virtue. "You don't do that with the girl you're going to marry."

No, not a nice boy in 1934. You're right. Sorry.

"Arthur?" Shirley's light voice floated down from above, took him by the scruff of his soul, and turned him around as Julia slipped into the light.

"Time for the dance," she said.

For an instant, Arthur's eyes were much older than the young face. "Remember me like this, Monk. There were as many shapes workable in me then as Julia's clay. What I lost then, I never got back." Arthur edged out of the light.

Julia looked after her brother. "He was wrong, of course. There was only one shape for him, and that got broken."

It didn't have to be.

"Everyone isn't you, Monk. Lauren told you that much. Don't pan the show until it's over. You get yours tonight like all of us." Julia turned her head toward a suggestion of preparate movement in the shadows. "Dance time. There's always a dance, even for animal acts like Shirley. What can you do with a girl whose artistic idols are Fannie Hurst," she jerked her head at the desk with weary disgust, "and Jack. Jesus. Places."

Julia stepped back out of the light as Jack, Shirley, and Arthur danced into it, *pas de trois*. Arthur tried to lead and danced a few steps with Shirley alone. There was only kindness in her smile as she disengaged herself and spun away to be caught smoothly by Jack. In his arms, her whole physicality grew more pliant, seeking contact wherever she could. Arthur hovered, waiting, but she didn't return to him. The anticipation dimmed in his eyes, replaced by bafflement, then cruel realization. The open wound was visible in his face as he backed slowly out of the light.

The light flowed with the two dancers. They moved toward the bed, paused and stood close together, swaying with the music.

"I don't write much anymore," Jack said. "Not real writing."

"You should." Shirley brushed her fingers through the gray at Jack's temples. "You're tremendously talented. Do you mind my saying you're very attractive too?"

Jack didn't mind. His eyes lit with more gratitude than hunger. He pulled Shirley closer, kissed her hard. She responded like a moth drawn to light, and they slipped down onto the darkened bed.

Arthur stared after them with a sick horror. He started a sound that Julia cut off as she thrust him away out of the light and turned with hatred and contempt toward the bed from which issued a coy giggle and then a throaty burst of tension and delight.

"You dirty, indescribable bastards. Get the picture, Monk?"

Got it.

"Then let's be tasteful and cut. Lights!"

When the lights shifted, Jack sat on the edge of the bed, moodily fastening the cuffs of his shirt. Her back to him, Shirley stepped into her dress and did it up. Her eyes were placid, his cloudy and troubled. Only the hunger was gone.

"I have to go home," Jack said neutrally, "and get on with what is laughingly called my life."

"Jack, it was—"

"I know," he said. "It was."

"I've never known any man like you, honest." She smiled nervously, smoothing her dress, touching at her hair. "I didn't think this would happen."

Jack turned to regard her over his shoulder. His smile was cool but not unkind. "Yes, you did. You knew it could and you knew it might."

"You must think I'm really awful."

"No . . . no. You're a fine girl. And I'm glad. Good-bye."

Jack moved to the desk in morose preoccupation. Absently, his big hands shuffled the pages together. Shirley slipped into the light behind him. She raised one unsure hand to touch him, then lost her courage. She glanced at Landry.

"Those were all the lines I had. I'm sorry about Arthur, but I never led him on. He was a nice boy."

What time is it now, Shirley?

"Oh. Well." She seemed embarrassed by the question. "This really isn't about me."

God and I have a thing for sparrows. What happened to you?

"I'll be seventy this year," Shirley said. "My husband is retired from the gas company. We get along all right. We had five children, two boys and three girls. Grandchildren now, and I get to see them as often as I can. Sometimes we used to go to the shore for a week in the summer. Nothing much ever happened to us. Good-bye, Jack."

Shirley closed the door softly behind her, trying not to disturb anyone. In the ensuing silence, Landry heard the raw, ugly sound of someone retching behind a closed door. Then Julia confronted Jack, fighting back her tears.

"Do you hear him? Do you know what you did? He remembered this all his life."

"All his life? It's all ahead of him. The best of mine is long gone." Jack rolled a fresh sheet of paper into the old Oliver. "Hate me downstairs, I'm earning the rent."

Julia backed away, fists beating at her sides in rising fury. "We're not going to stay here. We can't stay here." Her narrow head jerked about, looking for a place to go as the sound of retching went on and on behind a door that never opened again. Then the other sound came, the primal cry of another loss, freezing them all as the lights changed, and Jack twisted in his chair as he twisted inside, the pain naked in his eyes, as—

33

—the bald waiting room lights came up on Connie huddled in her old coat, clutching the tiny envelope. She opened the flap with stiff movements and removed the curled lock of reddish hair. It lay in her palm, wearing slowly into reality. Julia rushed in.

"It happened while you were right here. Jack and that little whore. I'm going to Aunt Alys and not coming back. Arthur too, he's already called her."

"What?" Connie looked at Julia through a mist. "Leave?"

"You should see Arthur!" Julia flung at her in a flat voice. "We *have* to get out. Once more old Arth and Julia hit the road like bums who can't make the rent."

"Let me alone." Connie doubled over, moaning. "Get away, don't you understand?"

"Sure," Julia acknowledged bitterly. "What the hell was I to begin with but baggage to be left with Alys, a flunky to feed the babies and change diapers while you played the flaming drama of your life—"

"What do you know about it. What have you lost, either of you?" Connie's voice lashed at Julia like a whip. "You don't know the meaning of the word. My baby's gone."

Arthur came to stand beside his sister—pale but composed. Whatever had cracked in him was mended, smoothed over, and never showed again. "I know, Mama. I'm sorry about that, but this has been coming for a long time. Jack just ended it. Ended it good."

257

Connie held on to Arthur's hand like an anchor. "Arthur, I lost my baby. Nine months I carried him, and now he's dead because the hospital let him die. Don't leave me, Arthur. Alys wants to take you away from me, never had children of her own— "

"Didn't you hear?" Arthur yanked his hand away from her. "Don't you ever hear *anything*? We don't fit anymore. We're not like you anymore."

"Not like me?"

"No."

"Why do you turn against me like this?"

"I'm not against you, Mama. It's just the only thing to do."

"Not like me . . ." When Connie understood it, she rose with sheer murder in her eyes. "You little pup, you'll be mine as long as you live. Mine! Out of my body like John. You want to live with my dried-up sister who can't be anything but a banker's wife?"

"Yes," Arthur said thoughtfully. "But it's not her, it's you. It's the smell of beer through the house and the constant arguing, arguing all night through the walls until we went to sleep just to get away from it. It's the slovenly way of you and the way you hate Aunt Alys because she wanted to be good to us. You're the jealous one, Mama."

"What do you know about love? Either of you. What could you expect from that little tramp? I could have told you what she was from the first day. Please don't go, honey. I'm alone now."

But Arthur had done his crying once and finished with it. "You were never alone," he said as if describing an insect to itself. "To use your phrase, you don't know the meaning of the word."

"Funny, no one's asking *me* to stay," Julia observed. "Love to be asked, just to make an even once."

"You?" At bay, Connie was capable of anything. "You were always a whining, selfish pain."

"You never gave me a chance to be anything else! What you grew into, a dirty old woman who didn't care enough about herself to change her underwear."

"You come to that," Connie admitted. "Expecting too much, feeling too much. I gave up."

"It was disgusting. On the rottenest day of my life, everything in my house was spotless."

"Antiseptic," Connie agreed. "Including very clean children

who never got hugged for the hell of it. That's a poor trade, daughter."

"You think I wanted to have all those kids?"

"Don't play martyr to the married state. Your diaphragm didn't fit right after the first one, but you were usually too drunk to care. You gave up too."

Arthur took his sister's arm. "We're going now."

"Don't go, Arthur."

"I know, Mama: you love me." Arthur's expression was a mask. "I learned about love in this house. It's in Jack's pants. It's in your tight fist, and you'll love us just as long as we stay in that fist, then the hell with us. Time after time you sent us to Alys for your own convenience. We know the way by ourselves now."

"Arthur, please!"

"You never learn anything." Julia shook her head with a sick marveling. "Ask me to stay. Ask me. I might have." She waited through a dogged silence while Connie only looked to Arthur. "I never told you, never even admitted to myself how much you hurt me and how I hated you. I put your picture on the mantel and all the coats of arms on the walls and told my children how wonderful you were. Later on, we seemed to let it go. We drank and laughed together and I listened to your problems with Monk. But we never touched or kissed or socked each other in the eye. You should've asked me to stay, but then you never had much use for women."

"Let's go, Julia," Arthur said. "Whatever life we had, this is when it started." He acknowledged his stepfather at the desk. "You were right about women, Jack. Just like going to the bathroom. You don't get hurt because you're not really there. You pick for looks and the hell with the rest."

Connie's children backed out of her light, leaving her to age and thicken in her shapeless housecoat. She put the little envelope on the table and poured the last of the beer into her glass.

"There was a commitment in me, Jack. Children were a result but you were the only thing I loved more than a stage. All my eggs in one basket with a great big hole in it. If I was cruel, it came from hurt. If I was too dramatic about every-thing, that was the way I felt about life: too much, too hot. But nobody takes what's mine."

Her dark eyes gleamed with tears. "But they have . . . and I can't have him back. The dirty, incompetent doctors, and you with that—I hope you enjoyed her."

Jack looked down at the desk. "It had nothing to do with you, Con."

"You never had the strength to say no."

"Or you to put a cork in the bottle."

"I *need*ed something."

"And I didn't?" Jack defended himself. "Most guys would've walked out on you. They killed me after '29, but I stayed."

"Don't whine." Connie turned away in disgust. "When I left you, I wish I'd kept on going, but where could I go with no money and two kids?"

"Was that the only reason?"

"You need a better one?"

"Yeah. You loved me," Jack said. "We never stopped sleeping together."

"What am I going to do when you wake me up in the middle of the night, yell for the kids?"

"Oh . . . Jesus Wept."

"*He* wept? You put a knife in me and broke it off." Connie's fingers twitched toward the beer bottle. "While I was in the hospital waiting for Johnny to die, you—" The bitter old woman hurled the bottle with an arm that would never lose its strength. It shattered against something. "Your son is in the envelope. And that's how the future was."

"That's how the future was." Jack sighed. "A little love, a lot of broken glass. And Monk just old enough to be in the middle."

"Monk! Come here!"

Connie pushed her beer-sodden bulk up from the chair. "Oh God, I'm stronger than all of you, have to be, but something's broken in me. It hurts too much to love like this and it's death when you lose. But Monk is me born again, he'll be like me. He'll love what I love and hate that son of a bitch as much as—MONK! I said come *here*, damn you."

The hoarse voice broke on a sob. Passing, it left a hardness that rarely softened again. "Patrick Landry, you come when I call you. Go get me some beer at the store. Two quarts, tell'm to charge it the same as always, and don't give me that funny look like you're so tired of going to the store, you little weasel. I'll slap you silly. I have to love you, but I don't like you. That—" Connie sat down again with theatrical timing, "I cannot manage today. Get my beer." She turned the vital, commanding eyes on her husband. "Do you have anything to say about the way I raise my remaining children?"

"Why don't you leave Monk alone," Jack said with a growl of disgust. "He's growing into a nervous wreck."

"Monk adores me," Connie stated with drunken certitude. "He loves *me*."

"And that's a victory?"

"You know what he thinks of you. You pathetic ham, anything busting out of her brassiere you can't keep your hands off her."

"Never as many as you thought," Jack admitted wearily, "but sometimes it was easier than making love to a hanging judge."

"Bastard. Monk knows what you are."

Jack swung around to her in the chair. "I wouldn't lean too hard on him, Con. You'll lose him."

"Never!"

"Don't push, Con." Spoken gently for the truth it was. "He'll turn."

"What would you know about Monk?" Connie jeered. "You barely speak to each other."

"That doesn't mean I don't watch him." Jack fed a fresh sheet of paper to the Oliver. "He's not as tough as you, but he's smarter."

The typewriter chattered. Connie cursed with a low, dark passion. The two sounds blended and went on for years.

34

The lights brightened from iso-
lated areas to full stage. Julia sat in her place at the table. As
Landry watched, his sister bloomed through the last of adolescence to handsome womanhood.

"That's enough," Julia decided, but the change went on
without her consent to bitterness in the lines about her
mouth.

The agonized boy who had been Arthur straightened, poised,
buried vulnerability under a hard aura of command. Like Julia,
he couldn't control it entirely. The lips curled with a telltale
cynicism.

Julia placed the exquisitely turned dancer on the table.
"Finished."

All of them now as Landry remembered them most clearly:
Connie fleshy and brooding, Jack sixtyish, his brother and
sister cased in their hard elegance.

Was that it, then?

"That was it." His mother nodded. "Arth and Julia left. Jack
took every hope I had and broke it like that bottle."

"No one ever hurt me again. I did the hurting." The words
sounded as burned-out as Arthur looked.

"And I found the home I always needed," Julia said. "A fine
husband, a picture-book house. A fortress where no one could
ever throw me out."

"None of you could deal with life without doing *East Lynn*,"

Jack growled. "And I was the heavy. I lived to be eighty-five. The view's clearer from there."

Arthur, was that it?

"It helped not to feel," Arthur answered. "The world doesn't care how you feel, a war doesn't. You rev up and fly, give orders and they're obeyed. That becomes habit."

And the women you married?

"Lived with, occupied space with. They never knew I wasn't there. Then one day, I looked in the mirror—"

"Five wives?" Jack sprawled his long legs out from the desk chair. "Four of them must've gotten wise sometime." The cigarette bobbed in his lips. "I lived forty years longer than you, Arth. You learn to forgive a lot, including yourself."

"Listen to him," said Connie with classic Hawkins contempt. "The Oracle of the Open Fly."

"When you're that old, you can't even find it. You can't do much but sit and think. Realize what you've always loved." The flint of Annie and Fiona softened in Jack's eyes. "Birdie was fun and no trouble, and I walked away from her with a nice memory. I could never walk away from you."

"You bet you couldn't." Connie laughed with the truth of it. "I could hate your guts five times a day, and I did, and I do. But somehow I couldn't *not* care. You didn't always have to wake me up."

Jack glowed under the compliment. "I thought you'd never say it. The defense rests."

"Why lie now? I'm dead," Connie measured herself. "I was stubborn but not stupid. We were always . . . involved. I knew how much you needed me. You never wrote a good line without running into the kitchen to share it with me. 'How does this sound, Con? Listen to this!' Never came home with some small bit of good news without telling it to me before your coat was off."

"Wait a minute," Julia interrupted. "These aren't the right lines. You left him after Shirley. You took the boys. How goddamned many times afterwards, *years* after, did you tell me you wished you'd stayed away?"

"I know. I couldn't."

"Neither could I, Con." The fact passed between Jack and Connie like an exchange of belated gifts. "Wanted to a hundred times. I never even got to the door."

Julia struggled with disbelief. "You're saying now, after all the years you knocked him and tore him apart—you're trying to tell me you *loved* this viper? That's not love, it's inertia."

"We're doing truth tonight, aren't we?"

Julia crossed her arms. "I do not believe it."

"I suppose not. You always had a marvelous density, Julia. Along with a passion for middle-class values."

"My husband never betrayed *me*," Julia shot back. I never let him feel that sure of himself," she added with dry-husk honesty. "He worked for me and provided for the children until the day he died. And you always made him feel like an oaf."

"I never denied Werner's qualities, only his conversation whenever possible. Not his fault, really. I never got along with Germans."

"Oh—*Ma*ma."

"Not that it matters now." Connie set down her empty glass. "We're out of beer anyway, and I don't suppose Monk feels like going for more."

No. I've heard it all.

"The Great American Family." Arthur turned his cool, superior smile on his brother. "Not nice but memorable."

All of that; and all of what you were, strength, weakness, high humor and brittle pride—the destructiveness, the bitter, brutal *perversity* of you all—

"Listen to that, Con," Jack said with paternal pride. "And you worried when he flunked English. But get on with it, Monk. We're close to curtain."

Cool it, I'm serious. It's all come down to me. To our dear Patrick, we leave our colors that he wear them. No thanks. They don't go with me anymore, but I can't stop caring or mourning. The *waste* of you. Not what you did or suffered or why, but that you let it twist you for the rest of your lives and so much of mine. Turned Arth into an icebox. Made Julia vicious and frail, so that she needed to create a fantasy she could live in but never leave. Oh, Julia—the lies you fed me out of the same bottle you guzzled from, and didn't you love the power. I was the green kid and you were the authority: putting Mama down, telling me she never loved Jack, never even married him. That Den and I were illegitimate—

"Julia, you didn't!" Connie was genuinely shocked. "You were at the wedding."

"Indeed she was," Jack recalled gleefully. "Emptying everyone's glass when they weren't looking."

"Don't I remember *that!*" Connie chortled. "You were sick all over your white frock, you precocious little lush. Mother-love failed me. I couldn't help thinking that if you died right there, I'd bury you in it."

That's when I began to back off, Julia. I loved you, but you were a closed door who needed lies to live.

Julia touched the clay dancer. "For me it was real."

And you, Arthur. Jack did you dirt once, but you screwed up the rest of your life yourself. It could have been great. Day by day, moment to moment, you could have *lived*. Jesus, and *I* was the spineless one? I've broken and healed more times than you got laid. People with half your deck to deal with do it every day. But not Golden Boy. By the time you headed for that motel bathroom, you were a miserable excuse for a human being, worse than Jack, caused more pain with none of the remorse. And when you tried to add up what passed for a life, it didn't compute.

"No, it didn't." Arthur was thoughtful. "What's the use?"

What?

"You wanted to know what I wrote on the tiles," Arthur said simply. "Tried to write. That was it: 'What's the use?' A month before that I was asking another question: What's the meaning? Still involved enough to ask. One day my wife was sitting at her dressing table. Quite beautiful; I married her for that. She glanced up at me in the mirror, and I knew—I *knew* she didn't see anything of me but the surface, possibly not much of that.

"That afternoon I was reading a report in my office at the base and suddenly the words made no sense at all. What's the connection? I asked. Twenty-seven years as an officer; trained to be sure that everything was trim, tallied, compensated for, or it was someone's butt. But the words meant nothing. Where's the point? I said.

"A few days later, I was flying alone over the field, just logging my flight time for the month, and I had the feeling again—terrifying this time—that it wasn't an airplane, nothing whole, just pieces of metal and plastic in someone's idea of order. Loose pieces that someone else told me made sense, and I was floating through space with less purpose than a bird. A bird is at least hungry, going somewhere. Down below me were millions of particles that someone said made sense. And if I nosed the ship down and ran her into the ground, that would make as much sense as anything else. Loose pieces.

Everything. Us. Unconnected. Where's the plan? I wanted to know.

"I tried to make love to my wife; actually tried to love her, to see and feel something more than a surface of particles, some reason to be there beyond motor responses. Nothing. She wondered if something was bothering me; not that she was very concerned. *Where's me?* I asked then. Don't you see? I couldn't stand or afford to function badly, never went up in a ship I hadn't preflighted from nose to rudder. I should have gone to the flight surgeon."

"Why didn't you?" Julia wondered.

"Why didn't I? That at least made hard sense. A wing commander can arrange for therapy, sure. And get straightened out and marked 'duty' again, but what do I tell him? That all of sudden nothing in the world including me makes any sense anymore? One way or another, it might be remembered when the promotion list came up. *That* made sense too. Once you're passed over at command level, you might as well put in for retirement, you've had it. What's the point? I asked.

"Nothing came together anymore. I couldn't understand people when they talked to me. Some of them must have had a great time gossiping. 'What's with old Iron Ass, he's flying in a fog this month.'

"One day in the Officers' Club, I was feeling really desperate. I needed to do something that proved I was *there.* Initiate *some* act with consequences. I picked up somebody's wife, bought her a few drinks. One of those silly southern women who have to impress you with their virtue and desirability at the same time. 'A lady on the street and a whore in bed,' as she put it, trying to look lascivious and virginal in the same breath, while I coped with nausea.

"Hell, I did what she wanted, made a date to meet her next day at a motel far enough off base to be discreet. Why not? Bitter, brutal perversity, Monk? I couldn't understand half of what she said to me. It made as much sense as anything else. And it was hardly the first time.

"I got to the motel too early. Went to the bathroom to clean up, thinking *where's the point?* I looked in the mirror, and that was the end. I wasn't there. Just . . . not there. Why should I be after all those years away. When I got into the tub with the convenient complimentary razor blade, I was thinking: *Why not drop the other shoe?* Which didn't seem unreasonable at all, even when the water went from pink to red around me. Oh—

out of habit, there was a moment when I felt I ought to live. So I posed the last question. *What's the use?"*

"Use?" Connie echoed. "I gave you that life. I was eighteen. Nothing went into it but love and hope, and you let it go down the drain like Monk's whiskey. On the worst day of my life—"

"Yes, Mama." Arthur cut her off, weary and bored. "The worst, sickest, most beaten. The last sixteen years of your life you didn't do anything but rot. What did they get you?"

"I mattered!"

"Oh?"

"I *was*."

"So was I," Arthur capped his argument. "Finally. In the act of denying, I knew I was. Or had been. By the time I reached that tub I'd been dead for years. Finally knew it, that's all."

Connie lowered her head, not to see him. "You shame me. Monk was right. Waste."

Arthur rose and smoothed the battle jacket over his narrow waist. "You and Monk were always so intense."

"Terribly alive," Jack murmured. Julia glanced at him in surprise.

"That's rather perceptive coming from you."

"Never occurred to me when I was living with them," Jack admitted, "but very true. Painful people."

"Well, I, for one, am exhausted from all this truth," Julia declared, rising and straightening her skirt. "I could really use a drink."

"For once in my death, so could I." Arthur looked at his brother. "It's not worth tears, Monk."

I can't help it. The waste. I loved you, you bastard.

" 'Love, you bastard.' Isn't that us?" Arthur cocked his head to one side, tasting the sentiment. "Love and curses. We always damned each other with a sense of style. Does the door open now?"

Yes. It's all said. All remembered.

"Waste!" Connie spat at Arthur.

"Don't you remember, Mother? I was a hero." Arthur opened the door and vanished through it.

"Wait for me," Julia called after him. "Good-bye, Monk." Hard as love was for her, she managed a crippled affection. "You were my little brother and you were good sometimes."

You too. I hated to put that flower on the casket and watch you go into the ground.

"The funeral was lovely. I arranged it beforehand. So very tasteful," Julia judged with visible satisfaction. "I like tradition. Good-bye, Mama. Think me a kiss sometimes."

"The kiss was always there, but you know me and women. Come have a drink sometime," Connie invited. "What the hell, we can argue."

"Love to." Julia bent to kiss her mother and disappeared after Arthur.

35

"**W**ell, Monk." Jack heaved out of the desk chair and put the cover on the typewriter with a final pat. "You made it. Always said you'd click. You've got the editors coming to you. And I taught you."

I wish you could have taught yourself. How many times did you say it? They cut the heart out of you. Cut away his buttons and they tore away his stripes and they gelded poor Jacky of his pride, dum-duh-dum. Always had to be the Big Man, always a little too careful to be noticed.

"While we're talking disappointments," Jack reminded him, "didn't I have a few?"

Face it, Jack: you *were* all you could be, a middling talent and a selfish child. So selfish you were pure with it like a Bach fugue. Shirley and all the other women, all the pathetic, transparent posturing—aspirin for an aching ego. I'm not judging you—

"You could've fooled me," his father noted.

No. Myself. Doing the same thing so often, going the same route. No wonder we did comedy. I watched you both die, and yours was the worst because I was old enough to . . . betray you with understanding. Not your death but your self-pity without proportion or comprehension. Because you couldn't stay on top. I watched you shuffle in your old slippers toward that death, and you never knew you were ten times the man when you died than the best night you ever played at the Palace. All your life, people said—even Mama—there goes a man. I wouldn't contradict them even now, but it didn't mean a damned thing to you when you weren't down center anymore.

You said every family does its own casting. Arthur was the hero, Julia the proper one, Denny the sweet guy, and me? I guess it was for me to stand a little apart and add you up. All of you in your pungent glory.

I know you all now, all the way down. You're mapped, plotted, containable. I love you deeply, but one way or another, none of you could take defeat, swallow it and get on with life. I'm not going to play your script anymore.

"I assume we can still visit now and then," Connie said.

When you're invited, Mama, but keep it polite. You're guests in *my* house now.

"You're right," Connie agreed with her husband, "he is a painful person."

"I always said he could really kill 'em off."

You won anyway, Jack. I'm good. You taught me. And Denny's writing now.

Jack brightened as if a bank of lights had risen on him. "Denny? Do you tell me that? Did you hear *that*, Con? Is he any good?"

He will be. He sounds like you.

Jack actually blushed with pleasure and pride. "Oh, well now. Like me?"

More than I ever did. You always used hyperbole like a sniper. His aim's not that good yet, but he can learn.

"He will if you take him in hand." Jack was instantly purposeful. "Teach him, Monk. Make him write *carefully*. Whattya know," he glowed. "Little Slobbotz with grits in his hair. Lord, that kid could make you laugh."

"All my children were exceptional," Connie asserted, "and only figurative bastards."

Jack held out a hand to his wife. "Coming, Con?"

"I'll be along."

"Come on, Con." Jack glanced prophetically from Connie to Monk. "The two of you were always bad medicine together."

"I think Monk wants me for next-to-closing. Right?"

You got it, Mama.

Jack shrugged and gave it up. "I'll wait for you, Con. But don't chew the scenery." His grizzly-bear bulk filled the doorway and was gone.

"Well, Monk."

Well, then.

"Do I get killed off too?"

It's harder with you. Harder to . . . separate us.

"Yes. I could adore Arthur without pain, but you were always a war."

I was you. That simple. I owe you for the passion and the music, the feelings too big for words that got written because Jack showed me how.

"That simple." She laughed soundlessly. "Everything I was—generous, cruel, possessive, arrogant, unforgiving. We never forgot a kindness or an injury, least of all from each other. Everything too big. We should have been opera singers."

Or hand grenades. Everything good in us had its own dingy demon to turn it against the people we loved. Who loved us. Like Lauren. No more, Mama.

Places. We're going to play the end.

Oddly, Connie seemed to hesitate, reluctant. "No. Live your life and let me go."

Places. Nineteen forty-five. You're on.

"Can't you leave it? That was the worst of me. I was dying."

And you'd take as much as you could down with you.

"So you want to take me on. All right." Connie got up and strode to the door with a hint of her youthful, energy. "Then let's do it in period. There's someone who deserves an entrance, but you never brought him on tonight."

Not Den. He wasn't part of it.

Connie shook her head. "I don't mean Denny. I said the original cast. You and me. And I'll still play you against the wall." Connie flung open the door and turned with her old timing. "Places, Monk."

Landry stared at the door that closed behind her.

You and me.

There was the sound of weeping, raw as Arthur's, from as deep a loss.

The boy hunched awkwardly in the desk chair, far too thin for his height, gangly legs and outsized feet twisted about the base. His narrow back was to Landry, but every half-formed feature, angle, or twitch of the adolescent body was remembered from the inside out: the large, restless hands, the neglected teeth that hurt, the savage day-long headaches that left him blind and nauseated; the manic bursts of energy spaced by thick fogs of self-destructive gloom.

He resembled Connie more than anyone else, a hint of Jack in the long bones and big hands. Now and then in the movement of the head, a darker, half-defined Arthur, the hair uncombed and bushing up over the unformed face. Connie's mouth soft and uncertain but shut down tight around his cigarette and the perils of a hurting world—sure, as only sixteen can be, that the world was a crowded bus with no room for him even if he had the fare.

Weeping now over a loss too great to contain. Doing it alone.

Landry's heart went out to the boy. *Could I picture Denny so well in an instant and forget you so completely? You never could shrug anything off, always absorbed it. All right, Mama, we'll play the end the way it was.*

Hello, Monk.

36

The boy wiped at his wet cheeks, ashamed to be caught with his guard so far down. He gave Landry a wary inspection, then splayed a big hand over a face. "Who're you?"

You wouldn't know me, not yet.

"Sorry." Another sleeve-wipe at the thin cheeks. "Boy, you caught me at a b-bad time."

The worst. She died yester—

"Please . . . don't."

And you've got to leave, right?

"I don't know what I gotta do," the boy managed in a strangled voice. "Don' even know who I am half the time. I can't stay here, but I'm old enough to leave school 'n' I will. Get a job, maybe the army like Arth. I don' know." Monk dragged deep on the butt and put it out. "Nothing to stay here for."

You learned a lot this year: people really die and love doesn't always get loved back. You learned to be alone.

Monk's foot began to jiggle, his fingers drumming on his knee, nervous energy not yet focused to vitality.

"I know what I did."

He masked a fresh upwelling of emotion, taking another cigarette from the pocket of his rumpled white shirt. Like his mother, he was already a chain smoker and an instinctive performer, covering his feelings with an act. His idols were John Garfield and Bogart. The cigarette dangling from the

273

corner of his wry-twisted mouth gave a flip shrug to the words
in the best tradition of Warner Brothers. He'd even learned
Garfield's trick of holding the lighted match while he talked, to
keep attention riveted on him.

"I used to believe in God until I was fourteen. Then I began
to wonder if He believed in me. Score: nothing to nothing."

Corny, kid. Get down to it.

Monk lit the cigarette when the match was almost burning
his fingers. "Last night . . . when it happened, I prayed. I
don' know, To Whom It Might Concern: please take care of
her. That's all I could think of. Take care of her."

And forgive you?

Monk nodded, still wary, but grateful for the understanding. "Yeah. I watched them carry her out on a stretcher. She
was moanin', she was in awful pain. I know she was in pain
because she got out of bed in the afternoon and . . . somehow
got's far as the kitchen. She didn't know me. Just made that
sound like an animal makes 'cause it can't talk but knows it's
dying. I wanted to do something and there was nothing except
to get her back into bed and wait for . . . I don' know what.
And listen to her. She shoulda been in the hospital already,
but it came too quick."

Wait for what, Monk?

The boy crushed out his cigarette and squirmed in the chair,
hands twisted together. "Nothing."

For what you caused?

"Whatta you know about it?"

For what you think you caused?

You God or something? I told you, I don't believe in God.
She did, and lookit the way God let her go. Whimperin' on a
stretcher like a sick dog. And . . . and I *saw* that, had to look at
it, and I said that's the only way you go out of this house."

You are a ham, just like her. But that wasn't it, Monk.

"I killed her."

No.

"I killed her." The truth shuddered out of the boy still
too frail to house it. "*I* did. I gotta go now, I can't stay
here. I killed her."

No, you didn't. You'll believe that someday. You'll understand. You can start now: you didn't—

The boy looked at Landry in embarrassment and surprise.
"You're cryin' too. I never saw a man cry before."

Julia said I'd get mine tonight.

But still a curiosity to Monk, something not done. "Doesn't it make you kinda 'shamed? Men aren't s'posed to cry. Denny does when he's mad. I do alone sometimes. But not men."

For sure not Bogart or Garfield. American heroes: nobody cries in a war movie.

"You gotta be tough." Monk said it the way his time had taught him. "I don' know if I'll ever make it."

Mama wasn't tough, just angry. And a fool. The doctor told her the blood pressure could pop like a balloon anytime. Remember that? Remember what he said? No booze, not even half a glass. Remember the diet he gave her? She pinned it up in the kitchen and that was the last time she looked at it. So who killed her?

The boy shook his head, miserable.

People do what they want to, Monk.

"What's that mean?"

It's hard to understand, the last thing people want to understand, so they lay the baggage on whoever will carry it. You carried Mama's far too long. How did you kill her? Come on, kid, tell me how.

Silence.

Come on; you said it. You must believe it. Tell me how.

Monk unwound himself from the chair. He moved awkwardly as he sat, hands thrust in his pockets, thin shoulders hunched, nothing of him focused, all scattered and diffuse. The face that had been a kaleidoscope of emotions a moment before showed only bafflement now. "I don't know."

Sure you do.

"I don't *know.*"

Think about it.

"Whadda *you* care anyway?"

You better believe I care. Was it a killing or a betrayal?

The boy's eyes darted at Landry, then away. ". . . Thought of that."

Not even betrayal. You want to name it?

"Lemme alone."

Think! You loused me up for years not thinking. You remember well enough.

"No."

One day, one moment. The two of you were so close; one Corsican twin stabbing the other and both bleeding from it. And neither of you could forgive because there was too much love.

"Love." Monk mouthed the word as if he'd like to be familiar with it but wasn't yet. "I mean, like in the movies people love each other so easy."

Especially the musicals. Two verses, a chorus, and the future's all gold. Not like that, is it?

"Why does—why did she have to come down on me so hard all the time, always me?"

You want a big fat headline? Because there's no real love without it. Sooner or later, if the love goes deep enough, it finds the other face.

"Oh boy," Monk jeered, trying to distance himself from the truth of it. "You talk like you were God or something. How d'you know everything I'm feeling? Boy, do I get told by everybody, like my ass is under glass or something. Everybody knows more than me. Mama, Julia. My brother-in-law, Werner." The pathetic puppy-face was lit by a flash of insight. "Julia says Werner knows a lot about sex 'n' stuff like that—but I'm beginning to think different. Tells a lot of jokes about it, not too funny. Tells me to take cold showers when I get horny. So I did. I got in the shower horny and came out horny and cold—what's so funny?"

That. The way you said it.

Exasperated: "Well, it's *true*."

That's why it's funny.

Monk looked tragic and misunderstood. "That's what I mean. Nobody takes me seriously. I never know if people are laughing with me or at me. Just wish Mama would leave me alone."

You got it. That's the scene. Look at her when she speaks to you.

"Look at me when I speak to you!"

I told you: one day. One moment. Not a killing, not even a betrayal. Say it, Monk.

The boy squirmed. "No . . ."

Then see it.

"I *saw* it," Monk suffered.

"You think you can take me on? You think you're stronger than me?"

Monk's head twisted away. "Shut up, Mama. Leave me alone." It tore out of the skinny boy, too strong for him to hold back any longer. He stumbled about to face Connie, against the wall where she'd always driven him, knowing he'd always come back to love her. One day, one moment when she was wrong.

"What did you say to me?" Connie hovered, a hard ugly gleam in her eyes, everything strong in her corrupted to this last bullying of the last thing she had to hold on to. The squat old woman enjoying the last of her power, knowing she'd win; pathetic enough to have to win even like this before the end.

"Did you tell *me* to shut up?"

The gangling boy was stunned by his own rebellion as something inconceivable. But it had shocked him at last into the clarity to see what she'd become: no longer a mentor or guide but a bully, aware of her own decline but unable to accept it. No resignation, only bitterness and cruelty, the need to dominate, clawing all the way down.

"God damn you." She moved in on him as Monk stood, shaking with loss and a rage frightening as her own.

"Don't, Mama."

"Don't what?" She slapped him hard. "Don't what?" Again. *"What?"*

"I'm tellin' you, get off me—"

"What! What! What!"

She smashed him back and forth across the face, too far gone to heed the warning or hear the sudden, feral snarl. Monk's long arm shot out, gripping her fleshy throat. The fingers began to vise. "I said *off.*"

Connie's eyes popped, but he held her at arm's length, squeezing tighter. She clawed futilely at the grip in his fingers. She managed a sound, an almost comic squawk more of surprise than anything else, and then she had no more air.

For a tortured instant, Monk held her impaled on the arm, then flexed with instinct and pent-up fury. He spun her about and caught her neck in the crook of one ropy arm. Every word was a sob.

"Don't—you—ever—touch—me—again. Ever." Tightening. "Ever!" A last brutal jerk and he pushed her away from him. Connie stumbled a few steps, holding her throat, breath rasping in her constricted windpipe. When she turned around, Connie still couldn't believe it.

"You dared do that to me?"

Blind with tears, incoherent, Monk still couldn't go to her. He could never do that again. "No more, Mama. Keep away from me."

They stared at each other, enemies across a hostile ground. Landry saw them whole, the shattered boy and the dying woman in this last battle, destructive and vicious as both of them could be. No truce at the end and no one to love either of them but Pat Landry.

Say it, Monk.

The boy only choked: "I can't."

Try.

"She hurt me too much."

Then I'll do it for you. We love you, Mrs. Landry. But it's your turn, so listen up.

Connie turned eyes full of bewildered hurt on him. "Why do you do this to me? To *me!*"

Because you're thick enough to have to ask. He forced this distance because you wouldn't give it. No one gives all the way down, not the last of themselves. They can't. You try to claim that—and you did, you desperate little bully—and anyone will bite back.

You broke things, Mama. There was something too big, too clumsy and brutal about you. You tore at people like a child with a favorite toy that has to be banged on something until it snaps, and now you cry with a child's loss.

Look at him, Connie, your own flesh. You couldn't break him all the way, couldn't stop him from growing away from you, hard as you tried. All you could do was twist him, make him think he hated your guts and carry *that* suitcase for years. Cripple him, make him temporary with every other woman because he never finished with you.

"He did this out of *spite!*" Connie wailed. "He's all I had left to live for—"

Liar! You can't play life that way.

"—and now he turns on me."

What would he know of loving but what you showed him? The defiance you threw at the world until hitting and hating became reflex.

"*What the hell does he know—?*"

Hell he knew.

"—the pain I'm in all the time."

You ask that of him? He knew it. Couldn't escape it. Monk was the one who had to watch your deaths, you and Jack; lived them minute by minute, unable to look away or forget one second of it. The Greek messenger whose function it was to see it all and live to tell it over. Worse, to understand it. To carry the scars from the broken bottle-end of your life. Look at him, Mama.

"I . . . can't."

Why not? With that nearsighted love of yours that had to pull everything up too close. Jesus Christ, you almost killed him. You weren't ever tough, just hard. That's why you were never a star. The world ate at you and you had to claw back. You want tough, there's Lauren. You can hurt her—and maybe I have, beyond forgiveness—but you can't break her or make her live anyone's idea of life but her own.

"Julia was right," Connie mumbled, buried in her own tragedy. "You are a bastard."

I'm you. One of your thoroughbreds. Your term, not mine. For thoroughbreds you sacrifice everything else to get the right lines. God knows why. The world is a dog act: they use mutts because mutts are smarter.

"Vicious."

We love you, Mrs. Landry.

"Vindictive."

We're you. Monk and I—every line we wrote, every part we played, every too-fierce loving was you. It's almost morning, Mama, and there's another caring I've owed too long. Put on your best costume, pick a good year, and get off with a hand.

Connie tried but her strength was gone. She tried by will alone to force the change, tear the years away from her coarsened, ruined body, but they were too heavy. "I can't do it," she gave up. The last life still glowed in the large dark eyes as she lifted them to Landry. "Could you believe in me for a moment, Mr. Landry? I seem to need it."

My privilege, Mother.

Landry took her hand—felt it strengthen and firm in his as the years and flesh melted away from her face and body. She never looked lovelier in the emerald gown, humming with pleasure and vitality. Connie lifted from the chair with the effortlessness of taut muscle, driving the brush hissing through the lustrous hair.

"I'm opening at the Winter Garden tonight," she brimmed, "and I think about five minutes before curtain, I'll peep out at the house and whisper: you all just sit back and watch, because I'm going to knock your *eyes* out. And then Jack and I will go to the Palais Royal. Paul Whiteman's there, and if we ask him, he'll play 'Avalon' for us."

She pinned up the shining hair, winking mischievously at

her son. "I don't know if I'm going to marry him. Sometimes I want that. I always fall so hard . . . then the overture starts and, hell, they've all got to wait in the wings."

The vibrant young woman flowed to the door, the weight of her coiled on springs. A slight frown shadowed her face when she looked at young Monk.

"Denny will be a brawler but soft inside, too easily surrendered. This one, they'll bite down into softness and find me. Take care of your brother, Monk."

She gave her hair a last reassuring pat. "You know me now, Mr. Landry. Call me when you need a star. But, please, no sweet old mothers. You don't ask a forest fire to play a match."

The door closed behind Connie. It seemed to Landry there ought to be applause. She'd expect it.

Monk said with a kind of awe: "I didn't know she was ever that beautiful."

You knew the worst of her. Now you've seen the best. She was worth it all.

"She died 'n' I never told her . . . I should've taken *care* of her."

The boy wiped his face with a sodden sleeve. "If I'd been better to her . . ."

You God or something? All those years you were the one who stuck close while the others dropped away. Arthur, Julia, Jack retreating year by year, Denny too young to understand and not interested anyway. You were there because you couldn't imagine being anywhere else. Then one day you could, and she couldn't take that.

Monk struggled with the truth. "There was a cruel streak in her. First I thought it was all my fault. But she enjoyed it."

Yeah, she did. Maybe she wasn't that mature yet. Man, I'm fifty, and *I* don't know if I'm grown up all the way. If she'd lived longer, you'd still have to play this scene. Maybe then Mama would be strong enough to let go. Some people never do. If you came out like hamburger through a grinder, you still made it, because you *were* as strong as Connie. And as much of a goddamned hardhead. Part of her loved that, part of her had to tear at it.

The boy only looked confused. "Don't get that at all."

Not now, but you will. Gimme a smile, kid.

"Ain't got one right now."

Please? You were the one I really short-changed in the love department.

"Boy, you really put a lot on a guy." Monk took a deep breath to fill his narrow chest. "Hell, it could be worse. No. On second thought, it couldn't."

Landry recognized the familiar fuck-you grin. Monk flopped on the desk chair, loose-jointed parts twisting into the adolescent contortions natural to him. There wasn't much of anything definite yet in the young face, but Landry recognized the capacity for survival. "Oh—shit and carry eight," Monk growled.

Think you'll live?

"Yeah, I'll live. But then there's the good side."

What's that, Mr. Bones?

"I won't be young forever. I hate being young." Monk squirmed. "I wanta grow up so—so I'll know how to handle things. Know what t'do. Some people say that's foolish. You oughta hear some of these jokers: 'These are the happiest days of your life. Enjoy them.' Like being grateful for a toothache."

You're right. Being sixteen is what makes reincarnation unattractive.

"Boy, does it ever. That's a good line." Monk brightened. " 'Being sixteen'—maybe I could just walk in at thirty."

That's even better.

"Yeah, I write almost every day now. But I don't know." Monk pushed the rebellious hair back from his forehead, which furrowed in dubious reflection. "Thirty's awful old."

Then you better get your ass in gear, hotshot.

Landry felt a marvelous, laughing love for the kid who moved like a Tinker Toy but with an eye to see that the world was sent to him with postage due and parts missing.

Monk unfolded from the chair in sections, jittering with nervous energy. "Yeah, I better get going. Just wish I knew the rules better."

You know enough for sixteen. You see the difference between what is and what should be. You know the people who warble about golden youth are assholes, that life's not a ball and you ain't Cinderella. But listen to the music anyway, because you're gonna make up your own dance to it. You'll bandage your cuts and soak your bruises, love the fine women and the good friends when they come, and be wise enough to let them go when they have to.

"I'm not a leaving kind of guy," Monk said, meaning it.

That's not what I said. Not possessing or owning, but love I'm talking about.

Monk regarded his older self gravely. "That why it hurts so much?"

It hurts everyone the same way. The difference is what they do with it. Sooner or later they make the decision to live with the hurt or play it safe. Jack said it once: "Most people live five-watt lives." He might have himself if he hadn't collided with a forest fire. Connie passed that on to you, blessing or curse. She couldn't handle it. Maybe you can. You'll love hard and leave hurting. But it'll be a *grand* show, Monk.

"No," Monk insisted stubbornly. "I'm not the kinda guy who leaves."

It's not that, dummy—

"I felt that's what you meant." Monk gangled his skinny frame to the door. "Did they leave you or you leave them? I couldn't leave anyone I loved. I was there to the end with Mama. I watched them carry her out, and I never got to tell her how much I loved her. I never wanta go through that again."

Wait a minute. What did you say?

Monk was already half out the door, twisting around to nod at Landry. "I gotta go 'n' see dumb Denny's not gettin' into trouble."

What was that you said about leaving?

Monk only shrugged; the thing was self-evident. "I couldn't. I could never leave."

But you *did*. All through your life you left them.

"You did, not me. S'long."

Monk slammed the door carelessly as usual.

All through your life you left them.

You did, not me.

No, there was something else, something he said.

Was that it? Everybody got a turn tonight. This is mine?

Something he said, about he never . . .

And I never got to tell her—

Something else. A flash like a subliminal frame.

You left, I didn't.

Never. Something about never.

I watched them carry her out.

Jack too. Slower, but I watched every minute of it.

I never want to go through that again.

He meant—

You left, I didn't.

Landry undressed slowly and turned down the bed. Outside his windows, the buildings had lightened to dull gray.

Never want to—

Was that it?

Never—

All of us locked in ourselves one way or another. Julia in her gingerbread house, Arthur in himself, Denny in a needle, and Monk . . . felt.

Never—

I never did go through it again. Ducked out, always left. Years or months or just days, I left or made them leave. I never let anyone put down roots in me. Why?

Your turn, Landry. You're still playing Connie's script. What did she do?

I'm not a leaving person.

Don't give me that bullshit. Not tonight, not anymore. You've left all your life. You're still leaving. You did it to Lauren tonight, and it started with Connie. What happened? What did she do?

I'm not a—

She died. That brutal, that simple. Think about it.

I have.

Sure, I've heard you for years. Beautifully philosophical: leaves die, grass dies, I'll go when it's time. You could always rationalize your own death, but not theirs. Not the ones you loved. Not the way death took them without leaving you anything to hit back at. Sound familiar? Sooner or later, whoever it was—Norma, Susan, Janice, Lauren—it would happen. You'd have to watch them die. Go away. Leave you. So you did it first, even chose younger women like Janice, because they were nearer the beginning of life than the end. Sure, they'd leave or you would, and that was fine. That was the script. Anything not to play that last scene.

. . . yeah.

Maybe in the morning you could call Lauren. Unless it's going to happen all over again. Of course, this time it may cost more than you want to pay.

No. Monk got the message across.

Try it.

Sooner or later I'm going to have to sit by Lauren's bed or she by mine, and one of us will watch the other die. Wreath it with flowers or score it for strings, it's a loss, a losing, and I'll always claw back at it with Connie's vengeful anger. With

Lauren it'll tear me up in little pieces, but I'll play the last scene.

Because it makes sense out of all the others. Pure soap opera, right? Let's play against the bad writing and get off with a laugh.

When it comes. The wonderful thing is that there's still so much time, so many possibilities.

Go to bed. They ain't gonna give us the medal, so we might as well grab some sleep.

37

Two o'clock the next afternoon, a clear, cold day beyond his windows. Landry sipped his coffee, tapped the pages of Denny's story to an even edge, and clipped them to the envelope. He dropped the story on the desk, unable to limit the swell of pride in Den's effort or the grin that capped it.

Doesn't know a thing about writing except how to do it.

Years, Den. A little glory, a lot of grind. Can you go the distance at last?

Who cares? All of a sudden, when the whole thing makes sense, I miss you.

"Aw . . . hell."

Hands in his pockets, Landry tried to find or deny reasons wherever he looked: the wall, the windows, the table.

He saw it then.

There on the table, partially hidden by the cruet and toaster: the dull green of it easy to pass over if you weren't paying attention. He hadn't looked at the table since getting up. Not closely.

Julia's clay dancer, where she left it. Perfect, every still-frozen attitude of leg or arm or meticulously crooked finger a promise of energy and movement, of possibility.

So many possibilities and so much time left to find them.

He picked up the delicate figure and carried it to the bed stand. He'd find a glass case; the piece deserved it as the best of Julia. One moment when she got it right. There might have been more.

"Thank you, Julia."

So many possibilities. So much time left to—

"Hell-l, *yes.*"

Landry snatched up the phone. When the switchboard woman answered, he gave her the Texas number he couldn't forget any more than his social security. Waste of time, he reflected. Noon in east Texas; Denny wouldn't be home—

"H'lo?"

Landry swallowed. "Denny?"

"Yeah, who's this?"

A long time, a lot of years. "This is Monk."

"Monk! Oh, *man,* it's great to—" Denny fell all over himself in eagerness and apology. "Did you get that thing I sent you? Look, I'm sorry. I didn't mean to bother you or take up your time or anything like that."

Denny, don't apologize for living.

The voice propelled on an urgency beyond the subject. "I've been writing since the last time in the joint. A lot of stuff I wouldn't show anybody, but this one seemed—aw, it's prob'ly shit. Forget it, Monk."

Landry had forgotten the quality of that voice. But for the Virginian thickened with deeper south, he could be listening to himself.

"Man, am I glad to hear from you. How've you been, Monk? I read all your books I could get my hands on. You're famous down here. Me, too; the brother of a famous writer." Den's laugh hadn't changed: resonant, arcing on definite notes through the scale. "Hell, down here you get famous if you can drink all night, which I does too much of. Oh, it's good to hear from you. How long's it been?"

"Twenty years," Landry said. "Almost."

"Twenty years." Denny mourned them all. "You wasn't too well disposed toward me last time we spoke."

That wasn't important now. "You clean, Denny?"

"Clean?"

"Junk."

"Hell, yes. John Q. Straight for years." Denny sucked in a long breath. He breathed like a heavy person. "Little fucked up from last night's beer. Shouldn't do that. My blood pressure's so high, it's icing over."

The old reflex took Landry. "Why don't you take *care* of yourself, dammit! What do you weigh now?"

"Two sixty."

"*Jeesus*," Landry sputtered. "You drive to work or just roll?"

"Man, I am a traffic hazard!" Denny roared, laughter always his umbrella in a rainy world. "Honest, sometimes you write like Dad. I mean the funny stuff."

"Yeah, Dad was a funny guy." *Still is, if you'd believe it.* "So you've been writing?"

"Trouble is, I don't know anything," Denny blurted. "Lot of stuff I threw away, really bad, but this one—" His confidence, never staunch, fled from him. "Hell, Monk, if you don't have the time . . ."

There's time. Landry realized he'd been pressing the phone too tight against his ear.

"Monk?"

"I'm here, kid."

"I'm proud of you."

Landry felt a rush of warmth, astonished it could mean so much. "Look, there's something I have to tell you."

"I guess you do, the way I did you," Denny admitted with resignation. "Go ahead. I deserve it."

"Your ending doesn't work at all."

"What?"

"Your ending sucks."

"What ending?"

"The story, stupid."

"Oh yeah, the—" Denny did a double take. "You read it?"

"That's what I'm saying. The kiss-off doesn't work."

Denny's amazement exploded in his brother's ear. "You mean some of it *does?*"

"It's a gas, Den. I was on the floor."

"Oh, God, you—"

"Needs a lot of work. Too much to explain on the phone. Got to go through it with you line by line just to sweep out the garbage."

Denny said it again in soft amazement. "You read it."

"You write like you used to comb your hair. You still got your hair?"

"Yeah, all of it. Gettin' real gray now."

"So's mine. You ever learn to comb it?"

"Nah, I keep it real short."

"Well, you're gonna learn to write the same way."

"Monk, I didn't mean for you to waste your time."

"You're wasting it now interrupting. I think maybe you could sell the story. With a lot of work," Landry underlined. "You want to learn or are you just screwing around?"

"Hey, wait." Denny was serious. "I want to learn. I read all the time, everything I can. If I can't get through it, I chuck it on a trash pile and start something else. I wrote every day in jail; that's where I finally woke up. Took a look at the fuckin' bullshit losers I was in with, and then the mirror, and, man, I couldn't see much difference. Saw your picture on one of your books. I look older than you, Monk. Like sixty. So I guessed if I was gonna do anything at all, it had to be now."

Denny trailed into silence. The humming wire tied them together with possibilities.

"I figure maybe I can deal one more hand. Help me, Monk. Dad helped you learn. Help me."

Stand on my shoulders.

"You there, Monk?"

So much time left after all. "Little brother, when can you get up here?"

Denny stumbled audibly over the notion. "You mean New York?" Outer space?

"I should go to Texas to teach you to write clear English? When can you come?"

"Gol-lee." Denny sounded very young just then. "Maybe I can."

"When?"

"Soon. Need another fishing trip to stash some cash." Denny grew more delighted with the notion in each breath. "Thanks, Monk."

"Just get up here, okay?"

"I think I can make it."

"Think yes."

"I will," Denny decided. "God bless you, Monk."

Landry felt an old, hard knot loosen in his chest, freeing it for a deep, sweet breath. "You too, Den."

"Can I call you? When will you be home?"

Most nights, he reflected bleakly, until (and if ever) Lauren forgave him. "Any night. After eleven it's cheaper."

"Right. Monk, I—" Denny hesitated. "I missed you."

"I missed you too, Den."

"I mean—look, I got no right to expect—you know—what I did to you and Dad, I was a real motherfucker."

"In your former line of work, weren't you acquainted with the statute of limitations on any given rap?"

"I heard of it." Denny chuckled.

"So if Ford could pardon Nixon, who am I to keep you under glass? Fuck it. You wrote a good story, so we'll work on it. Spend a buck and call me. Take care, Den."

"S'long, Monk."

Hands behind his head, Landry gazed at the ceiling. He felt light, ebullient. The first reaction was: *I got a family again. Call Laurie and tell her . . .* and some of the ebullience deflated. If Lauren didn't hang up on him, if she listened at all, he'd have some heavy dues to pay.

"Do I know how to louse up a good thing? Denny was an amateur," he admitted to the ceiling and his absurd self. "You, Landry, are a Florentine fuckup."

I found part of myself again, Laurie. I found my brother and, Christ, it was wonderful to realize how much I loved him. Please share it with me.

When he mustered the nerve to call her, the hotel told him Lauren Hodge had left an hour ago for the airport. There was a death in her family.

She must have heard last night. And I laid all that crap on her. Please come home, Laurie. I can handle it now. Come back.

38

Lauren felt confused and plain rotten about Pat. This would have been their first Christmas together. She'd looked forward to that. Now Christmas and New Year's were past, spent in Portland with the family, cheerful as possible in the wake of a funeral.

Such a big casket for that little body.

Don't think of that. It's done, finished. If there are angels, Mama is with them. Think about now.

There was one phone message from Pat, dated the day she left for Portland. That was December 20, over two weeks ago. On feminine principle, Lauren didn't return the call. *He* was the one who acted like such a—

Well . . . I helped. Dear God, I felt so miserable that night. I can't drink any better than Pat can. I wish one of us had more patience or common sense.

The days went by. Lauren doggedly bulldozed through the work at hand and tried to think clearly about Pat and their relationship. They were good together. They were not. The corduroy shirt, bought for him early in December, became the symbol of her ambivalence. Lauren could no more bring herself to gift wrap it than return it to the store.

Time passed. He ought to call her.

Well, one of them should.

All right—did she really want to call him?

Yes. Lauren dialed the Seville. A miserable anticlimax, but at least she learned why Pat hadn't called.

"I have a note on the board," the Seville switchboard woman informed her. "Mr. Landry is away. Can I take a message?"

"Did he leave word when he'd be back?"

"Not on the note. Can I take a message?"

"No," Lauren murmured through her disappointment. "No message. Thank you."

Relief with the disappointment: that explained it. He'd call when he got back. Of course he would. That was their unwritten rule. Whoever had the egg on their face did the apologizing.

Lauren dug out the video script about her mother and read it over. Perhaps her mood colored judgment; the emotion rang true but the piece was a rambling, shapeless mess. She could use Pat's surgical sense of what and where to cut.

If he ever cal—

Lauren was heartily grateful when the phone broke the oppressive silence around her. "Hello?"

"Hello, Mom? It's Meg."

"Meg! You sound like you're right around the corner."

"Well, I am, almost. I'm at the Dorset Hotel on—uh, let me see—Fifty-fourth Street. Come have lunch with me."

Lauren accepted, thinking as she put the phone down, *what in the world is Meg doing in New York?*

Margaret's reasons didn't ring true to Lauren. "In town for a few days' shopping." Three thousand miles to a city she loathed. In the Dorset Room with its restful green-and-cream decor, Lauren's daughter appeared spritely to the point of suspicion over poached salmon, actually chirping—*Meg never chirps*—about forays to Bloomingdale's, Gucci, and Saks. Listening to her, Lauren experienced a twinge of the apprehension she'd always felt when Meg and Marsh, as children, were too quiet for too long out of her sight.

Margaret's cheer struck her as forced. "Even with Grandmother's funeral, Jim and I were *not* going to let the children down for Christmas. *That* was expensive, and then, naturally, the car picked the day after New Year's to break down, you remember that because I was going to drive you to the airport and couldn't. With all the bills coming in, Mom, this whole last week has been done in checkbook green."

And so you're shopping in New York? Lauren's logic queried. *I don't believe it for a minute. Is she going to tell me or do I barge in and ask?*

"Bloomingdale's had some fantastic reductions—"

What's in New York you couldn't find in Portland?

"I bought this mohair yesterday. Like it?"

Yes, the maroon sweater was attractive with Meg's coloring, especially with the new hairstyle that brought her hair down to frame and soften her face. And no hat. More alarms went off in Lauren's maternal warning system. Meg in a sweater and the old slacks she usually wore for driving the kids to school. The whole effect was wrong. She might lunch this casually at McDonald's, but not the Dorset. Plus more effusive "Moms" than her daughter had allowed in years.

Signing the check to her AmEx card, Margaret asked brightly, "Have a busy afternoon coming up?"

Very busy: a hundred things she could do. Calls to make or answer, the script about her mother to shape up. Enough work to take her far into an evening not filled with the dear inconvenience of Pat Landry. But the need in Margaret's eyes was too clearly readable and canceled everything else.

"Nothing much," Lauren fibbed gallantly. "I'd really love to have you come home and visit with me."

Margaret said in a rush of gratitude, "I want to."

They took a cab to the Chelsea. Without a lunch table for anchor, Margaret stalked restlessly about Lauren's apartment, talking compulsively, keeping constant verbal contact with Lauren even through the bathroom door—

"It *is* a lovely view, Mom. Your plants are doing well. You always had a green thumb. I never noticed that picture before. How old was I then? Mom . . . do you have any bourbon?"

"Not a drop," Lauren confessed after a thorough search. "Just vodka and a little scotch."

"I'd like a scotch," Margaret said.

Lauren worried in earnest now. Her daughter drank an occasional glass of wine, now and then a weak bourbon before dinner. She never switched.

Gradually, circling the apartment like a troubled bird, Margaret came to rest in Pat's chair by the window. She sipped at the scotch, her dislike of the taste obvious, drinking for the effect. Lauren pulled the desk chair close to be able to touch her daughter. In her mid-thirties, Meg was Walter reborn. Her expression had set into the habits of certainty, unable to handle confusion.

"I'm glad we could come back here, Mom," she said at last. "I really had to talk to you."

Lauren heard the strained, breaking note in the hundredth

"Mom" of the day. She leaned closer to touch Margaret's cheek. "What is it, baby? Obviously not the lure of Bloomy's."

"I had to come to you because there's no one else. I'm in an awful jam. I don't know what to do. I *hate* that," Margaret flared. "I hate not being in control." Held in check so long, the flood burst through. Margaret curled sideways into her mother's arms, sobbing. Lauren let her go on, getting it out of her, leaving Margaret only to bring a handful of tissues from the bathroom.

"What is it, Meggy? Tell me."

"I have to," Margaret whispered tremulously, dabbing at her face with a sodden wad of tissues. "Have to tell someone."

A sudden, unreasoning terror chilled Lauren. This was her own flesh. Her mind flew to the worst. Death. Sickness. Cancer. A lump in the breast? One out of ten women . . . or no. She's pregnant and frightened she's too old. No, that's silly. Jim? Another woman? Jim's steady and responsible, but it happens.

Let it be that, Lauren bargained with God, *not sickness. I can't take any more dying now. Not Meg . . .*

She rose to stand by the chair, bending over her daughter and cradling the bowed head in her arms. "Tell me."

"I've gotten myself involved with another man."

"What?" Lauren wilted back into her chair, almost hysterical with relief. "Ohforgodsake—I thought you were *sick!*"

"Why are you laughing?"

"I'm not—I'm not," Lauren jittered, grabbing for a fresh tissue. "I was thinking lumps and cancer and—no, of course it's not funny. Just the first thing I thought of. Well. Who is this man?"

"Ed Wilkerson," Margaret said. "He's an old friend of Jim's and mine from the country club. He came over once last year when you were there."

Lauren's memory was inadequate to necessities, let alone random faces.

"Ed was just an old friend," Margaret stressed. "He and Ruth used to join us at the club for tennis and bridge. She divorced him last year. I never liked her that much. Well, sometimes Ed and I would meet at the club—when they separated, I mean—after tennis or whatever. At first it was just that he needed someone to talk to.

Margaret explained it with a scrupulousness that Lauren hardly needed. A man married for years, rocked by divorce, unused to being alone. A man used to coping, who suddenly couldn't. A panicky time for any mature person. He poured out his loneliness to Margaret, making her realize how lonely she'd been herself. The last few years with Jim, she said, hadn't been that happy. They were growing in different directions. But still—

"I don't know how it happened," she kept saying.

Lauren asked gently, "Are you sorry it did?"

Margaret groped for another Kleenex. "Could I have some more scotch?"

"Sure, but go easy, Meg. You're awfully tired. This is very hard on you."

Over and over, Margaret kept wondering how it happened, how the thing had come to this, as if reality and physical law and all the sanity she knew had suddenly been suspended. But no, she wasn't sorry for being with Ed.

"Something's got to resolve," Margaret choked, going rapidly through the tissues. "Things can't go on like this. Being with Ed made me realize how empty it is at home. There was one day after—well, after I'd started seeing Ed. I kissed him good-bye and started to leave. Like a wall pushing me back, so hard to leave him. Walking to my car, I felt dizzy. Naked. I didn't know what was real anymore. The world could just drop out from under me the next step I took, have you ever felt that way, Mom? Going home to be a mother to my children and a wife to Jim after—nothing made *sense* anymore. Not even going home."

The room was already growing dark through winter afternoon, but Lauren didn't want to turn on the lights. She put a match to the paper log in her fireplace; that would add a cheer both of them could use now. She invited Margaret to the bench by the hearth. "Come sit by the fire, Meg."

They sat very close together on the bench, Lauren's arm over Margaret's shoulder. "What's going to happen?" she asked practically. "What does Ed want to happen?"

That much was clear enough. Ruth wasn't coming back; that was definitely out. There was one other fact, the important one. "Ed's transferring to his company's office in Chicago. He wants me to go with him."

Lauren reverted to pure Portland. "Oh, wow. Does he have children?"

"There's Carl, he's fourteen. Ruth got him. Ed has visiting rights, but he wants to make a fresh start."

The whiskey, the growing warmth of the fire, and her emotional state told on Margaret's exhaustion. Her body untensed, her speech softened and slurred a little. "I want to go. Sometimes I feel that I've got to go. I can't now."

"When you think about it, he's not giving up a damned thing," Lauren interjected with good hard female sense. "While he's asking you to give up everything. Men are great that way. So it's pretty much all on you."

"Well," Margaret said carefully. "You left, didn't you?"

"No."

"But—"

"Think about it."

Margaret made a vague, helpless gesture. "I can't think straight at all, Mom. So I remember what has to be. Billy starts high school in September. Angela just started in the Girl Scouts. She's wanted to be one for so long, you should see how she looked, putting on her uniform for the first time and running downstairs to show Jim and me. And then, Jim and I are committed to remodeling the house because I wanted it. A whole new room built on, I told you about it. How did I get *into* this? I can't *believe* I'd ever be so . . ."

"Helpless?"

"Helpless is the word." Margaret dropped her head on her mother's shoulder. "Say something."

"What?"

"I don't know. Something. Call me a complete fool."

"As a matter of fact," Lauren admitted, "at this moment I haven't seen Pat for over two weeks. We had a fight. He acted like a complete ass and I guess I did too. Not much certainty I can give you or even myself right now. Except that I love you and I've missed you, and men are a definite liability."

At least Margaret could laugh a little at that. "Aren't they?"

"And they don't get easier to deal with." Lauren thought of the last evening with Pat, ended in livid fury.

"What am I going to do, Mom? I can't leave my children."

"How do you think I felt with Walter?"

"But you left," Margaret said.

"No. That was later. Much later, when you were grown. There were years before that, and they weren't good. Whatever there was between your father and me died along the way. There were men now and then. Good men. One of them was like your Ed. He wanted me to leave with him. I almost did. He was a marvelous man. He brought out all the feelings you told me about." Lauren savored the memory. "In all my life, I've never loved or needed any man so much. Every time I had to leave him and go home, it was a death."

"Yes."

"Look at me, Meg."

Margaret sat up and turned to her mother in the firelight.

"You always had trouble dealing with my life, didn't you? So did I. Mr. Landry is no one's paragon of stability, but he's honest, and he gave me one gift. People don't really *see*, Meggy. They react. They put labels on things and other people because that's easier than really seeing or thinking. Pat made me realize that what people call selfishness can be plain self-preservation."

Margaret digested that in silence. After a long moment, she said, "I was so mixed up when you left Dad."

"That was later. I never left you. You and Marsh were the reasons I didn't leave. Couldn't. I stayed and coped. What hurt the most was last year when you called me selfish. As if you were condemning my whole life. I'm not God, honey. If Aaron hadn't been here wanting me, I don't know if I would have had the strength to leave, or even if it was strength. But you were grown, I thought, and able to handle it. I don't know what you're going to do. I can't tell you what you should do. Will you give me the same break? Will you stop punishing me? Please?"

"Dad was so bitter. He couldn't understand any of it."

"Of course he couldn't. Your father only knew how things should be. He was full of should."

"I felt like I was the one left in the middle—"

"I know, baby."

"So hard to *explain* to people."

"No, that wouldn't be easy." Lauren took Margaret's empty glass. "Do you think you could explain it now?"

Margaret pinched her eyes between thumb and forefinger. "Mom, right now I can't even make sense of myself. I want to sleep for a week."

Forget explaining, Lauren thought. *You understand it now, that's enough.* "Why not lie down then. Come on, you're worn out worrying over this."

Obediently, Margaret let herself be led to the studio couch. Lauren slipped off her shoes and covered her with a light blanket.

"How long has it been since I tucked you in?"

"Long time . . ."

I'm glad you're home, Meggy.

"Feel so awful about Jim."

"Sure you do." Lauren sat down beside her. "Go to sleep. You'll feel better when you wake up."

Lauren felt weary herself, as purged as Margaret. "You know, I could use a nap too."

She stepped out of her shoes and lay down beside her daughter, covering herself with part of the blanket. She molded herself to Margaret's back and warmth. Under the blanket, sleepily, Margaret found her hand and closed her fingers around it. Lauren felt content with the moment. Meg would make her own decisions, knowing at least that they didn't have to be made alone in the dark.

Why go out for dinner? she thought, drifting off. I'll fix something here. That will be lovely: the fire going and my child to make dinner for. I don't think she's ready to leave what she's built, not yet, but Meg won't go back to it quite the same. Neither did I.

Lauren smiled tenderly against Margaret's back, knowing the probable course and even the predictable order of her daughter's problem. First the glow of this love affair, the secret happiness. Meg might even enjoy the novelty of thinking of herself as a scarlet woman and fallen wife for a while, like rich candy munched in secret, before the reality sank in—

—as it did for me. Thinking about one man all day long and half through the night, dying to be with him and unable to breathe one word to anyone. And still, lunches and dinners to plan and make, PTA meetings, the kids to get ready for school. To deal with and care about. Happy inside myself when I had to be mad at Marsh. Crying in the bathroom when everyone was laughing and having a good time. Never able to say it out. Being not at all sane, just pretending. That's the reality. Somehow the time passes. Pat said it: no one dies of a broken heart. At least Meg knows she doesn't have to go the whole thing alone.

Will I? Lauren thought just before sleep. What are we going to do, Pat Landry?

39

Julia's dancer stood on Landry's dresser in her new domed glass case. A narrow beam of afternoon sun had inched across the dresser surface while he watched, to touch the glass and figure with warm light, suffuse it, and pass on.

Over his cigarette, Landry's gaze went from the statuette to the phone. *So many possibilities:* the idea had stayed with him for days since he talked to Denny. *And the time to explore them.* What had he been afraid of for so long? Failure, being written out? When you came down to it, every moment in life was a choice from which the next could veer in any direction. Yesterday's failure didn't have to be tomorrow's.

Walking the windy shoreline at Harwichport on Cape Cod, he paced out the thoughts step by step along the sand. In time he would make Denny see that he didn't live on the edge of other people's lives but in the center of his own. In the same time, teaching this to Den, he could realize it for himself.

"Moment to moment," he said to Julia's dancer. "My choice. Boy, Edie. You're gonna hit the ceiling and go right through."

Landry put the next proposition to the phone. "So? I'll never make the bestseller charts. Sorry, Jack."

He lifted the phone and called Artists Associates, only a little apprehensive as he waited for Edith Fine to click on the line.

"Pat? Where've you been these last few days? I couldn't get you."

"I was out of town. Talking to some very astute seagulls. Thinking. Edie—you're going to disown me." Landry paused over the space of a breath. "I've mulled over the Falcon deal from every angle, and I don't want it." Edie's silence over the wire compelled him to justify. "No, I'm wrong for it. The project's wrong for me. There's all the time in the world, if I want it. But not for this."

More silence. Landry began to feel uncomfortable. She'd put a great deal of work into this contract. You didn't give grief to your agent. "I know you worked hard for me on this, but . . . if it makes sense, I've got to stay broke and—and scared for a while longer. Because the other way isn't worth it . . . Edie, are you there?"

"I'm here, Mr. Landry."

"Go ahead: cuss me out. You'll be the first today."

"I am grinning to my ears, Pat. And I just may grin all the way to lunch."

He felt much lighter. "Hey, I'm not crazy."

"Not at all."

"I'll get along, Edie. Just got to wait until the good stuff comes back. Until I can care about it again."

She said only, "Ride it out, Pat."

"I'm scared down to my socks, without idea one, but we'll earn out on *Camlann,* and there'll be something coming in on *The Harper's Wife,* so—"

"Pat." Edie wedged into his apologies. "You're telling me not to worry because you don't want to write junk? Forget it. I lost a little sleep over this one myself. We're in business for the long haul. Just get on with it. You're going to do good books and not-so-good, and now and then a fine book. How can you know when you're good if you don't fall on your face once in a while, huh? Will you for once trust your talent enough to wait for it?"

"Yeah," he said, grateful. "For once I will."

"It'll be there," Edie Fine knew. "So will the market. Are you okay for money?"

"I'll make it."

"Who doubted? If you do need, don't be shy, okay? Gotta go. Take care, Pat."

"Listen, one thing," he persisted. "When you talk to Bethany, tell her she ought to grab Darcy after all. I'm pretty sure she's still hot for the project."

"I will. Happy New Year, Pat."

The only unhappy New Year might be Bethany's. A word from him and Darcy would know exactly what to ask, and she'd get every dime. Landry relished the prospect.

"Sic 'em, Darce."

The next call would be harder. He couldn't expect anything from Lauren but a spit in the eye. *Take your lumps, man. Get it over with.*

Over with? Only if Lauren wanted it that way. For him, no more walking away.

"Let's do it, Strongheart."

He dialed Lauren's number. She came on after the second ring.

"Hi. Laurie, it's me."

There was a brief silence. Landry felt his future dangling in it.

"Well," she acknowledged finally. "You did it up good, didn't you?"

He couldn't read her exact mood. She hadn't said his name, never did when she was really pissed at him. "Laurie, I'm so ashamed of what I did that night. It was unforgivable. I called you the next day but you were already on the way home. Look, I've been out of town—"

"Oh?"

"I mean—in case you called."

"No. I did wonder why I hadn't heard from you."

"Just away. At the Cape. I can think up there. Laurie, you have every right not to want to see me again. But I wanted you to know how I felt."

"That was a bad night for me, Pat." He heard the reprieve in her voice. "I've been saying good-bye to you ever since. Trying to, but I find myself talking to you through the day. Thinking about you. My mother died that night."

"I thought that's what it was. I'm sorry, hon. Sorry I wasn't with you."

"And Margaret's been here," Lauren told him. "Do you ever get on guilt trips?"

"Lauren, I just got off the longest guilt trip in the world. My head's on pretty straight now. Can we have dinner?"

"Not tonight, I'm booked."

"Breakfast at Wellington's?"

"I was a bitch myself, but if you ever lay hands on me again, you'll get hit with anything I can pick up."

"Fair enough. What about Wellington's for breakfast?" He grinned into the phone. "While I can afford it."

Exasperated: "Oh, honestly! Are you broke *again?*"

"Not yet, but I may be in a while. Tell you tomorrow."

"I don't know what you *do* with your money."

"It's not that. I'll te—"

"Just throw it around—"

"Love you!"

"—until you're flat broke again."

"Wellington's. Ten-thirty."

"When are you going to grow up, Pat?"

"When I do," Landry told her, "I'm gonna be a cowboy."

Lauren chuckled. "I'm gonna be a fireman. A fireperson."

"Sure. And any fireman who's a gentleman will stand back and let you be first up the ladder."

As usual, he was early at Wellington's, into his second cup of coffee when (as usual) Lauren tore in late, puffing with exertion and cold, carrying a shopping bag. She'd barely set it down when Landry hugged her.

"So good to see you again, baby . . ."

"Frozen to the bone," she croaked while he helped her out of her coat and scarf. *"Fruz!* Oh, do I need some hot coffee." Lauren slid into the booth and signaled the stout little waitress who always took care of them.

"Margaret was here for a few days," she began, taking the morning's mail out of her bag. "Hi, dear," she greeted the waitress. "Happy New Year. My usual, nothing new. Sunnyside, rye bread plain, bacon *real* crisp."

While Lauren thawed over coffee, she described Meg's predicament. "We were close, Pat. She finally opened up to me and let me come close again. For all her problems, that was a wonderful feeling to hold her again the way I did when she was little."

She took a Macy's bag out of the larger one and passed it to him. "It was for Christmas. I bought it but didn't wrap it."

A corduroy shirt in powder blue, perfect for him. Lauren knew his body; she never bought anything that didn't fit or suit. He ought to remember that.

"Here's your present. I got it but didn't wrap it." He unrolled the rubber bands from the bag on the seat next to him and carefully unveiled Lauren's present. He set it by her plate. "Merry Christmas."

He relished the small, marveling O of her mouth as she gazed at the figurine. Slowly she turned it in a complete circle, studying the tiny, exquisite form from every angle.

"It's magnificent," Lauren said finally. "Such talent."

"Julia did it."

"What can I say. It's—"

"A small, perfect miracle."

"All of that," she murmured. "Your sister was that good."

"There was a sort of family reunion. Julia left me this. Will you keep it beside your own work?"

"Oh, yes." Lauren couldn't take her eyes from it even when he reached for her hand.

"Don't lose it, Laurie. Don't lose me. Hang on to me. I'm worth it. Goddammit all, *we're* worth it. We could walk away and be alone or find someone new. Or we can stick and try."

"Yes." Her gaze was still fastened on the dancer, entranced by the possibilities of light and shadow to play over it. "I thought of that. And all the trouble of meeting someone new. All those damned exploratory first dinners in the wrong, expensive restaurants."

"I love my shirt," he said.

"Carry my dancer home for me?" She lifted it back to him with ceremonial care. While he wrapped it like a set of crown jewels, Lauren rummaged through her mail, discarding junk, muttering over the appalling incompetence of university administrators. Watching her, Landry had the unexpectedly comfortable feeling that this went on for years. They wouldn't change; they'd always irritate each other and fight. Lauren would always be too sensitive when he least expected it, forever a pain in the neck reminding him of things he knew perfectly well, buying him socks because he never remembered, always late because she couldn't keep track of time. Finding a spot on his shirt or tie, or lint on his suit that a microscope would miss just when he was trying to tell her something *important*, for God's sake—and otherwise and forever driving him up the walls of male logic.

"Let's get some more coffee," she suggested, ravaging another envelope.

"Sure. Tell me about Meg."

Mozart's birthday again, only one day to Pat's, disco music vibrating off the walls of Crissy James's loft as she scampered to make fresh popcorn, hurled herself into the arms of new arrivals, dodged among the dancers, giggled with Lauren over Darcy Rambard's ensemble—

"She looks so *expensive*."

—to shriek with pleasure at the arrival of one more very welcome guest.

"Caroline!"

"Hel-lo, Crissy." They entangled joyously. "Happy New Year."

"I was so surprised when you called!" Crissy bawled over electronic guitar and a Hiroshima of drums. "Thought you were still in Tulsa."

"It's part of my deal with Norman. I get a break in London and New York every year. Criminee!" Caroline swept the party scene. "*Every*one is here. And there's my dear Patrick dancing. My God, he looks sober."

"As a Hebrew law," Crissy promised. "And with the same woman."

"Crissy, this is historic. Give me a drink and just a nibble of salad."

"I made a humongous lasagna!"

"Salad, honey. I'm going back to Tulsa with a new wardrobe and the ass to look good in it." Caroline's benevolent gaze narrowed to an appreciative glint. "Who is that marvelous giant of a man talking to Evan?"

"That's Forbes Schneider, and he's an editor and very married."

"So am I. Just window shopping." Caroline measured the man stem to stern. "I do like men I have to look up at. I'll have a short scotch, Criss. The London plane's godawful early."

Landry and Lauren came hand in hand off the dance floor, out of breath, to plop down at the long table. They toasted each other, her vodka to his seltzer-and-twist.

"It's not Glenfyddich," Landry regretted. "Gonna have to live with that."

"Sweetheart, don't be a martyr. Just you'll feel so much better in the morning."

Landry considered it. "Gonna have to live with that, too."

Lauren scrutinized his lap beyond the sweater waist. "Zip up your pants. Honestly, Pat, don't you ever look what you're doing?"

"Did I forget—?" He grabbed at the zipper. "I did. Thanks."

A swirl of color veered toward them from the edge of the dance floor. "Here comes Lady Glitz," Lauren noted without joy. "Why does Rambard always make me feel like a thrift shop?"

Darcy charged at them, resplendent in a scarlet velour jumpsuit with gold zippers, overlaid with mink. "PAT! I love you, and I've got to run—hi, Lauren—but Happy New Year and mazel tov for your birthday. But I've got to *tell* you, you wouldn't believe. In Hank Steinberg's office: the most incredibly beautiful man ever to call himself my new agent." Darcy actually sparkled. "I've been breathing hard all week."

"Don't tell me," Landry guessed. "He's a widower from commuter country, and only keeps kosher when his sister visits."

"Yah-h, who's kosher? His name's Brewster."

"Darcy! You wouldn't!"

"Who wouldn't?" She rattled her bracelets at Landry. "Rules are made to be broken."

"Your own agent? That's incest."

"A goy!" Lauren hooted. "Hallelujah! Up out of Egypt!"

"Don't ask. The man is off the cover of one of my books. Peter O'Toole with shoulders." Darcy swept the mink aside like Rodin unveiling a bronze. "Like my new outfit?"

"I was admiring," Lauren said tactfully. "It's so bright."

"Honey, I like to make a statement, and this statement comes to you courtesy of Pat Landry, who does lovely things for his friends. Also from Bethany Harris of Falcon Books."

Landry added more soda to his glass. "Good contract?"

"Good? Ha!" Behind the sequined designer glasses, Darcy's round cornflower eyes were not naive at all. "I let my new WASP agent get *her* drunk. I'm impressed, you know? You people are really good at business." Darcy wrapped herself around Landry in farewell. "Love you, but I gotta go. My sister's down from Albany. This month *she's* got problems, what can I tell you? Lauren, I love the way you can wear simple jeans. So sensible. Ciao-ciao . . ."

And Darcy Rambard swept away like prosperity routing depression.

Landry looked after her. "Helluva nice woman."

Lauren's smile was more sparing. "Yes, isn't she?"

"Darling Pat!"

Caroline's greeting was a clear trumpet over the disco music as she gusted down on them. "Patrick, give me a—how *are* you? Hi, Lauren. My God!" Caroline surveyed them with a certain pride in her own handiwork. "You two freaks are still together, and I'm so glad."

"It was him," Lauren admitted, "or an electric blanket."

"And he can dance." Caroline lifted an eyebrow at her erstwhile partner hulking near the dance floor. "Which is more than I can say for the viking over there. Saturday Night Feeble. A hunk but harmless. Pat, darling, can't stay, Norman's going to call. But do me a favor."

Caroline dug in her handbag and slammed a square of paper in front of Landry. "Tried this number all day, no dice. I'll be back from London in two weeks, the date's down there. Call the minister for me."

Landry squinted at the paper. "Minister?"

"The *Meth*odist, the one who took Dogger. He and his wife are going to Africa to be Christian to the Ethiopians or something like that, and he can't take Dogger, the natives would eat her. And you know, I miss the silly bitch to growl at. Who knows?" Caroline beamed. "Maybe in Tulsa she'll meet a nice German shepherd. When are you—?"

The three of them winced at a hundred-decibel blast from the speakers.

"What?"

"I SAID WHEN ARE YOU GETTING MARRIED?"

"Watch your mouth," said Lauren Hodge.

"*What?*"

"I SAID BON VOYAGE!"

40

"**W**ell, I was just thinking about it, that's all."

Landry loped down the long shopping arcade of La Guardia Air Terminal, Lauren trotting briskly to keep up, the long red scarf bobbing in her wake.

"It's a lovely thought, sweetheart," she said, "but do we have to decide right now?"

"I didn't mean next month, for God's sake, but sometime."

"Can we slow down?" Lauren puffed. "You're always in a hurry. The plane's barely touched down. Are you sure we're going the right way for the gate?"

"Yes, I'm sure," Landry said impatiently. "Just looking at the advantages. Hospitalization, things like that. Like in ten or fifteen years—"

"We're going the wrong way, Pat."

"No, we're not. I know La Guardia."

"Our gate's over that way."

"It is *not*." Landry consulted a sign and surrendered. "So hang me. It's the other way." They started back along the endless corridor. "So anyway—are you listening? I mean, how often does someone propose to you?"

"Never in an airport." Lauren was sure of her directions now. "Yes. Down this way."

Landry took her hand as they swung along. "All I'm saying is that, in a few years, ten, fifteen, it makes sense to get married. Think about it."

"So you propose a decade early. You have an early compulsion."

Landry looked badgered. "Jesus, sorry I brought it up."

"No, sweetheart. It's a lovely idea."

"Sure. Who's going to take care of us if it ain't us? Look, there's the gate. And we wouldn't have to live together unless we wanted to."

"I don't think we ever could," Lauren considered with candor. "See how early we are? They're not even coming off yet."

The mobile tube was just being rolled into place for the inbound plane from Houston. "Didn't I say we had plenty of time?"

They waited for minutes. The first passengers began to emerge from the tube.

"He'll be so glad to see you," Lauren said. "His letters sounded so lonely. When he comes, go put your arms around him."

"*Laurie*. Do you think I don't know how to greet my own brother after twenty years?"

"I was just saying—"

"Pick, pick, pick. Why not write my lines," Landry complained aimiably. "You want to do everything else."

"Twenty years." Lauren kept her eyes on the tube entrance. "In twenty years, I'll be almost seventy-seven. Maybe it will be time to slow down and get married. But not live together."

"Hell no—there he is! That's Den!"

Pictures told so little of the poignant truth. Denny lumbered from the debarkation tube, mauled and middle-aged, far too heavy. Pat Landry's heart went out to him.

He does look older than me, just plain beat up. But he's so close, love isn't a big enough word, and there's time enough for anything we want to be. Fat and old, but I can still see all the good things that will never change, and now he knows he won't have to cut it alone.

Still the Denny he loved: the blue eyes innocent, mild, and wondering. Denny saw him and hooted. The deep, joyful roar carried far down the corridor.

"MONK!"

Landry strode toward him, opening his arms.

"I hope Monk makes Denny take care of himself," Connie fretted. "He doesn't look well at all. But I love seeing them together."

Not all the family were enthusiastic about meeting the plane, but Connie insisted since she'd rarely managed to see all her children together at one time. For Connie Hawkins, a modern airport was sheer cultural shock.

"So many *stores*. Bright as the Winter Garden marquee. I never flew in my life. I should have. Somehow the notion suits me."

"Absolutely," Arthur agreed. "Mother would love it. The drinks are reasonable, and it's very comfortable when they're not shooting at you."

Julia enjoyed the sight of animated Lauren Hodge. "Will you look at that little mouse of a woman whipping those two big clunks into shape. The energy of her! At her age it's unfair to have that kind of figure."

"Very attractive." Arthur inspected Lauren with a wealth of expertise. "I have to admit I could like her."

"Like her?" Connie declared. "That woman is a headline act."

"She is that," said Jack Landry.

"Any woman," Connie dared any of them to disagree, "any woman who could civilize Monk—I always loved him, but what trouble!—that woman is aces in my book. I really must buy her a drink sometime and compare notes."

"That would be interesting," Julia considered it. "Monk could be very . . . nondescript. Frankly, I never thought he'd amount to a hill of beans."

"Ah, the hell with that!" Jack roared, glowing. "Just look at my boys. Den can still be anything. Write anything. Monk will make him work at it. The Monk would always work when he wanted something enough."

" 'My boys,' says he. He gets the tough from me, Landry," Connie claimed. "Unless you want to argue the point, and I hope you do."

"Con, Con—look at 'em. They're not ours but their own now. Different from us. You were so close to Monk you never saw all of him. He was practicing to be his own at seven." Jack swirled the image in his memory, savoring it like brandy in a snifter. "The Christmas he was seven we got him a toy suitcase, remember? Well, Monk decides: you get a suitcase, you travel. So into my workroom he comes and announces he's leaving home. I asked him: where do you think you'll go? Out to see the world, says he, and maybe Texas to be a cowboy. So I helped him pack his cowboy suit and cap pistol and jelly beans, and off he went. And he didn't come back until supper time. No, I never worried about Monk."

Jack gave his sons a last fond glance. "What say, Con? Want to pick a good time?"

A bare moment's hesitation. "Keith's Theater," Connie elected, that young even with the thought.

"That would be my choice." Jack bent to kiss her, thirty-five again. "You argued the night I first took you to bed and damn if you didn't argue getting *out* of bed."

"That was a classic year," Connie said. "Let's do it again."

"Why not? Who said vaudeville died. We haven't."

"Like your sons, Landry, you were a trial and a joy. Let's go play that night at Keith's." Connie kissed her husband again, a long meeting that forgot nothing good or bad. "Remember? The house was sold out, even standing room. What a hand I got. Three bows!"

"Two," Jack recalled.

"In your *hat*, two. You were there. You heard that house after my turn."

"Who was listening to them?" Jack tucked Connie's arm through his. "I remember you standing in the light, that's all. Shall we do it again?"

"Let's. And *then* we'll fight. Good night, children," Connie smiled farewell to Arthur and Julia. "Handsome, the two of you. I always said it. Come on, Jack."

They went on to Keith's to lay them in the aisles.

Arthur looked after his brothers moving away up the corridor: Pat with his arm around Denny, Lauren looking for signs, managing the whole show as usual. Arthur Cole's smile was never broad, nor was it now, though it lacked the accustomed hardness.

"You wouldn't think Monk would remember so much of us."

"No, but I'd rather not do it again, thanks just the same. I wish I had a mirror," Julia yearned. "Or that a mirror could have me." She swept the red-gold sunburst back from her brow. "How do I look, Arth?"

"Marvelous. Not a day over twenty. How about me?"

"Like a picture I kept of you, when you'd just earned your wings. It caught something I never saw after the war. Come home with me." Julia took his arm in a surge of affection. "I miss my house and kids. I'd like to see them again."

"No," Arthur declined. "I'm a little worn out with all this

emotionalism. I think I'll go walk by the ocean. It's peaceful there."

"Oh, come on." Julia tugged at her brother with the dawning of a fun idea. "Let's go haunt my daughters. They've never met you."

Arthur looked dubious. "Do you really think they need that?"

"Need it?" More than certain, Julia was committed. "Nothing ever happens to those girls. They'll *love* it!"

Parke Godwin

June 22, 1986

WITHDRAWN

GAYLORD M